Faded Coat of Blue

Faded Coat
of Blue

Owen Parry

AVON BOOKS ◆ NEW YORK

AVON BOOKS, INC.
1350 Avenue of the Americas
New York, New York 10019

Copyright © 1999 by Owen Parry
Interior design by Kellan Peck
ISBN: 0-380-97642-0

Library of Congress Cataloging in Publication Data:

Parry, Owen.
Faded coat of blue / Owen Parry.—1st ed.
p.   cm.
1. United States—History—Civil War, 1861–1865 Fiction. I. Title.
PS3531.A668F34   1999   99-25523
813'.54—dc21   CIP

First Avon Books Printing: October 1999

AVON TRADEMARK REG. U.S. PAT. OFF. AND IN OTHER COUNTRIES, MARCA REGISTRADA, HECHO EN U.S.A.

Printed in the U.S.A.

10   9   8   7   6   5   4   3

www.avonbooks.com

To the Welsh, Scots, and Irish
who built America
while the English weren't looking.

In Adam's Fall
We sinned all.

THE NEW ENGLAND PRIMER,
Seventeenth Century

Faded Coat of Blue

1

A SENTRY WITH TROUBLED BOWELS DISCOVERED THE BODY. A shock it must have been for the boy. He fired off his rifle and the Good Lord knows what else, then ran up through the mud and fog to his camp. I do not fault the lad, you understand. A soldier may be brave easily enough with his comrades all about him. But a boy new to service, touched with sickness and with the autumn chill upon him, such a one might be forgiven a wallop of fear when he tumbles over a dead officer in the pursuit of a winkle of privacy.

He should not have left his post, of course. That he should not have done. But they were all the greenest of soldiers in those days. As green as Gwent. Their days were full of drill and boasting, but well I know the nights of a soldier's doubt. So I understand what the lad felt, when he found the fairest of young men bedded down in the morning dark with a bullet through his heart.

The rest arrived at a run, slopping down through the mire the storm had left, and a dangerous pack they were. Lads in their unmentionables, with cartridge boxes flapping and rifles poorly handled. Sergeants bellowed. Company officers stumbled as they tried to run and draw on their boots at the same time, tripping over swords they had not mastered. Wet and weary they were. And some fool blasted a bugle.

I was not there. I am reconstructing events. But I have known many a camp surprised by a creeping enemy or a stray cow, and there was always a terrible confusion at the first. So I see them flushing out of their tents at the sound of their sentinel's shot, eyes hungry for more light and hearts in an uproar. I hear the voices of the weaker souls, crying out that the Rebels were upon them, and aimless shots.

When no one fired back, they settled a bit, and the light rose. Young Private Haney—for that was his name—blundered in leading a party down to his discovery. They slipped in the muck of the hillside, where the men had torn away each last twig for their campfires, and cursed relentlessly, though profanity helps no man. At last, they reached the body, down in the ravine, lying a pistol shot from the military road. They told me the dead man looked like an angel fallen to earth, but some of them were Irish and given to adorning language.

Later, they would all learn a muchness of death. More than any man should know. But let that bide. Their regiment was too new to have been at Bull Run, and the corpse was the first most of the men had seen. I do not count those taken by typhoid and the like, for that is a natural thing. This death was unnatural, and they knew it in their souls. The newspapermen wrote that the dead officer possessed the countenance and voice of a sweet, blessed saint. They had written that even before his death, after which no commentary might be trusted. The young man was known, and beloved, and should have lived long.

The soldiers who stood over his body were rugged lads from the highlands of New York, hill farmers. They were not great readers of the newspapers, and they certainly would not have left their fields for a lecture on the evils of slavery. They were men who worked hard, tillers with settled eyes and small expectations even in their youth, and their shoulders were oxen. They admired the officer in his death, but could not fix him with a name, and only stood about, uncertain what to do, looking down on his beauty. He was not of their regiment, and not of their world. Not even a sergeant dared touch his fine blue coat.

It took the officers to recognize him. Officers are terrible ones for spotting the bad in a situation, and not a few soon make it worse. I spoke with them later, in the course of my inquiry, and they told me how it was. At first, they, too, caught the fear of an attack and went about rallying the men—valiantly, to hear them tell it—but with the climbing of the light Captain Steele made his way down to the party gathered over the corpse. He thought he knew the face that lay before him, but he had been a lawyer before he took up arms and went cautiously about things. He waited until Major Campbell, the adjutant, joined him.

Now Campbell was a great Scotsman, and they are devils in the morning, see. He come down barking and settling his belt, sword in his hand. He had been a politician in his county, and that sort is ever more given to speech than to thought, although base calculation is not beyond them. The men moved aside for their major, and he saw the still, white face with its frame of golden hair, and brayed for all the world.

"Well, I'll be damned and resurrected," he said, and I am certain he was half correct. "That's Anthony Fowler."

It was a death that changed my life.

I was not there, for my regimental days were behind me. I had failed my new country at Bull Run, but a Welshman is a tenacious thing when you spin him up and I was a clerking officer now. I missed my Mary Myfanwy and longed to return to her, but duty is not a thing that will let go of a man if he holds the least worth. When the call sounded through the ward for men who could figure accounts, I stood to it. That I still could do for our Union. My leg pained me, I will not lie to you, but I would have walked through serpents like a Hindoo holy man to leave the stench of that hospital behind. Twas the smell of bad butchering.

So I was not in that encampment south of the Potomac on the second of November, in the Year of Our Lord 1861. Nor was I in any camp or fort of the hundreds ringing our capital. Nor was I in my bed at Mrs. Schutzengel's boarding-house, though as a middle-aged man of thirty-three I was ever glad of its warmth. No, ladies and gentlemen, that morning I was down at the depot below our unfinished Capitol, waiting for a trainload of trousers.

Twas but four in the morning, with the world black and shivering. There had been a great rain and blow in the night, and a window-rattling as if death himself had gone walking. It had barely stopped when I left my bed. The cold was enough to make a man want shelter, but the depot hall was locked to keep out the drunkards lamming from the provost marshal. Carters bunched in the streets, their horses slithering wet and wagons creaking.

There were always loaded wagons about the depot. The war was a great benefit for tradesmen, a matter I was studying in my new position, and space for goods on the trains was a precious thing. Men fought with their fists and their dollars for right of place. The Marylander bridges were not in steady repair, and even when they were up the government seemed to favor Mr. Cameron's Harrisburg line, which took the long way about, over the short route to Philadelphia. It made for a great wanting of trains. There was always more cargo than capacity. It was a new world of steel rails and high business, and we were learning it in the midst of a war, and there was more than a whisper of dishonesty in these matters. A man would have expected all of the cargoes to come into Washington to support our army, with little returning to the north. But all around me wagons rich with cotton and tobacco wedged toward the rails, and I did not think all was of legitimate provenance. But let that bide.

I stood under a gaslight, doing figures. The rain was not above a tardy splash, but no time is to be wasted, as my Mary Myfanwy would have said. There was cold, but a man must learn to appreciate his advantages. With the heat behind us for the year, Washington did not stink so badly, and that was a blessing. Now I am an old bayonet and a veteran of John Company's fusses, and my nose has not been stuffed with violets from the cradle up. But I tell you I have never smelled a great stink like that of Washington in the summer. It filled me with wonder, when first I met it face to face. Neither your Seekh nor your wild Afghanee would have lived amid such a terrible odor, but would have run screaming. A wild, dirty, unfinished little place it was in those days, our Washington. To a man who had seen London, Delhi, and Lahore, it was not much at all. Pardon me the sin of pride.

As I stood under that gaslight, with just a little stink rising from the canal and the leavings of the market, a wonder appeared before my eyes. A great carriage come up, with a pair of outriders in uniform and a brace of other carriages following. A trooper leapt out of his saddle and banged on the station door. He went at it with great whacks, while his comrades flustered about the big carriage, pulling on a pair of arms as if the occupant was unwilling to emerge.

Twas General Scott.

History stepped down before me, ladies and gentlemen. Six-foot-five and many a pound of it. General Scott come squeezing out the door of that carriage, fair blooming out of it, his cloak heavy with braid and his feathered hat before him. He was a great massive man, a good doer at table, and you could see what a specimen he had been in his prime. But he groaned and grunted now, and could not manage the carriage steps without the aid of a little army of staff officers.

His going had been rumored, his resignation expected, but we lessers had no facts to hand. Of course, we all wanted to see him go, in our heartlessness and our folly. He was too old, too fat, too tired for us. With the years behind me, I see his greatness now. But the country felt only impatience with him that autumn, and I longed to be one with my new country. Bull Run be jiggered—if you will excuse my ferocity—the Union wanted to march on Richmond. I knew better, of course, but what is knowledge compared to emotion?

We thought we had our man in General McClellan. But I must not go too swiftly.

Lights rose in the hall, and General Scott plumped for the doors, an old bear on parade. You could hear his limbs weep. A teamster hollered, "You're a-going the wrong way, gen'rul. Rebs is yonder." But none of his fellows took up the mockery. The carriages in trail produced faces half-familiar, politicians who perched at the bar in Mr. Willard's hotel, and ladies made fine, the sort who stuck to the north side of Pennsylvania Avenue on their promenades. Old Scott was going, but he would not go alone. His companions were making a social affair of it.

There is sadness in such doings.

The general did not see me. I am not great of stature,

nor a commanding sort. Nor was I a man of any importance. But I saw the old man's face. Twas the composition of sorrow.

Just as he was set to enter the station, we heard an uproar come on at a gallop, the shot crack of horseshoes on wet paving, then the muffling as they turned into the mud of the station yard. Accouterments jangled, and troopers riding in advance shouted a path through the wagons and carts and stray women of the sort who have lost their direction in life.

I am a man blessed with an instinct for where to look, and it has often been in the direction opposite from the public's attention. With the cavalcade just upon us, I turned toward General Scott. What I saw was far sadder than the loneliness of retirement. I saw hope. I understood him, you see, as one soldier understands another. I saw the quick, bright glow of hope that his President had changed his mind, refusing to accept his resignation and recalling him to his generalcy over the new multitudes in blue.

He was disappointed. General McClellan, our champion and as young as Scott was old, pranced up on his stallion. Even in the dark, the man shone, and his India-rubber cape looked like a lord's hunting kit. We all knew him by sight, great galloper that he was. McClellan was ever underway, racing over the long bridge to inspect the fortifications on the Virginia side, dashing up to the heights to welcome a newly arrived regiment, always on his infernal monster of a horse. Little Mac was the most visible man in the Union, a fellow who might have made a great career in the theater, had he not been fitted to the military. I had a fondness for him because he was a great man but not a big one, barely taller than myself. I thought him set to convince the world at last of the spark in the man of compact physique. And he was another Pennsylvania man.

McClellan made a perfect stop on his horse, gallant and just broadside to the old general, then he threw back his wet cape. The two men shared a taste for fine uniforms, and even this early in the morning they were resplendent. No Worth gown will match the magnificence of a general with an indulgent tailor.

Another man might have found humor in the contrast between the mountainous old soldier and the young rooster set to replace him. In truth, McClellan did not come up to Scott's shoulders. Not even with his French cap on. But Mac had zest, and old Scott did not. The young man carried it off with a fine salute. I was proud of him.

It seemed generous to me that McClellan should rise so early to bid a last farewell to an old soldier, but perhaps it was simply clever. No matter. I believed in its decency at the time. And once his face settled, General Scott appeared pleased, accepting the visit as a mark of respect from the boy who booted him, unwilling to think further on it.

I heard nothing of their conversation beyond the greeting, for admirers surrounded them, and the sound of an incoming train called me to duty. I had received a telegraphic message promising that a much-delayed shipment of trousers would arrive with certainty this time. We had soldiers standing guard in their drawers and sharing blankets under tentage that would not keep out a spit of tobacco. A week back, General Meigs, who was a hard and honest fellow, had condemned twenty-five thousand army overcoats that had been delivered shoddy. Think of the cost of such like. Our government bled money to buy the things the soldiers needed, but the relationship between payment and delivery seemed to have broken down. There was not an excess of honesty among the manufacturers, if I may be pardoned the frankness, and not a few seemed to regard the war first and foremost as a splendid opportunity to bolster their fortunes. Nor was our government composed entirely of innocents.

In the camps, sickness whittled at our regiments while the officers quibbled. My new duty was to clothe them, yet I could not do even that. It was a dark time, that first autumn of the war. We had no victories, and few heroes. The country was impatient with Mr. Lincoln. It seemed we could not bear another blow. But let that bide.

The trousers did not arrive. There was a shipment of cannon of a mark later found to explode upon repeated firings, and a company of zouaves sang a vulgar tune off pitch as they staggered from the train. But the cargo master had nothing for me.

General Scott boarded a fine private car behind his own locomotive, set to pull away ahead of the six o'clock train. McClellan bid him a handsome farewell, then strutted off, pausing only to inspect a driving wheel, for he had become a big railroad man before the war. Mr. Cameron, our Secretary of War and himself a railroad fellow, come hurrying to join old Scott, but he and Little Mac went out of each other's way like cholera shunning the plague. Only the barest of formal greetings passed between them, though they were both Pennsylvania men.

Now I worked on loan to Mr. Cameron's department under a queer arrangement with the Quartermaster General, and I would have liked to believe in the man. But I could not mistake that he had great acquaintance among those manufacturers least respondent to payment. I had twice been warned not to bother mill owners for due delivery. And Mr. Cameron had great interests in ore and iron and steel, as well. He would have been right at home in Merthyr's mill offices, or up in Crawshay's Castle. White-haired and weak of chin, Mr. Cameron had a narrow face and the eyes of a barracks lender. I marked it to Little Mac's credit that there was no great love between them. But let that bide.

The depot was a blustering place, what with the loading and the workmen shouting and the parlor laughter of the ladies attending the general. Bales tumbled from wagons and raindrops skirmished. Newspapermen, hardly creatures of the dawn, accumulated beside Scott's railway coach, weaving and pitching questions. Cars shifted, brakes shrieked, and steam rose. A courier boy ran up to one of the scribblers, and the man left quickly, as though the general's interest to the public had vanished in an instant, but I thought nothing of it at the time.

Nor did I think on the trouserless infantry, if I am to be honest. My thoughts were fixed on myself, and they were sour. I had been made a fool again, see. I had presumed to lead a company of men into battle, but I could not even secure a shipment of woolens. Perhaps I should have gone back to Pottsville and my Mary Myfanwy, for all the good I was to the Union.

I marched off in vexation. Along the first blocks of Pennsylvania Avenue, I had to keep to the high sidewalk, for the street was under water from the storm. A dead cat floated by and the slop water come right up to the base of the elms. Twas Saturday, and early still, yet farmers creaked in to market atop weathered carts, the rough wheels churning through the flood. Wet through, their wives shielded pies to hawk to the soldiers. Wagons of firewood, down from the counties, rolled behind nags too broken to sell to army purchasing agents. Drovers chased muddy beeves along the great avenue, a day's feed for the army, and language that was not Christian followed them. A boy sold chestnuts from a brazier for a workingman's breakfast. The fragrance took me in its thrall till I was tempted to buy, but we must be modest and firm in our expenditures.

The sky cracked above the Island. Light seeped over the roofs, fighting through the veil of chimney smoke. Bugles sounded in the distance, first one, then dozens, taking up the call one from the other like jackals. Our camps were everywhere, in the squares and on the great lawns, on the heights above the city and beyond the river. The army was growing like a great blue muscle, and the city swelled with it.

There is lovely when a city wakes to morning. But there was no peace for me.

Cheating the law, a saloon stood open for the devil's breakfast. A painted bit of a girl leaned near the doorway.

"Special price for the first of the day, sweetie," she told me.

I walked by, but she would not leave well enough alone, and called after me, "I'll make you feel like a real big man. You won't feel like a cripple no more."

Now I am not given to light conversation with such, although I will not be the hypocrite who pretends his youth was a model of Christian deportment, but something set off my powder that morning. Perhaps it was the undelivered trousers, or the child's voice issuing from the harlot's mask— if she was fourteen, I'm the Maharajee of Mysore. In truth, it might have been her lack of charity as to my person. All up, I turned on the girl, swiveling on my cane.

"How old are you?" I demanded.

"How old d'you want me to be?"

"Now, now, missy. Just tell us the truth, and there's a good girl."

"I'm old enough to show a fellow a time."

She had the look of a farm lass a week in the city and fallen in with its refuse.

"Look you," I said. "This is a bad business. If you're hard upon it, you can go to the Reverend Abernathy's mission for help. It's but a walk up 9th Street, where you'll find it clean and orderly."

She looked at me with the disdain of youth. "Oh, I know them kind. What all they want's a free tossing between the hymn howling, no thanks. And don't you talk queer like? 'Ye cane goo tah ta Revrent Meegillicutty . . .'" She laughed a laugh I would not wish on a girl so young. "Maybe you're a Reb spy?"

Now I understood the silliness about spies, for there was a great deal of rumor that autumn, and rumor would be such a girl's fact. But my speech has always been incontestably normal.

A man with a mustache as wide as his shoulders appeared in the door and addressed me in terms I will spare you. I turned to be on my way, but the girl called after me, with the sad spite of a child, "Go on, Cap'n Gimpy Leg. Look at the little sucker, would you?" I heard the sound of a blow then, followed by weeping and a man's voice commanding her to remove an indiscreet part of her anatomy to the interior of the saloon.

I am not blind. I have seen war, from the plains of Chillianwala to the hills of Virginia, and I know what it brings in its train. But I do not like that which is done to children, nor what is often made of them.

Seventh Street had begun to stir as I turned up its fine pavings. The daughters of the German shopkeepers were out clearing away the storm debris, scrubbing their windows and entranceways, ever the earliest, for they are a clean and industrious people. A few of them knew me to be Mrs. Schutzengel's boarder and greeted me as *Herr Hauptmann*. It seemed that all the Germans in Washington were quietly prosperous and acquainted one with the other. Great singers, they were, too, with their little societies for it, though they could not hold a candle to the Welsh. I think the Germans a fine people for an artisan class and keeping shops, and an honest race, but you will never make soldiers of them.

I turned at the Patent Office. My leg wanted an end to the walk, but we cannot indulge the flesh. A pair of ragamuffins who should have been to bed aped my limp and saluted. When I did not respond, they soon lost interest. It is an odd thing to remember. My injury that seemed so great to me then was nothing to what others would suffer in the war. We had no sense of the coming terribleness or its duration. By the end of it, a man with a bothered leg would hold no attraction for even the worst of boys.

I could smell Mrs. Schutzengel's house from half a block away, but this was a fine smell, the baking of bread and cakes, and a great frying. I never understood my fellow officers who mocked me for taking a simple room at an unfashionable address, for what more could a man desire in a boardinghouse than cleanliness, good cooking, and a fair price? Which left a nice remittance for my Mary Myfanwy. Now you might say the Welsh are tight in the purse— and I have heard that said—but your Germans and Welsh understand one another. A fair service for a fair price, and all are made happy.

I came in and the hall was cold, but I hung up my coat on the peg. The dining room would be warm now. Mrs. Schutzengel could be depended upon, and that is always a fine thing in life.

I was early, of course, with the other boarders still in their sleep. I surprised Mrs. Schutzengel in the kitchen, though I did not mean to do so.

She was a great door-filling woman, akin to the Low

Dutch we had encountered about our new home in Pottsville. When I come in, she was bent to the oven—a spectacle
from which a gentlemen of sense would avert his eyes—and
the effort of straightening her back left her out of breath
and red and tottering. Her hands grabbed the air.

"Oooch," she said, "*Mein lieber Gott, oooch, ist nur Sie, Herr
Hauptmann? Oooch, mein Gott, Sie haben so eine Angst in mich gejagt!*"

"Good morning, Mrs. Schutzengel," I said. "There is sorry
I am, if I gave you a fright."

She sweated like an old sergeant in the summer of Hin-
doostan, and the moisture clung to her cabbage of a nose.

"*Ist nichts, ist nichts!* Oooch, now I am always so bad to
speak German. I speak *Deutsch* to you, I am sorry. When I
am so frightened. Maybe it is them Rebels. Come *und* sit,
Captain Jones."

"No, no. I'm sorry. It's only that I thought—"

"Now you has been in the cold and all wet, I think? You
must become warm. Sit, sit. I make you a breakfast."

"Only a little coffee, see."

"*No! Nein* to only coffee. Your wife, *Gott erbarme*, she will
think, 'Who is this terrible person, the Schutzengel?' when you
are coming home all in bones like the *Sensenmann*. You will have
ein gutes Frühstück now. Think of your wife, of the little *Kind*."

"I think of them all the time, Mrs. Schutzengel. That I
do. It's only that I seem to be developing this American
craving for coffee, and I hoped—"

She resettled her apron, and a great apron it was, then
she planted her fists on her hips. I must say she was daunt-
ingly large. Though good of heart.

"Sit," she commanded. "Eat."

I stepped back in from the yard, prepared to leave the
house for the day, when I heard a ruckus in the dining room.

The other boarders were up and at their victuals, with a steady sound of cutlery. But Mister Mager, a drummer of uncertain wares and a fellow countryman of Mrs. Schutzengel's, was in high complaint.

"Where *ist* sausages?" he demanded. "I smells sausages."

"*Es gibt keine Wurst heute,*" Mrs. Schutzengel roared, for she was not pacific when aroused. "No sausages today."

"I smells sausages," Mager insisted.

I closed the front door behind me. Twas the politic thing to do. At my captive breakfast in her kitchen, Mrs. Schutzengel had thrust fine, bursting swells of sausage upon me, and I will not say I did not respond with appetite. Now Mrs. Schutzengel kept an abundant board, and she was generous with her potatoes and puddings, her biscuits and stuffings and breads—all gleaming with gravy or slathered with lard, as I see her table still—but the portions of meat she kept under firm control. I had eaten the day's entire ration of sausage, though not with ill intent or knowledge of the deed. Mrs. Schutzengel was a woman of great drive, and she was always driven to feed me. Perhaps she thought I was not done growing. I never understood her, but women are deep as a pit mine.

Now Saturday was a quiet day to work in the War Department. There were many who should have been at their desks, but the young gentlemen always found reason to be away, paying court to women honorable and less so, and when the officers are absent you must not expect great diligence from the ranks. I was not alone in the great brick building, but I might have been for all the work being done, war or no.

Evans the Telegraph, a good Glamorgan man, come by with a set of newspapers in the crook of his arm. I will admit that I examined them with him. But they had gone to press

too early to report on General Scott's departure. Nor did
they yet tell of the death that would so affect my life. I
soon laid them aside. If I am to be honest, my newspaper
was *The Evening Star*, and none of the morning folders. Now
if there was sensation in *The Star*, it was also a sheet that
knew how to tell a story, and Mr. Wallach had a scent for
news. Three good cents for four good pages, I always said.

A barricade of ledgers and bills my desk was, but Evans
the Telegraph said, "A letter I've had, Captain Jones. From
my Keziah's folk." His speech was slow and considered, as
becomes a chapel man. "They would send young Dafydd to
America. No work but bad in the valleys, see. How do you
think on it?"

I thought on it. "Mr. Evans, I would counsel a delay. For
war is a great temptation to the young. I expect an end to
it with the spring campaigning."

Evans nodded. "Just so. But young Dafydd is taken with
young Madlin Rhys. Of the Pontypridd line. You see how
it is."

I shook my head. "No good to come of that."

Evans drew out his pipe and I feared a long stay. There
were figures to reckon, battles to be fought with pen and
ink and rule. But I will admit I find a good talk with another
Welshman hard to resist.

"No," Evans went on. "No good. For there's English blood
on that side. Low people out of Hereford."

"Perhaps the boy should come on then. Better a war than
an English wife."

Evans lit his tobacco with one of those blazing American
matches. He nodded, puffed up the smoke, and sighed like
a heartsick dragon. "Just so, just so. Had the girl but been
a Pendoylan Rhys, *that* would have been a fine pairing . . ."

We settled that I would write to my Mary Myfanwy

about the matter. I wrote to her each day. She could inquire of her uncle, Mr. Evan Evans of Pottsville—no relation to Evans the Telegraph—who had set me to a fair job in the mining administration in my own time of need. The collieries were short of able hands, with the outflux of volunteers. There were not even Irish enough.

"And how is Mr. Lincoln?" I asked, as I asked at the close of each visit. Mr. Lincoln was a great one for visiting the telegraph office. The question was a notice that I had no more time, not even for a buttie.

"A great sad man. Full of jokes," Evans said. "I believe his health sustains. But a cloud hangs over him since the scrap by Leesburg."

He left me then, in his goodness, taking up his papers and puffing his pipe like a steam engine.

The department's accounts were a horror. Twas not only that a man began to suspect dishonesty and graft. Not a line tallied. Now as you will learn, I have little enough nostalgia for the service of old John Company or even the Queen, God bless her, but we never would have allowed the books of the remotest regiment to get into such a state. No, sir, I tell you. The provisioning sergeant would have been broken to the ranks and the responsible officer sent off to map the Kush. With the best will in the world, I could make but little progress.

I worked till the light left me, then shut up my papers under lock. I had not seen a general all day, nor a colonel nor major. Of course, the sharp ones would be over to General McClellan's headquarters. But how my new countrymen neglected the necessaries, from the Army's feeding to the good harnessing of its horses, was a mortal sin to me. Now it was a mighty task to go from a small establishment to a great battling army in a matter of months. We could not expect perfection. Yet the neglect of duty was everywhere, and I could not like it. War was still a lark to them. I would have liked to see only one general at his post that day, but all I saw as I left was Mr. Lincoln making his way to the telegraph office, shawl about his shoulders. He looked for all the world like a railway inspector on a county line.

I walked home past the supply yard put up behind Mr. Corcoran's new mansion, where an Irish sergeant called for cavalry boots and the devil. The gas lamps were on and carriages halted before the fine houses, delivering ladies from their afternoon visits. Cooking smells rose, and Fine Jim stood bandy on his corner.

"I'll have my *Evening Star*, thank you," I told the lad.

He looked at me. "You won't, sir."

Now that was not in the order of things.

"Ain't come out yet," he told me. "They're holding it back. There's a great story, they says. Coming any time now."

It ruffled me. Now a man must make allowances for wartime, certainly, but a regular fellow has his habits. My evening newspaper was a pleasant, indeed, a necessary thing to me. It was my day's rest to read in the parlor after dinner, while Mrs. Schutzengel sat in her martyred velvet chair and fingered her way through those great German tomes of hers, all the while keeping an ear to the boarders working off their debts in the kitchen. Then I would go up to my room and write to my wife by lamplight, for Mrs. Schutzengel saw no joy in a wasted penny and had not put in gas above the stairs.

Now the world was out of kilter. I am, I hope, a reasonable man. But I was unsettled without my newspaper. My leg pained me doubly much as I made my way home.

It is at such times that the decency in men redeems us.

I grumbled my way to Mrs. Schutzengel's block. Twas near the end of the last decent street, bordering a sharp drop in quality beyond, where God's image deteriorated until it reached the Irish snags down in Swampoodle. The lamps wore haloes in the damp air, and the wind sparked up. The rain would return as sleet, you could feel it. More storms we would have.

Ahead, I saw a gathering of soldiers, more than a dozen of them, just at the boardinghouse porch. I could not figure it. There was not a saloon nor one house of disgrace in our street.

Then I come up closer, and I recognized them just as they spotted me.

"It's Captain Jones," a voice called. "Down there." Private Pierce. His sound high and thin as a cheap bugle.

There stood a dozen lads from my old company, come to town from camp. To the Lord knew what end. But I will tell you fair, I was glad to see them. My heart leapt. Then I remembered the terrible, sad look on General Scott's face that morning and warned myself to be steady.

They gathered around me. Though a few had come by the hospital, a convalescent ward is a trial for young men and they did not last it. But now they had come. Try as they might, they could not hold their eyes from my limp. They were such young men, and so helpless.

Mrs. Schutzengel stood on her porch, a human bulwark.

"Oooch, Captain Jones. You are come home now, *Gott sei Dank*. These mens do not listen. They spits on my stones. On the stones I have scrubbed, they spitted. *Save me.*"

I braced up my back.

"Masters? You spitting again?"

"No, sir, Captain. No, sirree. Not much."

"And you, Farmer?"

Yes, a culprit there. I could tell by the face on him. Yet I could not be hard. I was so glad to see my boys.

"I will tend to them, Mrs. Schutzengel. They will behave. Now, what is wanted here, boys?"

They were lads out of the anthracite mines, or off the low farms, young Pennsylvania bucks, and speech was a burden to them. They shuckered about. Finally, Corporal Mays took charge.

"If the captain don't mind," he said, "would the captain climb up the steps there. So it's official like?"

I would have done anything for the boys. Anything legal and honest, you understand. But I could not let them see it. I put on my dependable face, the one I learned in the sweat and blood of the Punjab as a young fusilier.

I climbed the steps toward the scent of dinner. Private Berry moved to assist me, but I turned on him a face that stopped that quick. I would not be helped, for I was not an invalid, but a serving officer. With a slight crook to the leg, but no matter that.

"Will the captain face about, sir?"

"I am facing about, Corporal Mays. All in good time, see."

"Yes, sir. Captain Jones, sir."

I looked them over in the lamplight and shadows. Their uniforms still did not fit, still had not settled to their bodies, and flaps of cloth rose with the wind. Their buttons were badly polished at best. But at least they had trousers.

"Now, Mays . . . all of you . . . if you're in town for the drink, you know I do not approve of intoxicants, to say nothing of the breakdown in judgement that can lead a man to—"

"Begging your pardon, Captain Jones . . ." Twas Pierce of the bugle voice. Speaking out of turn. As always.

"What is it, Pierce?"

"Sir, Corporal Mays has something to say to you. If you please, sir."

Yes. I knew it, of course. But I am coward in matters of the heart, see.

"Go on, Corporal."

Mays put the boys into two ranks before Mrs. Schutzengel's garden fence. Then he come to the foot of the steps with a wooden case under his left arm. He snapped his heels together and saluted.

"Now, Mays," I said. "You'll do to unlearn that salute. I taught you wrong, and you're to learn the ways of our own army. Hide that palm, man. Finger tipped to the brim of the cap."

"Yes, sir. I've learned it right, sir. I just done it that way for you."

"Go on, Mays."

"Captain Jones," he began, with the heaviness of a man who has memorized his speech, "sir, we come to apologize. The whole company would've come, but we couldn't get the let for all. So we're the elected volunteers come to resent the entire—"

" 'Represent,' Corporal Mays. 'Represent.' "

"Pardon, sir. To represent the entire company." He began to step toward me, then caught himself. "We come to say we're sorry we run away. We're sorry we let you down. After how good you trained us. Wasn't right, what we done out at Bull Run. And to think of your leg . . ."

"My leg will be fine, Corporal. As for running, you will not do it again. That is enough."

"After how good you trained us . . ." he started again.

" *'Bayonets fore! Second rank, up! Third rank, ready!'* " That was

Roberts. Who was often light of heart and not the best representative of the Welsh race.

"Shut up, Bob," Corporal Mays told him.

"Roberts," I said, "we'll have no more of those improper commands. I taught you what I knew, and twas from another army. An expedient measure, no more. It's *Hardee's Tactics* for you now."

Mays could restrain himself no longer. He rushed up the steps, holding out the wooden case in both hands. "Sir . . . the boys all took up a collection. All the boys from home. Now that you're a big staff officer and all, and a hero, we thought you ought to have—"

"I am no hero, Mays. We'll have no such talk. A man is not a hero for doing his duty." The wind got in my eyes. "Why, couldn't I tell you boys of heroes, though. If you could have seen Sergeant Pomeroy at Chillianwala, a hundredfold of Seekhs all raging bloody about him—"

"Would the captain inspect his gift, sir?"

He opened the box before me. Twas little enough light from the gaslamp on the corner and the parlor fittings behind the curtains, but the metal and plate shone high. The boys had got me a revolver, one of the new Army Colts. But it was a special-made thing. It looked like a silversmith had taken his hand to it. And a goldsmith, too.

I am not one who holds firearms dear. They are the devil's instruments, and I had long thought that part of my life behind me. But that is another story. This was a gift of good intent, and no mistaking it. I lifted the pistol out of its velvet bed.

The men gave a little cheer, but one look put an end to that. We could not have a disturbance in the street.

Still, Pierce called out, "We even miss your singing, Captain."

The pistol was a heavy weapon, balanced long in the barrel, but sleek and very fine as such things go. And Mr. Colt was an honest manufacturer who delivered on his contracts, so I faced no reservations there.

"There is fine," I told them at the quiet. Emotion must be mastered. "Though it is a wasteful thing you have done."

"It's from all the boys," Farmer spoke up. "Ever one. The new captain, he wanted to chip in, too. But we wouldn't let him."

"You will be loyal to him," I said fiercely.

"Yes, sir. Only he wasn't part of what . . ."

"Yes, Farmer. But you are to mind your waywardness. You are given to an independence that does not become a private soldier." Then I said, "Thank you, boys. I thank you all. A fine gift, this. Though extravagant."

The tooling was beautiful. If such things can be beautiful. The pistol looked too fine to use.

"When you see it in the light," Corporal Mays instructed me, "it got lettering put on it. Siney done that, the jeweler's boy. It says, 'To Captain A. Jones.' And on the other side, there's, 'Hero of Bull Run.'"

"That is excessive, Corporal Mays."

Now I will not lie to you. The boys made me proud that night. Though they had been wasteful of purse. But the rain was coming again, and the little ceremony was over, and I recognized it before they did. I had to let them go. In truth I know it was more for them than for me, the gift. They were good lads, and longed to make amends. They would never see that I did not fault them.

"All right, men," I said. "You'll do the company and the regiment proud, I know it. But you're never to let Pierce anchor the line, for he cannot tell his right from left. And Berry, you're not to close both eyes when you fire. You are dismissed now. And do nothing in this city to shame your wives or mothers."

They come up to shake my hand, and most of them saluted. They were good boys, and had I not pitied them that first sad night I saw them struggling to drill themselves, I would have bided at home with my Mary Myfanwy and little John. But we all must go to our duty when we see it.

I watched them leave, with the pistol case clutched to my heart. Twas not a gift I would have chosen, you understand.

I was about to go in to Saturday dinner, when a figure like a ragged cat darted under the gaslamp. Twas Fine Jim, come with my paper.

"Cap'n Jones," he said, "I brung you something terrible."

𝓵

BY SUNDAY MORNING THE GLOOM OF THE NEWS WAS ON THE city, with the telegraph spreading it to the ends of the Union. The Reverend Abernathy was not a man to swerve from God's plan or his own, and he went ahead with his sermon on temperance—I leave it to you to consider the usefulness of a lesson on the horrors of alcohol preached to a congregation of Methodists who would not touch ginger beer—but at the end he had his say on the matter of Anthony Fowler.

"Is it not cause for sorrow," he asked us, "and for mighty lamentation, when a young and noble crusader for justice, a champion of those encumbered by the bonds of human servitude, when the purest of souls, a stalwart lily in the Lord's garden, is hewn down in his golden glory, slaughtered like a lamb in the service of his country, and murdered like a dog in his coat of honor?"

The ladies wept in their pews, and not a few wailed like Baptists, for they all knew the slain boy by image and report. Myself, I felt our loss, but I must admit that I sometimes found the Reverend Abernathy's enthusiasm for language alarming. In truth, I had yet to encounter a stalwart lily, or a lamb in the service of his country, or a dog murdered, let alone a dog murdered in a coat of honor. But let that bide. Old Abernathy was American-born, and even the Welsh blood on his mother's side could not save him from the native imprecision of speech. He was a man of conviction, though, and that counts for much.

"Weep today," he concluded, "ye children of Jerusalem. For tomorrow you must rise up and carry on a hero's labors. Seek to live your lives, my sons and daughters, in emulation of our fallen immortal's stolen young life. The Lord's mercy and blessing be upon Anthony Fowler." He looked up, with his strained eyes searching eternity. "Go forth now, go forth, I say, in a torrent of cleansing fire."

The congregation dawdled in the nave, for the rain was still knocking on the door. Sarah Williams wept up a storm. None of the other girls could compete with her. Young Sarah declared that she must die of a broken heart, for her love for Anthony Fowler had been immaculate and complete. The grown ladies cried in that dour way we chapel folk have, for all knew of Fowler and his accomplishments. Twas an abolitionist congregation, our own, come down on the right side of the schism among the city's Methodists. Washington was ever a strong Southron town, and even the children of John Wesley were sometimes blinded. When first I rose from my ward bed, a Georgetown chapel would not accept me in my coat of blue. I did not write of it to my Mary Myfanwy, who might have expected the like of high church folk, but not of our own kind. It was a terrible war that way.

The *Evening Star* had printed the story the night before, hard by the news of General McClellan's replacement of General Scott. And a frightful story it was. GOLDEN YOUTH ASSASSINATED! the paper proclaimed, UNION HERO MURDERED!

Captain Anthony Fowler, famed abolitionist, lecturer, philanthropist, and volunteer officer, scion of the Philadelphia Fowlers and sporting champion, late of the University of Pennsylvania, had been found dead of a gunshot wound. He had fallen in the darkness to an assassin's bullet, the victim of nefarious and insensate Rebel viciousness, murdered near the Virginia outpost line where he had taken his stand in defense of the Union. They wrote it fine and grand, they did, telling of his lecture tour with Mrs. Stowe and his eloquent defense of old John Brown. Another scribbler reminded us that Anthony Fowler had shone not only in grand society, but in the far poor winkles of the land, where he had campaigned for Mr. Lincoln and liberty, but, above all, for an end to the scourge of slavery.

Women adored Anthony Fowler, but he remained pure, vowing chastity until the day when all men would be free on American soil. Calling cards with his photo were a rage among the girls, and young men copied his dress, which had been fastidious but for an oversizing of the neckcloth. Then he put on a uniform and a new set of images went up for sale, the profit of each transaction reserved for the education of former slaves and their transportation back to their African homeland.

He had even touched my own life. My Mary Myfanwy had paid two dollars for tickets to hear him speak in a tent in Pottsville a year past. I could not go, for my work was not completed, and it clipped me to think not only of the extravagance of the dollar spent on my ticket, but of the ticket going unused. Then my Mary Myfanwy come back near hysterical, which was a shock just short of the resurrection of the dead on a Monday, for she was ever a decorous woman on social occasions. She had a fit in the front room. And that in the company of Mrs. Perry, no less, who, though she was of English extraction herself, went to howling and barking like an Irishwoman jilted and bereaved at one blow. Twas all young Anthony Fowler's doing, for he had described the infernal torments of human bondage till the audience thought the sky would open in an instant and pour down God's wrath upon the land. They noted his beauty, too.

"So pure he was," my Mary Myfanwy said, with her eyes all wet and sweet. "If only more men were so."

I did not take it to heart, for I knew she would not have had me quite so pure as young Mr. Fowler.

Then, when I left the convalescent ward for my work in the department, there he was. Not with me down in woolens and canvas, of course, but upstairs where they set out the sums for cannon and the great things of war. I saw him come and go, ever in the company of other young gentlemen of distinction, and would have spoken to him had I cause. For he was a beautiful man, such as I had only seen one time before, and that other the subaltern son of a duke, too fine for life and dead of the black cholera in fifty-four.

Perhaps, I thought, such beauty and purity truly were too fine for this life.

The rain let by, and I made my way homeward, thinking of the harshness of the world and Mrs. Schutzengel's Sunday roast. But I was not to have my dinner. For a great, wicked cavalry horse stood tied to the ring by the gate and a trooper sat on Mrs. Schutzengel's porch, heels up on the railing and spurs dangling. He looked familiar, but all I could think of was his impertinence in sitting that way. I could not believe Mrs. Schutzengel would allow such a thing. And surely she knew of his presence, for she had a nose for a bad intention a block away.

When I stepped near, he dropped his feet and stood. Familiar he was, but still I could not place him. He tugged down his short jacket and pulled on the brim of his kepi, then come down to me in the street.

"Captain Abel Jones?"

"That I am."

"Confidential matter, sir. General McClellan wants to see you."

Now that stopped me like a brick wall. I took the time to wonder if it were not a mistake.

"I . . . am not of the general's acquaintance," I stammered. "Perhaps you—"

"Well, he sure knows you, Captain. He wants to see you quick."

A prisoner of old instincts, I straightened my uniform and my bearing. "I am at the general's service, of course. When—"

"You're to come along right now. He's waiting for you. Got yourself a mount?"

"No, I—"

"Then take mine."

I fixed the man then. He was the trooper who had pounded on the station door the morning past, opening the way for General Scott. Now he was in the service of General McClellan, which was a quick evolution of fate and a curious thing.

"I'll walk, thank you."

He looked down at my leg. "You don't understand, Captain. The general—"

Now I must make a confession. And I suspect it will not be the last. I am not a man for horses. I hate the beasts. They are great stupid things, and we have no business upon their backs. Cavalrymen and horses deserve each other. Oh, I admit it—the creatures frighten me half to death. I would as soon wrestle a Sindhi cobra of fifteen foot than mount one of those four-legged demons.

I was rescued by Providence. A cab clattered down the street, fresh from stables and headed through to the prosperous quarter, for we were the walking kind in Mrs. Schutzengel's neighborhood. I waved my cane and let off a shout. Now a cab is a shameful extravagance, and walking is grand for the health, but fate left me no choice. I was so relieved to avoid the great nostril-flaring beast by the gate I did not even ask the price before climbing in.

The trooper led the cab to the big house on Jackson Square where General McClellan had made his headquarters. Out come two Frenchmen chattering. Twas a bad omen, I thought, for I have a difficulty with the French since the day I was forced to put a bayonet to one who was rallying the Seekh. I see the surprise on his face yet, the mystification in his eyes, and cannot sponge him out of my barrel. He was the first white man that I killed. But let that bide. High-smelling Frenchmen these two were, with their pointed little beards and gloves white as Easter. They forced me into the gutter, and my leg turned.

We must master ourselves. I followed the trooper inside, and it was a place unlike the War Department. All was activity, Sunday though it was. Clerks scribbled, aides bounded, and colonels bent over maps. These were bustling rooms, full of the good noise of work. They took no notice of me.

The cavalryman passed me off to a major who looked me up and down, and mostly down, I will admit. He was not twenty-five, and as confident of his own grandeur as any Frenchman.

"You *are* Captain Jones?" he asked. "Captain Abel Jones?"

"That I am, sir."

"Yes. Well. I have orders to conduct you to General McClellan."

He began to turn and I caught him by the sleeve. It was an improper thing to do, but he seemed such a boy that I did it without a thought. He looked coldly at my hand, and his eyes worried less about an offense to his rank than contamination.

I took my hand away and looked respectful, the way I used to do in my sergeanting years. "Could you tell me, sir," I asked him, "what the general's concern might be?"

"General McClellan has not taken me into his confidence." He considered me. "Might be something to do with the invalid service. Or a reorganization of the kitchen staff."

The aide cracked open a door, and I heard an impassioned voice say, "Not less than a hundred thousand of them on the Manassas line, Allan. I am threatened on all sides. And they hand me this rabble in arms."

"Beg pardon, sir," the aide said. "I have Captain Jones here."

The conversation broke off immediately, and a bad sort in a checkered suit slipped out past me. Had I been a teller of fortunes, I would have paid greater attention to the man. But the general pulled all of my attention and more.

He burst from behind his desk, thick-necked and steaming with energy, though his eyes were sleepless dark. Double-breasted, his tunic was done up tight but for one button left open above the stomach. His dark hair and mustache shone with pomade. I saluted, but he only thrust out his hand.

His grip was sure.

"Jones? Good of you to come, man. Sit down, sit down. The leg bad?"

"A minor matter, sir."

I will give him two inches on me, no more. He was a grand specimen of a man.

He signaled the aide to leave us alone. "Well, sit down, Jones. We must talk frankly."

I sat, though unsure of the propriety of it while the general remained standing. "Sir," I began, "the leg is growing better. There's no need to dismiss me from service. I could keep the books and do my part with no legs at all. I am a good soldier."

He thrust his hand into his coat where he had left that button undone, a very Napoleon. "Dismissed? Who spoke of dismissal? Jones, you're essential, vital to the cause."

Now any man likes to hear such things, and not least from a fine general.

He took up a new stance between my chair and the fireplace, legs spread and arms folded over his manly chest. "Jones, do you understand the responsibilities under which I labor? I must command my army in Virginia, yet now I am given the burden of all the armies of the Union, as well. I am surrounded by amateurs. And the President has no grasp, Jones. Though I believe his intentions are the best."

"It's a good deal for one man," I agreed.

He plunged toward me. "I can do it all, Jones. I can do it all. But I need men I can trust. Men . . . who can respect confidences."

"Yes, sir."

"You come recommended, Jones."

"Sir, perhaps there's been a mistake . . ."

He pulled a chair toward me as if drawing a saber. "I have been in telegraphic communication," he said, sitting down. "Encoded communication, Jones. There are spies everywhere. I had to locate a man of flawless credentials." He judged me with a surveyor's eye. "You're familiar with Mr. Gowen?"

I thought on it. "I know a young Mr. Gowen, sir. A barrister."

"The man himself. Franklin B. Gowen, Esquire. Philadelphia man, quite sound. Scrapper in the courtroom, though. Represents the coal interests up there in your adopted city. You do know him, then?"

"Not well, sir. He's a society man. I'm not—"

"Come, Jones. This is America. All doors are open. Anyway, Gowen knows you. And I know young Gowen. I trust his judgement." The general perfected the tip of his mustache. "He tells me you're a man who can keep a trust. A man of talent and discretion. Then there's your bravery during the Bull Run affair . . ."

"I keep honest books, sir. Bull Run was not the best of days."

"A man of military experience. In the very inferno of empire. 'Thin red line' and all that."

"That is behind me, sir."

"Crimean service?"

"No, sir."

"War at its cruelest, Jones. I was there, you know. As our government's observer. A cruel and vicious war."

"I did my marching in India, sir." I looked at him plainly. "I was not an officer."

His hand moved from his mustache to his goatee and his eyes changed. "You served . . . during the Mutiny?"

Twas not an affair I chose to remember.

"Dreadful affair," he went on, careless of my hesitation. "Women and children massacred . . . the barbarity of it. Cawnpore. The name will stand for villainy till the end of history."

"I was not there, sir. Not at Cawnpore." I almost told him I took part in the storming of Delhi, for a soldier's longing to talk about that which he has seen is a sore that never heals entirely.

"Dreadful," McClellan repeated. "We shall have nothing like that here. This will be a civilized war, fought on the fair field of battle, and on that field alone." He sat back, his big chest filling the chair. It was his legs alone that were little, and I saw now why he loved to sit on a horse. "And yet, Jones . . . there are occurrences . . . in such times . . . that require tact in their disposition."

He had done me a bad turn, with his talk of the Mutiny business. I saw them again, the little brown men strapped to the mouths of our cannon and blown to a thousand pieces. And our bayonets with such an appetite for human flesh. What they did to us was beyond all crime. But the Hindoo and the Musselman are barbarians, and we were got up to be civilized Christians. We hung them by the hundreds from gallows and trees and city walls, and there was no thought of a trial. At night we closed the town gates and set our fires and listened to them scream. We did not choose between the guilty and the guiltless.

"Do you understand me, Jones? Do you get me, man?"

"I am listening, sir."

"This unpleasant . . . this tragic matter of Captain Fowler," he said. The name woke me like a bell. "I need you to take it on, Jones. The inquiry. The official report. All of it." He looked at me with eyes I could not figure. "I need a man I can trust."

"Army regulations," General McClellan said. "There must be an inquiry." He rose from his chair and spoke with his back to me. "Of course, there *should* be an inquiry, Jones.

We must always seek the truth. Yet . . . this may prove a delicate matter."

"Sir . . . I am not a policeman, and do not know—"

"A policeman's the last thing we want. This is an Army affair."

"Yes, sir."

He turned to me and folded his arms over that grand chest a second time. "Jones . . . the matter would have been simple enough had young Fowler got himself killed in battle. Or on a raid, perhaps. But this . . . assassination business in the press. I don't like it."

"A painful matter, sir."

"Jones . . . there are those who believe I am softhearted toward the South." He took the fabric of his tunic between two fingers. "There are rumblings. From the comfort of their hearths in Boston or New York . . . men question my loyalty, my fitness for command. Though they do not take up arms themselves, you will note."

He moved away again and warmed his front parts by the fireplace. "The thing is . . . this is a tragic and unnecessary war. I shall fight. With all the skills imparted to me. I will bring my country victory on the field of battle. Yet . . . the necessity of it . . . is repugnant." He raised his head, an orator addressing the map on the wall. "People like Fowler made this war, Jones. With their passion for the nigger. Oh, I'm certain the boy had the best intentions. Pure of heart and all that. He was young. But slavery is a dying institution. We needed only to be patient with the South, to exhibit forbearance. The matter would have resolved itself in time."

He joined his hands behind his back and the fingers searched in and out of one another. "Now we have war. And there are those who still are not content, who would make it a holy war. Cynics who would exploit Fowler's death to create a martyr, to introduce a savagery to this war that would prevent any compromise. They do not want to defeat the South, Jones. They want to destroy it. To obliterate Southron civilization as the Romans did Carthage. They would sow the earth with salt, from Virginia to Texas. They would make of this war a cruel and bitter thing."

I nearly said to him that slavery seemed a cruel and bitter thing, for I am not free of a disputatious nature and hold prejudices of my own. But it was not my place to speak.

He turned and strode to his desk, lingered over a stack of dispatches, then suddenly sat down again. "I know the Southrons, Jones. Served with 'em. West Point, Mexico, the West. Now . . . I do not approve of the institution of slavery . . . but it was hardly our affair. In any case, they are gentlemen and not assassins."

His eyes calculated and judged me. "I do not say a Southron . . . perhaps a deranged fellow . . . could not have murdered Fowler. We can reach no conclusions without facts. *Facts*, Jones. I want you to keep an open mind. Examine all the possibilities. Ask yourself who might have profited most from Fowler's death." He canted his head and narrowed his eyes. "There is evil in the North as well as in the South. Young Fowler cries out for justice, not for a spectacle." A twist of a smile crossed his lips. "Why, for all we know Fowler may have been shot by one of our own sentries, by a mere boy with the jitters. Look into all the possibilities, Jones. Come to a wise conclusion."

"Sir, I have no qualifications for such—"

"Honor shall be your qualification. And discretion. Talent. Mr. Gowen assures me you have a fine understanding of people. And a rational mind." He leaned toward me. "I'm counting on you, Captain Jones."

"Sir . . . I would not know how to begin."

He snorted. "I have a mission for you. You'll go to Philadelphia. You will personally convey my condolences to the boy's mother. The funeral train leaves in the morning. There will be a to-do at every stop. Speeches and the like. Abolitionists in their full fury. The body won't reach Philadelphia until Tuesday at the earliest. You'll have a day's start. I've held the afternoon train for you." He drew out a handsome gold watch. "In fact, you should be on your way."

"Sir, I am not accustomed to the affairs of high society . . ."

He snapped his watch shut and buried it again. "Nonsense. This is America, not Britain. A pleasant manner and an honest heart will carry a man far."

"Yes, sir."

"And listen, Jones. The mother . . . can be a difficult woman."

"Difficult, sir?"

"She has . . . notions. And, of course, she shares her son's most extravagant beliefs. Be patient with her. I need you to extract a piece of vital information." He thrust his hand back into his tunic. Oh, he was a grand-looking man. "Find out if young Fowler had enemies. Among our own people. Jealous sorts, perhaps. Put it to her straight. Her crowd's wild with rage, ready to burn down Richmond and lynch every man, woman, and child in the South. Let her know that we will look to *all* points of the compass for her son's killers. We will get at the truth. In the meantime . . . restraint would become all concerned. Convey that to the woman. Gently, of course."

He stood up at a half right to me, back erect and chest thrust boldly forward. Twas a fine, soldierly posture. "I will not see this country destroyed by lies, Jones. This war is about Constitutional issues, not the emancipation of the

Negro. I am at pains to make Mr. Lincoln understand that, and I will spare nothing to make Mrs. Fowler and her zealots understand it, as well." He raised his chin. "We will fight to end our disagreements, if fight we must. But I will have no savagery."

He stepped toward me in a manner that told me to rise. He thrust out his hand again. "And Jones. You will report directly to me. You understand? You will discuss this matter with no one else. You're my confidential agent."

I had the grip of his hand and could feel the callouses where he held the reins and the smoothness of the skin elsewhere. He was a man who rode but did not work.

I did not let go of him immediately.

"Would the general permit an observation?"

"What is it, man?"

I freed his hand. "I'm in confusion, sir, and have been since I read the newspaper the evening last. Young Fowler was a staff man, was he not?"

The general nodded, impatient now.

"I saw him coming and going," I went on. "He worked there in the War Department building. Third floor, just down the hall from General Ripley."

"The train, Jones."

"Yes, sir. Only I was wondering, sir. What was young Fowler doing on the outpost line in the black hours of the night? In a terrible rain? And him a fine staff officer with no business that side of the river?"

McClellan's eyes shifted to the side. "Oh, I suspect Fowler may have been visiting friends in one of the regiments." His forehead creased. "And I'm told the fellow had something of a Byronic streak. Perhaps he was indulging it. 'Roaming through the mists in the face of danger.' Or . . . a spy might have lured him to the spot. Who can say at this point?" He settled a hand upon my shoulder. "Accident, assassination . . . that's all for you to sort out."

He steered me toward a side door with that art great men learn. "Jones, we must honor young Fowler's nobility of conviction. That goes without saying. But we must not be taken hostage by his death." His eyes cut deep. "The Union needs heroes, not martyrs. I fear for our country, Jones. I fear the madness of the times."

3

THEY HELD THE TRAIN FOR ME, BUT THEY DID NOT HOLD A PLACE of any comfort. Now a man should not complain when he can travel from Washington to Philadelphia overnight, but I found it a miserable journey. We were routed the long way around, and the company was not of the best, most of them political fellows disappointed in their requests by Mr. Lincoln. My appearance inspired vulgarities directed at the privileges of the military. I settled onto a bench before the two most honorable-looking passengers, a pair of card cheats departing under the supervision of the provost marshal's guards.

Twas cold dark when we arrived in Harrisburg, where we halted with the stove out in the car and no fuel to be had. In the small hours, those of us bound for Philadelphia were given notice to transfer to the Pennsylvania Railroad. I had not eaten since Sunday morning, for the prices demanded in the station houses for a meat pie or a jar of milk were such that no sane man would pay them, and now all was shut. I slept as best I could on a wooden bench, in a cloud of tobacco smoke. When I was a young man, I could sleep on a bed of rocks, but our bodies weaken with the years, and our expectations rise.

We pulled for Philadelphia at dawn. The traveling mer-chandisers were already at their drink, and, as we progressed through Little Germany, farm women climbed aboard at the lesser stops and unfolded meals wrapped in cheesecloth. I finally bought two boiled eggs and the butt of a loaf from a matron who spoke not a word of English but communicated expertly by coin. We did not reach our destination till noon.

No city looks good from the railway, but Philadelphia looked better than most. It was a great sprawling place, with smallholder plots abounding. As we come up on the depot, the buildings rose tall and dense, many of them fine, and the streets grew brisk with Monday business. The place had the feel of a true city, not of a poor, struggling town like Washington.

The moment I climbed from the car, a fellow stepped up to me. He was dressed all dark and sober, with a high hat in his hand. His bearing was very fine, he was groomed like a racing baronet, and his gaze was steady. He might have been a grand example of an American trading gentle-man, but for his Oriental face.

"Captain Jones?"

"That I am, sir."

He met my eyes with none of that shyness customary in your man of the East. He was fair proportioned, just of my height, and seemed a ready sort. But when I gave him a thorough look, there was something funny about him. His features were not entirely of the yellow race, if you under-stand me.

"I am Mr. Lee. I am to transport you to Havisham House," he said. He sounded like a missionary schoolmaster speaking carefully to the native children.

"And that would be Mrs. Fowler's establishment, Mr. Lee?"

"Yes, sir." He glanced down at my hands. "You are without baggage, sir?"

"A hasty departure," I said. "We might stop by a barber's, for a shave would do me no damage. None of your fancy society barbers, mind you."

"Of course, sir."

He was ready to lead me away, but my curiosity had been gathering during the journey.

"I expect Mrs. Fowler is terrible in her grief?" I asked.

He looked at me without a change of expression.

"There has long been grief in Havisham House," he told me. "Mrs. Fowler is not a companion to frivolity."

He was so fine of manner it surprised me to find that Mr. Lee was Mrs. Fowler's coachman, and not a private secretary or the like. He put me inside the carriage, then tossed a penny to the boy minding the horses, who promptly ran off shouting, "Chinky, chinky, yella stinky."

Mr. Lee snapped his whip in the air and told the horses to walk on. I was glad to be enclosed, without the need to look upon the beasts, for they were a great, huge pair of blacks, with the sleekness of a good stable on them but enough bulk to draw heavy artillery. Eighteen hands sure, they were the devil's own horses, and their eyes should have been red as flame.

The carriage was a lesson that taught all the difference between Philadelphia and Washington. In our capital, every society lady required a trap boiling over with luxury and brassed-up like a battery on parade. You could spot a Washington carriage a cannon shot away, exploding with the importance of its occupants. Mrs. Fowler's rig was black and of merely a useful size, and you had to come up close before you saw the expense in it.

Now I did not know Philadelphia in those days, though I got to know it later, and never had I seen such a wealth of streetcars, all drawn by dependable horses, not nags, and the rails crossing madly. Yet the streets themselves were rutted like market lanes in wet weather, potted and gouged, and Mrs. Fowler's carriage bounced hard. There was prosperity in the city, and I marked one building of eight stories, but the greatest surprise to me come from the number of Negroes shuffling about the streets with an aimlessness that said, "No work." It was an odd business, for this was the North and a free place for all, yet here the African seemed a superfluous man. In Washington, he was a busy fellow, though hardly free.

But let that bide.

Another great difference was the absence of military men. Washington crawled with them like maggots on Army beef. I saw but a dozen blue coats in the streets of Philadelphia, and those worn by men with a look of little belonging and less welcome. The patriotic bunting on the civic buildings and music hall facades drooped, worn by the weather.

Mr. Lee found me a barber hard by Chestnut Street, a tidy shop run by a Scotsman, from whom there would be no extravagant nonsense. Now your barber is a mountain of local knowledge, and you can get it from him if you go about it cleverly. I opened a chat as he stropped his razor and lathered me up.

Beyond the window, Mr. Lee wiped a splatter of mud from the carriage's lacquer.

"Mrs. Fowler's coachman seems regular enough," I said. "He might be a fine Christian gentleman."

"Aye." The barber tilted my head back and went to work. Between strokes, I mined his deposit of opinion.

"Young Mr. Fowler's death was a terrible thing, though."

"Aye," he said.

"A great shock to the family, it must have been."

"Aye."

"*And* to the fair city of Philadelphia."

"Aye."

"Anthony Fowler was one of her golden sons, was he not?"

"Aye." He scraped under my nose, for I am a clean-shaven man who finds the mustache and an excess of whiskers to be vanities. The fellow wore a look of powerful concentration, as if barbering required all the strategy in the world and every jot of his attention. The Scots are a stalwart, but singleminded folk.

"Young Fowler," I said, "must have been greatly loved."

"Aye," the barber told me. He guided his blade along my jaw. "By those who did not hate him."

The Fowler mansion resembled the Fowler carriage, slight in its external decoration but confident in its wealth. It sat on Walnut Street, a rush of leaves from Rittenhouse Square, although I did not know those names then. In a city of red brick rows, its brown stone stood apart. Small it was not.

Black crepe hung from the portico, and the windows had been shrouded within.

Mr. Lee escorted me from the carriage to the door, which opened without the need of a knock. Another Oriental fellow beckoned me in, bowing slightly and repeatedly. This gentleman was of high age, with a bit of dandelion fluff for a beard on his chin. There was nothing at all of the West in his manner or dress, nor did he share Mr. Lee's diluted complexion. He was the hoary Chinee out of a picture book, with his little brimless cap and a blouse of black satin without a proper collar. His pants fell just to the top of his ankles like those of a farmer boy, but his slippers looked the sort English colonels wore in the privacy of their campaign tents.

"Missa Fowluh wait you, suh," he told me. He smiled with ancient teeth.

The servant stood in the light of the opened door, but all beyond seemed black as the devil's own midnight. As he withdrew, motioning for me to follow, I could not see to make my way at first.

A boy—or perhaps it was a girl—I had not noticed closed the front door behind me. I might have been in a tomb.

The old man was a shadow with a pigtail. Hands like claws waved me on.

"Tis way, suh."

As my eyes learned the darkness, a fabulous world emerged. From the outside, I would have judged the house a severe place, but within it was crammed with trophies and brocades till it looked like the harem of the Emperor of the Manchus, if such folk keep those immoral establishments. I marched between a pair of guardian vases taller than myself, following the old fellow into the depths of a great hallway. It seemed to me that the floor slanted downward, but twas only a trick of the place. Great scrolls hung along the walls, some of them bearing heathen letters and others painted queer as the landscape of a dream. Incense stung the air, putting me in mind of places I had tried to forget. There was nothing familiar to a Western temperament but a series of family portraits up the staircase. It was an establishment where a man might have shivered in high summer.

I went knee first into a chair, knocking it cock onto the floor. The servant rushed to right it again, smiling up at me.

"Good, good," he assured me.

He opened a door.

This room was higher than it was wide, with widow's cloth blacking the lone window and two gas fixtures, set to each side of a second door, illuminating a secret world. Red silks worked in gold covered the walls, and a bronze urn as tall as myself supported a coiling dragon. The carpet, too, was red, with golden dragons chasing each other's tail around a great medallion. Filigreed lanterns hung unlit, their brass reflecting the gas flames. I had not seen the like in color and riches since my old regiment fought its way into the Ranee's palace.

"Please to wait," the servant said through his constant smile. Politeness soaked his voice, but he made it clear that I was to stand exactly where I was until given permission to step further.

He disappeared behind the door between the gas jets and whispered in a devilish tongue.

A woman's voice answered in the same incomprehensible sounds.

The old fellow reappeared, bowing yet again. Bobbing like a hanged man just dropped through the trap, he pointed into the darkness behind the door.

"Missa Fowluh wait you," he told me.

The room was colder than the November day without, and vast, and it smelled of ashes. It might once have been a ballroom, but the single gaslight would not let me survey it with accuracy. The walls seemed to recede as I looked at them. It took me a moment to locate Mrs. Fowler in the jumble and gloom, her face a pale blur amid deep browns and grays. It was only the interior dimensions and her slightness, but she looked to be very far away.

A white hand pointed to a chair.

"I am Letitia Fowler, Captain Jones. Do sit down."

My chair was of bare wood, high with a straight back. It was a wicked foreign business. My feet hardly touched the floor. As I settled myself, my cane slipped from my hand and struck the parquet like a thunderclap. I retrieved it without grace.

It took me a good minute to decipher the lines of her mourning dress. Until then, my eyes found only a spectral face and a band of white hair above her forehead. The rest was darkness. She sat rigidly, a queen before her public, ungiving. Only her hands admitted the distress of her loss. They moved along the arms of her chair in unpredictable rushes, like little white mice.

"George McClellan sent you."

I did not know if it was a statement or a question.

"Yes, mum."

"A respectable family, the McClellans. Connecticut stock originally," she said, "but sound. Young George sent me a telegraphic communication about you, Captain." Perhaps it was the faintness of the light, but her features showed not a wrinkle. Certainly, there was an agedness to her, almost an antiquity, but it did not reside in her face. You could see that she had been a crusher of hearts in her April.

"I thought the communication was from my son when it arrived," she continued. "A last message." A smile spooked over her lips, fading as soon as it appeared. "My son was fond of the telegraph, you see. He used to send me communications daily from his lecture tours. He was a great believer in progress and the perfectability of man."

"If I may say, mum, I'm sorry for your loss. And I know you have my wife's sympathy, as well. She thought the world of your son."

Mrs. Fowler sighed, but her back remained as rigid as a

corporal of the guard's. "I shall miss him, my Anthony. The world will miss him. His was too noble a spirit for this blighted sphere."

"Yes, mum."

She looked to the side. There was a great deal to look at in the room, once your eyes got a fix. High jumbles of furnishings, and tables piled with inlaid boxes and jugs and devil masks propped against China pots. When the gas flared a little, silver and gold flashed out of the shadows.

"The telegraph is a convenience," she said, "but an irrelevance. I have not left this house for fourteen years." She turned her face toward me again. "An indisposition left me immobile. But I did not feel incommoded. I have not missed the world. I saw it, Captain Jones, through my son's eyes. He described it all to me, all that he did, all that he saw. We shared the great world . . . as we shared his incorruptible ideals." The tiny smile came and went again, and a hand darted along an arm of her chair. "I suspect it was the best possible way to see our sinful world. Through the eyes of a youth pure in heart." Her eyes focused hard on me. "*Has* the world changed a great deal, do you think?"

"Well, mum . . . I suppose many an object is changed. But I expect men are the same as always."

She lowered her chin and her eyes disappeared under the shadow of her brows. "Yes," she said, her voice a whisper. "I, too, would expect little change in men. Still, we may hope. As my son hoped."

"Yes, mum."

"He was so like his father," she said. "Like unto the Christian martyrs." Her left hand scurried back into a billow of sleeve. "Perhaps you find it curious, Captain Jones, that I do not weep?"

"Yes, mum. I mean, no. I do not presume—"

"I have experience of tragedy, you see. I have grown accustomed to it, and expect nothing else of the flesh." She lifted a hand and indicated the dark treasures all around her. "This house is my memorial to my husband. I do not receive. You are an exception, made under exceptional circumstances. Society . . . is a loathsome snare. My time is occupied in the preservation of my husband's legacy, in writing down the history of his extraordinary deeds." She closed her eyes. "And now I must write of my son."

"I take it your husband was a visitor to the East, mum?" I had my questions for her, as directed by General McClellan, but I dreaded the asking and wished to delay.

"My husband," she said, sinking deeper into her throne, "carried Christ's word to the benighted. I went with him, to help him bear his cross. At our marriage, we pledged ourselves to Christ's work. He was a man of immense gifts, but of still greater generosity of spirit." She raised her chin like the proud girl she once had been. "We were both of us born to privilege, Captain Jones, but we made it our greatest privilege to serve God, to share His Word with those less fortunate. We went into heathen China."

Her face lowered again and her eyes found hard remembrance. "It was a terrible place, an inferno . . . wicked . . . diseased with the worship of idols. You cannot imagine the degradation of mankind unless you have witnessed it in Old Cathay, Captain Jones. God's creatures . . . wallowing in the devil's employments. Yet, my husband's heart knew only mercy, he saw only the good. He lifted the Chinese Heavenward, yet did not condescend to judge the least of them." She gestured toward her treasures again. "Look around you. Examine these manifestations of the love my husband bore toward their culture. He always said . . . he said that it

would 'take unto a hundred years' . . . but that China was
destined to become the greatest of Christian nations."

"Were you there a long time then, mum?"

"Seventeen years. Anthony was born there, you know. In
the mission residence. He was . . . the cause of my return.
Anthony was . . . not a well child. A late gift from our
Redeemer. Such children are often unwell. I feared the Lord
would take him from me. The filth of the place surely would
have killed him. And I loved him . . . immoderately. I had
to bring him home."

"Yes, mum."

"I saved my child."

"Yes, mum."

"And killed my husband."

Now there are times when a man encounters a shortage
of appropriate words. But Mrs. Fowler did not leave me long
in distress.

"My husband remained behind," she told me, "to con-
clude our affairs and to await the arrival of a gentleman from
the Society of Friends who was to assume the mission. But
that gentleman, too, was martyred. He died of sickness on
the river, before he even reached our station. Thus circumstances required my husband to remain in that slough of
idolatry. But mortal love can be as strong as bands of iron,
Captain Jones. After a year, he could not bear the separation
and took ship, abandoning his duties. He could not live
without me, you see." Her eyes sunk deep into her head and
her spirit slouched, though her back remained erect. "His
vessel was lost."

She lowered her chin until the shadows wrapped her in
a veil. Had she not spoken, I would have thought her asleep.
"Perhaps it was God's judgement. On my husband's prefer-

ence for his worldly love over his duty, on his choice of the profane over the sacred. A judgement upon both of us."

"A terrible story, mum." It moved me. For I understood loss.

She lifted her face again, as if her skin had grown a sudden craving for the gaslight, for the least warmth. "I do not tell this to you to gain sympathy, Captain. I only wish you to understand the tradition of sacrifice abundant in this family. My husband dedicated himself to the enlightenment of the heathen, and perished. Now my son has given his life to eliminate the hellish scourge of slavery." A hand darted from the folds of her sleeve to perch at the end of a chair arm. "My duty is to mourn them."

"Yes, mum." I was having a bit of a problem with my leg, for the high, hard edge of the chair was stopping up the blood behind my knee. I wished to make myself more comfortable, but dared not. We must preserve our dignity under such circumstances.

"Slavery . . . is a sin of ineffable darkness," she said, "a sin against God and man. I mourn my son. Yet . . . if his death can further the cause of African freedom . . . if the redemption of those poor innocents can be credited to his sacrifice . . . then let it be." For the first time, she leaned forward. It was only the slightest inclination of the neck, but seemed mighty in the stillness and gloom. "General McClellan informs me that you will head the inquiry into my son's death."

"I will, mum."

"You must discover his assassins. I will forgive them, Captain Jones, but the law demands that they hang."

The change in her tone startled me, for her voice grew as strong as a drillmaster's.

"Your pardon, mum, but in the confusions of wartime, it may prove difficult—"

"I rely upon you," she said, "to bring justice to my son."

"Mum . . . on that very account . . . though it is a painful question . . . I am put to ask if your son had any enemies, if—"

A window slammed shut elsewhere in the house. The noise struck me like the discharge of a cannon.

"Of course, Anthony had enemies," she said in an arctic voice. "There are always demons who would pull down the brightest stars in the firmament, devils grasping at the hem of angels." She turned her head just to the side, but her eyes remained fixed upon me. "Even in this city . . . this 'City of Brotherly Love' . . ." She laughed. It sounded as if an ancient machine had come back into use, creaking and unfamiliar with its own workings. "Do not trust this city, Captain Jones. For the people's hearts are with the South, and their thoughts are drenched in evil. Our Anti-Slavery Society never gathered the commitment of the least theater subscription. They shouted my son down. They spurned him, calling for Barabbas. They are black slavers in their hearts, all of them. Their name is Legion. We must annihilate them."

"Would there be any specific names, mum? Of those who wished your son ill?"

"Names? There are too many to name. Men . . . with their lusts for savage flesh. And the women . . . what poor boy understands the baseness in their hearts? They would have corrupted my son, destroyed him, but for the purity in which God armored his soul. He was born a soldier, Captain Jones, a soldier in the army of the Lord. His every day was a battlefield of temptations. But he remained pure . . ." She waved her head slowly from side to side, and her small hands raced. "I longed to stand there beside him, to support him in his efforts, to rise from this chair and walk beside him along the Lord's exalted path, to lend him my strength. But all I could offer was money and a mother's love."

Her eyes settled on me again, and now they burned the air. "Find his murderers, Captain Jones. Find his assassins, so that my son may rest in peace in his martyr's grave. For my part, I have undertaken to publicize his martyrdom. I am in correspondence with Mr. Greeley and Mr. Garrison, and with the crusaders of Brook Farm, with Mr. Emerson. Our family is known, Captain Jones, and not without power. I shall use all of that power to destroy the vile institution of slavery, and no general, not even a president, will delay me. I will say unto them, 'Get thee behind me, Satan.' Tell General McClellan that I shall not pause . . . I will not pause . . . my murdered angel . . ."

She was distraught, as well a poor crippled widow might be who lost her only son. But I had my duty as charged, and could not let the opportunity pass.

"You believe he was murdered, mum? That it wasn't an accident of war?"

"He was murdered," she said. "There is no doubt."

I could feel her desire to rise from that chair. Her hands scoured its arms for purchase. But her body would not obey her.

"I know he was murdered," she repeated. "I have been informed."

"And . . . who told you such a thing, mum?"

"My son. He came to me yesterday." She lifted a shrunken hand and pointed a finger toward me. "He sat in the chair where you sit now."

I am not a man given to superstitions, but when she said those words it scared the dickens out of me. The room went as cold as a January night.

"You'll think me mad," she said, smiling. "But there is more to this world than we see. The love my son bore me transcended the decay of the flesh. He could not part from me without a last farewell. So he came to me yesterday afternoon. He sat there and we communed in silence. He was as beautiful as ever, my dear Anthony, but immeasurably sad. Sad, and pale, and cold. At last he said to me, 'Mother, I am murdered. Avenge me.' Then he rose and left me. He walked through that door." She pointed into the darkness. "May I offer you tea, Captain Jones?"

"Will you visit the district headquarters, sir?" Lee asked me. "Or perhaps the Volunteer Refreshment Saloon? The Washington train is awaiting the arrival of a regimental contingent."

I gobbled fresh air. Twas a gray afternoon, but it seemed hurtfully bright to my eyes.

"Thank you, Mr. Lee. It is my intention to visit the arsenal."

"That would be along Gray's Ferry Road, sir."

"I believe that is correct, Mr. Lee."

"It is a long way, sir."

"If it's an inconvenience, Mr. Lee . . ."

He held up his hands. Twas an extravagant gesture in a man of such restrained manner. "Oh, no, sir. Of course not. Mrs. Fowler instructs me you are to enjoy the kindest attentions."

Two promenading ladies spent odd looks on us.

"Shall we go then, Mr. Lee?"

"Of course, sir."

I got into the coach, wishing its glass windows away, for I longed to drink down all the fresh air in the Union. The incense and ash smell of Havisham House would not quit me.

We passed a bounty of dwellings that would not have disgraced London itself, then, with the turn of a corner, arrived among sheds of two stories pretending to be houses, each a warehouse of humanity. I tapped at the front of the carriage with my cane, and Mr. Lee pulled up. We had reached a place where curious behavior might seem at home.

I got out and, shy of those hideous horses, climbed up on the coachmen's bench.

"I would see something of the city on our way," I told Mr. Lee, and it was true enough, though it took more than that to get me to perch over those barely harnessed beasts.

We had entered an Irish settlement of the sort that every city in the Union had acquired by 1861. Gutter saloons and a few ramshackle shops squeezed between shanties that would have shamed the backstreets of Delhi. Ragged women shielded infants with their shawls and men bleak of eye sat in the doorways, rising now and again to observe a country habit in an alley. A recruiting banner called for FENIAN VOL-UNTEERS, promising a bounty for service and giving the street its only color. Two dogs wrestled down in the slops till an old man pulled the bone from between them and shoved it into his pocket. Still, a sweet voice sang of Killarney as we passed.

I was patient of the Irish, having served among them, and knew they could be put to honest work with supervision. They could be sweet as children, the sons and daughters of Erin, and great in their imaginings. Yet there lay a despair in such folk that would not be quenched by all the liquor in the world. I hoped that America might make something of the Irish, for the Lord knows Britannia never did.

Mr. Lee soon took us out of that slough, and we trotted

fair by the river. Our route followed a bluff and I looked
down at the water to keep my eyes away from the horses.
Despite the season, men in a startling level of undress rowed
along in boats that were hardly more than splinters. I had
never seen the like.

"And what would they be, those boats?" I pointed.

"They are called 'sculls,' sir. Sculling is quite the fashion
among the young gentlemen."

I nodded. "And what is their purpose, Mr. Lee?" They
were too slight for cargo or the ferrying of passengers.

"They are for racing," the coachman said.

"And gambling?" I had little love for wagering, and saw
it ruin nearly as many a man as drink.

He teased the horses with his whip. "I do not know if
the young gentlemen bet, sir. Only that they race."

I sensed that we were not to grow more intimate, so I
went ahead and asked what I ached to ask.

"Mr. Lee, you'll pardon me for finding it a curiosity that
Mrs. Fowler keeps a carriage . . . and such a fine team . . .
when she does not go out."

The coachman responded with equanimity. "A carriage
belongs to Mrs. Fowler's position, sir. A lady cannot rely
on hire."

"Yes, Mr. Lee. But if the lady doesn't go anywhere?"

The coachman steered us clear of a brewer's wagon. The
teamster gave him a disbelieving look, as if the man had just
spotted an ape at his alphabet.

"It is not a matter of what the lady does, sir," Mr. Lee
told me, "but of who the lady is. We Philadelphians are
people of tradition."

The Schuylkill Arsenal was the nub of my trouser problems. I thought a surprise visit might effect some good—

certainly this was a fine opportunity—and I did not wish to waste the cost of my journey. I was not certain my interview with Mrs. Fowler had justified the expense to the government.

The arsenal was a great depot for the Quartermaster's Department and our primary warehouse for uniforms. Twas the very place that had promised me one delivery after another, only to send me thin air. Now I get into a state when I am made a fool, and I dwelt on my difficulties with the arsenal as we approached it. I did not come up short of anger, though I knew it was unchristian. My visit to Havisham House had not left me in perfect balance.

No sooner had we turned down the ferry road, than I saw a wagon loaded to the extreme of possibility with bundles of blue. Now I would have let it pass, glad to see a shipment of uniforms underway at last, had I not spotted the lettering on the side of the vehicle.

CAWBER STEEL & IRON WORKS, it said. PHILADELPHIA, PENNA.

"Halt," I shouted, grabbing the reins from Mr. Lee. I gave them a deathly yank and the horses whinnied. I hardly knew myself. "You, there. Hold up. Stop that wagon, man."

I do not pretend to be the cleverest of men, and the greater part of my schooling come by lamplight in my regiment, but it did not require Mr. Carlyle to realize that any wagon belonging to a foundry should have been delivering guns or shot to the arsenal, and not carrying fifty-score of uniforms away from it. I scented graft and corruption at its lowest.

I leapt down from the trap in such a rage I did not feel the hurt to my leg, and I went for the driver of the wagon with my cane. He had pulled up on command. Now he looked at me in wonderment, shying in fear of a blow.

"You'll turn that wagon around," I told him. "And quick."

It took him a brace of seconds to respond. "Captain, I got a delivery to make, and I—"

"You'll turn around, and no more talk on it. On the authority of Captain Jones of the War Department." Then I added, "And on the authority of General McClellan."

"Yes, sir. But there's a train leaving and these here uniforms—"

"No backtalk, man. You'll turn around." I pointed to a rutted field. "Follow my carriage, or I'll have you put in jail." I gave my cane a good wave in his direction.

He followed us as bidden. When we got to the loading yard at the arsenal, I roared past the sentry, bellowing like Glyndwr on the field of battle.

"Duty sergeant to me," I called, for I knew no officers would be about so late in the afternoon. "Duty sergeant to me at the double-quick."

A three-striper come toward me, settling down his cap. A corporal followed him.

"Thievery," I called. "Oh, I have you now, I do. That Oriental gentleman on the coach is my witness. It's thievery and corruption . . ."

The sergeant and his assistant saluted, feigning bewilderment.

"What is it, sir? What's the matter?" The sergeant had fear aplenty in his eyes. You would have thought the Confederates had just crossed the Schuylkill.

"That wagon. There, man. Loaded to the moon with Army uniforms. Brazen as brass, with the very foundry lettering on it. Theft, I call it. Larceny it is."

The sergeant and the corporal exchanged looks. The corporal was young and clean of feature, and it shocked me to find such a one mired so deep in dishonesty.

That wicked young corporal stepped forward.

"Begging your pardon, Captain. That man there had a drawing order. All regulation, signed by district head-quarters."

I whacked my cane into the earth and leaned forward upon it. "Oh, I'm certain it was drawn up fine. And a bloody, crimson forgery. I'll have the names of all involved. Of every man. And I'll have that wagon unloaded before a man in this arsenal has his dinner."

Along with my sense of outrage, I must admit I felt a certain satisfaction as Mr. Lee carried me back toward the railroad depot. I had caught them all with their fingers in the honeypot, and I intended to pursue it. If I could not give General McClellan much satisfaction in the matter of Anthony Fowler, I could at least see to it that the shipment and distribution of uniforms was put on a proper footing.

The autumn darkness fell upon us, and the coachman lit his lamps and detoured around the Irish settlement. I noticed little this time, deep in my calculations of crime and punishment, and when I woke to the world again we were back in streets with crowded sidewalks and gas lighting and busy shops.

"Have you additional requirements, sir?" Mr. Lee asked me, "Or will it be the station?"

"To the train," I told him. "And thank you, sir. You have been invaluable."

He could not take me the entire way, for a regiment was marching over from the docks to the depot and the carriages before us had halted to let them pass. I thanked my companion again and began to climb down. Then I decided it did not much matter whether he perceived me as a gentleman— and a coachman knows almost as much as a valet. So I clung to the side of the carriage and asked him a question.

"Mr. Lee . . . what was your personal opinion of Captain Fowler? I ask it as an agent of our government, and not from unseemly curiosity."

He looked at me for a moment before settling his eyes back on his team. He was a man of great dignity and pride, that half-breed fellow.

"Captain Fowler," he said calmly, "was his father's son."

The light was poor and the street a chaos, but I thought I saw a smile flit over his lips.

Twas a Maine regiment of boys tall enough for the grenadiers. They made a great singing show for the public as they marched, for they did not know what lay before them. They formed up nicely at the halt before the depot, but their company officers were baffled as to the proper commands to file them into the station yard. A few months before, a different Abel Jones would have stepped up and put them to rights. Now I inched behind the crowd of gawkers and slipped inside to guarantee my place.

A woman in a gray cloak and black bonnet waited with a basket of New Testaments for the soldiers. In her anxiety to begin her work, she offered one to me. I accepted it and pressed a dime upon her for her charity. She wished to refuse the donation, and I am not one to throw money to the winds, but I made her take it. For I knew my Mary Myfanwy would have approved.

My beloved wife was hard upon my mind. It was but four hours on a good-running train from Philadelphia to Pottsville, and I longed to see her. And the child, too, our little John. But I would not be an honest man were I not to say that my Mary Myfanwy come first to mind, and last. To come as close to her as this and not be able to take her in my arms, that was a deadly miserable thing. I ached to see those smart eyes quicken and hear her gasp at the unexpected sight of me.

Oh, I considered turning from my duty. For if anything could have turned me, it was the thought of my sweet love. And of the little boy I had not seen since April. My Mary Myfanwy had come thrice to see me in hospital, put up by the good ladies of the Wesley Chapel, and I wept like a babe at the sight of her, and she wept, too, saying only, "You're alive, my love, my darling . . ." By the third visit it was unbearable to get the scent of her by my bed, and to hear her whispering voice, and us surrounded by men caught in the twilight between life and death, and all of it public as a theater.

I longed to toss my cane and run through the streets from the Pennsylvania Railroad yard to the Reading depot, to cling to the side of a locomotive, if need be, and then to climb the little hill to our house and hold my Mary Myfanwy till my arms ached. I thought of a dozen excuses for such a detour, and told myself the loss of a day of my service could not much matter to the Union. My heart was wild within me. I could see her standing there, beckoning me to come . . .

I bought a stock of provisions from the railyard sutler and sat down on a bench, waiting for the train to Washington to be given free for boarding. The little Testament was a comfort to me, for I have often pondered the loneliness of Jesus.

4

NOW HOW WAS I TO REPORT TO GENERAL MCCLELLAN? WHEN
all I had to say was that poor Mrs. Fowler believed her son
murdered because he rose from the dead to tell her so? And
that she would like the general to set the army on the march
to capture the Rebels responsible and hang them. Or that
she seemed exactly the ferocious crusader he feared? No, I
did not think that would content our new general-in-chief.

My train reached Washington in light the color of gunpowder. I had jostled away the night, thinking about generals, the dead lad, and the time in India when Private Molloy
made off with the regimental silver. It had been no grand
murder inquiry, but I had managed things properly, and the
officers had not been distracted from their pig-sticking. The
proper method had been to go to the spot where the theft
occurred, then march outward. There had been no extravagant journeys to the likes of Philadelphia, and Molloy had
gotten no farther than the native quarter where the unhappi-
est of women made their homes.

If this Fowler matter would be clarified, it only made
sense to visit the camp where the body had been discovered,
and I felt I had better do it before reporting to Little Mac.

I wanted so to please the man, and had no wish to stand before him a failure.

And my curiosity was up now. For the loss of the boy moved me. There is too little goodness in this world, and we must sorrow when any goes out of it. But an orderly man does things in an orderly manner, and the world works the better for it.

I trudged from the depot to Mrs. Schutzengel's for a wash and a change of linen. I had taken my bath on Saturday evening, but a journey by rail is a dirtying thing. Nor was I about to waste a nickel on another barber when I could very well shave myself.

"Oooch, Captain Jones," Mrs. Schutzengel said when I come in, looking me over and counting my limbs, "*da sind Sie!* I am afraid you are hit over the head and stolen by them Rebels, when you are not coming home for your Sunday *Mittagsessen*. How I am worrying, *und* now you are here! Eat, eat!"

I took my morning victuals on the quick, going light on the sausages and hurrying through the last evening's paper, which my hostess had kindly saved for me. The first page bore its usual advertisements for unlikely cures for unmentionable diseases—and a shame on the army they were—but the second side was given over to descriptions of the progress of Anthony Fowler's funeral train toward Philadelphia. Twas as if the boy had already risen from the grave to carry his nation's flag into battle, such were the calls for vengeance. The South got the blame of it, which still seemed the logical thing to me, despite the general's reservations. But I did not like the passion in those accounts of the boy's journey to his burying—scribbling and howling of the sort you would not get from any fellow who had seen war for himself. Twas the rage of the stay-at-home hero. The worst are ever ready to avenge the best.

And I believed that Anthony Fowler had been of the best. Had his own mother's coachman not said he was his father's son, and that father lost ministering to the heathen in far China? And if words of hatred against him had come to a barber's ear, it is the sad business of humanity that those who stand up to right a great wrong will make enemies. Was not John Wesley himself the object of infamous slander?

I must confess my belief that slavery was a great wrong. For I had seen the shape and squalor of it among brown men, if not black, and did not like it. Twas my duty to be impartial as I examined Anthony Fowler's death, and so I sought to be. I marked the general's words. Yet I could bear no love for the man who put his whip to another human creature's back to gain his labor, no more than I could admire the pumped-up citizen willing to fight to the last drop of the neighbor-boy's blood. Myself, I would not have made a war over the emancipation business, but now war was upon us and I saw no going back. But let that bide.

I had half a wash at the backyard pump while Mrs. Schutzengel heated shaving water for the household. A raw morning it was, with chimney smoke bitter in the air and no lingering as the other boarders filed past to empty their night pots. Mr. Mager threw me a sullen look, for your German holds a long grudge when he thinks he has come up short at table, but I gave him good morning. I was gone into my thoughts, shivering and scrubbing. I remembered the heat of India. India was far too much with me these days, and I did not like such resurrections. Then, with a splash of water, I thought of the boys in their tents all around us, of the cold boredom of camp life. They had the heart out of me, for if there is little enough glory on the battlefield, there is still less in winter quarters. It is a drab, dour life. War disappoints long before it kills.

The least I could do for our boys was see to the getting of trousers. Before going out to the camp where Fowler's body was found, I walked down to the War Department. There was a great hullabaloo, with General McClellan establishing himself in his additional offices. I slipped in to my desk to record the matter of the wagonload of uniforms I had intercepted on the road from the arsenal.

A crucial point of the matter, and one that troubled me, was the lettering on the side of the rig: CAWBER STEEL AND IRON WORKS. Even in Pottsville, we knew of Mr. Matthew Cawber. The man owned not only foundries on the Delaware, but collieries, shipping, and shares in the railroads. He was rich and mighty and famous as Patti—surely not unknown to Mr. Cameron, his fellow Pennsylvanian and our Secretary of War. I wondered if he were not known to General McClellan, too, as a fellow Philadelphian. For all its vastnesses, our America can be a thick little world.

I loved my new country, and believed in it surely. Yet I could not help but ask myself if justice could reach so lofty a man as Mr. Cawber. I wondered, too, at the state of such a fellow's soul. It is a marvelous thing about greed, how a man with money enough to buy himself a county or two will still bend down to steal uniforms from his nation's defenders to add a few pennies to his pile. It left me raw to think on it.

I feared my report might come to nought, but a man must do his duty as it comes to him and not ponder. I wrote the matter down, then repaired the weakness in my language before sending a fair copy upward. I was so mad into the business that I put off Evans the Telegraph when he stopped by to discuss the way of the world.

With that duty done but the anger still on me, I footed it over to the Quartermaster's yard to see if any uniforms had arrived. They had not. The place was afluster, for General Meigs had come out for a surprise inspection, which he had broken off in a fury.

When I pressed him, the yard officer told me a number of shipments lay down at the depot, waiting for wagons. He believed he had heard something about woolen goods. So I walked the long walk to the depot to save the omnibus fare, but nothing was waiting at all. At that point, I gave up on trousers for the day. The morning was going and it was high time to pursue the Fowler business. I passed over the canal below the Capitol, heading for Virginia. On Maryland Avenue, a kind fellow hailed me and took me along in his trap to the head of the Long Bridge.

There is goodness in men, see.

I waited at the bridgehead for a wagon going my way. To study the greatness of General McClellan's army, you had only to stand there on the Potomac's bank and watch the procession of quartermaster vehicles coming and going, their trains interspersed with detachments of cavalry, all the horses steaming like mechanical engines, and the men's faces red with the cold. There was no end to it, only a mighty stopping and starting as sentries at the bridgehead inspected passes. I joined half a dozen other soldiers looking for transportation. We called out our brigade and regimental destinations to the teamsters. After a bit, I found a place on a Studebaker taking tents forward.

The Virginia shore was crowded as Judgement Day with soldiers and their camps. Companies of infantry suffered out their morning drill, while boys even more unlucky went about the camp work. Batteries jangled down the road, gunners in their greatcoats cursing the mud as it splashed over their fieldpieces. We passed the first line of fortifications, outgrown now, and the driver let me down where a military road veered toward a ridge. I walked up through the ruts, singing hymns for the joy and the practice, and asking my way to the New Yorkers. A brigade headquarters, where cigars seemed an indispensible part of strategy, pointed me onward.

As I approached the camp where Fowler's body had been discovered, I looked over the ground, imagining that, somehow, I would recognize the spot where he had been killed. Perhaps I was only weary, or maybe the befuddlement of the dead man's mother had infected my brain, but I really believed I might sense the place of death.

I saw nothing but mud and tree stumps and the dawdling smoke of campfires. Despite the chill, the air breathed heavy with the smells of kettles and latrines. A drummer practiced his signals, stumbling over the call to advance, and a sentry transferred his rifle from one shoulder to the other so he might warm a hand in a pocket. I was back in a world I thought I had left forever.

A staff officer galloped by. His horse kicked mud in my face.

The colonel's name was Goodman, and he was thin of hair and thick of waist. He invited me into his tent, although it was clear my arrival was a shock to him. I had no papers from General McClellan charging me with the responsibility for the inquiry, only my word. The colonel dismissed his orderly, pulled down the flap of his tent, and sat down in his camp chair to weigh my worth. It did not help that he was drunk at noon.

"Terrible," he said. "Slaughtered like a holy martyr. My regiment to bear the shame of it. And not a man of us so much as shook his hand. Never even seen him. How was we to know he was roaming about? What can a fellow do, I ask you? Join me for a drink?"

"I have long since signed the Pledge, sir."

He grunted and poured whisky into two glasses anyway. He downed his, then knocked back mine. "Now we're even," he said. His red eyes clouded with sentiment. "Died like a dog. With his crown of gold. Like a Vested Virgin. Like the nymph Adonis. Slaughtered like Caesar at the walls of Troy. My regiment to blame . . . never outlive the shame of it. Never even shook the fellow's hand . . . didn't even know he was there . . ."

He had a little square stove going behind his camp table. Its heat crisped the front of me while the cold seeped through the canvas and fitted itself to my back.

"Now, sir . . . if I may ask . . . why is it you say your regiment's to blame?"

He waved his hand at the mottled tentage. "What they're all saying. That's what you'll hear. 'Should've protected young Fowler. Should've rescued him. Whole regiment snoring away. Rebs with free run of the place. And the martyred boy . . . the poor martyred boy . . . lying dead on their doorstep . . .'"

I do not like imprecision of speech and there were no doorsteps in the camp. But let that bide.

"I do not see that it follows, sir," I told him, "that you could have protected a man when you were not aware of his presence."

He nearly jumped to his feet. But his legs would not support him. "That's what I say! What I tell 'em. But *they'll* turn it all around. You wait. You watch 'em. Say I'm a political man, not fit to lead. Shame on the regiment." He poured himself another glass. "McClellan, you said? McClellan himself? See how they're after me? They all want to nail me to the cross. All of them out to crucify me. Crucify me like a dog. Disgrace my uniform. Shame the regiment."

"Now, sir," I said, watching his neck throb as he drank, "I am to look impartially into these matters under the terms of inquiry. But I do not see the fault of your regiment. We cannot yet say what all the facts might be, but—"

"No-good New Jersey fellows. Over the ridge there. Saying we shot him down. Shot the boy down in cold blood. Afraid of our shadows."

"Is there any proof of such a thing?" I asked.

The colonel shook his head. "No proof we didn't, neither. Nothing the newspapers'll believe. Journalists all need hanging. Ruining the country. Traitors to the war effort. Every one of 'em. Worthless New Jerseys. Shame on the regiment. My honor as an officer . . ."

"Sir . . . before we go farther along . . . did Captain Fowler have acquaintance in your camp? A friend, perhaps? Might he have come by for a visit and—"

The colonel railed on, with great bellowing sobs and references to the Romans murdering Socrates and Hannibal dividing Gaul into three parts, but it come out that none of the regiment's officers moved in the high circles of the likes of Anthony Fowler. The colonel was a devil of a man with the classics even when intoxicated, but he could not explain the dead lad's presence at the edge of his camp.

"My honor . . ." he said. ". . . officer . . . shame . . . regiment."

I did a cruel thing, may the Lord forgive me. I poured the man another libation. Then I spoke to him as I would have spoken to a subaltern suicidal with gambling debts.

"I believe I can help you, sir," I told him. "I need but a bit of cooperation . . ."

*   *   *

Colonel Goodman was pleased to remain in his tent while I made my inspection, but he conjured a lieutenant for my escort. The lad's mouth never quite closed and he kept crying out, "This way, sir," though he hardly knew where he was going himself. Between his spurs and his sword, he seemed at constant risk of self-injury.

The first person I wanted to talk to was Private Haney, the sentry who had stumbled upon young Fowler's body. We found the boy singing in a sweet, thin tenor as he burnished a cookpot. One look and I marked him as the sort of young man born too mild to cut himself a fair portion of life's pie. I introduced myself and he dropped the pot in the mud as he saluted.

"Only a matter of some questions, Private Haney," I assured him. Then I told the lieutenant to remain behind while the private and I walked the ground, for a lieutenant is a meddling, infernal thing.

"Watch your step there, sir," the private told me. "Boys throws their slops down that way."

It was a foul and disorderly camp. Commanding officers always set the tone.

"Over here's where I was posted," Haney said.

"There's no sentry."

"Yes, sir. We only put a fellow back here nighttimes. Daytimes we just guard facing out at the enemy."

I looked down the slope into a ravine. Off to the right, the road up which I had come curved toward us, climbing a small valley. Washington lay hidden by a ridge, but all about me a new military city had sprung up. Some of the tent lines were as finely ordered as our summer encampments in India, when we left the cantonments to escape the heat and the cholera. Other camps appeared wretched.

Beyond the road, a gaggle of uniformed men attempted to club a ball with a stick, cheering each other on in dubious language.

"That would be the New Jersey fellows, I take it?"

Private Haney stuck out his face like a dog who hears a game bird but cannot see it. After he had taken a good look, he said, "Yes, sir. That's them, Captain."

"All right. Let's walk down to the spot where you found the body."

He looked at my cane, then at my leg, as if he could only understand the two things in succession.

"I will manage, Private," I told him. "Take me straight to the place, if you please."

"Yes, sir. You be careful now, sir. Major Campbell, he says we can't have no more trouble." He stepped out and I followed him. Every few paces he glanced back to see if I had kept up. There are times when the reactions of others to my slight disablement is more bothersome than the damage itself, for Abel Jones has always been an able man and no nonsense.

"I know I shouldn't of left my post, Captain," Haney said. "But when a fellow has the screaming trots, something got to get done about it."

I slipped in the brown sludge, but braced myself with my cane. Haney kept up his chattering. I only half-listened, for I was counting the paces.

We reached a level spot from which I could just see the military road to our right.

"It was here," the private told me, pointing at the earth. "Right down here. Put one devil of a scare into me, coming up on him like that."

"Here?" I positioned myself where he had pointed.

He considered. "Maybe two, three foot over yet. But thereabouts."

I made it fifty-seven paces. My stride had been regular in my marching days, but now I had a difficult leg, and the mud of the slope had an effect. Still, I had always owned a good eye for correcting ranges. The distance from the guard post to the spot where the body had been found was between one-hundred-thirty and one-hundred-forty feet.

"How was he positioned, Private Haney? Face up? Belly down? Head uphill, or down?"

"I remember that right enough. He was lying there flat on his backside, like he was just resting and looking up at the sky. Only he was shot dead. His head was up that way." He pointed toward the guard post.

"It was still dark when you found him?"

"Sort of like. Up home we call it 'rooster light.'"

"So you could not have seen him from your post?"

He looked at me. "Captain, if I could of seen him, I wouldn't of come down here."

"Can you shoot, son? Are you one of our American 'crack shots'? A frontiersman?"

He looked toward the earth. Blushing a bit. "I guess not. I'm not so good at seeing far away."

I had suspected as much.

Just across the military road, the soldiers were still at their batting game, which seemed a tedious affair.

"What are those New Jersey fellows doing now, Private Haney?"

He took a hard look. Squinting.

"Not much," he said. "Them fellows never do much."

"What do you see, though?"

"Looks like fellows standing around. I hear them good, though. Cussing terrible."

To kill Anthony Fowler, nearsighted Haney would have needed to shoot down a steep hill—and fine huntsmen shoot too high down a slope—and to do it in the dark. And there had been a hard wind, to say nothing of the rain earlier. Even had he gotten off a lucky shot, the corpse would have been pointing the wrong way. The head would have lain downhill, if the dead man had fallen on his back.

If a sentry had killed Anthony Fowler, it had not been Haney.

"Private Haney . . . I do not wish to be indelicate . . . but you just suggested your health . . . was not quite in order."

"I had them bloody trots. Something fierce. I was—"

"I am not unfamiliar with the symptoms. Now, how long had you been standing post?"

"Since midnight abouts."

I looked at him hard. There was no lie in that face. "Isn't that a long pull of duty?"

"Yes, sir."

"Especially for a sick man?"

He shrugged. "Everybody gets the runs around here, Captain. And I shouldn't of been out so long, but I lost at cards. So I had to take old Clarkie's duty, too. I was out here all night."

"Didn't you . . . I mean, given your condition . . . surely the little trip that led you to discover Captain Fowler's body could not have been your first?"

"Oh, no, sir. I was running like a fool. I was just jumping."

"Why didn't you use your company latrines?"

He briefly met my eyes, then looked down again. "Ain't got no company latrines, Captain. Just them what's for everybody in the regiment. Way across camp there. Somebody would of seen me leaving my post and there would of been the devil to pay." He stuck a hand down the back of his collar and gave himself a good scratch. "I know I wasn't supposed to leave away from where I was guarding. It was . . . it was a dilemma."

"So you traveled down here repeatedly during the night? Perhaps not to this exact spot, but . . ."

His eyelids half closed as he figured on things, then they opened again. "You mean did I come all the way down here when I felt the trots coming on?"

"Yes. That is what I mean."

He waved his head. "No, sir. It was too darned far. And I didn't want to leave my post. I knew it was wrong. No, sir. I stuck close."

"Then why come all the way down here the time you found Captain Fowler?"

He lowered his head toward his shoulder. "Well, sir . . . I didn't want the boys to see me. If any a one of them woke up. It was just getting light, like I said, and I couldn't just slip a few steps down the hill like before. So I come down here."

"It's a long way to come."

He looked up the slope. "Well . . . yes, sir. And I remember how stirred up I was inside. But twixt the guard post and down here it's just steep and steeper. I didn't want to take a tumble while I was going about my business. The boys are always laughing over me like it is."

From behind an earthen parapet, my escort peered down at us. When he saw me looking, he faded away again.

"All right, then," I said. "Let us recapitulate."

He looked at me with panic in his eyes. "I didn't mean to do nothing wrong."

"You were on duty all night?"

"From midnight, sir."

"And you came upon the body at dawn?"

"Thereabouts. It was that dirty kind of light."

"And, when you found him, you fired your rifle. Your regiment carries Enfields, does it not?"

"Yes, sir. I didn't mean to."

"Was that the only time you fired your rifle that night?"

"Yes, sir." He thought for a second, and a look of shock and terror fell over his features. "Captain, I sure didn't—"

"I know that, Haney. Did you hear anyone else discharge their weapons? At any time during the night? Did you hear a shot that might have killed Captain Fowler?"

"No, sir."

"No gunshots? None at all? You're sure?"

He nodded. "Yes, sir. I'd know a thing like that."

"Did you hear anything else during the night? Anything at all? Was there anything you *saw* that seemed unusual?"

He chewed the corner of his lower lip. "Sir, that was one terrible, awful night. All that wind, and the rain worse than Pap's temper. Tents all blowing down. And then the fog just sort of filled up the ravine. Things didn't settle down till towards morning. It was so miserable, I promised myself I'd never play cards again."

I clapped him on the upper arm. "And that would be a fine thing to come out of it, Private Haney, for the playing card is the devil's calling card. Now . . . when you found the body down here . . . you fired a shot and your comrades rallied to you?"

He smiled. "That was some kind of rallying, all right."

"So your comrades heard *your* shot. Without difficulty."

"Yes, sir."

"Was it still raining?"

"No, sir. Not really. Just kind of spitting now and then. And windy like."

"Private Haney, have you ever stood guard before?"

He looked surprised. "Sure, Captain. Lots of times. Hundreds, maybe."

"Did you ever hear any shots fired? In the distance? While you were standing guard?"

He thought about that. "I guess so. Fellows get nervous. Start shooting at things. It ain't so bad now as it was. Used to be a great to-do about every night."

"You could hear those shots from a great distance, could you not?"

"Yes, sir."

"Even in the wind and the rain?"

"Yes, sir. Maybe not so good always. But you heard them. You hear all sorts of things when you're out here at night. I hear fellows talking way over there, every word they say." He pointed toward the New Jersey camp. "And singing. You can hear a banjo a real long ways off."

"But nobody played a banjo during the storm Friday night."

"No, sir."

"Did you hear anything at all? Now think. Anything?"

He was a good boy and he did as he was told. After a minute, he just said, "Well, I heard some of the other fellows with the trots. They came running over to where the ground drops off, then went back just as quick, cussing all the way. And once some drunk fellas came along singing. Down on the road. Some crazy-drunk officer fellows, beg your pardon, Captain. Going back late to camp. Singing their lungs out in the rain like old fools."

I wished I were a smarter man. For I sensed there were other questions I should ask, but I could not close my fingers around the business.

"So you found him just here?" I was beginning to repeat myself.

"Yes, sir."

"Lying on his back?"

"Yes, sir."

"Shot through the heart, I am told."

"Right through. The brigade surgeon said it was right dead center."

"Ever see any Confederates around here?"

He shook his head. "No, sir." He looked around at the camps on the high ground. I glanced up and caught the lieutenant snooping again.

"Ever see any Rebels at all, Private Haney? Anywhere?"

"No, sir."

I poked a clump of turf with my cane. "And what did you do before you put on that blue coat, son?"

"I clerked a while. In Uncle Bill's store."

"And what sort of shop was that?"

"Dry goods, mostly."

"Why'd you join up?"

He gave me one of those innocent shrugs again. "Seemed like everybody else was doing it."

"You didn't join to free the slaves?"

Another shrug. "Ain't thought on that."

"Do you think slavery's a good thing?"

After a moment, he shook his head gently. "Well, I guess not. We didn't have no slaves back in Yates County, so I can't fairly say. But I guess it ain't Christian."

"You're not an abolitionist?"

"No, sir. I'm a Presbyterian."

"Who do you think shot Captain Fowler, the man you found here?"

He thought on that for a fair time, but only said, "That's too big for me to think on, sir. Are you going to arrest me now?"

*   *   *

The regiment's officers were useless, as officers often are. Although few shared the colonel's taste for whisky in the forenoon, all seemed to share his inability to think reasonably. The adjutant, Campbell, suggested that Confederate spies had sneaked all the way down from Canada to assassinate Fowler at a spot from which they could dash across the lines to take refuge with their own. As a lawyer, Captain Steele recognized the oddity of a man shot dead without a sound, but he had already solved the riddle for himself. Dark geniuses in Richmond had developed silent pistols with which to arm their spies. It was plain as day, he instructed me, and a threat to the entire Union. He begged me to warn General McClellan.

No one in the regiment had ever met or even seen Anthony Fowler, but for his image in the illustrated weeklies.

I left the camp and marched back down to the brigade headquarters I had passed on my way up. The officers were still at mess well into the afternoon and invited me to join them. When they learned that General McClellan himself had put me on the Fowler inquiry, it caused great excitement—not because of Fowler, since I clearly had not joined an abolitionist table, but due to their curiosity about McClellan himself. I knew little enough, but it was more knowledge than they possessed. I earned my soup.

"He's a splendid figure of a man," I concluded. "The very image of a fighting general."

"It'll be different now," a colonel declared. "With Little Mac in charge, we'll be in Richmond by Easter."

"By Christmas," a major with a bountiful mustache insisted.

Most of the officers seemed to be political fellows out of Albany, and they asked me to put in a word for their brigade. They wanted to be certain they were not held back in reserve when the general's inevitable campaign began, since it was important to their electoral futures that they appear on the battlefield. They lunched on stewed rabbit and peaches in syrup and washed all down with claret wine. They found it extraordinary that I did not take alcohol, but they soon passed over the matter in preference to questions about how Welshmen were likely to vote in America and what favors they might desire of government. At the end, I asked to interview the brigade surgeon and drew a laugh.

"Talk *to* him all you want," the colonel headed for Richmond told me, "for you'll never talk *with* him. We call him 'Silent Mick.'"

A lieutenant colonel sighed. "If he was more of a talking fellow, we could get him a fine ward when all this fuss is over. The party needs reliable Irishmen."

"Mick Tyrone's the only Irishman on earth you can't draw two words out of."

"One word even. The man's hopeless."

"He's off by himself in his butcher shop," the colonel said, savoring his last swallow of claret. "Lieutenant Vandervelt can show you the way."

I thanked the officers for the generosity of their table and followed the lieutenant between two rows of those wall tents the army had begun to use for headquarters business and the like.

"So," I said to him, "your brigade's got a quiet Irishman for its surgeon? There is strange."

"Oh, Tyrone's not so bad," the lieutenant said. He was a well-spoken lad, bred a cut above the politicals. "He'll fix a fellow up and won't let him down. Just not the sort you'd take into your club."

"Can you tell me anything about the man?"

The lieutenant carried fine leather gloves, but did not put them on. He slapped them into the palm of his free hand.

"Nothing to say, really. Keeps to himself. Reads a good deal. *Not* a drunkard. Hardly an Irishman at all, I'd say."

"Can you tell me where he's from? How he joined the brigade? Anything at all?"

The lieutenant pointed with his gloves. "That's his tent. Just there. You can ask him yourself."

The doctor was reading a book by his stove. We certainly disturbed him, but you would not have known it by the changelessness of his face. I felt that a great bloody torrent of slaughter would not have moved the man. I suppose that made him a fair cut of a surgeon. He was a hungry-looking fellow, narrow all over, though with a strength to him. He was cleanshaven like myself, but his eyebrows were thick and black, and the eyes themselves made me think of a seacoast in bad weather. All in all, he looked like he got a short ration when the Good Lord parceled out joy. He did not offer his hand but held his book in it, finger keeping his page.

The lieutenant began, "Pardon the intrusion, Major Tyrone, but may I introduce Captain . . ." He lost my name.

"Jones," I said. "Your servant, Doctor."

The surgeon made a sound at the back of his throat.

"Captain Jones . . . has an investigative charge," the lieutenant said, unsettled by the nick in his social form. "He comes to us from General McClellan, and—"

"The Fowler business?" the surgeon asked.

I nodded.

"Go on with your business, Vandervelt," Tyrone told the lieutenant. "You are superfluous, lad." The surgeon had a way of speaking that hardly used the muscles about his mouth.

His face might have been a mask. But there were gales in those eyes.

With the lieutenant dismissed, the surgeon noted his place in his book and set it on top of a folding desk. It was a French matter by a fellow named Fourier and made me suspect the Irishman of improper habits.

"Sit down," he said. "That leg won't need more standing."

I sat in the single chair and he took a place on his camp bed. A chest full of books and papers lay open. There was a smell of ether I had learned to recognize in the hospital.

"Well," Tyrone began, "are you here out of duty, Taffy? Or is it only the curiosity dripping from your mug?"

"The two, it might be."

He made that back-of-the-throat sound again. "You're slow, man," he said. "This entire army has a case of the slows."

"Will I address you as 'Major Tyrone'? Or as 'Dr. Tyrone'?"

"Call me Mother McGinty's little lamb, for all that it matters. It took you three days to get here, Taffy." He drew a watch from the pocket of his waistcoat. "Three days and eight hours since the finding of the body. And by now they'll have him in the ground, won't they? When's the burying carnival?"

"Today, I believe."

"Isn't that grand? They won't dig that one up again, now will they? Holy saint and martyr that he is? No, they won't pull that one up once they've got him planted."

"Why should they dig him up, Dr. Tyrone?"

His throat rumbled again. "The question, Taffy, is why were they in such a haste to put him under? When it was as pretty a murder as ever a doctor did see."

"You believe he was murdered, then?"

He laughed. Twas a solitary crack of a syllable. "And don't you, then? Or have you come limping all the way over to me for the love of fine society?"

"What makes you think he was murdered?"

Those fierce eyes set on me till I felt like a great hound had me caught in its jaws.

"Went by that New York regiment, did you?" he asked.

"I did."

"Knockos who can't tell their well from their turd pits. I'll not settle in New York when this is done, for I never would trust the water. And what did you ask them, man? What was it you found there that brought you to me?"

I met him eyes-front. "No one heard a shot. The body was hardly a hundred feet from the camp, and no one heard a shot until the sentry boy found him and let off his rifle."

He gave me another thunderclap laugh. "Is that all? You might as well go on with you, if that's all you gleaned."

"I know he was shot through the heart. That you yourself said so. And I know it's a lucky shot by daylight that strikes a man so. A miracle by night, it would be. And the sentry boy's nearsighted as a schoolteacher."

"Any more, Taffy?"

I could not think of more.

He stood up and paced the little world of his tent. "And what if the man was shot with a pistol? Close enough to have powder burns over his tunic. And yet there were no powder burns on the front of his greatcoat, nor was there a bullet hole through its front or back to match the one that passed through the rest of his uniform, to say nothing of his heart. And why so little blood on that coat, then, when the rest of him was soaked with it like a butcher's apron? And what if no blood leaked out from under him onto the ground where they found him? What would you say to that, bucko?"

I looked at him.

"There was no *blood*, man," he went on. "Or not enough of it." It was a queer thing how his face stayed empty of feeling, though his voice went thundering and his eyes clouded black as a monsoon. "Not a drop on the ground where he lay. With a great raging hole out his back. And all the sweet life drained out of him. Not a drop of blood anywhere but for the stains clotted up on his uniform. And that uniform itself more dry than not, but for the back of it where they tossed him in the mud. And all of this during a night of drowning rain. Doesn't that set you thinking, Taffy? Doesn't it make you wonder just a little? Or don't such high and mighty saints as him bleed like the rest of us?"

"I am not fond, sir, of being called 'Taffy.' I understand you to mean the boy was killed elsewhere and not by the camp. That the body was moved from the site of his death and put out to be found with a purpose."

He clapped his hands and looked heavenward, for the Irish are born upon a stage with the Lord as their audience. "I'm in the presence of Newton himself! Of Galileo!" He leaned down over my chair. "Could I make it plainer, man? The boy was murdered with a pistol to his chest and hours after the deed somebody put a spanking new overcoat on him and dumped him there in the mud." His mask cracked with a look of disgust. "But none of that matters, of course, for all they want is a great shining saint."

"Have you told this to anyone, Dr. Tyrone?"

"And who would I tell, bucko?" He pointed out through the wall of his tent. "Do you think *they* want to hear it? No, man. Read the newspapers. They want him crucified like Jesus. By the Romans from Richmond." He shook his head with Fenian exaggeration. "It could send a man to the drink."

Now there are men who are marked by their pasts. I am

one. Tyrone was another. I would learn his story later. But already I saw in him a born doer of right, and an ally. I was not to be mistaken.

"The brigade officers told me, Dr. Tyrone, that you are a man of few words. It would appear they are mistaken."

This time I got both a laugh and a grunt. "The poor, bleeding buggers," he said. "What man with a brain in his head would waste his breath on politicians?" He sat down and braced his hands on his knees, giving me the hard look. "Now what are you going to do about our murder, Captain Jones?"

TWAS GROWING DARK WHEN I REACHED THE RIVER AGAIN. FROM the bridge I could see the campfires on every side, far brighter to the eye than the gaslit streets ahead. The sky was contrary with rain, now it would start, but after a few drops it would stop again. The teamster who carried me was bound for the Navy Yard and set me down after we cleared the sentries at the bridgehead. I had a walk before me, and not a welcome one.

I turned toward the Mall, for there lay the shortest path to my destination. The mud was a burden to my leg, I will not lie to you, and crossing from the brick castle to the nearest canal bridge forced me through a swamp sloshed up by cavalry drill. The street was but a hint between puddles. Smoke rose from the army butchering sheds and the fresh smell of death roamed like fog. Cattle, oblivious to the massacre of their fellows, snugged down against the weather below the unfinished obelisk. I would as soon have joined them as pass through the next few blocks.

They called the quarter between the canal and Pennsylvania Avenue "Murder Bay," and while there was no bay to be seen, there was murder enough. Not that I feared the knife, or even the temptations of the alleys, with their slower forms of killing. No, it was the discouragement of the place that scorched my heart. Each man and woman, and not a few children, strove one with the other to reach new depths of iniquity. The army had brought with it a great spread of bawdy houses and saloons throughout the city, as armies will, but the establishments of Murder Bay were worse than anything on the Island, or even, they tell me, in Swampoodle. No provost marshal's ordinance could reach them.

Murder Bay was the resort of the penniless and hopeless, and of all those who would not be seen in honest daylight. Not that I have been pure in deed from the cradle, mind you. Twas only that the lost souls of Murder Bay took that which was ugly and made it worse. There was sickness in the place, and despair, and walking by made it harder to recognize God's mercy than a Christian man finds comfortable.

I kept to the edge of the place, but this was a luckless day. Tuesday though it was, a trickle of soldiers had found their way to the plank bars and gambling dens in defiance of general orders. Through windows patched or half boarded, I saw boys who should have been at home entwined with women who would never have a home again. Blackbearded, black-eyed barkeeps gauged their prospects, while touts leaned in the yellow light of the doorways.

Along a stretch without gaslamps, women emerged from the darkness. A bold creature seized my arm, whispering, "Won't you be my sweetie boy?"

I broke away from her roughly, and she laughed. I would not be a rude man, but the picking of pockets is a great trade in Washington, and pity the unsuspecting. They say even the mayor is not above it.

Not a dozen paces, and another unfortunate stepped out.

"Special treats for special boys," she told me, "Half price for soldiers."

Life's ravages were plain upon her and needed no more light to be recorded. Her skin hid under whitewash and her lips were slathered crimson. She put me in mind of the medical advertisements on the first page of the *Star*. When she touched me, I jumped like a lad on the edge of his first battle.

"Nothing you want won't shock Red Kate," she said. "There's no shame in it, dearie. Could it be a bit of the other you're after?"

I would banter with none of them, those evening phantoms, and marched through their offers of "oriental performances" and interviews with children. Before I reached the glow of an oyster house they were laughing. One sang, "Come to look and not to buy, and home alone with Willie."

The next time, I told myself, I would give up the money for a cab.

I went straight to General McClellan's old headquarters, for there were things he needed to know. But I could not get past the first room. None of the faces were familiar. A staff major in a fine uniform intercepted me, to the titters of one of the Frenchmen I had seen about. The major asked my business, his tone uncharitable.

"I'm here to see General McClellan," I said. "On a confidential matter."

The major laughed me up and down. "He's here to see General McClellan, this one. Did you ever hear the likes? Are you drunk, little man?" He looked about for the approval of his peers. "Are we taking cripples into the army now? Or midgets? Has it gotten so desperate?"

"The general charged me to report to him, sir."

The Frenchman laughed and prettied his goatee. They are a cruel folk.

"Another escapee from the asylum," the major went on in a stage actor's bellow. "Call out the guard."

A lieutenant colonel put down his papers and stepped forward. "The general's not here," he said, "and he'd have no time for the likes of you, if he was. For God's sakes man, this is army headquarters. You can't just stroll in. Now get along."

You can tell, I think, that I do not look a grand or polished man. Yet I am honest, and loved by an honest wife, and I wished to do my part for my new country. Such men as those officers ever struck up a fire in me. I have never understood why Americans, of all people, wish to set themselves up as aristocrats and pretend to be more than themselves.

I caned my way down the steps to the street. A blast of rain struck me as I turned toward the War Department. But there was work to be done, no matter the hour. Twas an easterly blow come up and the wet of it pinched my eyes. I might have gone back to Mrs. Schutzengel's instead, to fetch my India rubber cape, for all the good my visit to headquarters had done.

A voice behind me called, "Captain?"

I turned about too suddenly, wrenching the leg.

Twas a different major. Out in the rain without his hat. "What's your name, Captain?"

"Jones, sir."

"Well, Captain Jones," he said, levelling his hand to his brows to keep the raindrops from his eyes, "do you really have business with the general?"

"I do, sir."

He, too, wore a splendid uniform and he was anxious to go back inside. Yet he lingered. "I'll see that he knows you were here. And don't mind the boys. They act that way whenever the Frenchies come around."

"Twas nothing," I lied. For he seemed too decent a man to bother. And he grew wetter by the instant.

"All right then, Captain Jones. I'll tell him."

"You'd best go in, sir."

"Yes. Listen, Jones. That remark about your . . . your impairment was tasteless. Can I fetch you a cab?"

"No, thank you," I told him. "I would rather have respect than a cab, sir, and you have given me that."

He knew not how to answer and went in. There is decency in men, and goodness, and we must never forget that.

I no sooner sat down behind the mass of papers swelled up in my absence than Evans the Telegraph poked his shoulders through the door.

"*Noswaith dda,*" he said, "I saw the light."

"Good evening, Mr. Evans," I said.

He looked over my desk. "There's a great business before you there, Captain Jones." He stepped closer and pulled up his nose. "Wet sheep, is it?"

"Sheep there are none, Mr. Evans. But fools, perhaps." I had a welter of work waiting, but the man wanted to talk, and he was my friend. Now I am a great one for duty, but the humiliation at McClellan's headquarters was not entirely behind me. I decided that a pause in the long day was not unreasonable. And a bit of speech with a buttie is a fine, warming thing. "Come in and sit you down, if your time belongs to you."

He swept a hand across his whiskers and left a smile where it passed. Dropping into his accustomed chair, he drew out his pipe.

"I have written to my Keziah's folk," he said. "To give

them your considerations on young Dafydd." He struck off a match on the heel of his shoe.

"And I have written to my Mary Myfanwy, who will speak to her uncle."

"It is a curse when a boy marries badly," Evans said through the first smoke.

"And a blessing when he marries well." For I knew that to be true.

He smoked and sat and looked at me. There was a matter to be gotten out.

Finally, he said, "Captain Jones . . . do you think it ever right to break a trust?"

I thought on that. "I would say no, Mr. Evans. Except under the most exceptional conditions."

He smoked and nodded. "But if the conditions were powerful exceptional? If they were terrible exceptional?"

"Then I should study to see where the good lay."

"Well, I have studied it, then." He leaned toward my desk. "Now I saw a telegraphic message sent off by the general himself some days ago. A confidential thing, it was. To be delivered by hand to a lady in Philadelphia. Your name was mentioned, Captain Jones."

"That would be Mrs. Fowler."

"The very same, Captain Jones. And the telegraphic said you yourself and none other were to inquire into the young man's deceasement."

"That is true, Mr. Evans."

He puffed. "As you are my buttie, and a fellow Welshman from the head of the valleys, I will tell you about another message, then."

"From the general, as well?"

He took the pipe from his mouth and looked about him. Assured we were alone, he said, "No. From Richmond."

He had a true Welshman's flair for the dramatic, for we understand the quietness inherent in revelation. We would make fine actors, were the profession not indecent.

Evans let his information soak well into my brain.

"There is strange," I said after a time, "I did not know that we were in communication with the Confederacy by telegraph."

"We are not, Captain Jones."

"Will you explain it to me, then?"

"That I will. Their lads rode high into Maryland. All for the purpose of taking over a stretch of our wire and sending this message."

"It sounds of great import," I said.

"'Twas addressed to General McClellan."

Now that was a rare thing, and my curiosity rose higher still. But for honor's sake, I asked him, "Are you certain it is fitting I should hear of it?"

He worked his pipe a long time. "I have thought hard on it, see. It is your business, Captain Jones. If you are entered into this Fowler matter."

"The message concerned the murder?"

Didn't he give me a look then. "Are we talking murder, then?"

I had failed to govern my tongue. "Well, murder it may or may not be. We shall find out in good time."

"And doesn't it all make sense now, with the Rebels just pleading over the wire?"

"What did the message say, Mr. Evans?"

He lowered his pipe to the level of his knees, a sign that more than one sentence would come out of his mouth, cursed slow Welshman from black Glamorgan that he was.

"'Twas from Jefferson Davis himself," Evans said. "Begging General McClellan to believe him and swearing to beat the band that not he nor anyone under the Southern flag had lifted a hand against the Fowler lad. A clear thing, it was, that the business has put the fear into the great Rebel himself, for he offered a parley of cooperation to set the business right. To read it, a man would think the fellows in Richmond are more afeared of having the blame for the Fowler boy's deceasement than they are of all the armies in the Union."

I nodded, but my words formed slowly. "You have . . . been of great assistance to me. I am indebted."

He thrust the stem of his pipe toward me. "I knew it was a tale that needed telling to you."

"I thank you again. You are a true buttie, Mr. Evans."

He rose to leave me to my work, without waiting for me to ask about Mr. Lincoln. Then he hesitated.

"There is yet another matter," he said. "General McClellan clears all of the messages now. It is a strict command that he shall be the first to see the telegraphics. And he forbade us the passing of this message to Mr. Lincoln. He said there was no need to trouble the President with it. We were not to breathe a word of it, upon penalty of martial justice." He glanced about him a last time. "Is that not a queer business, Captain Jones?"

I was set to agree when I saw a shadow pass the door. A moment later, a cavalryman appeared. Twas the man I had seen twice before, once at General Scott's departure and again when he fetched me for my interview with General McClellan. Now the curious thing was the quiet of the fellow, for a cavalryman makes a loud approach, what with his spurs and his steel and his swagger. But I had not sensed this one's presence until his shadow caught my eye.

"Captain Jones," the cavalryman said, "the general's waiting on you."

*   *   *

I thought they would have their comeuppance then, the officers in their fancy coats and braids, when they saw me come marching in escorted to see the general. But it was not to be.

The cavalryman led me across 17th Street to a carriage parked unpleasantly close to a house of shame. The general waited within the trap, alone.

"Sit down, Captain," he said, pointing to the forward seat.

"Yes, sir. Thank you, sir." I took my seat just as the carriage drew off.

"Jones . . . pull down that blind, would you?"

He closed the other side himself, leaving just opening enough for the fumes of the lamp to escape. The general wore an evening cloak. Where it fell away in the front, gold shone on midnight-blue cloth. He looked as though he had been gotten up for a portrait. And he had taken a generous hand to his cologne water.

"I have been informed," he said, "that you were badly treated, Captain Jones. Shamefully treated. By my own staff."

"A fine major come to my assistance, sir."

"It will not happen again, Jones. You have the personal apologies of the general commanding."

"'Twas nothing, sir."

He leaned toward me and the lamplight burnished his dark hair. "The thing is, Jones, I have decided that you are of most use to me if we go about things more quietly. Perhaps headquarters isn't the place for your reports." He sat back and smoothed a fold of his cloak. "I understand . . . that you raised a number of questions in a regimental camp today."

His intelligence was fine. I hoped it was as good when it come to the Rebels.

"Sir, I was asking into the circumstances of Captain Fowler's loss. A proper inquiry—"

"Yes, Jones. Yes, the inquiry. Vital matter. But I cannot overstate the sensitivity of all this. I hardly expected you to go straight from Philadelphia . . . to the field, as it were."

"Shall I stop asking questions, sir?"

He raised his chin like a tiger on the sniff. "Not at all, Jones. That's not what I meant. It's only . . . that we want to be more discreet in the future. Don't come to my headquarters. My staff need not be a party to this matter. I will take it upon myself to contact you."

"Yes, sir. Begging your pardon, sir, I have come to a point where I think the business wants a police fellow. I haven't the skills—"

"Nonsense, Jones. That's the last thing. Police, indeed. The army's capable of sorting out its own affairs." He fanned away my concerns with an ivory hand. "Listen . . . how did you find Mrs. Fowler? You may be frank."

The carriage bounced along, good of spring. "Well, sir, she was a great lady. The very picture of mourning. But addled with grief, as we might expect."

"How 'addled'? Don't be polite, man. Was she mad? Was she ranting?"

"Sir . . . I am not fit to judge such a thing. The woman was disturbed by events, certainly. Her son . . ."

"Has she got the boy's death through her head?" The general had a habit of leaning forward, then sitting back and folding his arms, only to lean forward again. Twas as if the carriage was too confining for him. "I didn't warn you, Jones, because I wanted you to meet her without prejudice. But Mrs. Fowler . . . is given to spiritualism. And other curious beliefs. Occult matters that strain patience and credulity." He swallowed with that big neck of his and it was like watching a great snake gulp down an infant. "Now . . . did she appear to understand the situation? Might she listen to reason? Or do we need to suggest an interview by a medical committee . . . to establish the state of the poor woman's faculties?"

"Well, sir, she knows the boy is dead, though there's a bit of churning in her mind. And she's certain as chapel on Sunday he was done in by assassins. That's sure." I looked at the general, wondering again why he had chosen me as his delegate. "She's hard set on punishing the Rebels, sir. She's all for a great hanging and bloody vengeance."

He dropped his chin down onto his collar. "To be expected. They're a hard bunch, the Fowlers. Christian on the outside, cannibals within. I expect she rambled on about dark conspiracies on the part of slaveholders . . . all sorts of claptrap."

"She does believe the issue of slavery counts up, sir. Given her son's lecturing and crusading and all. And she's personally strong against the evils of Negro bondage." I considered the splendid man sitting before me. It is hard to be honest with a general. "To be fair, sir, a reasonable person might well share her—"

He waved the thought away. "I've made myself plain on the matter, Jones. I know the men of the Confederacy. Served with 'em. They are . . . misguided, at present. But they are not assassins." He cocked his chin again. "They will fight us on the field of battle, if we force them to it. But they are not murderers. The Southrons are men of honor— would that I could say the same of all our own. This war is an unspeakable tragedy, brought about by New England impatience and the belligerence of the sedentary."

"Sir, I could not help but feel sympathy for the poor woman, given the family history and such. I was inclined . . ." I come up short of proper words to disagree. How weak we are in the presence of power. I think it is an unrealized source of evil.

McClellan sent me an odd look. "Jones . . . Mrs. Fowler takes a certain position in society. It is a high, though not a usual one. She is . . . indulged." He sniffled as though the autumn had gotten at him, and pulled out a fine handkerchief. "It is a family conceit that the Fowlers live apart, secluded from worldly concerns. That is a fiction, Jones. The woman has a web of acquaintances, some of them from the lowest quarters of the press . . . while others include the madmen who drove us to this war with their intransigence. She is . . . maniacal in her prejudices. Far more intolerant than any Southron. And she has long been treated generously by men of goodwill. But there are limits to what even Lettie Fowler can be allowed. Her sort have done their best to wreck the Union. With their venom, and their deification of the African. The time to call their bluff may be approaching."

He turned his commanding eyes upon me. "Do not misunderstand me, Jones. I do not justify secession. I am prepared to give my life's blood for our glorious Union." He tucked his hand into the gap in his tunic. "But the death of Anthony Fowler must *not* be exploited for vicious purposes. And we must not limit our search for the killers to those who might seem the most obvious perpetrators."

"Well, the boy was murdered, sir, that's sure."

The fine pose of his face did not change. "Yes, Jones. But by whom?"

"I cannot say, sir."

"You are to look everywhere, Jones. *Every*where. Exclude no possibilities, do you understand? The killer's motives may have been of the greatest cynicism." The lamp flickered and lit him up handsome. "I take it you do not . . . believe he

might have been shot by a sentry? Mistakenly? Not a chance
of it?"

"No, sir. For he was shot with a pistol, and close."

That surprised him.

After a good pause, he said, "How do you know that,
Jones? I understood no ball was extracted."

"No, sir. But a surgeon saw the body. He marked it sure
as a pistol wound. And there were powder burns on the
boy's uniform, which speaks to the distance."

His jaw locked for a bit. Then he said, "What else did
you learn today?"

"Captain Fowler was not killed on the lines. The body
was moved and put there. With thought on the doing. That's
the bones of it, sir."

He pawed at the little wedge of beard on his chin.
"You're certain of all that?"

Of a sudden, I smelled a great stink. It overpowered the
general's cologne water. Twas a mammoth smell of horses.
Even with the carriage shut up and blind, I knew where we
were. Passing the remount stables, the devilish long clap-
board barns thrown up to hold thousands of the beasts for
the army. I could hardly imagine a more terrible place and
always gave it a wide berth.

Now there was no reason to go to those stables unless
they were your destination, for they stood between the edge
of the city and the river marshes. I realized the coachman
was driving about for the sake of it and keeping to the
back ways.

"Are you certain?" the general repeated.

"Well, sir, I believe that I am certain. For many saw the
pieces of it, but could not assemble them whole. No shot.
And no blood on the ground under the body, see. A fresh
greatcoat put on him after he died. There's clarity in it, for

him that looks. A murder it was, sir. But we do not know where it was done, or what Captain Fowler was doing at the time, or whose hand held the gun."

McClellan pondered that. The carriage pulled back onto a street with a regular surface for a time, then jounced over dirt again. But the ride was not so rough and this part of town was less fertile of odor.

The general tapped a signal to his driver with the hilt of his dress sword. Then he settled again and said, "You've done a splendid job, Jones. Excellent work. Mr. Gowen was right about you."

"Am I shut of the business now, sir? I expect you'll want a more capable sort—"

He shook his head, drawing down his eyebrows like curtains. "Not at all. No, we have to uncover all the facts, all of 'em. You've uncovered a conspiracy, Jones. Surely you see that?" His hand fretted on his tunic but did not slip inside. "Find out who's behind it. Where *did* the murder take place? And why? You're the man for it, Jones. We *must* find the truth. And then we must use that truth for a higher good." He nodded, as if weighing the wisdom of the ages. "Root out the truth of it." A little smile lifted his mustache. "No matter who it might embarrass. Anthony Fowler *will have justice.*"

"Sir . . . I am not a policeman. I do not know what to make of this further."

"Nonsense. You're a born policeman, Jones. Allan Pinkerton himself couldn't have done better. Listen, I've given this a great deal of thought. Strategic deliberation, you might say. In the morning, you will report to the Ordnance Office. Where Fowler worked. Take over his desk, his duties. Look through his papers. Don't stick on niceties. There's no shame in it. If justice is the purpose. Get to know his fellow officers.

Examine the details of his life. See if we can't learn anything that way." He straightened the fit of his cloak and I sensed we were soon to part. "And I think it best if we go about this more quietly, Jones. As I said. You can see the sensitivity of the matter. We don't want our purpose misunderstood." He tested the set of his mustache with his little finger. "Use my name only in an emergency . . . and wait for my summons."

The driver reined in the horses, calling them up. The carriage rocked then settled.

"Sir, if I may . . . there's another matter most unpleasant, about the uniforms for the troops and a terrible instance of dishonesty—"

The carriage door opened. I saw a fine town home, brilliantly lit, and heard a gay tune.

The general stepped out. When his boots reached the street, he arranged his uniform a last time and corrected his posture to perfection.

"Ordnance Office in the morning, Jones. You have my full confidence. Justice must be done."

I rose early and went breakfastless to the War Department. I could not leave so much of my former work undone, and I sat to my old desk first, matching accounts and eating the sugar biscuits my Mary Myfanwy had sent me. For all my tiredness, I could not be in bad spirits, for my weekly package from my Mary Myfanwy had been waiting for me, along with a cold chop preserved by Mrs. Schutzengel, upon my return to the boardinghouse the night before. My Mary Myfanwy kept a wise household, and saved all her letters to me through the week to send in one package, for it spared good money. When the packages arrived, each made a holiday. If I could not settle my love in my arms, I could rest my heart in her words and admire the gentility of her hand. She wrote on good paper, as a lady should, and spared not the expense of that. Her letters were lovely things.

The package had been a great treasure, not only because of the biscuits, which even Mrs. Schutzengel, a great jealous baker, described as "Maybe almost German good," but because of a pencil sketch one of the young colliers had made of our son. Twas clear young John would be a handsome scrapper, blessed with his mother's aspect.

I will not lie to you. I clutched the picture against me and wept.

Twas difficult to keep my mind on the work that morning, for the Fowler matter had bitten deep into me. There was much I could not figure. I still did not understand why General McClellan had sent me to Mrs. Fowler, nor did I fully understand the general himself. He had a great way of saying things and not saying them, and thanks to Evans the Telegraph, I knew there was more to the business than the general was ready to lay on the shop counter. Still, he was a busy man, with the whole war on his shoulders now, and I hung my cap on his telling me that we must get out the truth, no matter what it might be. A general might have his reasons for keeping a fact or two in his pocket. And he seemed to have a great faith in me. Flattering that was.

At eight o'clock, with the stoves lit and a lamp a needless luxury, I went up to my new place of duty. The ordnance staff's rooms lay just a staircase from Mr. Cameron's office, so important was their business. I was coming up in the world.

There was no one about, but the office door I wanted was unlocked.

I let myself in. Four fine mahogany desks filled the room, nothing of your military issue. There was a fine window, with an airy view of branches close, though they were bare now. Mr. Corcoran's mansion stood just across the avenue. Twas a grand spot to sit and work, well-heated, light, and clean.

I determined Fowler's desk by simple figuring. Two of the other desks had tobacco ash not long smoked by the smell of it, and the third had a fine china cup with the last day's coffee half in it. Fowler's desk, though laden with papers and books, had a bareness when it come to personal effects. It might have belonged to a good Methodist.

Sitting down in the dead man's chair, I hastened through the drawers, but found little of Anthony Fowler. The desk was full of work, badly organized. The lad would never have made a clerk. The only items that spoke to his character were those books on the desktop and a pair of fine pens.

I picked up the first of the stacked books. *Phrenology Of The Non-Caucasoid Races*, it said. The second was called, *The Christian Path To Moral Reform And Temperance*. My Mary Myfanwy would have approved of that. Next down was a volume of Mr. Emerson's. Then there was a book about Africa and savage tribes and the like, followed by a text in German as heavy as a rock. Young Fowler had been modest in his pleasures.

I heard footsteps along the hall and stacked the books again, but the boots went past. The sounds of a staff began to rise from the neighboring offices. I set myself to study the official papers upon the desk, since the dead boy's work was to be my work now.

It seemed Fowler had been the officer charged with the first review of purchasing orders for cannon. There were letters from foundries and arsenals, and pleas for guns from field commands, the latter thick with endorsements. Few things seemed to have been resolved, and the requests and complaints began to repeat themselves. I wondered why on earth a freshly minted captain of good family, born for the cavalry, would have been placed in a position that wanted a terrible lot of experience and promised no glory.

I last took out my watch at thirty-seven minutes after nine. There was a great bustle of business sounding through the walls and out in the corridor now, but still I sat alone. I settled back to the documents.

There seemed little confluence between those cannon which had been approved for order, those which had been ordered, those which had been paid for, those which had been delivered to the government, and those which had been forwarded to the troops. I could barely make out if we had bought one Napoleon at two thousand dollars, or two thousand Parrotts at one dollar. Young Fowler might have been an excellent orator and exemplary Christian, and perhaps he would have made a good soldier, but he would never have made a quartermaster in the village militia.

A great thundering ruckus of laughter and footsteps come down the hall, and the door burst open.

Three young men rollicked in, happy as miners on payday.

The instant they saw me, they stopped, and a terrible quiet settled on the room.

In battle, you learn to spot your enemy's leaders. I do not mean so much the high-horse generals, but the natural sort, the ones who need killing if you are to turn the melee and buy your bayonet a rest. Now the boys that stormed in—and they were all but boys, ranks notwithstanding—sorted themselves out in a moment. A major, a captain, and a lieutenant. The major was a dark fellow, the confident sort who ruins women's lives just by strolling through the parlor. He was the ranking man, but he would have been the leader of that pack had he been but a private soldier. Twas he that spoke.

"Who're you? What are you doing at that desk?"

The others drew up to either side of him, but remained a touch behind. The captain was a rusty-headed lad of the type who never starts the bullying but is glad to pile on. The lieutenant looked thin to consumption and his eyes had no steadiness. That one might have been playing dress-up soldier in his father's uniform.

I rose to my feet. "Abel Jones, captain of Volunteers, at your service, gentlemen. I am sent to join you in your work."

"That's Fowler's desk," the lieutenant said. He had a high voice that would never make a singer. His remark aimed more at his companions than at me.

"I understand Captain Fowler is no longer with us," I said. "I am sorry for the loss of him."

The major strode forward. He had hair and a mustache the blue-black of anthracite. Strong of body, he seemed about to strike me, the gentleman's cut of him notwithstanding. I felt a permanent rage in him, barely contained by manners. He halted before the desk.

"What in the name of God could they be thinking?" he said, looking down at me. "Sending us a burlap just off the boat. To take Anthony's place."

His companions cackled a bit.

I stood there as tall as I could make myself. I was sorry I had unbuttoned my tunic at my work, for a soldierly appearance matters at such times.

"I have some experience at figures and inventories," I said, gesturing toward the stacks of documents. "And the papers seem to want attention."

The major laughed, and there was no charity in it. "A clerk?" He turned to his comrades. "The man's a *clerk*." They snickered as wanted, and the major looked back to me. "Do they think this war's going to be won by *clerks?*"

Now I wished to be a Christian man and temperate in my remarks. But Washington had already filled me up with these men whose greatest battles had been with their tailors and who crammed the government offices and hotel bars by the hundreds. Certainly, two of the three men before me would have done for the field, leaving the paper duties to such as me.

"The war will not be won," I said, "by prancing peacocks, but by soldiers of the line and the officers leading them."

The major went as white as the best quality flour. It was a thing to see. The two behind him waited for his judgement.

In a voice from the soul's winter, the major said, "You . . . little monkey. How dare you question my honor?"

It's always "honor" with that sort.

Oh, there was madness in him, true enough. He drew out his sword. The sliding metal rasped as he pulled it free. The blade shone in the dull light.

It was an insanely disproportionate act, amazing. The seconds stretched themselves thin.

He raised the blade, slow and queer, and I saw a blind brightness in his eyes. I had seen that look before, in the eyes of fanatics and smokers of hashish.

His hand trembled and sent a shiver down the blade. It was stupid, that drawing business. Twas the gesture of one who did not understand his circumstances and who rarely had need to care, of a man unaccustomed to facing the consequences of his actions. Nor did the major understand the use of the sword. He held it like a butcher's cleaver. And now that he had started the business, he did not know how to stop. Had he not been shivering, he would have made a very statue of vengeance, standing there with that blade held high. He had gone too far, and did not know how to retreat.

I took up my cane from behind the desk and marched out to meet him.

He glanced down at my leg. Twas a mistake. In a blink, his sword had gone banging free against the wall and I laid him down on his back. Never underestimate a Welshman. Or a former instructor of bayonet drill.

I stood over him, with my cane tipped against his throat. His butties made not a move.

Now I should not have done it. Even dispensing with the difference in our ranks, it was a foolish way to introduce myself. But my Christian nature thins when you push me hard enough.

"Honor," I told him, "is like wages, boy. And must be earned."

They made a joke of it all, as gentlemen do. Pretending to ignore me, they settled into that nervous sort of banter that is too loud and clumsy of rejoinder. They called each other by their last names, copying young Englishmen. The dark major was Trenchard, the rusty-haired captain was Bates. The lieutenant, a starved bird, was Livingston.

They had arrived late for duty because they had been "sculling" on the river. A sentry had taken a shot at them and they found that a great joke. Perhaps the man had thought their boats to be secret vessels, or torpedos? They laughed at the stupidity of the recruits, all immigrants and farmboys, who could not recognize a sporting boat.

They spoke, too, of the Schuylkill River. It did not take me long to understand that they were all old friends, all from Philadelphia, all from a university they called, "Penn," and that Anthony Fowler had been one of them. Yet, I could not see that at all. These boys seemed to care about nothing but themselves, while Fowler had set out to save the world.

I listened closely, given my charge from the general to learn all I could about Anthony Fowler. But my own curiosity was in play, too, I will admit it.

When it come time for the middle meal, they got up together to go. They had put up some plan while I was deep down in my work, for Bates, the captain and the great laugher of the three, gave the others a wink. He hefted a great stack of documents from his desk and walked over to where I sat.

He dropped the papers before me.

"There you go," he said. His voice had the confidence of a sound banknote. "Since they sent you here for your skills, old man, you can use 'em on these. Won't be jealous in the least."

They all laughed.

Major Trenchard followed with another stack. "Scribble, scribble, Jones. Set us right, won't you?"

The lieutenant aped the actions of his friends, but did so timidly, as though I might jump up and sink my teeth into him.

I was ashamed of my earlier outburst, for control of the self is both manly and Christian. But Providence had taken up my cause, making these three officers its servants. I had been aching to have a look at their papers. Where they meant insult, I took a gift.

"Good appetite, gentlemen," I wished them.

They went off laughing, as they had come.

Major Trenchard and Captain Bates did not return in the afternoon, and I did not expect that Lieutenant Livingston would come back, either. I took it they had the authority to grant themselves a holiday and kept to my work. I finished the sugar biscuits from my Mary Myfanwy, for I admit to loving a good sweet, and stole but a moment to go down to the yard around three.

When I returned, Livingston was sitting at his desk, or near it, anyway. He was drunk as a priest on Christmas.

"Good afternoon," I told him, and went back to my work. Twas clear I would need weeks, if not longer, to begin to untie the knots that had developed between contracts, deliveries, and requirements.

The lieutenant sat at a slump. I barely marked him from the corner of my eye and thought him asleep. His uniform was wasted on him.

The choice of country did not matter. Wherever you went, it was the same. The wickedest sons of the gentry hid out on the staffs, while the poor sweating buttics went at it with sticks and stones to make widows. I would not preach disorder, and I see that society must have its organization, but I do not always like the injustice of the world.

A voice as thin as workhouse soup come to me. Twas the lieutenant.

"Why did you have to bother us?" he pleaded. "Who are you, Jones?"

6

"WHO ARE YOU, JONES?"

Twas a fair question, but I put the boy off with more blather about the figuring of accounts. I remember him well, Lieutenant Livingston, sitting there wretched with drink and looking like he had been put together with broomsticks. He was a sad one, and you knew at a glance he was one of those lads who never know how they have arrived where they are and have not a hint where they are going. He was a fellow who would make few real decisions in his life, and most of those bad ones. Perhaps I would have a tidier tale to tell had I taken more time with him that afternoon.

"Who are you, Jones?" Like most men, I could not say more than where I had been and what I had done, and I did not say even that much to Livingston. I was a man of thirty-three, in the prime of life. I sought to be a good Christian. I was a captain of Volunteers. The rest was accumulation.

"Who are you, Jones?"

I did not tell the lieutenant, but I will give you the shreds of it.

My father preached a chapel in Merthyr Tydfil, tending

the souls of workmen and worse who trickled down from the ovens of Cyfarthfa or up from "China," those black slums by the bridge. I remember my mother only as kindness in a gray dress. They tell me she ministered with even less fear and more heart than my father, and that even the Unitarians were scandalized by her indulgence toward the poor. Now it is an easy thing to paint your parents pretty when they are dead, but I never heard a man or woman worth a listen speak badly of my father and mother. They must have had great faith, for their times were bitter.

Half the children of Merthyr died before their fifth year in those days. The mills made the town terrible. I recall the hellfire of the furnaces at night and the blackness of the days. My parents had already lost two children, a boy and a girl, when I fell to them. By all accounts, they loved me the more for it. We might have made a happy family, but my father was not born for such a fate. During the rising, when I was but three, he took the side of the workers and lost his chapel for it. They tell me he stood in the street, begging the Highlanders to stop firing on the women and children, but that may be an exaggeration. Perhaps he only tended to the fallen. It would have been enough in '31.

He found work as a carpenter in Ebbw Vale after that, for his hands were as good as his heart, and carpentry, too, had been our Lord's work. On the Sabbath, he praised the Lord at a chapel in the hills, up where the poor could not pay for their faith. I remember his strong arms carrying me toward the sky. The sky is nowhere so blue as it is above the Welsh valleys in summer. In my memory, he is forever carrying me toward Heaven. I make much of the recollections I have, see, for they are few.

The cholera struck in '32. My father and mother tended the sick, Christians to a fault, and died in their turns. My father went first. I do not remember his going, but my mother's death is burned into me. There was fear in the streets, and charity was tested. I was four, and small, and could not undo the locks to get out of the house. My mother stared at me with those great open eyes that never moved and the vomit dried over her. The look of her is scorched into me, and I remember sitting by her in the dusk of the parlor, waiting for her to awaken. I recall how cold she was when I pulled at her hand. They told the Reverend Mr. Griffiths it was three days before I was brought out of there, but I do not know how they reckoned it. Then they put me in the pest house and waited for me to die, too.

I did not sicken. Eventually, the Reverend Mr. Griffiths appeared, a black man in a black carriage. I thought he was death come for me, as a child will. I am told I wept and fought to stay out of his rig, though I do not remember that part of it myself. At first I was put out to a farm family on the high scratch above Tredegar, and I stayed there long enough to dust all threat of cholera from me.

I remember cows.

Then come the fateful day. The Reverend Mr. Griffiths was church, not chapel. He said he took me in from Christian charity. He repeated that every time he beat me. I do not think I was a bad child, see. But I remember the whippings well enough. I feel them still. He would bare me and bend me, saying, "Abel will be caned, and I will cane thee, Abel." He was a man of rigor.

But that come after. When the black man with the black carriage drove up to the farm to fetch me, he was not alone. He brought with him a woman who looked as though she bore a great and painful burden. Twas his wife. A girl of two rode with them. I had never seen a thing more shining and beautiful, and have not to this day. My Mary Myfanwy looked down at me and pulled up her nose and said, "Dirty."

She was my guardian angel, ever wiser than her years. She was as kind as her father was cruel or her mother frightened. For Griffiths never harmed the girl, but loved her. He taught me little enough, but twas from him and his affection for his own child that I learned there is love lurking in the hardest heart.

He took me in and raised me after a fashion, but hated the doing of it. I was a clever sort—"the wicked cleverness of the lower orders," he called it—and did well when put to my books. Children did not eat at table in such houses in those days, for that was a sure sign of poverty, and my joy was the little cat's corner I shared with Mary Myfanwy in the kitchen. She gentled my heart, and wept when her father beat me over causes I could not fathom. I believe her intercessions lessened my punishments, hard though they remained. Years later, she told me that her father once had asked my mother's hand in marriage, but had been turned down. Looking back, I believe there was a great loneliness in Mr. Griffiths's heart, though little mercy.

My world broke apart again soon enough. Miss Mary Myfanwy Griffiths was forbidden my company at the little table. Her father said I gave her common habits, and that my father's blood was telling in me. I still saw her when Griffiths was away, for the mother was not so hard of heart, but the distance grew between us.

When I was ten, I was put out, apprenticed to a tanner. Mills nor mines would take a boy so young and small in body then, but the tannery was a low business. Hughes the School begged Griffiths to let me study on. I heard the conversation myself. But Griffiths said I was become a man, and had the evident weakness of judgement that had damned my father and dragged my mother down, and that work was the only thing for me.

I was glad to be shut of the beatings, but would have endured them for the sweetness of the schoolroom. For I loved to learn and got my lessons quick. They tell now how all schoolmasters were brutes in my time, but it is not true. Mr. Hughes had more kindness in him than any fifty deacons. His eyes grew wet when he patted me goodbye.

The tannery was a horror. Better I had gone to the mills. I have always been sensitive to foul odors, and a tannery stinks like brimstone. It is a place of death without hope of rebirth, of flaying, blood and horror, of skins stretched and pounded as if torment does not stop at death. I was always small, and when my achievement was too little in the yard, Williams the Hide shut me in with his draft horse, a mean biting beast, in a stable that was dark and never clean.

My Mary Myfanwy brought me a book, but ran away when she saw the place and me. I thought I should never see her again. But I did. She steeled herself to it. She knew what she wanted even then, the girl did, and she would have it no matter the cost. Mr. Williams did not make a commotion, though not out of kindness, I do not think. Rather, he feared her father's imagination, that any whisper of her presence by the tannery would bring the blame down on him for conspiracy and collusion. He closed his eyes and let our secret be. For the Reverend Mr. Griffiths was a man of authority in Merthyr, sponsored by no less a gentleman than the Marquess of Bute himself. So I saw her, once a month perhaps, me in my rags and her proper as a duchess.

When I was sixteen, I had grown muscle enough for the mines, and they liked banties to work the narrow veins.

Williams the Hide let me go as worthless, though I was not, and I went from blood and leather to dust and darkness. I was a Dowlais man, which held promise then. But there were too many Church people about above ground for my good. My Mary Myfanwy come to me on the wrong side of the moon, and a hard heart saw me kiss her. Now twas a daring thing, and wrong perhaps, but she wanted it of me as much as I wanted it of her. Twas but a child's kiss, our first, and the tongue that reported it to her father should be damned for meddling cruelty, Lord forgive me. The old man packed my Mary Myfanwy off.

I went after to find her. I walked as far as London—a place of frightening confusions to a boy—and halfway back again. But I failed.

A vagabond in despair, I lied about my age in Bristol and begged the recruiting sergeant to add an inch to my height so I might sign for India. He liked my miner's muscles, but had never seen a boy so anxious to enlist. He feared I had done a capital crime. But twas only that I saw no hope in life. My love was all I knew or wanted then, and I saw that I could not have her, and even come to believe that I should not, for her own good sake.

I wrote her a letter. I was taken with the novels of Mr. Scott in those days, for I had little gravity of spirit, and I wanted to be a gentleman of the sacrificing sort. I wrote my goodbye to her in words bigger than I was myself, scarce knowing their meanings. Her mother, God bless her, sent it on to her, and for that one act I beg the Lord's eternal salvation for Mrs. Griffith's suffering soul. Eventually, an answer found its way to me on the banks of the Jhelam. But by then I was a changed man.

Chillianwala. Who has heard of that battle today? Yet it was a desperate business—and a blunder, to tell you the truth. Defeat would have meant our massacre, and we knew it. Twas my first big fight, and I remember it brightly, though the brightness was the crimson of blood. The shooting was the least of it, then we were well at it, with the green tangles all about us and no time to reload. The Seekh got into us, and us among them, and it was stabbing and clubbing and biting by all. There was killing beyond the counting, and mercy for none, with brave Campbell struggling to put right what a fool of a general had done wrong.

At one point, we pressed together so thick that a great yellow-robed devil and I crushed up against one another. His eyes were mad and his breath hot and stinking, his mustache slavered with gore. The brim of my cap pushed into his turban and we screamed into each other's face. So crowded we were that we could not raise our arms to the business of murdering one another. We must have gone like that a full minute, each cursing in his own language, hating and glaring and shameless. Then I worked my bayonet up under his chin and rammed it through his brain.

We were all of us covered in blood and even in the tumult of combat the flies would not leave us—black and biting and big as buzzards they were. Men fell to bullets and blades, and I learned how ugly we are beneath our bit of skin, how rancid. Others fell to the heat and thirst, or just to exhaustion. The lines were gone. Men in a crawling stupor clubbed one another to death. We screamed our throats dry and bloody, and we left our wounded behind to save ourselves.

God forgive me, I loved it.

There began my second life, that of Jones the Bayonet. I was a small man, but found I did not lack courage. Perhaps it was sense that I lacked. I became a hard man, and a good soldier by the standards of the regiment, and the youngest of its stripers. I did not drink, and I had my letters soundly and could add. That I could fight, as well, and shame the big men to stand by me crowned it. I was cherished for qualities that shame me when I think on them.

I stopped answering my Mary Myfanwy's letters after a time. We signed on for long service in those days, and I knew I would not see her again. Then there were other matters in my life that do not need discussion. But I will tell you that I caught the rich scent of India as only a young man can, the curry smells and the stink of the pyres, the softness of the old and the callous brutality of the present, the drabness and beauty so mixed up you soon stopped trying to make sense of it all and just lived. I would not return there now for all the loot of old John Company, but there was a time when I thought I would never leave.

I served in gleaming garrisons and in the dust and blood of the frontier, the youngest sergeant in the regiment's records. I taught the bayonet, and kept the books for a gin-soaked quartermaster, and learned that the sins of officers do not want seeing by the other ranks. My beloved never stopped writing to me, or sending me books to read for my improvement. Her father died of a seizure and my Mary Myfanwy took a gentlelady's position to an industrial family in Monmouthshire. She did not marry and swore she would not until I was hers for the marrying.

I stopped reading her letters.

I experienced a loss of my own that does not require description here, and it only hardened me. I was the devil's infernal machine when it come to soldiering. Danger was my drink, violence under a flag my vice, and wasn't I rewarded for it?

The Mutiny caught us unawares, for we had ignored the

hissing in the bazaars. An Indian fellow I knew from the trader class as much as told me that doom was dropping upon us, but I paid no more attention than did the rest. We who served in India were Britannia's bastard sons, yet we believed our superiority to the brown man so great that we were invincible. We thought our feet were planted on solid ground, but we were walking on the surface of the deepest of oceans. We had grown dependent on miracles.

Our siege was short and we broke it ourselves to link up with a column marching north. Twas then we heard of the massacres. Sepoys murdering their officers, safe conducts broken, women and children hacked up alive and stuffed down wells, and the slaughter of all white skins. It was a queer business, with both the Hindoo and the Musselman raised against us and only Johnny Seekh, so recently broken, steadfast beneath our colors. Cawnpore, Lucknow, Delhi . . . for months it was a close business whether we would last in India. But we regrouped, and London sent regulars.

That is when I met my fate. Oh, I was a good one for killing in those days. Yet, I was never a cruel man, see. My doings were on the field of battle, dutiful, and I do not recall meanness in me. I never killed a man who was not interested in killing me, and I was never one for inflicting punishments and the like. Now, it is possible that many things had been at work in my soul, not least a certain loss of the year before, but something happened to me.

We put down the rising with a thirst for blood no one would believe of civilized men. We slaughtered the natives whether they surrendered or not, then left the bodies for carrion. We burned villages and shot down those who tried to flee. Punishment slipped into torture. We stuffed the mouths of dying Musselmen with pig fat, and made your Hindoos lick the blood from the pavings, all to deny them the last comfort of their religion. Twas horror at the full, and many a man was brilliant in his cruelty. And all legal, it was. Under orders. In the name first of John Company, then of the Great White Queen. The records tell nothing of what we did, only of the sins of the brown men. Perhaps it is better so, for we must believe in ourselves if we are to rule.

Where we suspected fanaticism, we blew our prisoners from the mouths of guns. Beyond Delhi, we shot down so many of them we had only our emergency reserve of cartridges to see us through until the next resupply column arrived. In a rusty pot of a town, my detachment gathered up a dozen of their holy fellows. Perhaps they had preached Mutiny. We did not know for certain, but believed that most of them were guilty. The captain in charge judged them on the spot. He ordered me to use them for bayonet instruction.

I nearly did it, for twas orders. We tied the old Hindoos up well enough. And what with the tales of white maidens ravaged and all the natives' butchery, I would not have lacked volunteers for the business. Twas a hot day in a poor place, with their women crying and not knowing how lucky it was that we were too sweated to kill them, too. I remember the face of one old holy buck. His skin was dirty canvas, unwashed for a lifetime, and his eyes were patient with all the stupidity of the East.

"Go to it, Jones," Captain Barclay told me, "and we'll get on to some bloody shade."

I could not do it. My bayonet would not descend. Nor could my tongue give the order to the others. I do not pretend to any sort of revelation or experience of life's higher meaning that day. My limbs and tongue simply would not obey me. Then my brain would not give my body any further orders. I was so gone into myself I forgot the soldiers around me.

"Sergeant Jones, what in the blue, bloody blazes—"

"No, sir," I said.

I recall the shock on the captain's face.

"I cannot do it," I told him. "I will not do it, sir. And I shall not do it." I did not throw my rifle down. It simply fell from my hands. And then I could speak no more.

I could not even move. When Captain Barclay recovered from his astonishment, he had me bound up like the brown fellows. I'm sure he spoke further on the business, but I was gone out of it, and much that passed is opaque to me now. I was no longer in the world of regiments and bayonets.

They killed the poor niggers anyway.

I did not speak for days. Then, one morning, my senses come back to me and I was as normal as a cup of tea. The only thing different was that I knew I was done with killing.

The colonel was a good sort. He treated the men fairly and had done me not a few kindnesses over the years. His skin was as brown as any native's from a career under the Indian sun. He spoke firmly, then all in a rage, then pleadingly.

"No, sir," I told him. "I will no longer fight."

A major, who claimed he drank for his fevers, shouted for all the world, "But . . . but this is mutiny! He's as bad as the nigger bastards himself!" He was all for hanging me as an example, for he said that any other fate would have a corrupting effect upon the men.

There was a horrible fuss in the regiment, with some of them saying I had always been nothing but a puffed-up coward and that you never could trust a Welshman. A few of the boys offered pity when the other backs were turned. My rank was gone, of course, and they put me to navvy work to humiliate me. I carried sacks of meal in the plague heat. Then they put me to emptying the privies with the lowest of the natives.

I did my work in silence. To this day, I cannot explain the business. I only knew that I would not kill again, that I could be a soldier no longer. Had they burned me alive, I would not have changed my mind.

I asked for a Bible, but they would not give me one.

In the end, no one wanted to shame the regiment by making such a business public. Nor would the colonel hear of hanging me. He told me he was sparing me for all the good years of service I had done, and he got the surgeon to write me down mad of fever. That is how my service ended, shipped home as an invalid on cheap passage, "insane, but not dangerous." Half starved I was, when that filthy boat touched England.

I did what men do. I ran to a woman. I did not even think on it. Nor was there the least shame in me. Only fear. That she was gone. Married in the last smattering of years. Or otherwise dead to me.

She was sitting in the garden of a fine house, reading to her charges, when I walked up on her. I was ragged and foul from marching over a great piece of Britain.

Dropping her book, she come running.

She hugged me and wept, and said, "You, is it? I knew you'd come . . . I knew . . ."

Her mother had died and there was nothing more to bind her to the valleys. I would have found work, but she feared the rumors that would haunt my return. She wanted two things, my Mary Myfanwy, marriage to me and respectability with me. She had become a chapel woman herself, I think from contrariness toward her father, and we were married by a good man with doubt written all over him.

Her savings and a little legacy went to buy two passages to America, where her uncle had prospered. She believed that talk would ever taint us in Wales, but that people in America had better things to do than bother about the likes of us and rumors out of India. For the Americans had their own red Indians to worry over. She was a brave one, my beloved, all for a new world.

Oh, she was right about America, this blessed place. Twas the land where every man started again. Her uncle set me to work in a coal company countinghouse, down low at first. The books were scrambled and, despite the heavy business, the company was headed for bankruptcy. I fixed what I could, and that was enough to gain trust and a better position when the crisis passed. Pottsville was a boom town then, with collieries going up along the valleys like great wooden castles and immigrants fresh off the train every day and down the pits the next morning. I remember it as a place ever in motion, with locomotives pulling off long coal trains, and the canal still busy, too, and the beer wagons bold, and the miners' wives down from the patch for their twice-a-year look in the shop windows. When we walked out, my love and I, upon the mountainside, rows of green ridges spread before us, lovely as Heaven on a Sunday. The blackness had not yet covered the hills and the wind blew down from Eden.

By the winter before the war, I knew everyone needful in town, and they knew me, and the miner with his cap held low and a question about his pay could come to me for a fair hearing—and theirs was a hard life, I will tell you. We had a worthy chapel, though the Americans called it a church, with a good man in the pulpit. We had friends. If the hours were long, the work was honest, and my beloved and I thought we were in Paradise in our house of three rooms and the kitchen. No young person could love as we did, nor share with heart so full. When we were alone, my Mary Myfanwy did not object to me reading the evening paper in my shirtsleeves, and the souls of many a chicken must have smiled down at the stews she made of their earthly remains. Twas that winter young John come to us. I could not tally my blessings.

I had become a solid one for religion, though not fanatical, and I got to believe my happiness was the Lord's reward to me for turning from the soldier's life. I knew one thing certain, and that was that I would never again raise my hand to another human being, unless it was a fist to protect my family. The scent of war was upon us that winter, and had been, and the worst cold could not kill the stink of it. It seemed a madness to me, that men so blessed must fight with one another. Yet I know enough of men's hearts to understand there is more than simple goodness in them, and I know enough of their heads to know there is more in them than sense.

My Mary Myfanwy was a great one for raising up the Negro, as was the Reverend Mr. Edwards. I believe he preached *Uncle Tom's Cabin* as much as he did the Bible. Now I was not against the abolition business, for slavery was a foul matter in any color, but there were no slaves in Pennsylvania, only the hard struggle of the mines, and I marked that none of those crying out for blood had ever seen blood shed. I would have freed the black man if I might have done so by command, but I would not have fought to free him. It seemed, in truth, a distant matter to me. My fighting days were behind me, and I wished no quarrel with any man. That was a hard business, keeping my temper while they blabbered about the purifying effects of righteous war, for they knew nothing of the matter.

Come a raw March Saturday, well I remember, and long in the afternoon. I had closed up the countinghouse and wrapped myself warm for the walk home. The wind ripped down the valley from the high pitheads, and I thought on debits and dinner. Now there are sharp, cold days when it is a pleasure to be out only because you know what a joy it will be when you are back inside, and this was such a day. The world lay black, the wind howled as if a terrible hurt had been done, and spring seemed far away.

I saw them drilling in a field, men and boys in their work clothes. I knew them. A few were miners, but most not, for the miners were too weary for such a business. No, they were the fellows of the town, and when I did not know their names I knew their faces from the pews or shop counters. McDermott, the hotel keeper, read orders from a book, shouting as if to a cook in the kitchen. The responses were as inventive as they were varied. The boy with the flag could hardly keep it upright in the wind.

Would it have been better if I had not come upon them? It struck me deeply, seeing them like that, all youth, good intentions and ignorance. I knew of the militias, not least the fine Washington Artillery, but kept away. Now this lot set themselves in my path, a little orphan of a company. I watched them for a bit and would have laughed had the matter not been deadly. I knew what waited for them. They would not learn the needful from a book.

I turned away in anger. The wickedest place in hell should be reserved for those who paint war in glory and cause young men to dream of it.

But the business would not let me be. Over a fine pot pie—a Dutch affair learned from Mrs. Barrett's house-

keeper—my beloved noticed my change of temper. Twas
not hard. For we were gentle talkers of the day's events,
sharing all our little matters between us, but I held my silence that night. I feared to speak, see. There was such a
rage in me. Of course, she marked it. And she asked. And
I told her.

She did not reply, but I could feel the fear in her. I
understood it as clearly as ever I have understood a thing in
my life. For the same fear was in me. The war was not a
distant matter of the Negro now.

Young John set to wailing and she put down her fork
and went to him.

I saw them again the next Saturday, and they were no
more skillful for the passage of time. If those boys had no
idea how it all would end, neither had they any idea of
where to begin. They had less order in their ranks than
Irishmen lined up for free beer.

Still, home I went. April come in cold. I kept myself
long at work. In the evenings, I would ask my beloved to
play on her melodeon, song after song, as long as the infant
allowed. I sang to the grace of her fingers, hymns or songs
of polite matters, just now and again one of those risky tunes
of Mr. Foster's, which do have a lovely curl of melody to
them. I did not want to read, though that had been our
custom for the late evenings, after sleep had quieted young
John. I did not want to read because I could not. I only sat
there thinking about those boys drilling with their hunting
pieces.

I wondered where the goodness lay, if I might be worse
damned for sending them to their deaths unhelped by my
bit of knowledge. They were the sons of the neighborhood,
of our congregation, and I refused to reach my hand to
them. I wanted to run to them and shout that war was a

terrible, monstrous, unforgiveable thing, that none of us had need of it, and that men must learn to reason before their souls perish. I did not want them to go to war, but knew they would. It was coming, oh, it was coming sure. The newspapers were screaming for it. And those boys would go to the slaughter unready.

My thoughts were only safe when I lay wrapped in my nightshirt, holding my beloved to my breast.

The Saturday after Carolina fired on Fort Sumter, I stepped up to help them learn their drill. None of them knew I had been a soldier, for it was not a thing I spoke of, and they thought the matter humorous at first. I suppose I did not look a military man to them. But I can manage young men. By the end of the afternoon, most of the boys could face about without doing the next fellow in line a damage, and they knew when to speak and when not.

I made it clear that I was only helping them with their evolutions, and that I would have no part of any war.

We crossed Bull Run Creek at a ford that morning, but did not go straight into battle. The cannon made the boys jump. Then the sounds of musketry spread. Our regiment shunted about in the rising heat. I did what I could to keep the boys calm. Whenever we stopped I bothered them with inspections. For thought is the enemy of duty.

The battle noise was shocking, and different to me. Missing were the sounds of swords and chants, the grisly humanness of it. Apart from a high distant keening that came and went, it sounded as though two vast foundries had gone to war. I had heard guns and volleys in my time, but this had the ring of machines making war on machines.

The morning passed with sudden movements forward, followed by flank marches and more halts. Into the trees we went, only to come back out. Stragglers wandered past us, for every battle has its share, and the first wounded followed them. That made the boys go quiet. I could feel them aching to plunge forward, to get into it and put the waiting and wondering behind them. They doubted themselves, as soldiers have done since the battles of flints and stones, and each man felt his separateness now.

I could not say where I was on the field, for I had no map. But our colonel rode over and directed me to move my company into the woods and to the right, to secure the regiment's flank.

I marched the boys through the underbrush, with the sergeants coming on behind to collar shirkers. It was a jungle of a place. I reformed the company on the near side of a creek where the fall of the land would channel an enemy toward us, then I sent out pickets and gave the boys, "Rest in place." We were beyond range, but their hearts refused to understand that.

The waiting was terrible for them. A thundering battle raged above us on the heights, and quitters come stumbling through the depths of the woods, crying out that we had been defeated, that the day was lost. Cowards always claim such. I knew that nothing had been decided. We had spent the morning moving forward, and, by the sound of things, we were just as likely to go forward again.

My immediate concern was to stop the boys, who were thirsting under the heat, from drinking out of the creek. I scented death in it.

A battery went into action above us. We could not see it, but the sound was enough to unsettle the company again.

"We gonna get in it, Captain Jones? We gonna get in it?" The young man's eyes bulged like those of a driven

animal. There is a quality of fear that makes a man run
toward the object of his terror.

"We will await our orders," I said. "Steady, now."

"Think we're winning up there, Captain?" another soldier
asked. "Don't it sound like we're winning?"

"The generals have the matter in hand, Pierce. There is
muck on the butt of your rifle. Attend to it."

The army that had marched toward Manassas Junction
was as raw as a newborn calf, and I was astonished that the
generals thought it ready for battle. But let that bide. My
heart was beating as hard as any, though I could not let the
boys know. I had never felt so lonely on the edge of battle,
for I had always had my butties to banter with me. This
time I stood alone as the officer commanding. And there
was still a greater difference about me now. I had something
to lose. I stood up as straight as I could, and kept my face
a mask, but my thoughts fled to my wife and child.

Light speckled down through the trees. It would have
been a lovely place, but for the noise and the reek of blown
powder. We waited in our little green world.

"It's even hot in the damned shade," a private declared.

I turned on him. "We will have no profanity, Roberts.
Sergeant Childs, you will inspect the men's rifles for cleanliness." A groan rolled down the ranks at that. But I only
wanted the men busy and not prey to their thoughts.

Battle? They did not even know what real heat was like,
let alone battle. In the Punjab, the heat dropped more men
from the ranks than the enemy did. But these were Northern
boys, got up in wool, and it was hard enough for them.

The smoke drifted down to us, feeling its way between
the tree trunks. The rifle fire grew so intense its crackling
nearly smothered the sound of the cannon.

A great thrashing come through the brambles to our rear.

Twas an officer, a lieutenant colonel, whom I had never seen. "Every man to the front!" he cried. "General's orders. All regiments to the top of the hill."

He was flustered with the heat and his own importance, and sweat soaked his muttonchop whiskers. When I inquired about our regiment, he assured me it was already on the move, that there was a crisis on the heights, that every man was needed.

"Would the colonel kindly keep his voice down?" I said. "No need to rile the men, sir."

He looked around as if about to leap away from me. "Yes, of course . . . of course . . ."

"Now, sir, my last orders from my colonel were to guard this flank. May I ask on whose authority—"

"Everybody's supposed to go forward. General's orders. That's all I know."

I heard a great deal more crashing and clanging farther off on the flank, beyond the end of my line. The lieutenant colonel heard it, too, and glanced about in panic. A body of men were moving through the woods. In a moment, I saw them, a full regiment in blue, overtaking our position.

The security of the flank was no longer an issue. It angered me that I had not heard from our colonel. But he had been a banker four months before. Things great and little are forgotten in battle.

When I invited the lieutenant colonel to go forward with us, he said, "I'm bee-stung. I'm a wounded man." And he disappeared.

I had Lieutenant Michaels form up the men in two ranks, then called, "Company . . . *forward!*" The creek had a slop of a bottom and we come out of it heavy with mud. I almost lost a shoe. I tried to keep pace with the regiment to our right, since there was nothing on our left where our own regiment should have been. The men had to work through thickets and over fallen logs, but they stepped along in good spirit, closing up the ranks as quickly as the ground allowed. Even with the growl of battle above us, I could hear the familiar sounds of canteens bouncing and the chink of metal on metal, the great rustle of soldiers on the move. There was more smoke now, and the firing thickened with every step we took up that slope.

A squirrel fled before me.

We broke out of the trees below the crest of the hill, but could not yet see the battle—only little knots of men meandering and a sutler's wagon with the horses shot dead in their traces. We were as good as in it, though. Bullets hissed above our heads. The regiment to our right had been well drilled and its ranks hardly rippled as they climbed. It made me proud to see them. Then their green banner flapped out beside the national colors and I thought, "My God, they're Irish." I smartened up my boys right quick, for I could not let the sons of Erin shame us. We made our separate way through virgin rye.

All clear of the woods now, I saw trouble. On our left, there was a gap of two hundred yards between us and the next ranks of blue. Nor did I recognize the regimental flag in the distance.

There was a break in the line.

We crested the hill and I heard a gasp from every throat behind me. The smoke had settled heavily in a swale, and the battle was inside the cloud of it, lit by muzzle flashes. Men stumbled back toward us, materializing suddenly, a few of them wounded, others running and throwing down their rifles. Behind me, a frightened voice said, "God, that there's a *leg*." The blood would seem brighter than the sun to my boys, I knew. It would have been easiest on them to pitch them right into the battle.

Someone needed to cover that gap to our left, though.

I halted the boys, with no more time for explanations. They had to trust me now, though they were great ones, these Americans, for wanting reasons for the doing of a thing.

"Connors, to me," I shouted. My voice was still that of a sergeant at drill, not of an officer.

Private Connors ran up, face pale and lips the color of liver. He was a fine runner, Connors.

"See that officer over there? On the horse, see? You run down and tell him there's a gap in our line. He can't see it from where he is. Tell him there's a gap on his left and we'll try to cover it until a regiment comes up to close it. But a regiment must come up. Do you understand me?"

He nodded. But it was a great deal to remember.

"A gap on his left," I repeated. "We have only one company. A regiment must come up. Now run you down there."

The officer I had set Connors to chase after suddenly raised his hat, waving his men forward. His red hair caught the sun. The Irishmen went to it like great raging tigers, but after a minute I saw their flag no more.

A cannonball bounced across our front. The men watched it go. Then they began to laugh.

"Ain't that the damnedest?" I heard. Twas Pierce again.

It meant a gun was positioned to enfilade our advance. And it would not be a joke when a ball laid down a squad in line.

"Company . . . left . . . *face*. Forward . . . *march*. Guide on me."

I led them into the gap in the lines, positioning them just behind the crest, where there would be no killing of them until they were needed. I watched the battle from the height, with my sword sheathed and my arms folded so the boys would see no nervousness in me. I glanced back at them often enough to warn of the consequences of bad behavior.

I wanted orders, for the truth is I lacked the confidence an officer needs. I ached to see our own regiment or any other in blue break from the trees behind us to close up the line. We were in a bad way in a bad place and nobody seemed to mark it. When Connors come back, panting, he told me the red-haired colonel cursed heaven and earth and said he had no troops to spare.

"He said he'd send to General Tyler, though," Connors went on.

"Did he understand that it's a serious matter?"

The boy nodded, sweat dripping from his chin. "Oh, he was mad to the devil about it. He's a wild fella. He's just having a grand old time, and cursing a blue streak. But he didn't like that talk about a gap." He looked at me oddly, face pink as good roast beef from his exertions. I did not like his eyes.

"Is there water in your canteen, lad?"

He looked at me in embarrassment. "I drunk it all, sir. I'm—"

"Here." I gave him my canteen, for I did not want to lose him. "Now go back to your place, Connors. You've done well."

The battle appeared to be centered on a house several hundred yards away. When the smoke tore, I could just see its outline amid a great muddle of men and guns.

Lieutenant Michaels stepped up. He was a good lad, and might have made a fine officer.

"Sir," he said. "Captain Jones. The men . . . they're

wondering . . . why we aren't going into the fighting. They think—"

His head whipped back and blood and skull exploded down toward the men, wetting them thirty feet away. Gore slicked my cheek.

"*Anderson, Boyle, to me,*" I shouted. They were the two sorriest men in the company, and we could well afford to lose them.

"To *me*, I said."

They came reluctantly. All at once, there was a great deal less enthusiasm for getting into the battle.

I liked the boy and could have wept over him. But it would not have done.

"You two will carry Lieutenant Michaels to the rear. You will treat the body with respect." He was the only son of a judge, and grief would crush the old man's heart.

Boyle and Anderson looked at me. I read their minds. They had no objections to going to the rear, and wished they had never volunteered for the war. But they were reluctant to pick up the boy with his head shot away.

"Do what I say," I told them in the lowest voice they would hear over the rage around us. "Or I'll have two others do it and you can join the front rank."

Still they hesitated. But I knew they would do it then.

"Empty your haversack and put it over his head, if you don't want to look at him."

They took him away. They were lucky men. Within a minute, a gray rank—a broken attempt at a rank—emerged from the smoke hardly a shout away.

I rushed my boys up to the crest.

"Aim low now," I told them. "Steady, lads. *Steady.* Aim at their knees. *Fire by rank. Company. Ready. Rear rank. Aim. Fire. Load. Front rank. Aim. Fire. Load . . . Rear rank . . . aim . . . fire . . .*"

They did it well, my boys, if such work can be called well done. Men fell before us. The gray line shivered and faded. A few of them fired back or shook their fists. Oh, they were game, but as green as us or greener. Soon they were drowned in the smoke again.

"Cease firing!"

The boys cheered themselves. I made them reload, check their pieces, and dress the line again. I blasted the sergeants until they woke to their business. Every man needed to be busy now, with all thought driven out of him.

I expected the Confederates to come back stronger, having glimpsed the weakness of our line. But it was a battle of confusions. The next men to emerge from the smoke wore blue. They were running toward us, disordered, throwing off their equipment.

"Hold your fire, boys," I shouted. Still, a few men let off rounds. I would need to see to the discipline of that. *"Hold your fire."*

I ran along the front of the line to stop them, and a fool thing it was to do. But luck was still with me.

In a moment, the first of the fleeing men come upon us, shouting of disaster and black horse cavalry, of ambushes and slaughter.

"Steady," I shouted. "Not a man to move. *Steady.*" I raised my sword. "Eyes on me."

A carriage, empty of passengers, raced across the field. More men ran toward us now.

"Stand fast," I ordered. This was the worst of any battle. Panic was as contagious as cholera. And those who ran died all the sooner.

A few men faded from the back rank and I gave our sergeants the devil. But they were hardly true sergeants, and they were doing their best. The fear was on everybody.

I tried to stop as many of the fleeing men as I could, taking the flat of my sword to them. But even the officers were broken.

The blue ranks on our right fell back, but in good order. Their green flag was up again.

A runner found me.

"You in command here, Captain?"

I nodded. "I am the officer accountable."

"Colonel Sherman's compliments, sir. He asks you to hold as long as you can, to cover the withdrawal. He says it's all buggered."

"My compliments to the colonel. Tell him we will stand."

I meant it, but did not know if I could fulfill the promise.

The flood of broken men thinned. I ordered the company forward, beyond the top of the crest, and had them stand ready. I noticed that more of the boys had faded away. We were not much, but I wanted to be seen. If we had not much strength to fight, I hoped to frighten the enemy from our front by a show of confidence, advancing at least a few steps while the units before us were collapsing. I hoped they might think us the vanguard of a fresh regiment.

The Southrons came for us then. Yelling like wild Afghanees, and no order to them. Some in gray, some in brown, and some of them just dressed for farm work. I had the men fire by rank again, for the effect was solid and it kept good discipline. And, by God, if we did not stop them once more. Then they come back at us again, with all the fury of battle on them. We sent them backward that time, too. It was nothing like the butchery of Chillianwala or the Mutiny. But there was blood enough.

The smoke had drifted, leaving a path of sunshine across the top of the hill, and I saw that we were only the fringe of the battle. But the retreat was shifting in our direction, and the powder clouds followed it.

On our right, down the hillside now, the red-haired colonel formed his men into a square, and imagine my astonishment. It was properly done, too, and his boys kept up a good fire. The Duke of Wellington himself would have thought it well done.

The Rebels shifted away from them.

"Fix . . . bayonets!" I shouted.

I heard the dutiful clank and scrape.

Another round of firing erupted and smoke drifted over us like a cloud. I marched back and forth, before the men and behind them, trying to keep their courage up, calling them by name.

The smoke grew worse. The breeze, what little there was, had shifted again. Soon all we could see were hellfire flashes to our front and off to the right. The noise seemed denser for the darkness, and you could feel a physical shock when the cannon let off. Six-pounders, I judged them. Not as many as before, but they had been wheeled closer to us.

Another runner found me. Twas a miracle on that field. The same colonel wanted to know if we still could hold. The situation was desperate, the courier told me, the army was in collapse.

"We will hold," I said, "so long as I am standing."

Hardest on the men were the lulls in the fighting. They needed occupation to keep down the fear. I had seen but three of them fall to bullets. But if I had forty men left, it was a generous estimate. Cowards ran through our ranks, casting away their haversacks and cartridge boxes, anything they could undo while at a run, and they took the weaker men with them.

I heard cheering, but sensed it was not our own. I kept

talking up the boys as best I could. To be honest, my pride was up, for we had not done badly. And say what you will, battle is an intoxicating thing.

The smoke had taken a terrible liking to us, thickening around our heads. I struggled to see. Then a dreadful rumbling arose within the cloud.

I saw nothing. Not even pips of light from rifle fire now. There was only a rushing thunder upon the earth and the black smoke.

A battery of mounted artillery burst upon us. Sliding over the crest they came, their horses terrified and whinnying, all eyes and teeth, with men in blue clinging to the caissons.

They smashed into the company.

What the Rebels could not do, the gunners did in an instant. Our ranks collapsed as men dodged to save themselves. It was sudden and unspeakable. I ran after the boys, shouting for them to reform the lines. Twas then that a team of horses and a caisson wheel knocked me down and went over me.

I remember a horse spewing blood from its nostrils. And the gunshot sound of breaking bone. Through it all, I shouted useless commands to rally, lying there in shock and failure.

You can see I was no hero.

A sergeant I had never seen before and never saw again rescued me. He had the confidence of a regular and an enormous pistol. He held the gun on two frightened boys from Connecticut and forced them to carry me off the field. In truth, they did more damage to me than necessary, but they were frightened and it was not done on purpose. I could not believe what had happened to me, and I wept with shame and anger. Nor was I in comfortable mind, for a man does not like to see the bone of his own thigh come through his pant leg.

They must have lugged me a pair of miles before they found a place for me on a meat wagon. And thus I joined the long retreat.

In the darkness, the wagon stopped at a barn lit with lanterns and rough men took us down. The pain was full with me then. Many a man was mad in his screaming. I pretended their screams were mine and kept my silence. Then they come for me and threw me on a table made of boards. The blood on it gripped my hair and soaked through my tunic. They cut away my trousers.

"I cannot . . . lose my leg," I said. It was difficult to speak and I had to concentrate on the one thing that mattered.

The bloodiest human being I have ever seen looked down at me.

"There's no time to fiddle," he told me. He sounded weary.

"I'm going to keep my leg, see."

He considered the break.

"Fracture that bad," he said, "I splint it up, it's just going to rot."

"I *need* my leg."

"There's many a man here who—"

I grabbed his arm with all the strength I had left.

"*No,*" I told him.

He shook his head at my folly. "Wouldn't you as soon have your life, man? Leg or no leg?"

I could not help it. The tears broke free. "There's not enough of me as it is," I told him. "You can't take any more away."

After a moment, he sighed and said, "All right, Captain. But you're taking your own life." He turned to his helpers.

"Hold him down, boys. He'll be screaming to change his mind in a minute."

The next day, it rained and Confederate cavalrymen stopped by the barn. They had a look at us and left again. Eventually, a wagon carried me the thirty endless miles to a hospital set up in a hurry in a Georgetown church. Twas a special place for those expected to die of their wounds, and soon it stank of gas gangrene and fouled bandages. But a Welshman is hard to keep down.

7

SINCE THE DAY I PUT HIS BACK TO THE FLOOR, MAJOR TREN-
chard stood wary of me, elegantly spiteful, and Bates and
poor Livingston copied his pattern. There was a truce between us, but an unhappy one, for they did not trust me,
and liked me less than I was trusted. I kept my place and
did my work. But there is the devil in men. Bit by bit, they
tested me, as children will, to see how far they might go.

Trenchard sat back in his handsomeness, with his fine boots
braced on his desk and a smile thin as barley water. Twas fine
outside, a high November morning, but we were in.

"Jones?"

I looked up from my work and theirs.

"Fond of poetry, by any chance?" he asked me.

I put up my pen, careful of the ink, for I knew Trenchard
was but started.

"Poetry is it?"

"Yes, Jones. Poetry. You know the stuff. 'Roses are red,
violets are blue . . .'"

A brashness of leaves struck our window. Golden they
were. "I am not a great reader of it, sir. Though I have been
through my Homer. There is good in him."

Trenchard made one of his playactor's faces for his friends, a great orbit of the eyes under lifted brows.

"Homer! Think of it, gentlemen. Our toiling scribe has 'been through his Homer.' The diligence of it! The ambition!" Handsome he was, I will admit, as he turned his face to me. "You read him in Greek, of course?"

My work called me down, while the brilliance beyond the window called me out, and I only wanted away from their meanness. But Trenchard would have his joke before lunch. There was nothing to be done. Then he and Captain Bates would prance off on their horses for the rest of the day, leaving Livingston back to mind me.

"Twas not in the Greek, sir, but in Mr. Pope's rendering. I would commend the *Iliad* to all soldiers, for they will find in it all the cruelty of war and the vanity of heroes."

"Yes, Jones. Homer, by way of the little country church. Just the thing, I'm sure. But I didn't really have the Greeks in mind—although we're all pleased to find your class reading anything at all." He gave his whiskers a loving stroke. "Thing is, Jones, I find myself in need of your assistance."

I sat and waited for him to make his speech, for I would not step to put my foot in his trap. I knew he would bring the trap over to me in good time.

"You see, Jones, I've come upon a poem from the land of your origins. Strikes me there's wisdom in it. I thought you might identify the author. I'd like to read more of him." Trenchard was a man with no music in his voice, and none in his heart. The sound of his yap was polished, but brittle. "Like to hear the poem, old fellow?"

"There is work I must do, sir."

"Won't take a minute, Jones. Then back to your scribbling. Here it is:

"Taffy was a Welshman,
Taffy was a thief,
Taffy came to my house,
And stole a piece of beef."

They laughed like bad children, the three of them. I knew the doggerel for a cradle rhyme from the wrong side of the Marches. Twas nothing. Still it angered me.

"I can tell you, sir," I said, "that the author was an Englishman who had not the courage to sign his name to his doings."

"But you do get the beauty of the piece, Jones?"

"And this I will tell you, Major Trenchard. If ever a Welshman took a bit of beef from an Englishman's house, twas because only that much was left of the cow the Englishman stole from the Welshman."

"No need to get your back up, Jones. We're speaking of literary matters. Aren't we, gentlemen?"

Oh, they murmured along like the cowards they were.

Trenchard stood up. "Well, Jones . . . I'm sure you have the office business in hand. Scribble, scribble, right? Captain Bates and I may not be back this afternoon. Liaison matters. Coming to lunch, Livingston?"

I took my meal in the yard to get the loveliness of the day. Mrs. Schutzengel had put a fine leg of chicken in my sack, and did that not come as a surprise. I had the last of the bread and cleaned myself with the cloth. Then I sat. I would take my time to feel God's sun before the winter fell.

Evans the Telegraph come by. Pleased to see me.

"Well, sit you down," I told him, moving over on the bench. But he waited a moment, stretching himself like the grocer's cat.

"There is beautiful," he said. "Do you not miss home on such a day, Captain Jones?" He sat down beside me and took out his pipe.

"My home, Mr. Evans, is by my wife and in America."

Evans was the slowest man to fill a pipe that ever I saw. He nodded in rhythm to his hands.

"As it should be, Captain Jones," he said. "For a wife that does not scratch is a blessing. But I had another meaning. Do you not miss the valleys gone pretty with the autumn, when even the Monday washing has beauty in it? Do you not miss the silver in your breath in the morning, and all the world handsome as a well-sung hymn? Is there no more of Wales in you, then?"

I watched the blue sky above the city streets. " 'Season of mists . . . and mellow fruitfulness . . .' "

The curious face he gave me.

"Poetry," I said, "though by an Englishman."

"I think on home, Captain Jones, until the tears come bothering me."

"We are Americans now."

He gave his pipe a light. Tobacco seasoned the air like hearth smoke. "Cannot an American remember the fondness of old things?"

"I would look forward, and not back."

Evans sighed. "That is the India in you. You broke away young. Twas India and the Hindoo took the love of the old country from you."

"All that India took from me was the innocence of a boy and the folly of a young man. No, Mr. Evans, proud we Welsh may be, but I am for these United States. For if I remember the beauty of our hills, I remember the heaviness of the English boot, as well."

"This war rends America. No good will come of it."

"Sorry I am for the war. But we do not know what will come of it. Anyway, my heart is here."

He shook his head. "There is an obstinacy in you, Captain Jones. You are worse than a chapel deacon. That you will not admit the longing in your own heart. There is no Welshman alive who does not miss his valley on such a day. Not even a Merthyr man."

"And how is Mr. Lincoln?" I asked.

A shower of leaves fell on us, and we laughed like butties.

"Oh, Mr. Lincoln is himself. More cares on him than a mother of ten." He put his face closer to me. His tobacco had a wash of rum on it, and I will admit to liking the smell. "But it is a hard thing to see General McClellan with him. For I think there is little respect there, and less patience. The general will treat Mr. Lincoln as a schoolboy."

"The general has his cares, too. But let that bide. There is work now."

He laid his small hand on my arm, asking me not to rise. "Wait you, Captain Jones. The Fowler lad is still much in the newspapers, I see. And on the lips. Is there no revelation?"

Leaves scoured past the bench. One caught on my trousers. "They have made a martyr of him," I said. "Mr. Greeley and the lot. They have been judge and jury, and the verdict is murder by the Confederates. It will put hatred in the killing to come. McClellan sees that rightly."

"But . . . the telegram. From the Rebels. Has nothing come of that?"

"Oh, the Confederates did not do the murder," I said, not without a strain of anger. "There are lies from here to the top of the hill. It is a black business."

"Natural, though, to blame your enemy," Evans the Telegraph said, with the weight of thoughtfulness in his voice. "And him a keeper of slaves."

I stood up. "I will see fairness, Mr. Evans. We need not like the Confederates to deal with them honestly. They had no hand in this thing. I may fight a man without bearing false witness against him. There are greater sins and lesser."

Knowledge lit his eyes.

"Ah," he said. "Then it is progress you have made." He looked at the bowl of his pipe, then back to me.

Across the street, Lieutenant Livingston shambled toward us. Coming from the direction of the Willard Hotel bar. I think I have never seen a man with less confidence. He passed by without seeing me. Like a great pale mole.

"There has been progress," I told Evans, my voice low.

"Do you know who did it, then?"

Fool that I was, I said:

"Yes."

"Congratulations," I told Livingston as I entered our office again.

He gave me those befuddled eyes. Confused first that I had not been in my chair waiting for him as always, then by my salutation.

I moved for my desk, with its paper hills and valleys. "Your engagement," I said. "I have only been told of it. My congratulations. Marriage is a thing of wonder."

"Thank you . . . Jones." He never called me "sir" or "Captain," but I let that go. There was not consequence enough in him for disputation.

"She is a pretty one, I hear, your Miss Cathcart."

He brightened. Twas a rare thing, rarer than the glory of the day, for he was a sad man, though how sad I did not yet know. "Betty—I mean, Miss Cathcart—she's an angel. Wonderful family, too. Quakers." Suddenly, his eyes alarmed. Over nothing. For small things frightened the boy.

"Philadelphia Quakers are a different sort, Jones," he added quickly. "Not like . . . the ones you might know. The Cathcarts are people of excellent standing. Aristocratic, really."

"Authentic dynasties, I hear. These Philadelphia Quakers."

He nodded, a happy child. "Got 'em on my mother's side, too. She was a Blake. But the Cathcarts . . . their family came over on the same ship as William Penn."

"My congratulations again. A grand society match it will be. And will the wedding wait on the war's end? Or will the golden day come sooner?"

Something happened to his face. Twas the look of a man bitten by a flea after he has just put on clean linen.

"Oh . . . her parents . . . they want June . . . I mean, Betty and I . . . we could . . . they have nothing against my wearing of the uniform. 'Fighting Quakers,' you know . . . it's just that . . ."

Something wrong there. At first mention of the business, his enthusiasm had lifted him out of the drink that was in him, but now the alcohol came back to his voice.

"Speaking of families," I said, "I'm told Major Trenchard's father has the biggest merchant bank in Philadelphia."

His eyes dreamed in drink again. "Second biggest. Oldest, though. Rich as Croesus. Though a gentleman . . . shouldn't say so." He smiled to himself. "Charlie's father got us put here. He's great pals with Mr. Cameron . . . although the Secretary doesn't have . . . quite the social standing, of course. Politicians. And Governor Curtin. Knows everybody, old Trenchard. And Billy's father is the shipping fellow. But you must've known that. 'Pride of Philadelphia' and all."

"And your father is in the railroads?"

His mouth lived while his eyes died. "The railroads are a sport for Dad."

I did not want him thinking too clearly, but neither did

I want him asleep. I slammed down a ledger. Just hard enough to startle his eyes back open and lift his hands from the arm of his chair. I already knew everything he had told me, for I had spent the heft of November studying the business. But I had other aims for the conversation.

"None of you are assigned to this office, though. Not officially. As I am not. For Congress has not authorized an increase in the number of officers for the Ordnance Department." I watched his face, the slack of it. "We're all ghosts here."

A smile dressed his lips without reaching his eyes. " 'Ghosts.' You're a good one, Jones. I'll tell the boys that one. 'Ghosts.' "

"Perhaps you will go to a regiment soon?"

He laughed, the sound fragile as a consumptive's chest. "You don't think I'm a real soldier. Do you?"

"We can be made such."

He shook his head. "I know I'm no soldier. But Father . . . he wants to run for the Senate. Stevens isn't in the best of health, you know. Old Thad. Now there's a loony for you. Educate the poor . . . free the Negro. One of these days he'll choke on his own nigger-loving heart during one of his rants. And Father will take his place."

I acted as though the papers before me were of more interest than the conversation. "But his son must wear a uniform, if the father is to run?"

"You're not stupid, Jones."

"I see the sense of it."

"And Charlie and Bill . . . a fellow has to wear the blue coat. In times like these. But you can carry a thing too far. Anthony . . . he was always one for carrying things too far."

I opened the bottom drawer of my desk. "Lieutenant Livingston . . . can you keep a secret?"

His eyes opened at that one. "What?"

"If you do not object . . . I will take just a preacher's swig of whisky to pass the afternoon." I brought out a bottle it had pained me to buy.

"Why, Jones . . ."

I passed my hand through the air. "Forbidden. I know it. But if you are not one for telling, I will not be. A small one is it?"

He tried to rise.

"Sit you there," I said, getting up with bottle and glass in hand, God forgive me. I poured him a fine glass, near twenty cents worth, and set it by him.

"Our secret," he said, toasting the four walls. "You're not such a bad sort, Jones. Every man his vices, right?"

"Right."

How he drank, the boy. He did not notice that my own glass went untouched. Nor did he care, I think.

"And all this fine Philadelphia society," I said, "that would include Mr. Matthew Cawber? Of the iron works?"

He shook his head with a great wildness, as if the whisky had turned to fire on his lips. "Not Cawber. Society won't have him. *Can't* have him."

"A rich man like him?"

He drank to rinse the taste of the last drink from his mouth. "Cawber . . . can't be invited. Nobody has him to dinner. Unwelcome. No club . . . no club will . . ."

I slammed down the ledger again.

"He is a great man of industry, though," I said. "This Mr. Cawber."

"He's a stinking crook. And worse. A seducer. Of honest women. Stole his wife, the bastard. He . . . he might live in Philadelphia . . . but he isn't *part* of Philadelphia. Never will be."

"Did your friend . . . was Anthony acquainted with Mr. Cawber?"

He gave me the astonishment, and honest it was. "Jones . . . Anthony would never . . . Anthony wouldn't have said so much as, 'Good morning,' to that sort."

"But wasn't young Fowler a great democrat? What about the abolition business? The freeing of the Negro?"

He waved that away. "Touch of the eccentric in all of them, the Fowlers. First-rate family, though. Excellent blood-lines. Smacking rich. Just quirky."

"But Anthony certainly wanted to free the slaves? He was sincere in that, was he not?"

Livingston's eyes regained enough focus to find me in the brown light of the room. "Sit 'em right there beside you. Anthony would have done that, all right. So close you could smell the jungle. Treat 'em equal to the white man."

"Then why on earth be so set against the likes of Cawber? A man of his own race?"

He blew out two lungs of bad air and followed up with a burp. "Cawber . . . just isn't our sort. Why . . . his father . . . did you know his father worked on the *docks?* Anthony . . . could not have . . . Jones, would you be a friend and share a touch more of your whisky?"

I gave it to him, God forgive me.

He drank and savored and sighed. "Look . . . Anthony had a great fondness for his pet Negroes. Like his father with his Chinese heathens. The Fowler men . . . they all have this unaccountable need to save somebody." He turned his eyes to me and the blue of them shone weak. "Don't you see it, Jones? Your nigger's one thing . . . I mean, he's not going to climb up and push his way into your house, is he? But Cawber's sort? They'll build a bigger house right next door to you. Annoy the ladies. Want their brats to play with your children, go to the same schools. Buy their way in with all their dirty money. Upset the order of things." He smirked. "You might as well invite the Irish to the opera."

"I have noticed . . . in going through Captain Fowler's papers . . . that he paid a great lot of attention to Mr. Cawber's doings."

He grunted. "Anthony saw him for the crooked swine he is. Anthony *hated* him."

"There is a certain matter of cannon."

Livingston sat up straight. I would not have thought the boy capable of it. "Now you're onto it, Jones. Now you see. Anthony was going to put him in jail. For fraud against the government. Then we'd see what all the Cawber money was good for. Let him try to buy his way out of prison. Like he tried to buy his way into Philadelphia society."

"Your friend . . . Anthony . . . had quite a pile of evidence. Requisitions outside of the normal process. Bills of approval signed by Secretary Cameron himself. And more than a dozen cases of exploding guns—all from the Cawber works. Men were killed. It's all here."

"Cawber's a damned crook. Anthony saw it. Anthony . . . was a hero."

"Was Anthony . . . did Captain Fowler ever express any personal concern . . . fear, to put the honest word on it . . . regarding Cawber?"

He treated me to a dumbfounded look, with his glass stopped halfway to his mouth.

"Anthony wasn't afraid of anything," he said.

The one thing I did not understand was the behavior of General McClellan. Now certain it was that he was busy. Yet his concern for the Fowler business had seemed so great, and his worry that the boy's murder would be used for wicked purposes so urgent, that his lack of interest in my doings bewildered me. There was a great campaign in the newspapers to follow Anthony Fowler's ghost on to Richmond. Every Union man with a mouth called for vengeance, from Maine to the banks of the Missouri. Yet I had heard not a word from the general for almost two weeks. I yearned to lay my suspicions before him, for I believed I had seen through the matter. But the only time I glimpsed Little Mac he went dashing by on horseback, kicking up leaves and dust, with one of those French devils beside him and a troop of aides galloping to keep up.

Oh, I wanted to talk to the general with a fury, for I saw the murder clear. But he had forbidden me his headquarters. All I could do was to wait. And the waiting was hard.

I wanted to see justice done.

I outlasted Livingston that afternoon. When he finally staggered off, I shut up my papers and books in the safe I had cajoled for the office and stepped out into the dark. The little warmth of the day was lost, and winter was teasing us. On Pennsylvania Avenue, a line of oxen towed a great gun toward the city's defenses, and I paused to watch it pass. Then I made my way toward Mrs. Schutzengel's house and dinner.

When I stopped for my *Evening Star*, Fine Jim said, "You're struttin' just like a minstrel, Captain Jones. You'll be running next."

Twas a lie, but well meant.

"I'll have my paper now," I said, and he held it out to me. I gave him his three pennies, and a fourth for his kindness. I am no believer in spoiling a young fellow, but I had a weight on my conscience. The matter of paying the devil a dollar then pouring Satan's whisky into Livingston was wrong, I knew.

"There is cold," I said to Fine Jim. "You'll want to dress more warmly now."

His red hands slipped into his pockets and he did not answer me. I had been too much with my own thoughts and now I was sorry I had spoken, for I had shamed him. Had he a coat, the boy would have worn it.

I tipped my paper against the brim of my hat and marched on. But the devil had gotten into me as sure as he had waited in that whisky bottle for poor Livingston. I was not far along before I turned right toward Pennsylvania Avenue again. I had bought a uniform of decent quality at a fair price from a tailor fellow on 13th Street and soon enough I stepped into the shop of M. Feinberg and Sons.

The old man remembered me and smiled most kindly, putting on a queer voice that might have passed for an imitation of a Welsh accent among the far Eskimo. "Not a penny more! Not a penny more!" he called from behind his counter.

"Evening, Mr. Feinberg," I said.

He considered the fit of my tunic. "To steal from me again, you come here? At such a price, I should feed my family? Still it hurts me."

"I need a coat."

He reached for a stack of army overcoats and held one up. "A beautiful coat," he said. "Quality."

"A coat for a boy."

He turned, and if his eyes were not question marks. "A boy? A son? A son must have the best quality."

"Actually . . . I'm wanting a coat for a newsboy, Mr. Feinberg. Just a little fellow, see. There is cold now. He feels the want of a warm coat."

"A relative? A nephew, perhaps?"

"No. Just a newsboy. They're a poor lot and—"

"No? Not a relative? Captain Jones, what am I to think? You bargain with me like a man with a knife." He held up two blue-veined fists. "You hold every penny in your hand until it thinks it's a goldpiece. And now—such a man as this—he tells me he wants to buy a coat for the paperboy? Maybe he thinks Moses Feinberg is a fool?"

"He's cold, see. That is all there is in it. Simple Christian charity it is."

He gave me a look then, but called for one of his sons from the rear of the shop. There was a great running back and forth. After a go-about over weight and size, we settled on a black wool affair that would cover most of the parts that might freeze on a boy. The cloth was rough, but warm. And it was big enough to give Fine Jim a year of growing into it.

With fear in me, I asked the price.

The fellow's brown eyes sparkled.

"Fifty cents," he said. "And no bargaining."

Twas a two-dollar coat, if ever a two-dollar coat there was. Mr. Feinberg hardly let me open my mouth before he added, "Inventory reduction. Who wants such a coat? Take it from my shop. An evil day when I wasted good wool on such a rag."

Another of his sons wrapped it with string and I hurried back into the street, for I wanted to catch Fine Jim before he left his corner. Now you will laugh at me and say there is foolish in Abel Jones, but I have seen the Jew from India to America and find him no more wicked than another man, and sometimes less so. I think him honest, though it surprise you. He has the carefulness of the eternal guest, see, and that confuses men born safe in their property. They think him devious when he is only cautious. Perhaps America will be a home to him, too, although I understand not all would have it so. For men need to blame and to feel bigger than one another, and sorry it is that we are made so. Look you: I recognize the sadness in the Jew. For it is the sort you will find in a Welshman when the singing is done. Our homes were taken, too, and our religion mocked. We, too, were said to be of lower clay.

The evening froze around me. Fine Jim was still at his spot, dancing to beat the cold.

When he saw me coming on the wrong way, his face went into troubles. "Something the matter, Captain Jones? Something wrong with your paper?" Perhaps he thought I would ask for the fourth penny back.

"The paper is as a paper should be." I held out the package. "Here is warm."

He opened it, and there was pleasure in him, but a wavering, too.

"Go on with you. Try it for the size."

He held it respectfully before him.

"My old man says I'm not to take charity."

"And what does your mother say, then?"

He shook his head. And I understood that I had been indelicate again. I was hardly a Solomon that evening.

"Well, there is no charity in it," I said. "It is a gift between friends. There is a difference, see."

With the suddenness of a cat, he pulled it on. Large it was. But not to tripping over. It looked warm.

"You won't miss your paper any day," he said. "I'll get it right to you, Captain Jones. Anytime you can't come by. I promise."

It is trouble to understand the world. I wanted only to do good. But the next time I saw the boy, the coat was gone from him and his left eye was swollen. He would not look at me. It was a hard country then. But let that bide.

After dinner I took my place in the parlor across from Mrs. Schutzengel, who was reading one of her queer German pamphlets. The *Evening Star* was as it always was, with the advertisements for the sale of waterproofs, oysters, and quack cures on the front page and the news of the war next back. I was just reading about a fellow named Grant and a to-do along the Mississippi the week before when a fist started up at the door. I would have gone to answer it, but Mrs. Schutzengel was the guardian of her own gate and would have it no other way.

I heard a voice ask for me. There was a familiarity to the sound, but I could not conjure a face or a name. A moment later, the brigade surgeon I had met over the river stepped into the light. His medical bag hung from his left hand.

"Dr. Tyrone," I said. "Now this is a surprise. Mrs. Schutzengel, this is Dr. Tyrone, a surgeon to our troops."

He bowed. *"Habe die Ehre, gnädige Frau,"* he told her.

Mrs. Schutzengel blushed and answered him with a stammer.

"German is it?" I asked him. I was surprised for, although he was a surgeon, he was, after all, an Irishman.

"Need it for the medical books. If a man's serious about his butchering. *Verzeihung, gnädige Frau.* Your Germans have the doctors, the schools . . ."

I recalled that he had been reading a French book in his tent. Now that was a thing, it was. An Irishman who spoke French and German. Perhaps there was foreign blood.

"Listen, Jones," he said. "I've business in town. Thought you might like to join me for an evening promenade. If that leg of yours allows." He browsed over Mrs. Schutzengel's pamphlets as he spoke. He was a man who could no more pass by a book or journal without examining it than a dog could pass by a bone.

Suddenly, he laughed. Almost a roaring, it was. And he looked at Mrs. Schutzengel.

If her face had been red, now it was crimson.

"*The Communist Manifesto,*" he said. "Now there's a fine recipe book for the lady of the house."

Mrs. Schutzengel snatched the pamphlet from his hand. "*Sie haben kein Recht,*" she barked.

I knew nothing of the work and had little of the exchange until Tyrone laughed again, delighted, and said, "Do you realize, Jones, that your landlady is a flaming revolutionary?"

I looked at Mrs. Schutzengel, at the stolid largeness of her. But her eyes had gotten up a defiance, as if someone had tried to rob her larder.

"It is only in America that the peoples will be free," Mrs. Schutzengel said. "Even no-good Irish peoples, *so ein wertloses Volk . . .*"

"Now, now," Tyrone said. "Nothing against it, milady. Read what you will. So long as the sheets are clean and the food abundant for my friend the captain. Will you walk with me, Jones?"

And we walked, with Mrs. Schutzengel giving the door a good bang behind us. Tyrone was thoughtful for a few blocks, then he said, "I can tell you her story, poor woman."

"You know her, then?"

He shook his head. "No need of it. Tis a common enough tale. Common as hunger. Has she not spoken of a husband?"

"There has been such mention. An untimely end, I believe."

He laughed again, but this sound was as dark as the night. "Yes. 'Untimely.' In the streets of Berlin or Frankfurt or Mannheim. Or on the Rastatt barricades. Might be they just hung the poor bugger after his catching."

"Who, then?"

"Your Prussians. Back in forty-eight or forty-nine. The revolution that failed. Though it will come again."

"I was in India then."

We turned down 7th Street. "And I was in Vienna," he said. "Studying. With my sympathies already up, though that's another tale entirely. Nearly finished I was. And then they poured out into the streets, waving flags and shouting about the rights of man. A grand lark it seemed. The words . . . had the brightness of cherries. And victory seemed easy. We honestly thought we'd won. Then the army came back to itself. They shot their way through the streets." He went a few steps in silence. "I went on to Budapest. For there was a great need of doctors there, with all the fighting." He was gone into the past. "If ever a hero's fight was fought, your Hungarians fought it. The Germans, the Austrians . . . everybody else had given up. But not your Magyars, bucko. First they fought the Austrian troops, and didn't they give them a grand hiding. Then your Russian bastards marched in to save the dirty crown for Frantzen." He lowered his face in the darkness between lamps. "Your Russian would rather kill than drink, and rather drink than breathe. It was nothing but a slaughter. I ran away and left them to their dying. Heroes they were . . ."

"I am not a great believer in heroes," I said.

"Each man to his own. But heroes they were, sure. All over Europe that year. But your Hungarians above all. Fighting for a shred of decency to cover their arses with. Oh, the revolution will come again." He turned his head toward me and there was more than gaslight in his eyes. "Is the walking too much of a bother?"

"There is no bother. Are you a revolutionary then, Dr. Tyrone?"

He laughed. He was a great one for laughing, Mick Tyrone, and had more different laughs in him than a chapel has hymns.

"Next time," he said, "I won't run away."

As we turned from 7th Street into Pennsylvania Avenue, Tyrone made a fist at a door. The glass overhead read, WASHINGTON BUILDING.

"There's a man I'd drop in the river with his hands tied back," he said.

I said nothing, but he must have felt my curiosity.

"La Bonta," he said. "Calls himself a doctor."

I knew the name instantly, for the man's advertisements were a constant in the newspapers. He claimed to cure diseases of shame.

"When he doesn't poison them," Tyrone said, "he gives them false hope. And back they go to the sheets. He's a plague upon the camps. The provost marshal should close the bastard down."

Dr. Tyrone's language disappointed me, but we cannot hold the Irish to the same standards we apply to civilized people.

"Surely," I said, "he must cure some. Or he would not have the business."

Tyrone let off his darkest laugh of all. We passed a saloon and a girl in the door gave him a funny eye, far too familiar.

"There is no cure for syphilis, Jones. None. His sort prey upon the hopes of the afflicted. And hope is all he has to sell."

He shocked me with his bluntness, for I had not heard

the name of that illness spoken half a dozen times in my life, and then quietly.

"It is a terrible thing to be without hope," I said.

"And a worse thing for a man to believe himself cured only to infect his wife or sweetheart. Or for the harlot to think the fading of her symptoms means the end of the disease." There was deep anger in the man. "There is no cure, not a one from here to Heidelberg. Not mercury, sure. And damned well not Dr. La Bonta's potions. You make a wrong choice, and you die. Some go fast, some slow, but all of them go, Jones. And their going's uglier than the Queen's backside."

I was not unaware of such matters, for I had seen that ugliness, too. India did not lack for it, and a regiment's tragedies do not all occur upon the field of battle. But one did not speak aloud of such things.

"There is no need to insult the Queen," I told him, "for she is a lady."

He stopped cold. "Oh, a lady, is she? Just like all of them, then, your lords and ladies of fair England. Dancing while the Irish starved to death, and shipping their grain overseas for profit. No war was ever so ugly as the Famine, Jones, let me tell you." He laughed bitterly. "Syphilitics can live for decades. But have you ever seen an infant starve to death, man? With the mother's teats nothing but dried-up little purses? They go fast, the little ones do. And the mother goes next, and half of the heartbreak. Your Russians in Hungary were kind put next to your English landlords. But I suppose you were in India for that, too?"

"I have heard of the matter of the Famine." The regiment had seen a great influx of Irish soldiers from forty-seven on.

"Hearing won't do. You had to see it. I ran to Vienna to get away from it. Already half a doctor, I was. But I couldn't stand it. The bloody raw helplessness of it." No laughter now. "Oh, I've done my share of running, Jones. As you can see."

He turned across the avenue toward Murder Bay. Emrich's Billiard Hall glowed like the portals of Hell before us.

"That is not a good way to go," I told him.

Yet another variety of laugh from the man. Perhaps the Irish are so rich in the voice because twas the only thing the English could not take from them. It is why the Welsh sing.

"I'm not going a good way tonight," he said. "I asked you to come along because I think you might prove a good companion, and those are few. And because the Fowler boy's bloody murder will not go out of my mind." We passed an oyster bar, well lit. Shouting pitched against the rollick of a piano. "I read the papers, Jones. And I know better. And I know that you know better. And now I want to know why we seem to be the only two buckos in the world who do."

I began to speak, but he stopped me. "I'll make no embarrassment," he said. "But I want the knowledge of the thing. Who killed that boy, and why?"

"I cannot speak of it," I said. "Not yet. But I believe there will be justice in the end."

He shook his head. He was the sort of man who found belief difficult. Except belief in his revolutions, I suppose. Men without Faith must substitute a dream, and mad dreams there are in plenty. There was a great loneliness in Dr. Michael Tyrone, though I hardly felt the depth of it then. Few men needed God so much and failed to find Him.

"Now wouldn't that just be a rare thing," he said. "To see justice done. Well, come on, man. I'll take you where there is no justice, and never will be."

*   *   *

He turned down an alley. Twas a foul stretch of darkness, its shadows alive.

"Dr. Tyrone," I said, "perhaps you have seen me wrongly . . . for I am not a friend to such places."

His laugh was sweeter now, with real humor in it. "Shut your worries, bucko. I'm no whoremonger. Tis a darker business than that."

And he explained. Twice a week he journeyed in to visit the houses of shame frequented by his soldiers. He was trying to keep down the rate of disease in his camp and the others.

"And it isn't only the soldiers I'm after helping," he said. "If some of the girls are as bad as any man, others have come to the business in a thousand sorrowful ways. We must not judge them as if they were children of privilege." The darkness whispered around us. "If you half knew them, Jones, you'd understand the need for revolution. And your landlady's fondness for *Herr* Marx. The miseries of the bordello can be as grim as those of the battlefield. And the girls set out on the streets have it harder still."

"The trade in human flesh in inexcusable under any circumstances."

We stumbled through the darkness. Amid dreadful offers. Tyrone spoke bluntly to me, the way a doctor will speak when he's got his students on a tour of a hospital, careless of the ears of the patients. "And what if your flesh is all you have to trade? Should you starve for virtue, Jones?"

"Yes. For a woman's virtue is her jewel."

He gave me a snort of a laugh. "You've never starved, I see."

A female form put itself across our way. "Two at half the price," she said. "And you boys won't have to hurry."

Tyrone stopped. "How's the little one, Nellie?"

Closer she come, and I got the stink of her. "Oh, it's you, doctor. I'm sorry. I didn't see proper. I didn't—"

"And the little one?"

"Weakening."

"You promised me," he said, "that I would not see you here again. You are a danger to all."

Twas a conversation between shadows, the voices rich for the lack of sight. Her voice had been frightened from the first, and went worse now.

"Don't put the police on me. Please don't you do it, doctor. I have to eat. And the baby . . ."

Tyrone told me of the case as we walked on. The woman had another variety of sickness I will not mention, and her baby had been born blind. Every man who went to her took the sickness from her. Now I have seen enough of the world to know of such things, but I never heard them spoken of as Tyrone did, as though they barely deserved to be hidden. He would have trumpeted them in broad daylight, I think, for he had that confidence in knowledge and reason you find in many who have lost their Christian faith. But even his fine Latin phrases could not dignify the business.

"Don't you see, Jones?" he asked. "Ignorance is the enemy. The poor things don't understand the least of it. Much is preventable. Some is curable. And the rest is containable. But not if we shut our eyes, man."

I often wanted to shut my eyes that night, but Mick Tyrone did not shut his. He was fearless, in his way. I refused to go into the houses with him—for a man must fear moral contamination a hundred times more than the physical—but even their streets and alleys reeked to gagging a man. Entire houses stank of humanity gone sour, of sewage and sweat and worse. Yet there was ever a great coming and going, even through the grimmest doors, and that on a weeknight.

It is a curious thing how men and women will pursue an act meant to be one of love and beauty in surroundings of hopeless squalor. It is as if they hate what God has given them.

I sought out quiet corners where I might wait for Tyrone to be done. Of course, there were many unpleasant proposals to be declined, the oddest of which come from a wretch who thought I must be a doctor, too, and who wanted me to inspect her at the back of an alley.

"I can't stop the damned itching," she said, and was embarrassed when I finally made her understand I was no medical man.

Tyrone stepped out of the last house. Twas a dreadful shack of a place, next to a coalyard and hard by the canal, all wrapped in the smell of human waste. His face was green in the lamplight.

He shook his head. "I can't imagine how they stay in business," he said. "Every one of them sick. And most of them look it. And they'll do things at the paying that the imagination strains to touch, yet they're shy as maids when it comes to a doctor's examination." He looked up into the darkness, as if cleansing his eyes with the stars. "Two young boys are in there drunk, and they'll regret it all their lives. They wanted to fight me when I suggested they leave."

"You are quite the good Samaritan, Dr. Tyrone."

The thought of such a thing brought a snicker. "I'm just bribing my devils to leave me alone. Off we go, Jones."

We turned into a better street, although better was a relative matter in Murder Bay. Immediately, I grasped Tyrone by the arm, pulling him back into the shadows. A cat shrieked and ran out between our legs.

"What—"

"Quiet you," I said.

Toward the end of the block, Major Trenchard and Captain Bates had gone up the front steps of a house. I had a good eye and knew it was them. I watched their backs shrink through the door.

"Who were they?" Tyrone asked me.

"Fools," I said. "Friends of Anthony Fowler. Although he was a different kind of fool entirely."

Dr. Tyrone's face took on the playful. "Well, that's fitting."

"And your meaning, Dr. Tyrone?"

We walked again. "That they should be friends of the Fowler boy. With all of his abolition talk. Tis a house where gentlemen visit Negresses."

I made no answer and he mistook my thoughtfulness.

"You find that shocking, Jones?"

"No, Dr. Tyrone, I do not."

We got board pavement underfoot again. My shoes would need a fine cleaning before I might step into Mrs. Schutzengel's hallway.

"Yes," he said. "Of course. India. And the English rose in short supply." He smiled. "I suspect you might be a bit of an abolitionist yourself, Jones."

I refused to be baited. "I would see no man enslaved," I said. "But I am one for minding my own business."

"Tis every man's business. All men are brothers, Jones."

The lights and life of Pennsylvania Avenue spread before us again. Provost guards rode by where they were not needed.

"You are an abolitionist, then, Dr. Tyrone? As well as a revolutionary? Might that explain your interest in the Fowler boy?"

He shook his head. "The Fowler case has to do with a murder of the body . . . slavery with the murder of the soul."

"But you would fight to abolish Negro servitude? Kill one man to free another?"

He clapped me on the shoulder. "Why do you think I'm wearing this damned blue coat, bucko? This Union of ours is man's last hope. Oh, Jones, tis a shame we are not drinking men, for we would have such talks."

He shifted his bag from one hand to the other and grew serious again.

"I would abolish more than slavery," he told me.

We said goodbye in front of the National Hotel, with that bummer there as always. Twas late for me, and I had not yet written to my Mary Myfanwy. Nor did I think I could craft a letter that night. It seemed wrong, and dangerous, after what I had seen. As if such matters might seep in to taint our world. I wished to talk to my beloved, to let out my heart to her, and to ask her questions I could ask no other. But the war would not have it, and the pen dared not tell it.

I was thinking about Trenchard and Bates, curious that Livingston had not accompanied them on their revels. Of course, the boy was engaged to be married and perhaps he was given to goodness, after all. Marriage, or even its prospect, can make a great reformation in a man. Yet, they were friends, those three, and thick together in their doings. Livingston's absence gave me a matter to think on.

So far gone was I in my weariness and wonderings that I did not see the fellow on Mrs. Schutzengel's porch until I started up the steps. My footfalls on the planking woke him, and we both jumped.

Twas that cavalryman, come to gather me up for General McClellan.

9

THE TROOPER HAD A CARRIAGE WITH HIM, ALTHOUGH GENERAL McClellan was not in it this time. The man mounted his horse and rode ahead, with the coachman following and me trying to order my thoughts. I had a great deal to tell, and I was confident in my determinations, but a general will have things told properly and no nonsense. I worried over my words, for justice depended upon them.

We stopped beside a fine house on the corner of H Street and 15th, and the trooper led me to the tradesman's entrance. The house appeared dark from the outside.

"You can report here now," the cavalryman told me, "when there's something needs telling. Just don't never go to the front side. This is the general's new house, and his wife and family's coming."

When the door opened, I saw the gas fixtures turned low ahead of me, throwing just enough light for a man to walk. The trooper led the way. The house smelled of a recent cleaning, with lye biting the nose.

"You be quiet now, Captain. General Marcy's asleep and he's a coot when you wake him." He led me up the first set of stairs and pointed to a door. "Knock soft like."

I did as I was told. General McClellan's confident voice bid me come in.

Twas his very bedroom. He was at work at a table furnished with a kerosene lamp to strengthen the gas glow. A young man in a captain's uniform stood by him, bending over a document. I saw a blood resemblance.

"That's enough for tonight, Arthur," the general said. "Off to the sleep of the just."

The captain went out, nodding as he passed me.

"Jones . . . good to see you again. Sit down, sit down." He pointed to a chair all velvet and fringe by the stove. Then he turned over the paper on which he had been working. "I must do it all myself. I can count on no one. They do not understand war, Jones." His eyes shone above dark crescents. "But you understand it. Don't you? The horror and splendor of the field of battle?"

The chair was a fine one, and soft. "I have seen the horror of it, sir."

"And here I am . . . the general-in-chief. Pressed to campaign before we're ready. Why, I even had to plan the grand review myself. Though I must say it went off splendidly. Did you see our little show, Jones?"

"Work wanted doing, sir. But I hear the Army marched well."

He sighed. "Yes. Work. The work of building an army. Would that there were more like you, Jones. I am surrounded by amateurs and incompetents." Even in his bedroom, he wore his full uniform, a model for us all. He sat back and slipped his hand inside his tunic as he liked to do. "Who killed Anthony Fowler?"

I looked him in the eye. "Mr. Matthew Cawber. Of Philadelphia."

His face did not answer with the shock I expected. A good general is master of his emotions.

"I do not mean, sir," I went on, "that Mr. Cawber pulled the trigger himself. But I believe he was behind the murder."

"And why is that, Jones? Tell me." His mouth remained open, as if he were smoking an invisible cigar. That was the tiredness in him, I thought, and pitied him the want of good subordinates.

"Anthony Fowler was a crusader. The boy could barely help himself. He was born to it. Abolition was his first cause. This was his second, for he saw it as just. Then he discovered evidence of corruption. Of great and terrible corruption, sir, harmful to the Union. Cawber Steel and Iron has been selling the government faulty cannon, at exorbitant prices. Many a Cawber gun blows up by the third or fourth firing. A dozen men have been killed, sir, and others maimed. And I myself saw evidence of lesser corruption on the part of Mr. Cawber, of stolen uniforms and—"

"I know Cawber," McClellan said. "And I don't like him or his sort. Ruthless. Piratical. Parasites upon the land. He puts on a great show of contributing to the abolitionists and their printed rags, though his own workmen are little better off than slaves." The general chewed the side of his mouth. "Cawber's greed and ambition are . . . inhuman. But murder . . . that's another matter entirely."

I leaned forward. "Sir, Captain Fowler had built up a mass of evidence. I have it locked up in the office safe. And one of his friends came right out and told me Fowler intended to send Cawber to prison. It became the boy's third cause, all wrapped up with saving the Union and freeing the Negro, see."

"This war is not about the abolition of slavery, Jones."

"No, sir. As you say. But young Fowler saw it in such a

light." The room was wicked warm and I wished for a drink of water, but dared not ask for it. "Consider it, sir. Here's Cawber, a man who's clawed his way up from the gutter, who's built himself a fine fortune and great mills for iron and steel and the like. And more than anything now he wants respectability and social position. Then along comes a bright, young crusader with a mind to put him in jail. And ruin his business, like as not. Men have killed for far less."

McClellan let his tongue come out and rest between his lips. The meat of it looked fat and pink under his mustache. It was incongruous: our general in his handsome uniform, with his hair down sleek and dignity in the very air about him—and his tongue peeking out like a small boy's over his penmanship.

"And you say you have evidence?" he said finally.

"Of the corruption. Not directly of the murder. But the thing is sure. A greater investigation—"

McClellan waved me to silence. "It would rock the Union . . . if true. The murder of our own golden youth. Corruption in the War Department. The public riven. *And* our nation's honor discredited abroad." He shook his head slowly and his hair took the flicker of the lamp. "This nonsense with Mason and Slidell is bad enough. Seward's not the man to handle anything more. The British could use the scandal as their excuse to come in on Richmond's side. Oh, Palmerston wants to do it, you know. Cotton. Manchester. Bankers and worse. As if war were a matter of national economy." His hand slipped from his tunic and fell into his lap. "Cawber, indeed. A Cameron man, of course. No telling where *that* might end."

"There is shame in it, indeed, sir."

He writhed in his chair. "My God . . . I never believed the Confederates did it. I did not want these hatreds stirred up. But neither did I expect . . ." His eyes sought mine. "Do you realize what a scandal it would be, Jones? I almost wish I could blame it on Richmond, after all."

"Justice must take its course, sir. An expansion of the investigation—"

"Nothing of the kind. Not yet. I can't have others brought in on this until we're certain. There are spies everywhere, Jones. The streets of this city are full of men of questionable interests. We can trust no one." He rubbed his eyes and permitted himself a slight yawn. "The matter may call for exceptional measures. Extraordinary measures. I want you to stay with it, Jones. You've done magnificently. Keep up the splendid work."

My hands were empty and my heart was emptier. "Sir . . . I don't know what more to do. The matter is far bigger than me, and I've come to my end of it. Surely, you can see that."

He canted his head. "Nonsense. *Toujours l'audace.* We must go on the attack, Jones. But we will do it skillfully. Strike the enemy where he is weak. If Baron Jomini were in my position, I'm sure he'd do exactly the same."

"And would this baron fellow be the Frenchman you go riding with, sir?"

He laughed. "Not likely, Jones. Listen. Here's what we'll do. I'll contact Cawber telegraphically. Make it clear he is to see you, and no nonsense." He thought. "Tomorrow's Friday. You can take the morning train. The railroaders have the Baltimore to Philadelphia line running again, though it's slow over the bridges. You can see Cawber tomorrow evening. The Cawber works are just down the Delaware from the city. I'll have a military conveyance put at your disposal."

"But . . ."

"Confront him. Lay out the evidence. Let Cawber know

that we know what happened, make him think he's already trapped. Then we'll see what he does."

"But I have no direct proof, sir. I cannot—"

"That's the point, Jones. We can't be timid in the face of the enemy. We have to accept risk, if we want results. If there is a weakness in our position, we must go on the offensive. Why, do you imagine I would take the field and hesitate to press the foe? Outnumbered five to one, I would attack with the resolution of Ney, of Napoleon himself. We must show ourselves confident. Frighten him, Jones. Scare Cawber out of his wits. Then we'll have him." He smiled. "I wouldn't be surprised if he confesses on the spot. Imagine the shock of it."

I sat for a moment. I sensed he expected me to say something, but my thoughts were a jumble. I did not mind confronting Cawber, who had done an evil thing. But my mind had already reached beyond that part of the business.

"I cannot help," I said, "feeling sorry for the boy's mother. An affair of nations it well may be, sir, but it will break Mrs. Fowler's heart a second time when she learns the stuff of it." My mouth screwed into my cheek. "She's old, and sick. And she believes her boy died for a great cause, murder or not. It is a black matter that he died for a man's greed."

McClellan stood up. Twas the signal that I should go.

At the door, he took my hand.

"Justice must be done," he said.

The Cawber Iron works were black. Their waste blackened the river till the moon found no reflection, and the smoke from their chimneys blackened the stars. Within the walls the ovens glowed with hellfire. The war was good to the works. Even on Friday evening, the melting and pouring and pounding of steel hinted at Armageddon. Furnaces gaped, and sparks thrilled up. The laboring men appeared tiny and fragile beside the machinery, and their rags were black with the coke, their backs bent. They hurried about in the sudden, frantic gestures of those afraid. Their skin was gray as beef forgotten in the pot and their faces were but dungeons for their eyes. As they tugged at the chains of the great kettles, they looked as though they had already been judged and cast down into the pit. What man could live so?

The works were a chilling sight to me, for they echoed Merthyr and sorrow. It seemed my fate to live in an age when the whole world would be ground up by industry, and covered with soot and ashes.

Mr. Matthew Cawber was blacker than his works. Hair black as spent powder, and plenty of it he had. Whiskers wrapped his face, and rogue hair crowded out from his cuffs and down the back of his big hands. Tufts grew between the joints of his fingers. One cheek bore a scar of the sort a miner takes from a coal-face slash. It started from the corner of his eye, and all the whiskers in the world could not hide the depth nor the startling blue color of it. His eyes themselves were savage things, and dark. If not for his fine tweeds and the clean fingernails, you would have taken him for the shift bully down by the ovens. He put me in mind of a wild Pushtoon. I would not have chosen him for my enemy.

"Go to hell," he told me, lighting up a cigar.

He had waited me out, burning, as I spread my facts and conclusions before him. Not a word was to be had from him before I was done, not a sound—unless there is a sound to inner fury. There seemed to be no fear in the man. Only rage, and plenty of that. He reminded me of those soldiers who are louts in garrison and lions on the battlefield, men who despise all authority but their own, and who slaughter the enemy when they really want to kill their own colonel. His face had gone scarlet, but for the lifelessness around that slash.

He stood up from behind his desk. If he didn't look like the devil himself, with his hellfire works and the black night beyond the window at his back.

The devil with a blacksmith's shoulders, he was. Or Vulcan, the Greek fellow, all muscle, lust, and bile.

"Now," he said, "it's your turn to listen to me, you pompous little fool. Just like that damned snot McClellan sending up a cripple to do his dirty work for him. Knowing a gent can't knock his teeth out his back end."

I tensed and nearly rose. But the force of the man fell on me like a Madras monsoon.

"You think I don't know what you've been up to?" he said. "You think Matt Cawber can't buy all the eyes and ears he wants in Washington? Whole worthless city's for sale." He drained the smoke from his cigar then fair spit it back out. "Oh, I know you, Jones. Known you since you made that damn-fool scene over at the arsenal." He picked up a portfolio from his desk and threw it into my lap. "Open it. Read it, if you're capable. Those are legal government contracts. For Cawber wagons to haul goods to and from your damned arsenal. You think the government has wagons enough for the work at hand? Hell, man, they don't even have harnesses for their nags. They came to me, to Matthew Cawber, hats in hand. Because Cawber Steel and Iron owns more wagons than the U.S. Government. And if they were fool enough to pay me too much for the cartage, shame on them. That's just business." He smiled like Satan in a bad mood. "That wagonload of uniforms you turned back? They were on their way to the railyard. Ready to go to Washington. To fill your own requisition. But would you listen to anybody? With all your damned self-righteousness? All you did, man, was to slow your own work down."

I looked at the papers. And felt the sort of rottenness in my stomach you get from drinking bad water.

"Now, Captain Jones. As for your famous exploding cannon." He tossed me another file of papers. "Every one of those guns was cast according to the specifications set down by the Ordnance Department. Hell if I know how you got it wrong. I never did run a cannon factory until now. But I'm learning." He pointed his cigar down at his works. "You just go down there. Go down where we're casting the guns. Ask for Schminke. Or for Dassenbrock. Or LaFonte. I've brought in the best cannon experts from Europe—at my own expense, mind you. Sent my agents out to find them and hire them on. I'm doing the work you people should have done for yourselves. There won't be any more exploding guns from the Cawber works. No thanks to the War Department."

He tossed the cigar, unfinished, into a marble dish. "Are you mad, Jones? Do you think I want us to lose this war? And lose half our national market? Just to see those British bastards move in? When the shooting and shouting's over, I want those damned fools down in Georgia or Louisiana to buy their steel from Cawber, not Sheffield. If secession came off and this country split forever, it would be one damned disaster for business. Hell, you won't find a stronger backer of Honest Abe and Union blue anywhere in this country."

The second set of papers contained diagrams and formulae which I could not fully decipher. But they were to do with cannon, certainly. And they carried the official seals of the Ordnance Department and the War Department both, and proper signatures.

With a roar, Cawber kicked over a table loaded with papers and account books. A white storm filled the air. The man had the kick of an army mule.

"*Damn them,*" he said. "Damn every one of their black Philadelphia hearts." He wheeled around to face me again, eyes hot enough to burn the air. "Let's get down to the real business, Jones. This turd you just laid about me killing the Fowler brat." He made a noise between a choke and a growl. "First of all, what makes you think a snot like that's important enough to kill? Why would it even be worth my while? You can see for yourself there's no legal case against me. A judge would laugh to beat the band if you waved this in front of his bench. And Anthony Fowler knew it. Not more than a month ago, he sat right in that chair you're sitting in and tried to pull this corruption nonsense on me himself. And I gave him both barrels. Boy was like a damned sheep after I laid it all out for him. Him and his Philadelphia crowd. Oh, high and mighty they are. High and mighty and righteous as the angels. But didn't the little puke end up asking me to contribute to his war chest for the free Negro before he slunk out of here. And damn me if I wasn't fool enough to give him something, after all he said against me. For slavery's a bad business, and bad *for* business, and we've got to bring it down. Can't ask an honest workman to compete with slave labor. But that little snot Fowler was nothing but a confidence man. He should've been off selling cure-alls in a medicine show."

"Anthony Fowler was a hero," I said. "He was incorruptible."

Cawber laughed. He really laughed.

"Oh, was he now? Like his father, I suppose?" He shook

his head, smirking down at the wreckage his tantrum had left on the floor. "Jones . . . you're like me in one thing, at least. You weren't born with a silver spoon in your mouth. Suckers like us, we tend to think folks like the Fowlers or the Trenchards are our betters. We let them slip the con over us. We don't like it, but it works on us anyway. Me, I was fool enough to believe a fortune honestly got and a good marriage would be enough to open their doors to my little son and daughter. Didn't I give to all their charities when they came creeping around? Gave to their academies and schools and orphanages. Hell, I've funded the abolitionist movement damned near single-handedly. And still they won't shake my hand in public. Because my old man worked his life out on the docks. Broke his back unloading old Bates's boats. That makes me not quite human to the inheritance crowd. And my children are the same way to 'em. Tainted. Just because the Cawbers weren't here in time to steal land from the Indians and kiss the British on their backsides."

He smiled and his whiskers spread like wings. "I hear you've been to visit Mrs. Fowler?"

"A grand lady," I said, "and I will hear nothing spoken against her."

"You'll hear what I decide to tell you. You know why she keeps that carriage you rode around in, Jones?"

"There is social position to be answered. A lady must have her carriage, though she cannot use it herself."

"Oh, use it she does, man. Once a month. In the black of the night. When she thinks nobody sees. The whole city knows—though you won't get a one of them to say it. They stick together, I'll say that for them, your Philadelphia society folk. They know if one of 'em goes, they all go. So they just pull down the shades and slobber over their family trees while Lettie Fowler rides off through the dark like the witch that she is." His eyes set on me as if he were aiming a gun. "Know where she goes, Jones? In all her fine Philadelphia dignity?"

This time I had nothing to say. I looked at the cigar gone black-nosed, forgotten in its dish.

"She goes to a beautiful little country estate near Bryn Mawr. A lovely place. With high fences. High fences with sharp spikes on the top. Know why those spikes are there, Jones?"

I shook my head.

"Well, it's not to keep us peasants out. The place isn't a country estate at all. It's a loony bin. For the rich. For the relatives that have to be gotten out of the way. That's where you'll find the real history of Philadelphia. And you know who she goes there to visit, man? Her husband."

"Mr. Fowler died. In a shipping incident."

He smiled. "Go there, Jones. I'll give you the address. Your uniform might get you in. One way or the other. Old Fowler's eaten up by every disease known to man. He's killing mad. The old bitch sits outside the bars and just looks at him." He showed me his teeth as a mean dog will. "Now can you figure out why she can't walk? And why she left China? Talk to a medical man. One who handles confidential cases. Oh, old Fowler loved the Chinese all right. He bedded every yellow whore he could find. Half a dozen at a time, from what I hear. And from what I know of Letitia Fowler, I can almost understand it."

"That is indecent, sir."

He strode over to me and put a hand on each arm of my chair, bending down to give me the sulfur of his breath and a good look at those pagan eyes. "No, Jones. I'll tell you what's indecent. Coming here to accuse an innocent man of murder, *that's* indecent. Who do you think's building this country up from nothing? Men like me, or phony aristo-crats like them? They're nothing but damned leeches. But maybe you'd like to hear more? How they brought old Fowler out of China in a cage? Or about the secret society the Trenchard brat and young Bates and the Fowler boy founded at the University of Pennsylvania? Now there was a scandal that got hushed up mighty fast. Must have cost a fortune to buy off the families of the girls. Half the medical faculty had to be retired on the quiet. Or how about old Lettie Fowler's opium smoking? Oh, that family brought back plenty from China. Plenty. And not just the junk crammed into that haunted house off Rittenhouse Square."

"I have never met . . . a perfect man, Mr. Cawber. An-thony Fowler fought for the freedom of the less fortunate. He dedicated his life to the cause. There is much to be said for that, and youthful indiscretions are to be forgiven." I was desperate to find some goodness somewhere. For the man's words twisted my bones.

Cawber ran his hands back over his scalp. The hair fol-lowed his fingers like the pelt of a wolf.

"Well . . . it's time somebody in that family did some-thing good for somebody. But if Anthony Fowler had come anywhere near my daughter, I damned well would've shot him, and done it myself. Whole Fowler clan's riddled with disease and dementia. The mother wants to raise the spirits of the dead, and the boy wanted to raise up the Negro. The father just wanted to raise every whore in China and set her down on his lap. I say, let 'em go and good riddance. Let 'em rot, and be glad there's no more of 'em."

Cawber drew out his pocket watch. Its gold case gleamed.

"Waste of damned time," he said. "Listen, Captain. You go back and tell that peacock McClellan that Matt Cawber

said he's a horse's ass and that I don't believe he has the
stomach to fight through a quilting bee. And if this is all
some kind of plot to get me to sell out my railroad interests
to his bunch, he'll damned well have to try again. Matt
Cawber won't be bluffed or bullied by the likes of him." He
smiled down at me. "You know . . . the truth is that Georgie
McClellan has no more credit with those old Philadelphia
families than I do. They're just playing him for a fool. They'll
see where he goes and drop him when he turns useless."

He picked up the cigar he had forgotten, registered its
death, and put it down again.

"McClellan does have friends, though. Ambitious men.
Like himself. Less scrupulous men than me. He'll always
squeak through. Somebody's always going to cut him in on
the game. He'll die a pillar of society, though it won't be
the society he craves."

He stroked his whiskers with his thumb, considering me.
And his face took on an expression almost of pity. "Do *you*
have any friends in high places, Jones? Is anybody going to
deal you a winning hand? It looks to me like you've been
everybody's fool. And soon you'll be out with the garbage.
On your way now."

I am a flawed man. I know it. But I will not hide from
my follies, or try to make them pretty. There is dullness in
me when it comes to spotting evil. I always want to believe
a man better than he is, or as good as he might be. I wish
virtue where often there is none. As a Christian, I have a
weakness for redemptions, and would raise a man up rather
than put him down. More than once have I imagined light
where there was only darkness. Nor was Cawber wrong
when he said that our like must beware the blandishments
of the great.

The Good Lord knows I had believed in General McClellan—and wished to have faith in him still.

How much had I been led to believe, and how much had I come to believe on my own? How much art was in the evil surrounding me?

Twas a hard night, though I passed it in a clean bed. I found refuge in the little hospital set up behind the Union Volunteer Refreshment Saloon. Now that establishment, I must tell you, was run by charitable citizens—it was not the sort of saloon where drink is dispensed. No, a place of brief comfort it was, for regiments headed south, and the strongest liquid poured was apple cider. The hospital of fifteen bunks was for soldiers taken ill on their journey to the war. But there were no sick or convalescents that night, and each pale bed lay empty, and they let me a place for kindness. Perhaps they saw the sickness in my heart.

They gave me supper and tea—for the good ladies feared the stimulating effects of coffee on the male of the species—but I managed hardly a bite. I could not believe that General McClellan had treated me so shabbily, that he had made such a pure fool of me. Yet, neither could I believe that Little Mac was ignorant of all that I would come up against in Matthew Cawber. If the general knew even a quarter of the truth of it, he had no good cause to send me on such an errand. What could be the point of it?

I believed Cawber, see. For if I want to believe the best of other men, that trait is balanced by my ability to recognize the truth when finally I do see it, or hear it, or smell it. I believed almost everything Cawber said. And yet I suspected there was error enough in the world for him to have his share of it, too. I would not believe only evil of the Fowler lad. No matter if his family had its devils and his schoolboy pranks had been harmful to the undeserving. I have never known a perfect man. Somehow, I continued to believe that Anthony Fowler had died wrongly, and undeservedly, and well before his time.

Before I went to bed, I sat over my cold leavings of tea and watched a Negro fellow sweep the floor of the saloon. He was old as Methusaleh and stooped, with a halo of hair that put me in mind of dirty wool. He looked a simple sort—I realized his race had not the makings of generals or men of government or business—but he was undeniably my human brother. Mick Tyrone was right about that. Now well you may laugh at Abel Jones, for you have seen in me fool enough. But I could not see the justice in keeping such a one as that poor sweeper in chains or subject to the lash, or in rending him from the bosom of his family. The Good Lord knows this is a hard world, and I do not see the virtue in making it harder for any of His creatures.

Tens of thousands of people had believed that Anthony Fowler had dedicated his life to the abolition of slavery. They had *believed* in him. He had convinced the multitudes, and he had even convinced my Mary Myfanwy, who can tell a sound egg from a bad one while they're both still in the basket. And I believed in him still.

Perhaps it was the fairness of his countenance those times I saw him passing into the War Department, for beauty confounds us and we often confuse it with virtue. It might have been the adulation of the high-born against which Cawber warned me. Or it may have been the need I have to believe in something beyond our human smallness. With my vanity ravaged and my pride in ruins, I still wanted to know who had killed Anthony Fowler, and what had driven them to such a deed. I still wanted . . . to see justice done. But I felt lost, and friendless, and without hope. I had meant to do good, and emerged a braying jackass.

An invisible limb had been broken out from under me, and I had fallen hard. I did not know if I could get back up.

I drifted in and out of sleep and dreamed of horses streaming blood, of terrible fires and laughing men. Twas one of those nights when the difference between sleep and wakefulness is slight as a bubble, when your nightmares follow you well into the morning.

I woke to the sounds of a steamship putting in and the calling of stevedores, for my bed lay hard by the docks and Saturday was for business in Philadelphia. For a moment, I wished my beloved and I could but climb aboard and sail for California or a place more distant still. But, like Tyrone, I knew I had run far enough. I had come to the land where the running ended.

Perhaps that was what the war was really about. Twas an entire nation of runaways, America in 1861, and your place in society depended upon what you had run from and when. Perhaps General McClellan was right that the war was not really about slavery. Perhaps it was a struggle between the dreams of men who would run no more.

I resolved to go to the Reading depot and take a train to Pottsville. Even if the only run consisted of empty coal wagons, I was willing to wrap myself up and ride in one of those.

I felt ill in my stomach from the shame of the role I had been put to play—though I did not understand it yet, I sensed there was evil behind it. I needed the rest that only love can give. So I ran to my Mary Myfanwy, as I always did. We men and women are incomplete things, and must be made whole every so often if we are to continue in our adversities.

McClellan had not specified that I return directly to Washington, and I clung to that as an excuse. For I am the sort who cannot defy too directly. Duty has its comforts, after all, and what would a man be without a sense of it? I might spend one Saturday night in Pottsville, quiet like, without failing the Union. In the comfort of my beloved, I might take the strength to recognize that which was right, and to do it.

G

THE RAILROAD ENTERED THE MOUNTAIN GAP WHERE THE SCHUYL-
kill had carved its way, and my heart beat like a lad's. The
tracks followed the canal, with its coal barges and mule
paths. The boatmen looked up sternly as we raced past. At
the hoot of the whistle, children poured from shacks nestled
under the slopes. Pallid faces those, and too similar, for an
odd breed lived in the hollows by the canal, fond of remote-
ness from the law and the church. The driving wheels
counted the miles with me, pounding like native drums in
the vale of Peshawar. The ridges were bare now, but beautiful, and copper leaves covered the valley and floated on the
waters. The last geese lifted from the marshes.

We burst into a valley and braked into Schuylkill Haven.
The town was clean-painted and heavy with Dutchmen. La-
borers unloaded crates and bundles, taking their time about
it, or so it seemed to me. With Pottsville not five miles
away, I ached to get out and run, bad leg or no. Then the
whistle called for the clearance of the tracks, and the cars
snapped into motion again. Plump town boys ran along beside us until their breath quit.

Twas afternoon and we entered the shadow of the next

mountain, with the canal a highway of anthracite below us, its water silted gray above the locks. The sky, too, was gray to the rest of the world, but summer blue it was to me. The valley narrowed and shanties rose beside the rails. The Palo Alto iron works—a dwarf to Cawber's giant—loomed under turbans of smoke. Saturday half-shift that would be. I moved to the other side of the carriage and saw Henry Clay high on his pillar and the backsides of the houses along South Centre Street. Then the commerical buildings began. There was money coming in.

Coal had marked the valley even then, though it was not so glum as it would be later. A great potch of shoppers filled the streets and delivery wagons jostled for rights at the corners. The carriages of the colliery owners kicked up the last dust of the season. We pulled into the station, with its curtain of saloons and drummer's hotels, and it was all as dear to me as Jerusalem.

I almost took a hack, such was my haste to get home, but the price was up with the war and I worried that my Mary Myfanwy might think me an even greater fool than I was if I rolled up in a hired trap like Lord Folderol. So I walked. And not a few startled looks I got, and many a citizen would have talked me to death in the street. I ran to the edge of rudeness to get free of them. If there was pain in my leg, I did not feel it. Across Centre Street I went, with its grandeur of banks and company offices, of good shops and law shingles, then straight up Norwegian, where the addresses were respectable but not extravagant. I might have been blubbering like a babe, for all I knew. My thoughts were not on myself. I lacked the sense to stop and put right my hair or blow my nose.

Oh, the face of her. Looking up from her scrubbing as if the ladies of the chapel had caught her prancing, with strands of hair loose from her bun and moist pearls waiting to be kissed from her forehead. You should have seen the look of her. First that high flash of anger at the interrupting she got, then the shock of her seeing, then the trembling of the lips and all around the eyes as she rose to her feet.

"There is beautiful," I said, "and beautiful you are, Mary Jones."

She held me fit to break my ribs, and sobbing she was. Then I saw my son behind her, and was not master of myself.

How she held me, though. If ever I doubted her love, though I did not, that one hug would have filled me with trust for a lifetime. Never was the smell of soap and water so akin to lavender and roses.

"You're an evil man," she told me, crying. "Wicked and evil. Coming upon me like this."

And the boy, standing little in his wonder—my son standing—stared up with his mother's eyes. My Mary Myfanwy sensed me pull toward him, but she would not let me go, not yet.

"My love," I said.

"I look like the rag woman."

"Then it's such I will have, my beauty."

She wept again, with her face buried against me. "Oh, God," she said, "oh, God, I've dreamed of this day." And she kissed me at last. Hungry. Starved.

She had not thought to put down her scrub rag, and the wet of it was already through my coat. But I would have drowned in dirty water for the taste of her.

The boy's face glazed with fear. He put a little hand to the corner of an eye, and I could not have that. I broke her hold as gently as I could.

"Is it a strange man you have taken into the house, Mary Jones? And who is this strapping buttie?"

Then we were three together, and no man hated war as I did.

"There is foolish," my beloved said to me. With her black hair loose and streaming. "What good is to come of confronting the man? A general he is. And you with twice his heart but not a tenth part of his power."

Twas Sunday morning. Sunday morning, already. We were still in private circumstances that do not want description. Though I will speak again of the loveliness of that hair, that shining midnight hair that is pure Welsh from up the valleys. And the whiteness of her skin, and the eyes green.

"He shamed me, woman."

Yes, those green eyes. One of your fancy book writers would compare them to jade. But I have seen jade and it is a dead thing, while there was nothing more alive in the world than my Mary Myfanwy's eyes. Fiery emeralds, they were, with sparks of gold.

"Go on with you. Shame is it, Abel Jones? Well, there is shame and there is shame, and I say the man shamed himself the more if he lied to a good man such as you and used him wrongful."

"Will I take it like a dog, then?"

"You will take it like a man, and keep your tongue in your mouth."

"It chews on me."

She rose to her elbow. In the soft light. With the child still blessedly asleep. "And what is it, then? That's cause of this great chewing? The shame and embarrassment that is nothing but selfish? Or the knowing that the boy's murder goes unanswered?"

She was a loving woman, but firm. No empress matched the backbone of my sweetheart.

"The shame and embarrassment first," I admitted.

"And then?"

"I would know what happened to the Fowler lad."

She smiled. Oh, she knew me, that one. "Then swallow the false pride down, Abel. For the pride of man is dust. And let this General McClellan think you a fool, if he will. And you will sit there knowing more than him, and who will be the fool then?"

"It could be that he did not understand . . . the range of the business."

But I had shared the meat of the story with her, and most of the trimmings, too, and we both knew better.

"There is foolish. The man has proven himself a liar, if only by all he left unspoken. You mark me, Abel Jones. His like will come to naught, for all his airs." She lifted away a tumbling richness of hair that had sneaked too close to her mouth.

"And what would you have me do, woman? There is badness every way I turn."

She thought for a moment. A great thinker she was, and deep. Then her eyes come out to play again. "I wish I were a man. For I would help you then."

"A man is it? I would have you a woman and as you are."

"You wait, boy. And hands to yourself while we're talking." Her hair fell forward again as we tustled and she brushed it back once more. Without lowering her defenses. "Go on with you now. A bad little boy you are. But I will tell you what I do not like. And that is this lieutenant. The one who is to be married fair, and who drinks himself dumb by dinner. There is a story there."

"And?" I said. For I knew she was the smarter of us, and I could listen to her without false pride. She never gave me bad advice, and how many men can say that of anyone, let alone of a wife?

"And then, Captain Jones, I would look into those other friends. Young gentlemen who go to a Negro bawdy house. And on a weeknight."

I blushed at her bluntness. But her skin held white as the first snow. I have never known another so decorous in the parlor and so honest upstairs, if you will excuse me the liberty. In her it was only good sense, not hypocrisy.

"There is something wrong there, see," she continued. "And if they were true friends to Anthony Fowler, it is wrong twice. For I do not believe he would have fought to lift the Negro from his chains only to see the daughters of Africa bound to a worse slavery still. Trouble there."

"More still, my little one?"

She thought for a moment. And wasn't I proud of her? What a man she might have been, with that mind of hers, though me the poorer for it.

"I would like to know," she said. "What those fellows were singing."

She lost me.

"In the rain," she went on. "You told me the sentry boy heard singing and naught else. In the night before Anthony Fowler's body was discovered. He heard officers drunk and singing. And I would like to know what they were singing, for I do not think they were so drunk. And I would like to know how he knew sure they were officers, if he could not see them. That is what I would like to know."

I shook my head. Putting to her a silent question. For I did not yet see her wisdom.

"There is simple," she said. "Out in the fierce of the weather they were, these drunken, singing officers. And why? I will tell you. Because they put the lad's body down where it was found. Carrying him along as if he were only the drunkest of them and unable to walk by himself. Clear it is, see. That is why there was no bullet hole in his overcoat. They had disguised him up as a drunkard, and all muffled over they had him, and what sentry would think twice of it? Singing they went, but not so drunk or not drunk at all, and I would know the song that was on their lips. For by it I might know the men. And if I knew the men I would know the killers."

She was a clever one, mine. And me the greater fool still, for having all the pieces and none of the puzzle together.

"I would two things of you, Abel," she said. "Go carefully. For I will not lose you again. It is too long I have waited. Second, I would have justice for the Fowler boy, if justice can be got."

I looked at the steel and softness of her. "He . . . may not have been the perfect one people think."

She scooted her elbow up and rose higher. "And who is perfect? Short of Jesus Himself, I ask you?" For the first time, there come a real scold over her. "I saw that boy, didn't I? With these two eyes. And heard him with these two ears. And there was goodness in him. I will tell you that, Mr. Jones. There was goodness. And if he suffered all the temptations of the Damned, I will believe he rose above them as best he could."

"Mary, really . . . your language, girl."

"Find out what happened to him, Abel. Your Christian duty it is. For like as not he was killed for his goodness, say what they will. And my language is no more than what is in the Bible, thank you, and good enough for archangels."

I sat up so straight my nightshirt caught under me and gave me a yank at the neck. I reached for the stand where I had set my pocket watch. We had forgotten the hour.

"Late for chapel," I fair shouted, tossing back the covers.

But she caught me. And tugged me back down.

"No chapel today."

Those endless eyes moved closer. Above the rose of her lips.

"I will not share you with them," she said. "Not yet. Not now."

"Talk there will be, Mary Jones."

"Let them peck. For they're only caught between wishes and regrets."

With the splendid timing of infants, young John began to cry in the room next. But my beloved only held me the more tightly for it. At my concern, she whispered:

"He will learn patience, your son."

Later, I played with the boy, and talked to him, and held him. He was strange with me, of course. I ached to make an impression on him, for I wanted to be remembered. My job seemed the safest of the war, yet war is cruel in its jokes. If never I saw him again, I wanted my son to have some recollection of his father, however slight. But he was too little, and I realized I would be gone from his mind as soon as I was gone from the house.

Twas hard.

I had to leave the two of them for an hour, though I would have stayed within those walls forever and been glad of it. First, I went down to the station, with the good folk of the city still in their pews. In fair luck I was, for Iestyn Hughes was the yard master that day. There were no passenger trains going south from Pottsville, but he promised me a place on the bunk car of a coaler, if I would come by three. It would take me to Philadelphia, but then I would have to wait until morning for a train to carry me on to Washington.

He was a good man, Hughes the Trains. But he broke

my heart when he told me three o'clock. I had hoped to steal the afternoon all whole.

I yearned for home, but had another stop to make. I intended to catch Mr. Gowen just after he come from church. A constable guided me to his residence directly— all full of questions about the war, he was, and why hadn't we taken Richmond yet?—but the housemaid handed me disappointment.

"Already gone, he is, sir, is Mr. Gowen."

She was an Irish girl, with freckles and a starched linen apron.

"And where might I find him, then?"

She gave me the doubtful eyes, unsure of the propriety of giving out such information. But the constable, bless him, told her, "It's all right, missy. He's an officer, our Jonesie, and it's all official."

Which is what I had told him, more or less.

How the Irish have had the fear beaten into them. It shows most on the women, since they do not drink. Her lips shivered as she spoke, though not from the cold.

"He's gone to a Sunday hooley up the Masters, he is. But he's a great one for keeping his Sundays all private, sir, is Mr. Gowen. If you please, sir . . ." Her hands worried in the pockets of her apron.

"We will not trouble him with the source of our information," I said. "There's a good girl."

She curtsied as though she had just learned the gesture and had not yet got the knack.

"You know where Mr. Masters lives?" the constable asked me as the door shut on us.

Everybody knew where Masters lived. Up the hill, as the rich always do. He was a coal boss of a far higher order than my Mary Myfanwy's uncle.

I went alone up the streets, with the climbing stiffness in my leg, and the size of the houses grew. I felt the watch tick against my stomach, time running away, and every moment of my life squandered that was not spent with my wife and son.

The Masters house had no Irish girl to reckon with callers. A fellow in a fine get-up opened the front door.

He looked me over quick, sharp as a tailor in his judgement of cut and cloth.

"Yes, sir?"

"I would like to speak with Mr. Gowen, please."

"Have you an invitation, sir?"

"Official business," I lied.

He considered me again, snoot in the air as if he owned the house himself. There is no senator so arrogant as a well-placed serving man.

"One moment, sir," he said. Then he shut the door on me.

Mr. Franklin B. Gowen, Esquire, stepped out to the chill of the porch. He was a grand-looking man, young and a comer, with a figure gaining substance. But his eyes were cold as winter. His face was all annoyance at first, colored up by irritation, but he placed me after a moment and changed his demeanor, as lawyers will. I had already heard the rumor that he would be our next district attorney.

"Why, Jones," he said. "What the devil is this? Our county's hero and left on the doorstep? Come in, man. Old Masters will want to shake your hand."

He smelled of alcohol. On a Sunday.

"Sir, I cannot. Time I have none, but for a question. If you will excuse me."

He folded his arms and looked down at me. Still thinking how to be. I did not trust him then, though I hardly knew him, nor did I like him of a sudden. It is almost as if I had a presentiment of all that was to come after the war, of the violence and injustice and the coal country torn apart, of my own home burned. But that is another story. Let it bide.

I could not know that I would be the one to find him, decades hence, hanging dead in a Washington hotel room.

"Well . . . what is it, man?"

"Sir . . . did General McClellan ask you for a recommendation? Did you give him my name?"

Confusion swept his eyes. Then his features cleared again and he grew a smile I did not like.

"McClellan . . . that's rich. Haven't heard from the man since a railroad case in fifty-nine."

"I was told . . . that you recommended me."

"Yes, yes. But that was to old man Trenchard. A Philadelphia acquaintance of mine. He was looking for somebody who would do as he was told, as I recall. Someone who knew his place. Somebody already in Washington. I couldn't think of anybody, but my clerk recommended you."

I put it out of my mind. I had not an hour and a half at home once I got back, and I refused to waste my thoughts on anything but my wife and son. My Mary Myfanwy had raised fine ham cutlets from a neighbor, and we had farm eggs like the molten gold of myth, and biscuits, and salted butter from the crock, and her plum preserves. She was sick with the poverty of it, for a cook and keeper of a good house she was, and didn't she want to please me? It hurt to see her so, ashamed when she should have been proud as a duchess.

Twas our Thanksgiving dinner, we both said, four days short of that finest American holiday. And so much we had to be thankful for. When I spoke the blessing, there come a vibrato to my voice that had nothing to do with the singer's art. In the middle of the meal, over a pink bite of ham, I broke into tears, unmanly.

I wished to be alone with my beloved again, but there was the child. And I wanted to be with him, too. He grew restless with my holding of him after the meal, willful as a cat, and my wife scolded him for it.

"He needs you by," she sighed, for she could be cruel when she had a mind to be.

The boy tottered off. Faced with a wooden train, he let his legs go out from under him. Then he sat looking at the toy, for it was more interesting than a strange father.

I knew my wife had something to say. Something that she needed to say, but did not want to.

"Go on, girl," I said. "Speak your piece."

She looked down at the rose swirl of the carpet.

"Sometimes . . ." she said, ". . . I wish you were a coward." Her green eyes come up to me wet. I made to rise and hold her, but she shook her head. "After. First, I'll get the talk out. I wish you had never gone with them, Abel. I wish you were little and selfish and mean like the rest of them, and mine to hold each night. I wish you had been a man of sense and that you had come home from that hospital. 'He's done his share,' I hear the voice inside me. 'Is it away from you he wants?' And it tears me to bits and pieces. For I know you love me, but Satan gets inside these walls, and I doubt everything then." Fair weeping she was now. "I worry you won't come back. That something will happen. I thought I had you all safe to myself at last. And this war came." She beat her fists down on her knees. "I hate it. I *hate* it. I hate that you are gone from me. I don't care about freeing the Negro or their damned Union or anything but you. But us. The three of us. That's all I care about in the world, God help me. And all I care about in Heaven, too."

She let me hold her then. I lifted her to her feet and wrapped my arms around her slightness.

"There is silly," I said. "That I would not love such a treasure."

"I love you so much . . . I know I'll be damned for it."

I stroked her hair. "Then burn together, we will," I said, and meant it. Though I am not one to talk so on a Sunday.

"But not John," she said seriously. "He won't burn."

"Not little John. For he is an angel come among us. A fine son you have given me, Mary Jones."

"Come back to him, Abel. Come back to me."

"Always, my love."

We kissed while the child ignored us.

When it was time to go and a little past, she ran up to our bedroom and come down with a small package wrapped fine.

"'Twas for your Christmas that I had it done," she said. "But you will have it now. To remind you."

"Reminding, is it? I'll give you reminding."

This time she blushed at the way I touched her. For we were in the parlor, after all. And children have eyes in the back of their heads.

"Go on with you," she said, suddenly brusque. "There's pots to clean, and I'll thank you to be out of my way."

I ran to the station, and a sight I must have been on my leg. Running with my carpet bag and the package from my beloved and the church bells going three before I had even reached Centre Street, let alone the yards. The first snow-flakes of the year teased down.

Hughes the Trains had held the locomotive for me. Now there is goodness. He put me aboard the back wagon with mutterings about the tardiness of Merthyr men and a cloth of pasties he pressed on me for the journey, and Mrs. Hughes a famous cook and his lunch it was, but he would give a gift to see me off. A cause for astonishment it is, how one man can be so good and kind and another so bad. We are a funny lot, mankind.

Two railway men—and not the cleanest—shared the wagon with me. They got up the stove, and asked the questions strangers will, then they dozed, for their turn at work would come. As they lay on their dirty blankets, I opened my package.

Twas a photograph in a silver frame. Of my Mary Myfanwy. Not of the child. There was only her. She knew me hot and cold, the woman.

Beautiful she was. Sitting there stiff in her one good silk, she looked more beautiful than Eve in a gown of stars. Perhaps the hard preachers are right, when they say we cannot escape our fates. For she seemed a fate to me, though a blessed one.

I forced myself to wrap the image again, for the train was sooty. But the picture was there behind my eyelids when I closed them.

The snow let by, only a flirt. I noticed without caring. And soon it was dark. The train clipped the joints in the rails, one after another. Oh, the power of our thoughts to cast us down. I was glad the railway men were not awake to see me. For a man must keep a certain bearing, and an officer must be more stoic still.

My heart broke a thousand times before we reached Philadelphia.

The first hack driver I approached laughed when I asked if he knew where Mr. Matthew Cawber lived.

"No secret where that fella lays his head," he told me.

Indeed, it was no secret. Cawber had built himself a palace in the heart of the city, just beyond Rittenhouse

Square, on the far side from Mrs. Fowler's home. He had bought himself a block and built halfway to heaven.

I was daunted. There was no telling if he would talk to me, and certainly he had every right to put the dogs on me, so shameful had I been toward him. But there are things which must be done, and every man must eat his humble pie.

If Mrs. Fowler's home appeared severe from the street, Cawber's had all the ornament of a painted gypsy wagon. Spires, there were, and the gables of an English manor, and even a level of false battlements that put me in mind of the great Mughal fort of Lahore. What money could buy, the man had bought.

I marched up to the front doors. Twice my height they were. My cane gave them a tap.

A manservant opened the door, and strike me blind if he hadn't a powdered wig on his head.

"I would like to see Mr. Cawber," I said. "Tell him it's Captain Jones, if you please."

"I regret to say, sir, that Mr. Cawber's secretary is unavailable."

Mr. Cawber had hired himself an Englishman to mind his door, and one of the low, beady sort who trade on false manners and copied speech. It is hard to like the English as a race, except for Mr. Shakespeare and a poet or two, and their conquest of the world speaks ill of mankind. Perhaps they have more Welsh blood than they let on. That would explain the poetry, at least.

"Well, it's not his secretary I want to see, man. It's Mr. Cawber himself."

"I'm sorry, sir."

He made to shut the door, but I thrust my cane into the gap.

"Just tell him," I said. "Tell him it's Captain Abel Jones."

I heard the unmistakable rustle of a woman, and light steps, and a voice the angels might have envied.

"What is it, Cedric?"

The snooty fellow opened the door. And showed her to me.

Mrs. Cawber she was. You just know such a thing. And lucky the man. If twice in a lifetime a fellow sets eyes on such beauty, it is a muchness of luck. She stood there before me with features no sculptor would rival, her hair the blond of new hay. Her cheeks were unmarred by paint and soft as the inner petals of a flower, and her eyes were impossibly blue. As if she had risen from the depths of the sea. She wore a gown of lilac silk with purple trim and a pattern of shells, and her long neck was bare but for a sapphire that would have sent the Queen into fits of jealousy. I saw her all at once, as you see things only rarely, and my jaw must have been hanging like that of a boy at his first circus.

"The gentleman," the doorkeeper said, "insists on seeing Mr. Cawber."

She looked straight at me then, with the expressionless face a goddess turns on a mortal. Twas not a matter of infatuation to admire her so, mind. Nor was there disloyalty to my beloved in it. She was a painting in the gallery of Heaven. No man of flesh and blood could aspire to such, but only look on in wonder.

"May I help you, sir?" she asked.

If it did not take me a year to find the words, I know nothing of time. But she waited. No one as slight as me could discomfit her.

"Begging your pardon, mum. Sorry I am for disturbing you. And of a Sunday night. It's only . . . I must speak with your husband. It is a great matter, see. A terrible great matter . . ."

"And your name, sir?" When they call the final roll, may such a voice call me.

"Jones, mum. Begging your pardon. Captain Abel Jones."

She never looked over my uniform or shoes, as lesser sorts will do.

"Please come inside," she said, glancing at the doorman. And didn't he open the door quickly then. "I shall speak to my husband."

I watched her go. Now you will think wickedness. But there was not a ghost of it in me. I watched her as you might the fading of the last sunset. A second servant opened a great carved door for her, and her trailing hem disappeared. I never saw her again, but remember her to this day.

Cawber come out with an expression black as the hair running all over him. A very Vulcan he was.

"Damn me, man," he called from across a mile of marble foyer. "Are you chasing bad judgement with bad manners, or what the Hell?"

"Sir . . . I'm sorry," I said as he closed on me. "I have come to say I am sorry."

He growled and only slowly turned the sound into words. "Apologies are worthless." He stood grand before me and crossed his arms. Mighty as a blacksmith. He wore a velvet smoking jacket, perfectly cut, yet it looked odd draped over his chest and shoulders. The man was meant to run naked as an ape, excuse me, and I mean that as praise. I have never felt such energy in a man standing still.

"It is right you were, Mr. Cawber. I have been made a fool."

"You were born a damned fool, Jones, not made one. Georgie McClellan just knows how to pick horseflesh." But he gave the eye to the doorkeeper, who promptly disappeared. "What is it you really want?"

"The apology is meant," I said. "Be it worthless or no. But I have come to ask a favor."

Those nettle eyebrows rose. "Well, you've got gall."

"It may be in your interest, sir. Though I cannot say with certainty."

The corner of his mouth made a hook. "Know what my wife said to me, Jones? She said the saddest-looking man in the world was at the door, asking for me."

"Mrs. Cawber . . . was gracious to me."

"Well, she's gracious to everybody. Doesn't mean a damned thing. What's your favor, man?"

"Sir . . . it seems to me that . . . if I can find out who really did kill young Fowler . . . that it might also tell you why somebody went to the trouble of setting me after you."

He smirked. "You want me to help you solve that self-righteous snot's murder?"

"Perhaps . . . those who wanted to hurt him . . . are the same people who want to hurt you. Or to scare you. Or annoy you. Or whatever it is they want."

He thought about it. Then said, "Unlikely."

"Well, then . . . isn't it revenge you want? On the high families of Philadelphia?"

His mouth changed just enough to bristle the whiskers on his cheek. "That's putting it raw."

"I think there is something wrong there," I continued. "I do not know what it is. But young Livingston, at least, was hot to set me after you. And there's something wrong with the boy. Frightened, he is. And given to bad habits. There is an odd business with his friends, as well."

"Young whoremasters. And half of them inbred. Fowler probably came to a shabby end and those buggers just wanted to hide it, so they set you off on a wild-goose chase after me. That's all. No shame on old Philadelphia, if they can help it."

"That's it, sir. I think the same, see. I cannot yet say how, but there is a tying together somewhere."

"Well, just suppose, Jones. Just suppose I wanted to waste my time on this. Which I don't. What is it you want from me? Precisely?"

I tried to square my shoulders and meet him man to man. But he was a beast.

"I can study the Washington end of things myself," I told him. "But not the Philadelphia matters. The place reminds me of India, see. Where the outsider never knows the truth of the goings-on. Not even the half of it." And for a moment I did dwell on India in my heart. "I need to know the fit of things, Mr. Cawber. Young Trenchard. Bates. And Livingston. The girl he's promised to marry, Miss Cathcart. Anything more about the Fowlers. And the elder Mr. Trenchard's relationship to General McClellan, for there seems to be one. Such like, that's what I need."

A sound rose in his throat and he raised his jaw.

"I'm not going to waste a lot of effort on this," he said. "Frankly, I don't care who killed the Fowler pup. Good riddance. But neither do I like their dirty business of trying to drag me into this sewer of theirs. So no promises, Jones. But . . . if anything turns up . . . I just might pass it on to you. I'll think about it. Now, is that all?"

Twas almost all.

"Mr. Cawber," I fair stammered, "if you would not think it impertinent of me . . . I feel compelled to say . . ."

"That my wife is the most beautiful creature on God's green earth. Well, at least you've got eyes in your head, Jones."

"I'm sorry, sir, if I have been improper."

He laughed. That smoky laugh of his. "Know who she was all set to marry? Before I picked her up in my arms and carried her off?"

I did not know.

"Anthony Fowler," he said. "The little ninny. Olympia would've eaten him alive."

"But . . . his pledge . . ."

Cawber rolled his eyes. "Never to marry. Until the Negro stands free and tall. Well, all that came after I saved Olympia from the rot of the Fowler dynasty." There was a different light in his eyes when he spoke of her, even when the words were tinged with anger. "And now look what they've got rubbed in their noses, the aristocrats of fair Philadelphia. A happy marriage between one of their own and a docker's son." His smile filled the hall. "Is it any wonder they hate my guts?"

Twas late. And cold. Smoke drooped from the chimneys and the night smelled of coal fires. A brown fog roamed the streets. I heard the whistle of a constable—for only a policeman whistles so—and I listened to his footfalls. But I did not see him. The streets of Philadelphia were empty, and the big houses shut. I might have been the discoverer of a lost city, like those fellows who wander the Holy Land or Egypt.

I am good at finding my way, and I found Mrs. Fowler's house in short order. I stood on the corner away from it, watching the fog drift across its front. Still as a mausoleum it was. With no light or life. But that house was the same even by day. With its windows eternally veiled.

My leg hurt. The season was teaching me more of the new strangeness of my body. The cold was right there inside the bone where it had broken.

Footsteps tapped along the brick sidewalk, their rhythm broken and hesitant. Slowly, a man shaped himself from the fog, limbs then a torso, and last of all the head. Twas a fellow with bottle shoulders and a plug hat. Carrying a squeezebox. The instrument hung silent on him, but when he paused before me it gave a sigh.

"Is it a sweetie you're looking for, boyo? I can take you to the lap of the very innocents, I can. Young and dewy-clean from the Old Country. Riley knows them all."

He smiled at me with a blackness where teeth should have been. By the smell of him, he must have had whisky for blood and bile.

"Go on with you," I told him. "Away from here now."

But his smile did not leave him. "If you don't want them tonight, sure you'll want them tomorrow, laddybuck. Old Adam's in all of us."

"Go on now."

"Little ones," he said. Then he sang in a ravaged tenor, "Mother change the sheets for shame, our Molly's a maiden no more . . ."

I put the tip of my cane to his chest. Just above his concertina. "Off with you."

He gagged out a laugh and went along singing of Galway. Once I heard him stumble. His instrument groaned.

The house was like a fortress, and nothing to be had from it. I headed for the alley to its rear. With the fog thickening until the gaslamps were but a gauzy paleness.

In the alley, there was no light at all. Fine the neighborhood might have been, but the back lane was as broken as a ploughed field, and the air smelled of decay.

I sensed my way as much as I saw it. The ugly sound of horses come to me from both sides, for there were stables here. Only now and then a muffled voice sounded inside the lesser walls of servants' quarters. The horses took pride of place for their stalls, and the help got the leavings. The rich are so.

God forgive me, I prowled about the windows. The doing of it made me shiver. For I remembered the man they had caught doing such back in Merthyr, when I was still at the tannery. Justice was rough, and did not wait on English law. A patrol of men got up like Rebeccas took the peeper to the high hills and put out his eyes for him.

I found what I was looking for. Where the thinnest sliver of light cracked out of covered windows. I saw a Chinese woman bent over a bowl, eating with her fingers.

It took me a minute to feel my way around to the door. If door you could call that shabby gathering of boards. I put my cane to it, but not too hard.

The world seemed quieter of a sudden. No footsteps came to answer. So I tapped again. And then again. Only when I was about to tap a fourth time did the door pull back an inch.

I had heard no footsteps.

There was light then, though little of it. And I saw the very face I wished to see, a bridge between two worlds.

"You remember me," I told Mr. Lee. "I want to talk to you."

"This . . . is irregular," he said in that fine manner of speech that had startled me from the first.

"That it is. But we are going to talk, see."

With a slowness you could barely call decision, he opened the door. Then a jolt seemed to pass through him.

"Come inside. Quickly, please." He slapped the boards shut behind me.

What a stench there was. Mrs. Fowler had a grand house, with all the latest conveniences, I'm sure, but there were none such for the servants. Add on the queer smells of their cooking, and it would have gagged a Hindoo. And jabbering they were. In the room beyond the entryway. The funniest talk you ever heard, but with no mistaking the fear in it.

Mr. Lee stood before me in the half light, a different man. He wore a stained and collarless shirt, with one sleeve garter up and one slipped down. Stepping backward to give me more space, he glanced over my shoulder. As if danger waited beyond the door. He did not have me into their room, but I could see enough of it to pity them. There was an easy dozen Chinese folk, and not got up in the splendors of the East like the Fowler mansion. No, they were dressed in cast-offs the Irish wouldn't wear, and the furniture was broken. The only ornament I saw was a picture of Jesus on the wall, with the glass cracked over his face.

"Why have you come here?" Mr. Lee asked me. Sweating in the cold. When last we were together, he had been the picture of composure.

"Only to ask you a question, Mr. Lee. And one of your own making."

"I do not know the answer."

"I have not asked you yet."

"No questions," he said. "Go away. Please. You are making it dangerous for us."

"And why would that be?"

"No. Go away."

Perhaps I seemed as foul to him as that fellow with the squeezebox had seemed to me. There is no telling how another sees us.

"I know why Mrs. Fowler keeps a carriage," I told him. "And I know about the place in Bryn Mawr."

"Mrs. Fowler is a noble lady."

"That is not the point, Mr. Lee."

"Everything is fine here."

"Is it now? Then you shouldn't mind a question."

"This is not your business."

I looked at that frightened man. With his American voice and the loneliness of a skin not white nor yellow. I remembered him speaking of "We Philadelphians" when first we met. Far from home he was, for such as he had none.

"There are those who have made it my business, Mr. Lee. Now I will have one answer from you. When I asked you about Captain Fowler, you said to me, 'He was his father's son.' What was your meaning there?"

"Nothing. No meaning."

I shook my head. "Mr. Lee, you do not strike me as a man given to empty speech." In the room behind him, an infant began to shriek. "I will have the meaning of it."

"Please," he said. "My family is at risk. Mrs. Fowler will make us all leave. And where will we go, sir? Where will we go in America?"

"Answer my question," I said. "And I will bother you no more."

He looked down at the floor. And I realized with a shock it was earthen. Oh, Christian charity was high with Mrs. Fowler.

I do not think I am a cruel man. I pray that I am not. But things had gone too far to fail over a nicety.

I took him by the shoulders. The cane in my hand was as thick as his arm.

"Talk to me, man. Or I will have a bang on Mrs. Fowler's door that will wake the dead. And I will tell her it was you who told me about her midnight visits and her husband's condition."

I must have made a commotion, for a shriveled creature

peered around the corner at us. I think it was a woman. Her nose was eaten away.

"Why was he 'his father's son'?" I shouted.

"The weakness," Mr. Lee said at last. "I only meant the weakness."

10

I DID NOT REACH WASHINGTON UNTIL THE AFTERNOON. MY train took the direct route from Philadelphia, but it was delayed north of Baltimore. Partisans had done a mischief to the rails ahead of us and a troop train left the tracks. My fellow passengers declared Maryland a no-good Secesh state, whose citizens deserved no better than the horsewhip or the noose. And it is true that Baltimore frowned on those in Union blue. But why is it, I ask you, that those willing to do little themselves want the most done to others? For it is one thing to call for hanging Jeff Davis from a sour apple tree, though quite another to catch him and knot the rope yourself. But let that bide.

I used my time to think and plan. Not once did I allow myself to take out the picture of my Mary Myfanwy, for I knew that would set me to moping and dreaming. And there was work to be done.

I needed luck, see. Not a great deal of it, but just enough to open the door a crack. I saw now what a fool I had been and how much I had left undone. I had been governed by my anger over a shortage of trousers and had behaved with a shortage of sense. I had been only too ready to blame Mr.

Cawber. So it was that I neglected the simple questions that needed to be asked. Now I would ask them, however late. To begin with, I needed to know *why* Anthony Fowler had been murdered. Twas clear enough that some men did not want the truth to come out. Yet that did not mean they knew the truth—only that they feared it.

I needed luck, and I got it, though I did not realize it at first.

There are days in late November when the air is made of gold dust and beauty fills the heart. On such an afternoon I got down from the train, planning to stop at Mrs. Schutzengel's for a wash and then to take the next step in my investigation before going back to the War Department. For there was a fear in me that General McClellan would relieve me of my duties, now that the dirty work had been done to Mr. Cawber. And a Welshman is not a quitter. Now that I was in the stream and wet, I intended to get to the other side.

An omnibus presented itself to me at the foot of Pennsylvania Avenue. My leg was queer again and I almost took a seat as far as 7th Street. But the distance was little, and it did seem a waste. I waved the driver on.

Never was I so wise to save a few pennies.

I marched up the sidewalk, fighting the special tiredness a man gets from travel, and paused only to look in the windows of French and Richstein, where I intended to purchase a few of my beloved's Christmas frivolities. There was a new novel on display, *Silas Marner*, for seventy-five cents. Pricey that, but a pretty edition, and we must make allowances for the holidays. I knew Mr. Eliot was a favorite of my wife's, though I never could be got to read him. There is too much puffery and pretense in a novel for me. It is very much a lady's province, and I always suspect the men who write the things of unsound habits. Such scribblings would be better left to a feminine hand.

There were three books by that Balzac fellow, too, in new translation. They were piled up shameless, for all the walking world to see. I will say one thing for the valleys of Wales: the chapel deacons would have made short work of any bookseller who put French matters in his windows. Only imagine what a Frenchman will put down on paper, once he learns to write.

Then on I went past saloons, haberdashers, and jewelers. At the mouth of 6th Street, Brown's Hotel faced off with the National. The same bummer as always lazed in front of the National, threadbare and natty at once, with his eyes quick and his hand out. When I passed him by he spit tobacco juice with a great bluster and noise. In the street, a gang of Negroes worked to repair the cobbles.

And then it happened. A train of commissary wagons clattered down 7th Street, blocking my way, and I almost turned up the near side. But something made me wait them past. As I crossed at last, my cane caught in the pavings and called my eyes down.

When I looked up again, Lieutenant Livingston come popping out of the door on the corner.

Our eyes connected.

No man ever looked away quicker than that boy did. His mouth opened and you could feel the stammer come up in him. Then he decided to say nothing to me at all, but turned his back and took off down the avenue. As though I were a very hound of Hell.

There is strange, I thought. But not for long. For I recognized the doorway that had poured him into the street.

Seventh and Pennsylvania.

The Washington Building.

Dr. La Bonta, the quack.

Private diseases, handled confidentially.

I saw Livingston's troubles clearly then. With the wedding to Miss Elizabeth Cathcart of Philadelphia coming toward him. It almost let me feel his taste for drink.

Mrs. Schutzengel was in a state.

"You are coming back, Captain Jones! *Ooooch, Gott sei dank.* I think you are going because I will have the revolution, and shame on that Irish man who is making this trouble over innocent books. I think he is against the proletariat."

"The what?" For I thought it was another of her German words.

She filled the kitchen with all her yeasty dignity. "The verkers," she said. "The verkers of the verlt."

"Beg pardon?"

She said it again, and I got it.

"There is wrong you are doing the man, Mrs. Schutzengel. Dr. Tyrone is on your side."

"If this man is a doctor, I am the queen of Prussia. *Und die verfluchte Königin von Preussen bin ich nicht!*"

"But he really is a doctor. He studied in Vienna. He's a bit of a revolutionary fellow himself, see, and—"

"*Der ist doch kein Revoluzzer! Ooooch, Ich kenne diese Typen.*" She was a frightening spectacle when aroused. "*Die lesen, ja, und philosophieren, und schaffen nichts! Kampfbereit muss man sein!*"

"Please don't upset yourself so, Mrs. Schutzengel."

I did not know whether she would shout on or break down weeping.

Instead of doing either, she calmed and said, "You will eat now? You are hungry? How I am wishing I am cooking for the whole proletariat *und* for poor Mr. Marx, *der arme!* He is surrounded by the capitalists of London *und er leidet so. Der liebe Engels hat mir alles mitgeteilt . . ."*

I begged off my feeding after downing a pair of biscuits and a cut of stewed beef, but my curiosity was up, of course, and I could not help asking:

"Now . . . Mrs. Schutzengel . . . surely you are not plotting a revolution . . . here in America?"

She looked at me as if I were the silliest man on earth.

"Here? In America?" She shook her mighty chunk of head so hard a pin flipped from the strictness of her hair. "In the world, we will make the revolution. But not here, *Gott erbarme,* for these Irishes to break all my windows."

The lamplighter had gone to work by the time I left the house. I had done no more than wash and set the photograph of my beloved on my bedside table, but the November days were short. The cold followed the darkness. I made a detour to buy my newspaper from Fine Jim.

He stood on his corner, eye swollen and coatless.

"And how are you, lad?" I asked him. There was no more I could do, for I had shamed the boy enough. Our foolishness is boundless, though we mean it oh so well.

"Tops, Captain Jones. I'm tops."

His smile was as thin as army coffee.

I put my paper in my pocket and went on my way to G Street, where Anthony Fowler had taken his rooms in a fine town house. Twas a place I should have gone at the first opportunity, but my head had been hard and my eyes shut.

Now that was a rooming house different from Mrs. Schutzengel's. A Negress in a starched cap opened at my ring and the chandelier I saw behind her head would not have disgraced Mr. Cawber's palace.

"Yes, sir?" the girl said. Her voice was soft, with the

inflection of those high-flown Southern ladies and none of your minstrel-show grossness.

"I would like to speak to the proprietress, if you please. A Mrs. Reynolds, I believe?"

She allowed me in, but had the art to plant me just by the door. "Excuse me, sir. I will inquire," she said.

No hurry to her. Nor dallying, neither. Just a stately going, as if she owned the house herself, and the city besides.

From the next room I took the murmur of female voices. A chair creaked and shoes clacked on a parquet floor.

A woman fine in her years approached me, all Belgian lace and silver hair.

"May I be of assistance, sir?"

This one did look me up and down, lady or no. She might have been buying a horse on a day no good hooves were to be had.

"Mrs. Reynolds?"

"Madame Reynaud, sir."

The maid stood quietly in the background, in case her mistress needed help in booting me out the door.

"Yes, mum. My apologies."

"I have no accommodations available at present. I'm so sorry."

"Yes, mum. But I am not in want of such. I have come to ask you about a recent lodger, Captain Anthony Fowler."

Now there was play in the muscles of her face, though you needed good eyes to spot it. A slight movement at the corners of the mouth, a tightening around the eyes. There were calculations doing in that head.

"I cannot . . . discuss the affairs of my guests," she told me. "Those are private matters."

I had not expected much more, truth be told. "Mum . . . the lad was murdered. Cold and ugly. There is a difference there, see. I am not after the secrets of the living."

"I'm sure Captain Fowler had no secrets of any kind. He was a gentleman of flawless comportment." She was just taller than me, but she looked down at me as if from a perch high up on the wall. "We all regret his tragic . . . loss. But we dare not slight decorum. Good day, sir."

And she turned from me just like that. There is manners and elegance for you. A wall put up to keep honesty out.

"Decorum, mum? The boy's dead," I called after her. "Murdered, he was. Do you care nothing for that?"

With her white hand on a brass nob, she turned to me again. "Good *day*, sir."

The colored girl let me out, though I had no need of help. Funny eyes she laid on me, though. As if she had a mind of her own about things.

In the street, a lone carriage clattered by. There was little to-do on a Monday evening. Any other night, with the streets fuller, I might not have noticed the gentleman following me.

I turned down toward the Avenue, with its thousand excuses for pausing by a window and studying the reflection. And I purposely took my time going. Had the fellow been more experienced, he would have kept to his pace and passed me by without a glance. That's how your dacoit would have done it in India. But this was a country of amateurs still, of amateur soldiers and amateur criminals.

I was but four blocks gone when I heard a quick clapping of shoes behind me. Women's shoes, they were, with that higher sound and a feel of hesitation even at a run. When she was almost upon me, I turned.

Twas the Negro girl from the rooming house, with a cloak thrown about her and a hood over her fine white cap.

"Captain . . . please . . . wait," she called.

I glanced back up the street and saw the man trailing

me stop clumsy as a corpse on the sidewalk. It took him a long moment to think to step into a doorway.

"Go away, girl," I said. For I sensed the beginning of danger.

But go she would not. "Please, sir. Please. I want to help. Captain Fowler . . . he was a saint, an angel. No one should die like that, no one. Especially not a man like him . . ."

"What do you know?" I led her into the shadow of a flight of front steps. "Quick now. Tell me."

"I don't know anything," she said, and her brown eyes were huge and sad in the poor light. "But Annie Fitzgerald, she might know something. Annie knew everything. I declare, that girl had eyes and ears . . ."

"And who would this Annie Fitzgerald be, then?"

"His maid. Captain Fowler kept a butler and a maid, but the butler's gone away. Nobody knows where. But Annie's still in town, I think. Annie . . . she adored him. Everybody adored Captain Fowler. He was a perfect gentleman. Always. Even with me."

"And where would I find Miss Annie Fitzgerald?"

"In Swampoodle. She said to leave a message at Mother Flaherty's, if I heard of any work she might have. But it isn't easy, sir. People in Washington . . . none of them want Irish help. They prefer us coloreds around the house. It's higher class."

"And where is this Mother Flaherty's? Have you an address, girl?"

She shook her head. The hood of her cloak nearly fell back, but I caught it for her. I hoped that the man following me had not seen her face. "I don't think there are addresses in Swampoodle," she said. "A body just asks." Her eyes lost what little steadiness they had. "Anyway, I'd be afraid to go there."

"All right," I said. "Thank you, miss."

"It's for him, sir. For Captain Anthony. Don't let anybody

ever say anything bad about that man. He was . . . noble,
sir." Her alarm at her own boldness mastered her. "I have to
go now," she said. "I had no leave from the house."

"Go, then. But don't turn around. Go on ahead of me,
and turn the corner. Then go back by another street."

She raised her eyes. Pretty enough, she was, and I could
imagine the bother some of the gentlemen lodgers made for
her. Her praise of Fowler carried a special weight.

It was funny how the women all seemed to think Fowler
a saint, while men liked him made small.

I caught the girl just as she was walking off. My touch
startled her. And offended her, I think.

"I'm sorry," I said, taking my hand away. "But one last
question, if you please. Do you know anything of a Major
Trenchard?"

When I said the name she shivered.

Mrs. Schutzengel expected me for dinner, but we cannot
let our bellies govern all. With my leg pestering me, I did
weaken and take the omnibus from Willard's to the foot of
Capitol Hill. Along the way, I seemed to have lost the gentleman following me. And I did consider that the whole
matter might have been a fault of my imagination. Getting
down well clear of the horses, I hauled myself toward Swamp-
poodle, up past the railyard and into a dank world. No omni-
buses ran there, I may tell you, and I understood that no
cab would risk its alleys after dark. Up there, Tiber Creek
oozed yet uncovered, reeking of all that was offensive in
man, and the newspapers often told of a nameless fellow
floating dead among the corpses of dogs and rats.

At the insistence of the night constables, the gas works
had put a few lamps in Swampoodle, but there were far
fewer of the posts than you found in respectable parts. The

lights claimed little islands from the darkness, separate and sparse as watchfires on the Black Mountains, only adding to an intruder's sense of isolation. Nor did I see one provost guard or policeman in my journey through those alleys.

Now I have seen slums, from London to Delhi, but Swampoodle might have won the hoopla prize at the fair. There is funny, see. For slums come to us in two kinds. Both are ugly, and I would not paint them pretty, but there is a sort in which hope resides, where the people look beyond the disappointments of the day and believe, no matter the odds, that tomorrow will be better. Swampoodle began with a feeling of hopelessness and grew worse with every step I took.

Twas the only place I ever knew where the Irish did not sing, though I did hear the scrape of a cheap fiddle. The reel broke off in midphrase, as though the player's heart had failed him.

Harlots there were, but more listless than brazen. Wrapped in rags, they stood quiet against this wall or that, as though the energy was not in them to champion their wares. Only the beggars spoke in their cracking brogue. I did not belong there, had never been before, and hoped not to go again. For I will believe in America, see. And Swampoodle was a place to trouble your religion, let alone your faith in mortal things.

The children played by the whores. There were no saloons as such, only shacks with smoky lamps and planks on barrels, but the stink of whisky and beer clung to your skin. Ahead of me, a man flew backward out of one of the drinking shanties, followed by three big fellows who got him down in the muck of the street and kicked him wherever their boots could find a space.

"Kill the Derry bastard," a woman shrieked, "oh, put it to him good."

Then the loose women thinned away with the cleverest of the beggars, and soon not a child was to be seen. A long pitch there was between the streetlamps now. I had seen no sign of an establishment named after a Mother Flaherty. And, I will admit, I was reluctant to ask for directions. If there was any remaining trace of Welshness in my voice—though I heard none myself—Irish fellows of this sort would not like it. For the Irish would rather fight than sing, and rather sing than talk, and rather talk than think. If the good Lord lets them into Heaven, they will raise a rebellion in a fortnight, only to divide and fight amongst themselves, crooning tearful ballads all the while. In the meantime, they will practice with their fists whenever they can.

"The charity o' Christ for a cripple o' the war," a clump of old clothes called to me.

And wasn't there a shock in the sound.

Familiar it was.

"Private Molloy," I barked, for some things are ingrained in a man.

A human figure, and not a bad one, erupted from a mountain of tatters. If I had taken a shock, that devil Molloy fair shimmered with amazement.

"*Sergeant Jones,*" he cried, saluting like a fool. "Sure, and I didn't know ye. An't I sorry for it, and no disrespect intended."

I took a great gander at him, with just light enough to peg him sure: that same red bundle of hair the natives begged to touch, and those eyes ever moving in search of wicked opportunity. He had his soldier's posture still, with the leanness of the man who never wears down on the march. A splendid soldier he would have been, but for drink, dishonesty, and his birth.

"It is Captain Jones now. And 'sir' to the likes of you.

And what is this 'cripple o' the war' business? I see no crippling here, Molloy."

He hung his head. The Irish are like children. "Sir, and don't a man need an occupation? For the food and drink don't fall from Heaven, no more than they will from a priest's black lap. It was only my occupation I was pursuing, when ye strutted up on me all unsuspecting." He come closer, and looking hard he was.

"You should still be in Delhi jail," I told him. "A silver thief. And from your own regiment, when there were Highlanders in the next cantonment."

"Oh, and would ye have me back there then? In that black jail? Instead of here in Amerikee, all free and prospering like? Ever a hard man ye was, Sergeant Jones. But the black cholera come back, thank the Blessed Savior, and they wanted for volunteers out of the prison for to help with the burning and burying, and I must've died o' it meself, for wasn't I reborn on a dirty dhow to Maddygascar, and from there I as much as swum to Baltymore, when I heard of the good livings to be had."

"You're a bad sort, Molloy. Always were, always will be. Though you had the makings of an excellent soldier."

Closer and closer he come. I had no fear of him, for I was ever better with the bayonet, and my cane would put him down in a trice. But I did not like my sense of him now.

Suddenly, he laughed.

"A captain now, is he? Sure and isn't that grand as a monkey on a throne?" He could not stop laughing and, in a moment, tears come sparkling out of his eyes, stealing the bit of light between us. "Oh, and here's poor Jimmy Molloy fooling off with a bit o' silver, and heavy on my conscience it was, and not a thing to be doing but for the awful craving after the drink in me and the heat driving a fellow mad.

Then it's off to the hoosegow with me, off to the black Englishman's dungeon." He laughed to beat the band. "But who is the connie man here, I ask ye? Tis not Jimmy Molloy. No, sir. The master stands before me, and off with me hat to him. And him a fine captain now. Him what said he was all give up on fighting, and wouldn't raise his hand against a mouse, and all with a straight face he says it. And even the good colonel coming to believe it. So out o' the army he goes, free as a priest with his promises o' salvation. Oh, the beauty o' it. A man could weep at the sly, deviling beauty o' it. And a captain no less, and an't that a bargain well made?"

It was clear that he did not understand me.

"None of your nonsense, Molloy. I need not explain myself to the likes of you. Though an explanation there is for honest men."

"Oh, Captain, sir. Will ye not spare two bits for old comradeship? So a starving man can put a bitty crust of bread in his gob?"

"Molloy, you don't understand. I was sincere in the matter. I never believed I would take up arms again, never intended to. But I saw a duty here, a different sort of duty, see . . ."

He gave me a wink. "Sure, and Jimmy Molloy don't need the explaining over a thing like that. For they'll hear no tales from me, not a one. For Jimmy Molloy knows how to value an old comrade. Jimmy Molloy can keep a trust." His head lolled in a mockery of sorrow. "And I'm just thinking o' the day the Pushtoon caught us shy o' Attock Fort, and both o' the rivers all running with blood. And there's my little Sergeant Jones, me darling man, all lathered in gore, ramming home the bayonet like a very devil and shouting, 'Who'll stand by me, men? Who'll stand by me?' And wasn't it Jimmy

Molloy what was the only one flocked to the call? And didn't
we beat the black boogers down, the two o' us? And wasn't
it Private Jimmy Molloy what carried the good sergeant back
what that couldn't walk no more, and what saved him from
having his head cut off or worse? Wasn't that a scrap for
the remembering, now?"

"And for your service, I spoke in your defense, Molloy.
You would have had twenty years, not ten."

" 'Let bygones be bygones,' says Jimmy Molloy. For you'll
never have gratitude in this world, but only the grief o' your
doings. But an't there a shilling too heavy in your pocket,
Sergeant Jones, and wanting to buy me a little handful o'
crumbs for me supper?"

I gave him a dollar. There is pain. But the truth is there
was more soldier in him than in a hundred of your baronet
colonels or viscount lieutenants. Twas only the drink that
drove him down, and his lack of moral faculties, and his
base parentage.

"I know you will squander it on wickedness, Molloy. But
eat something first. And think on your sinful ways. For a
man can start afresh in this country. And muscles you have
still. There is labor to be had, see. And honest soldiering."

He shook as if I had struck him. A shying horse the man
was. "Oh, no more soldiering for me," he said. "No more o'
your 'Yes, Sergeant,' and 'No, sir,' and what all, and your
brass an't shiny or your musket an't clean. No, there's a
mistake Jimmy Molloy'll not make again."

"Work then."

But he went queer on me. "And speaking o' sin," he said,
"though I would not class it such, benefit o' clergy or no,
I'll have ye know ye had my sympatee. Sure, and didn't ye
have the sympatee and the bleeding tears o' the entire regiment, when that brown girlie died on ye. For beautiful as

all the angels she was, and kinder than the archangels, and terrible it was to see ye standing on parade, and barking like the great dog o' a sergeant ye was, and the tears pouring over your face like monsoon rain. Oh, damn the black cholera, says I, for nothing should touch the likes o' that Ameera and the little one what went with her to break the heart o' our good Sergeant Jones."

I said nothing for a time.

"Tis truly sorry I was, and am. And weren't we all?" he continued. "For any man with eyes could see how ye loved her, nigger Hindoo or not."

"That will do, Molloy. And she was not a Hindoo."

"Oh, sorry I am to think on it."

"I said that will do." I could not speak further. We may harbor memories in us for years, and think we have mastered them. But let a fellow who was by us in the battle speak a word, and our losses were but yesterday's.

I closed my eyes. Until I fair mastered myself. Then I just said, "That was in another lifetime, Molloy. It is behind me, and I will leave it so. I would thank you never to mention the matter again, if ever our paths should cross."

"Ah, pain there is still, then? And don't I understand it, too? Twice sorry I am, Sergeant Jones."

"There is no Sergeant Jones on this earth."

"Will ye not join me for a glass, sir? As my guest? For to kill the pain o' remembrance?"

"Drink has been your bane, Molloy. It will not be mine."

"Oh, ever a hard one ye was, sir. Ever the hard one. But only when it come to your native lady, I remember the great mooning boyo ye was . . . with your whiskers perfumed and your scarlet coat the fit o' perfection . . ."

"I'll leave you now, Molloy. Good luck to you. Do not waste God's gifts."

"Nor yours, Captain, sir." He held up the fist with the dollar squeezed tight. "A terrible good man ye are still."

"Listen . . . have you heard of an establishment called Mother Flaherty's?"

"Mother Flaherty's? Man, ye'll find no comfort there, nor little brown sweeties, for tis worse than a convent, it is. Tis for the boarding o' girls from the Old Country not yet fallen to the streets. Though fall they will, for all your talk o' Amerikee. No, ye'll find none like your Hindoo goddess there, sir."

"Molloy, I am a married man. With a child. And happy and content. Have the charity to let the past go."

"Dwelling on it, am I? Then forgotten it already I have. And Jimmy Molloy will be glad to drink your happiness, sir. For an honest man deserves as much, and honest our Sergeant Jones was ever, and bless him. Even if he fooled the colonel himself."

"How do I get to Mother Flaherty's?"

He told me. Twas not far, but the ways were rough. "Be careful with ye now, sir," he said. "For not every man here about lives according to the stipulating o' the Holy Mother Church. Go careful with ye."

"Have your dinner, Molloy," I told him. "Before the drink."

I walked away.

The discomfort in my leg no longer seemed of consequence.

Mother Flaherty's was still another sort of rooming house. It looked to have been a country stable in better days. Now it was a barracks of beds, clean though, with its windows barred against the world. Mrs. Flaherty, whose crucifix rose and fell with her breathing, had a great suspicion of me at first, but finally she relented and agreed to let me interview Miss Annie Fitzgerald, so long as she, the matron, might remain in the corner of the room for the sake of propriety.

"She's a good girl, that Annie," Mrs. Flaherty told me, "with clean habits. But she's found no work and I'll have to turn her out at the end of the week. If I let one stay without paying, they'll all expect the same, and none of us will eat. And it's bad enough with the typhoid going around now, and one of them taken off to the infirmary not a week past and dead in a day. And her a regular-paying girl."

Annie Fitzgerald was a straight, plain young woman, with hair the color of moleskin and a pudding of a face. She was the sort of maidservant wise parents would have in the house when their boys got to a dangerous age. Her face was bright with expectation when she come up to me.

She curtsied and I nodded for her to sit down across the table. A few other girls peeked in from the next room, but once they had their look at me they soon went off. Mrs. Flaherty worked on her embroidery by the glow of a kerosene lamp, for there were no gas fittings in these parts.

"Are you needing someone for to work, sir?" the girl asked me straight out. "There's nothing to housekeeping I can't do or won't. And I'm decent, and give to the church."

"There is sorry I am, Miss Fitzgerald. But I have not come to talk about employment."

The expectation faded away, and all that was left of her was the look of a worried mouse. "Yes, sir," she said. There was a meekness to the girl that promised the streets would devour her, and not one illusion of joy would she have of the doings.

"Miss Fitzgerald . . . I would like you to tell me about Anthony Fowler." Her eyes perked up again at his name.

"Anything you can think of that might help me understand him. I'm trying to find out who killed the boy, see."

She looked at my uniform. "Are you a constable, sir? Or a bailiff, like?"

"I am an army officer. But think of me as a constable, if it makes it easier to understand matters."

"I would rather think of you as an officer, sir."

"As you will, Miss Fitzgerald. Now . . . so far as you could tell . . . did Captain Fowler have any enemies?"

She did not even need to think about it, but shook her head with conviction. "Only friends he had, sir. Great friends, all of them. And admirers. Of all kinds. Always gone he was. The invitations would be lying in a great pile on the sideboard. 'Where shall I go tonight, Annie?' he'd say to me. 'Shall it be to dinner with Senator Such, or to an at-home with Mrs. Much?' Kind, he was, sir. And funny, when the mood was on him."

"Never a cross word, then?"

"Never, sir. Never to me. Although he was a terror on the subject of freeing the Negro. Would that someone would take the part of us Irish like that."

"Now he had a few close friends, I believe? A Major Trenchard, for one?"

She got the same frozen look on her face as the one that had come over the colored maid.

"Is something wrong, Miss Fitzgerald? Something about Trenchard?"

She looked down. "I had no liking for him, sir. Begging your pardon."

"Did he . . . ever disturb you?"

A rueful smile crossed her face. "Oh, nothing like that, sir. Though he was always getting after Imogen. Wouldn't let her alone, he wouldn't. And her not interested in the least, but fearful for her position . . ."

"Imogen?"

"Madame Reynaud's maidservant, sir. A colored girl, she is. But kind. And clever. It's half so clever I wish I was."

"But . . . if he didn't bother you . . . why didn't you like Major Trenchard?"

She studied the hands in her lap. "Because he was wicked."

"And how was he wicked?"

She did not reply for a time. I watched the blush spread over her white skin.

"How was he wicked, Miss Fitzgerald?"

"He wanted Captain Fowler to let me go."

"And why did he want him to do that?"

"He said I wasn't pretty enough." She glanced across the room at Mrs. Flaherty, then leaned slightly toward me, whispering, with her eyes lowered. "Major Trenchard said a housemaid was a hoor. And hoors should be pretty."

"There's a good girl. You're perfectly presentable, Miss Fitzgerald. But is there nothing else, then?"

She had the shyness of one accustomed to being ignored. "He and Captain Fowler would argue."

"About what, girl?"

She shook her head again. "I was always up in my room in the garret by then," she said. "With the door locked, like a good girl, sir. I could hear their voices, but not the words. It was terrible sometimes, though. And the two of them such great friends, otherwise."

"Do you have no idea at all what they were arguing about, then? No idea at all? It could be very important."

She rocked her head from side to side, eyes cast down again. Twas her way of thinking hard.

"Oh, I don't know, sir," she said. "Only that it was something to do with the marriage."

A possibility opened before me. A matter of great delicacy.

"Would that be the marriage of Lieutenant Livingston, then?" I asked her.

Surprise lifted her head. "Oh, no, sir. The marriage of Captain Fowler."

The girl knew nothing else, not a detail. But she was certain as sunrise at the end of the night that Anthony Fowler had meant to be married, and quick. Now I had not heard a word of such a thing, except in the negative, for Fowler had sworn not to marry. A public oath it had been. There was Cawber's reference to stealing his bride from the boy, of course. But that must have been years back, for Cawber had told me he had a son and daughter.

Marriage? To whom? And why argue about it with the likes of Trenchard?

Twas dungeon dark in those Swampoodle alleys, with ugliness under the soles of my shoes. I would have watched my step, but had not light enough. It seemed a mile between gas lamps now, and the shanty stoves were burning wood and even rags by the smell of it, along with a few lumps of coal. The smoke settled in the lanes like fog in a river valley.

There is such a thing as too much thought. I had been paying too little attention to the here and now, and had lost my way. With not a living soul to lend assistance. Unless rats have souls.

I paused.

In that instant, they were on me with their clubs.

11

THERE IS LUCK. FIVE OF THEM COME AT ME, BRAWLERS AND BUL-
lies and cowards that they were. Three might have finished
me quick. But five were too many, and they got in each
other's way in the tight space of the alley. They did not
expect a fight, so I put one of them on the ground in a
blink, though I took a few good thumps doing it.

Now one man or even two might be set to rob you. But
five mean it's killing they are out to do. I pivoted, and par-
ried, and thrust when I could. Listening to their curses, and
the crack of their bats on the bar of my cane. It is a good
thing they were not Johnny Seekhs or Pushtoon men, for
those boys would have had the head off my shoulders and
been done with it. My attackers were big fellows, but sloven
in their fighting manners.

I did wish I had my leg back sound, for the sake of the
twisting and turning, but wishes are wasted things. All I
could do was to keep the fight to the center of the alley
and not let them back me against a wall, where I would have
neither leverage nor room to maneuver. And I watched out
for my hands, for the great danger when you are contesting
with musket stocks or clubs is the blow that breaks your

fingers and leaves you helpless to hold onto your only means of defense. I have seen too many men fall because they knew not how to place their paws in your hand-to-hand fuss, men who had not been attentive when their good sergeant lessoned them. So I fought with all the skill I had remaining, and the old reflexes were better than I deserved. When I had to take a blow, I took it on a shoulder, for I am strong in muscle, if small.

I had seen battle enough to know I could hold them for a minute, and no more. Then they would put me down, with my skull broken open.

As if four of them still standing to bother me were not enough, yet another devil come out of the darkness, screaming like Katie in the tub when the preacher walked in.

"I'll do the lot of you," I told them, and took a mean whack across my spine for the saying of it. One of them kept trying to get in behind me and knock out my knees.

Twas a tumult then. What your staff officer calls a "mêlée." Screaming and banging and blood mixing free. And the funny thing was that it seemed as though they had begun to fight among themselves, for I saw clear as day how one of them cracked another over the head and laid him out in the slops. The fellow next to me turned, bewildered, and I gave him a proper startling with the ball of my cane.

I could not decipher it, with my enemies going after each other now as well as for me. Perhaps they were drunk in the dark, I thought, or only thoroughly Irish. Blood come wet and annoying into my eyes, and the salty taste of it lined my mouth. I only knew that I must not go down, and I concentrated my life's effort on that.

I rammed the tip of my cane into the loins of a man who had swung too wildly and sent him to his knees. Wailing he was, and calling on all the saints. Then I gave him one over the pate and he dropped like a barley bag. One of the two apes still left on the top side of their shoes took off at a run. I lunged forward to finish the last of them.

The devil stepped aside, as neat as a veteran soldier.

"For the love o' the Holy Family," he cried, "put up your shillalah, Sergeant Jones."

That no-good Molloy it was.

"What are you doing here, man?" I said, panting. It is after the fighting that my shaking comes on.

"And is that gratitude, I ask ye? Shouldn't the man be down to his knees, howling a hundred Hail Marys and a thousand novenas? Holy Jaysus, if ever a man wanted saving, wasn't it this banty, cruel Welshman before me?"

All I could think was that he had drunk up my dollar with the haste of an undertaker running after a rich man's corpse.

I am not good after a fight. It is only then that I realize how frightened I have been. The heart is like an animal, raging in its cage of ribs.

"And there I was," Molloy went on, "dollar in me hand, and great plans for it, too. When another fellow comes by just after ye, and him looking as out o' place as a painted hoor in a Dublin church. And wasn't he walking in your very footsteps, though?" Molloy was breathing hard, too, but he refused to let shortness of breath interfere with his love of the gab. A braggart he had ever been, and the worst sort of barracks barrister. " 'Oh, and there's trouble, sure, Jimmy Molloy,' I says to meself. But didn't I follow after, just like I come to ye that blood-covered day above Attock Fort? And won't I be having even the saying o' thanks for me troubles?"

"Thank you, Molloy. You were ever brave and loyal, if a drunkard and a thief."

"Now that's better, Sergeant Jones. Like old times, it is."

One of the men on the ground gave a groan and rose an inch, only to collapse again.

"Well, there's a one o' them left alive," Molloy said. "One o' us must be losing his touch."

I stepped over to the man who had moved and put the tip of my cane into his neck. Just below his Adam's apple. And I gave him a poke.

The fellow jerked like a snake with its head cut off.

I followed his neck with my cane. Making him gasp.

"Who set you to your dirty work?" I asked him. "No mistake, now. I will kill you and find goodness in the work."

"Don't know," he said, choking on his own blood and spit. He tried to rise up enough to hack the waste out of his throat, but I pinned him back down.

"Who put you after me, man?"

He gave a faint shake of the head. Twas the best he could do. "Don't know his name," he muttered.

"That one's a black Donegal man," Molloy said in disgust. "They don't know the names o' their own mothers. A blight on the Irish race, they are."

"I will give you a last chance," I told the fallen man. "Tell me who sent you after me. Or I will put my cane through your throat and leave you to drown in your own blood."

It is a good thing, at times, to have been a sergeant. For you know how to use your voice when another man would have to resort to a knife or a gun.

"The handsome one," the beaten devil cried. "The handsome one wanted you dead."

I gave Molloy another dollar, and the wanton fellow was not shy about taking it. He walked me to the edge of Swampoodle, ripe with unwelcome reminiscence, then I

made my way back to Mrs. Schutzengel's. I was not in the
soundest condition.

Just as I come up the porch stairs, *Herr* Mager, the drummer fellow, stepped out of the front door. When he saw the
wreckage of me in the hint of light, his face filled with
delight and he made one of those I-knew-it-all-the-time
sounds Germans make at the back of the throat.

"I have always knowed you was a stinker, Captain Jones,"
he said. *"Nun weiss ich es bescheid!"*

There was something about the man that forever put me
in mind of a chamber pot.

I had company waiting inside. Dr. Tyrone was sitting
in the parlor with Mrs. Schutzengel, and thick as thieves
they were.

"Der Marx hat die Arbeiter idealisiert," Tyrone was saying.
"Doch, Fourier sagt—"

When they saw me, they both shot to their feet, which
was a small miracle in Mrs. Schutzengel's case.

"For God's sake, man. Let me look at that gash."

"Ach, du lieber Gott," Mrs. Schutzengel cried, *"Der arme ist
ermordet!"*

I made the sounds of demurral a man must make, but I
was beaten down in body and soul. I stood obediently under
the gas jet as Tyrone felt his way along my hairline.

"Hot water, *Frau* Schutzengel," he commanded. "And
bring your finest needle. And thread." His fingers made me
wince. "It's going to hurt worse than that before we're
through, laddybuck," he told me. "Damn me, I wish I had
my bag along."

He was right. I sat there doing my best to be manly,
with Mrs. Schutzengel clucking and closing her eyes each
time he dug the needle back into my flesh. Tyrone had skill,
though. I will say that for the man. It seemed hardly a min-

ute, though a miserable one, before he was tying off the thread.

"You'll do," he said. "And how's your stomach? Any feeling of sickness, man?"

"I would not go to a banquet this night."

He snorted and worked his fingers over the rest of my skull.

"They make the Welsh hardheaded," he told me. "No other damage?"

My shoulders were as stiff as a day-old corpse. But I did not want to raise any more fuss.

"Well, then," Tyrone said, "if you haven't had excitement enough for one night, there's a pressing matter I'd like to bring to your attention. It involves a little stroll. But the thing will interest you no end, if Mick Tyrone's any judge of human curiosity."

"It won't wait, then? I will admit to a tiredness in me."

He nodded. He was a fine-looking man, though narrow like, with early snow on his temples and eyes full of thought. "It will wait," he said. "Though Monday is the best night for it. No customers. We would not be interrupted. Or observed."

My curiosity come up. As he knew it would. "And with what will it have to do?"

He glanced quickly at Mrs. Schutzengel, then whispered: "Fowler."

"You'll have to change your uniform, though," Tyrone said. "What with the blood and the damage. You look plucked halfway to the pot, man."

I looked down at the oilcloth set over the parlor floor.

"What's the matter, Jones?" Tyrone asked.

"Well . . . see . . . I have been busy . . ."

I managed to meet his baffled eyes.

"I have but the one tunic still," I said quiet like. "Though I have a fine second set of trousers."

Tyrone rolled his eyes. "You Welsh," he said. "You're tighter than absentee landlords."

Mrs. Schutzengel had remained with us, and she made one of those little noises, hardly a whisper, that women make when they want your attention.

When we were both looking at her, she said, "I think I am helping." Yet, there was an unusual hesitation in her voice, as though it were painful to make up her mind.

"And how might you help, *gnädige Frau?*" Tyrone asked.

"*Frau bin ich, doch nicht so gnädige.* You are . . . coming upstairs . . . with me now?"

The thought was, at least briefly, alarming.

"You wish to make justice, I think," she said to us. "And all justice is helping the world revolution."

Now Mrs. Schutzengel was a woman of girth. But these Germans are different from us, see. Fat she was not, if I may employ so unkindly a word even to banish it again. No, she filled the staircase with solidity, a human leviathan, with the muscles of one who worked hard and ate accordingly. Mick Tyrone was close to six feet tall, with the gait of an athlete, but the man lacked volume and Mrs. Schutzengel would have had the advantage in a fair fight.

She climbed more slowly than usual, though, puffing a bit and lingering on the landing as if she might yet turn back. But she only repeated:

"*Komme doch mit.* I am helping you, *meine Herren.*"

Now I had never even peeked into Mrs. Schutzengel's bedroom, let alone been inside that forbidding preserve. Twas the one door in the house that remained shut to us all.

She asked us to wait while she lit the lamp, then she

went into the dark room and shut the door behind her. We could hear the little lighting-up sounds, but then there come a new silence, a stillness, as if her heart remained undecided.

Tyrone gave me a look that said, What on earth is this all about?

When Mrs. Schutzengel opened the door, tears streaked her great chunk of face.

"*Herein,*" she said.

The room was flawless in its cleanliness and order, with dark furniture built to pass down through generations, though her plush chair looked defeated. A painted bridal chest languished in a corner and a mirror doubled the glow of the lamp, while an intense-looking young man with long hair and a student's cravat stared down from a gilt frame. The curious thing, though, was the bed.

A man's suit of black worsted lay flat on the cover.

"*Mein Josef,*" Mrs. Schutzengel said, "he is coming no more, I know. But my heart is never believing he is killed." She looked at me. "He was a perfect man. Made small, but big in the heart. Like you, I think."

We three stood awkwardly for a minute, not knowing what to do next or quite what to say. But Hilda Schutzengel had learned practicality from her long journey toward the world revolution, and she broke the spell she had cast.

Snatching the jacket from the bed, she fair hurled it at me. The trousers followed.

"You will go now to your *Zimmer,*" she said, "*und* wash *und* change your clothings. I will make your uniform good while you are going away."

"Mrs. Schutzengel, I couldn't possibly . . ."

She just gave me a no-nonsense-from-you face. "Better you are having his *Anzug* than the moths. *Marsch, marsch!*"

*　　*　　*

After Swampoodle, Murder Bay seemed an improvement. Monday late it was, and all but the most forlorn women of the night had gone in, so we were little bothered.

Tyrone led me directly to his objective, with hardly a word beyond his ritual cursing of Dr. La Bonta as we crossed Pennsylvania Avenue to enter the province of sin. He did observe, though, that Mrs. Schutzengel had a fine mind, and that she was better read than many a man he knew from Trinity. He said she was a niece of *Turnvater* Jahn, though the name meant nothing to me.

"A hard life, that one's had," he said. "But you knock a German down and damned if they don't get back up while the next fellow's still flat on his back seeing stars."

He stopped us in front of a house on a lesser street. Three stories of wickedness, I made it out to be, though I did not recognize the place at first. Mind, I had been through a long day wrapped up with a bump on the head.

"You don't remember?" Tyrone asked me.

I felt as though I should.

"It's the house you asked me about. Where you saw those two friends of Fowler's go in."

Ah, yes.

"Well, forgive me, Jones, but I took it upon myself to make inquiries. I have been of service to the old girl who ranks the place. And I think we've come up aces. Come on, man."

He started across the street. But my feet would not follow.

"For God's sake, what is it now?" Tyrone asked.

"Is it going in there we're after?"

"Well, what do you think, man? That I brought you here to admire the architecture?"

"I . . . have no traffic in such places."

He came back over to me, flaming. "Do you want to solve the Fowler lad's murder, or not? Because if you do, you'll hitch up your trousers and follow me. And we'll have none of your chapel righteousness inside, for they're human beings as much as you or I. Come on, then."

Lord forgive me—and asking my Mary Myfanwy's pardon—I followed him.

Now life's requirements later dragged me into a number of such establishments—for the Fowler case was but the beginning of my new career—and I have seen dens of sorrow with straw in a corner for a bed, and I have seen Mrs. Mansfield's New York house, which catered to the princes of finance and was fit for kings. The one thing all such traps have in common is their odor. Perfume it as much as you will, and be the household staff ever so diligent, you will always have at least a hint of that cat scent to trouble your nostrils. It is a whiff that draws a man, see. If you will allow me the shameless truth. We are drawn to that danger above all others, and lose our judgement in a twinkling. What old Mick Tyrone saw as self-righteousness was but my grasp of Adam's fall, and the ease with which it happened.

Half a dozen negresses lazed around a shabby parlor, clad in their indecencies. They hardly registered our arrival, though I heard Dr. Tyrone's name whispered. But for the girls, the downstairs might have been the home of a grocer who had lost control of his accounts. Clean, though.

The matron of the household was a colored woman of great presence. In size she might have been the twin of Mrs. Schutzengel, though she had a polish and precision that my dear landlady lacked. Her hair was drawn back tightly and her dress matched its sober gray. She wore an ivory cameo below the folds of her neck.

"Oh, Dr. Tyrone!" she said. Then, "But I have not had the pleasure . . ."

"This is Captain Jones, Effie."

"Why, another of our brave officers! And this one in disguise!"

"We've come to talk to Lucy."

The practiced look fled her face. "Oh, Dr. Tyrone . . . there won't be trouble with the provost marshal, will there? They'll put City Hall on me, I know it, and those no-good Southrons cannot *stand* to see a free woman of color making her own way!"

"No trouble," Tyrone said. "The girl's had troubles enough."

She shook her head with exaggerated drama. "I knew it was too good to be true. I said it to her, I said, 'Lucy, you might as well sell yourself south as believe in such fancies . . .' "

"Trenchard or Bates in tonight?" Tyrone asked.

Her eyelids narrowed. "Those creatures. I have a mind to forbid them my door. What that Trenchard asks my girls to do. It's nothing but corruption. Ruining my little chicks for decent trade."

"When were they in last?"

She fingered the cameo at her neck. "Those boys in trouble?"

"We'll see."

"Well, I for one would put them in Old Capitol Prison and throw away the key. That Trenchard . . ."

"When were they in?"

"A few days back."

"Not since?"

She shook her head again, but less theatrically. "They don't come by here so much now."

"May we go upstairs?"

"Of course, Doctor. My door is *always* open to you." But she could not help adding, "Wasn't that Fowler boy a gallant, though? Like a hero right out of a book."

"Lucy doing any better?" Tyrone asked, making for the stairs.

"Oh, Lord. That girl. How am I going to keep her on when she just cries and cries? My gentlemen callers don't want any part of crying girls. At least not the decent ones." She touched Tyrone lightly on the forearm. "Doctor? Afterwards? Could you spare a minute for my Theodora? I think she has been unlucky."

We went up two flights and stopped before the door of a front bedroom. The old woman knocked twice. When there was no answer, she signaled us to wait a moment. She went ahead into the room, which was black, and lit the lamp, cooing all the while at a figure I could not yet see. She might have been soothing a baby in a cradle.

Then she opened the door to us, and I saw the young woman, and Dr. Tyrone said:

"Meet Anthony Fowler's betrothed."

What words would ever do? Surely none of mine. She let me understand the bedazzlement of Solomon at the sight of the Queen of Sheba, and the breaking of Marc Anthony, and the siren bed of Dido. Passing strange it was. But one night back I had thought to have laid eyes on the most beautiful woman on earth, that grand wife of Mr. Cawber, yet here was competition and more. In Merthyr we said that fair things come in twos and foul in threes, and so it was. If such judgements lie not beyond a man's ken, I will tell you that this girl with her milk-coffee skin was even the

lovelier of the two, a very enchantress. Then I come closer—
at the slow, mind you, as if the vision of her might vanish.
And I saw her eyes staring past the lamplight. An unexpected
blue they were, and steady. Those eyes were twin to Mrs.
Cawber's, and Anthony Fowler would have seen it from
the first.

A happy heart sits at home, they say, but a broken one
roams the wilderness. And what a marvel Anthony Fowler
had found on his frontier.

You will expect that the sight of her put me in mind of
things Indian, and of certain losses of my own, and it did.

"Lucy," Tyrone said in a gentle voice, "this is Captain
Jones with me. He'll not hurt you, girl. He only wants to
talk."

She nodded from the depths of a dream.

"You might leave us now, Effie," Tyrone told the mistress
of the house.

"You will look in on my Theodora?" she asked, but she
went. For she knew her business.

"Sit down, Jones," Tyrone said. Then he put the gentle-
ness back in his speech. "I'm sorry to make you speak of
these matters again, Lucy, but Captain Jones needs to hear
the facts from your own lips."

From the lips of an Ethiopian queen.

"Tell him," Tyrone said, "about that night. The night
Captain Fowler never returned."

She inclined her head slightly toward the sound of his
voice, with all the tragedy of the ages on her face. Then
she spoke, in a child's tones.

"My boy-boy. I be all ready to be going with him. Going
to New York City." An immortal sob shook her. "He say we
be married in the great Plymutt Church, in Brooklyn in New
York. We be in all the newspapers, my boy-boy telling me.

He say our wedding bring peace to the white man and the black. That we be the marriage of Africa and Europe here in 'Merica. We going to show all them folks how love be the conqueror of hatred. He always be talking pretty that way, my boy-boy."

"Tell Captain Jones what happened that night, Lucy."

She seemed to wake, then to drowse again. Her voice might have been the trick of an invisible spirit in the room. "We be all ready. He so pretty, I knows, my boy-boy. With that soft hair. Lord, I remembers him so pretty under my fingers. But the carriage don't come up like it supposed. And he say he just going to find out about that carriage. And he kiss me sweet and call me his little angel wife. That what he call me. And my heart just beating for him, how I loves that man and never no other. He was going to lift me up. To save me, he say. Like a fallen angel. Then he go out after the carriage, and I hear that gun-shooting down there, and I just know. I just know it be him . . ."

I could not wait for her to resume.

"What did you see, girl? For the love of God, did you see anything?"

Tyrone turned to me with a funny look on his face.

"Don't be an ass, Jones," he said. "The girl's blind."

"You see it, then?" Tyrone asked me when we were back in the street. He had washed his hands after tending to the other woman, the sick one, and he reeked of lye soap.

"I see it," I told him.

"And what are you going to do about it?"

"Will you be at your camp tomorrow afternoon?"

"I will."

"I have business your way. With that sentry boy. The one that found him."

"You could come out in the morning."

"No," I said, with the cold in my leg again, "there is another step that must be taken first. I will have to wait until Trenchard and Bates go off and leave Livingston to me." We passed a cheap saloon all scented with damnation. "Tell me, Dr. Tyrone . . . might a man go to this Dr. La Bonta for anything other than . . ." I could not force the word out.

"Syphilis?" Tyrone said. "Well, maybe for a bad drip. But not for anything else, I don't think. You wouldn't risk being seen at that address unless you had a severe case. Why?"

I tapped my cane over the bit of planking that pretended to be a sidewalk. "Would you judge me a heartless man, Dr. Tyrone? From what you know of me?"

The question seemed to surprise him. After a moment, he said, "Not at all. On the contrary. Though you can be a bit of a prig."

"Well," I said, "tomorrow I must do a cruel thing. Though for a good end."

Tyrone laughed to himself. "You sound like a doctor."

Twas then we saw the corpse. Lying on her back she was. Just shy of a lamp, as if she had been drawn to it like a moth or a fly. Of course, we did not know she was dead at first. For drunkards there were plenty, of both sexes.

Her clothes were disheveled, but there was no look of violence upon her, only of the slattern. Tyrone knelt to her quickly.

"Don't think I know this one," he said. In hardly a second, he added, "Good Lord, she's dead."

He went over her diligently, but rapidly. You could see the brigade surgeon in him then, the man who must work fast after the battle's butchery, and make decisions without delay.

"Is it one of those . . . atrocious diseases, Dr. Tyrone?"

He laughed another small laugh, but looked under her eyelids before he answered me.

"Would that it were," he said. Standing up, he wiped his hands on a handkerchief. "That's typhoid."

12

THE PHOTOGRAPH ALMOST FINISHED ME, THOUGH I WOULD NOT have traded it for an Orient of wealth.

They were snickering when I come in that morning, although there was less of it from Livingston than the others. The lieutenant looked at me with hatred and fear.

"Here, Jones," Trenchard said, in that half-English accent of his, "what's this now? You look like a rag-picking Jew in that uniform. If you're going to work here, you should at least have the decency to come properly attired."

I went about my business, taking the portrait of my Mary Myfanwy from a canvas bag and setting it out on my desk. I had resolved to carry her back and forth with me each day, never to part from her. As to my uniform, I thought Mrs. Schutzengel had done a grand job with the mending, and my buttons were polished, as always.

"Looks like that cow of a landlady of his took a rolling pin to him," Bates said. He had ginger hair and a ginger voice. "You weren't being improper now, were you, Jones? Not taking liberties?"

I bent down to the safe to retrieve my work. They had not had the combination of me, nor had they asked.

"Well, anyway, I suppose the uniform hardly matters," Trenchard said. "I hear the good Captain Jones won't be with us much longer. He's going back down to woolens, where his sort feels more comfortable."

The safe was empty.

"What's this now?" I asked. "What's this?"

They all laughed. Trenchard said, "Ripley's orders. Contents of your safe to be seized. Someone suggested that you were cooking the books, Jones. Though I have no idea who that could be. How's Philadelphia, by the way? Didn't you feel just a bit out of place? Although Matt Cawber's hardly your better."

"Who has my papers?" I demanded.

Unexpectedly, Livingston said, "Colonel Kempner. Down the hall. He's got the charge now. We're all going off."

I looked at him, at all of them. I would have liked to thrash them each. For there was anger in me, and spite.

Trenchard smiled. "I'm for England, Jones. What do you think of that? To assist our ambassador. In time for the winter season. And Bates here's to have a promotion. With an inspectorate of coastal artillery."

"I'm going back to Philadelphia," Livingston said, "to oversee recruiting."

"Where do you think you'll end up?" Trenchard asked me.

"Go to the devil," I told them, pardon my vulgarity.

I fair roared down the hall, leaving my cane behind and staggering like a poor-born half-wit. But I had the sense to calm myself a shade and knock properly on the colonel's office.

When he called me in, the man was sitting over my papers.

"Oh, Jones," he said. "This is propitious. Listen . . . I don't understand these accusations at all. It looks like you've been doing wonders . . ."

"Sir, with respect, could you draw out the Cawber file? Cawber Steel and Iron."

He frowned and gave his whiskers an idle scratch. "I don't remember seeing anything like that. Were you working on the Cawber account, too?"

I rushed his desk as though it were a fort to be stormed. He let me leaf through the papers. Everything was in order. Except for the Cawber file. There was no trace of it.

"What the devil's the matter?" the colonel asked me.

"This is a rotten business," I said.

The colonel sat back and gave me a pitying look. "Have you only just figured that out?"

I heard their wicked voices before I opened the door, and, oh, they were laughing.

"She's an absolute witch," Trenchard's voice declared. "Why, she looks like a damned humpback."

"A witch and a warlock, the two of them," Bates said.

"He always makes me think of an ogre," Livingston said, "or some evil dwarf from a storybook."

"Imagine meeting the two of them in the street," Trenchard said, "you'd have to cover the children's eyes. Why, I've never been so drunk that I'd—"

That was enough. I threw open the door so the handle banged a hole in the wall.

They were standing behind my desk. Trenchard had my wife's photograph in his hand.

"Put it down, you bastard," I told him. *"Put it down."*

He gave me a close-lipped smile, held it out, and dropped it on the floor. The glass shattered.

I leapt across the room. Oh, if ever a man flew, I flew then. He was too low a cur for the fist, so I slapped him so hard it drew blood.

Then we all stood.

"I . . . challenge you to a duel," I said. Madness it was, but I was gone from reason.

Slowly, Trenchard's face composed itself. He brushed his lip with a handkerchief and grew a terrible smile.

"Won't that be jolly?" he said. "And I believe . . . as the challenged party . . . I have the liberty of choosing the weapons? And appointing the spot and the date?"

The other two were not really with us. The heart of it beat between Trenchard and me.

"What weapons you please," I said. "And damn you."

He glanced at Bates, not bothering about Livingston. "Just below the obelisk will do, I think." Then he lowered his eyes to me again. "Today? Last light?"

"The sooner the better."

Livingston piped up. "Charlie, dueling's against the law. And against regulations. They'll stop it if they see. There could be trouble."

Trenchard's smile stretched another half an inch. "Oh, I don't think we'll have to worry about anything. We'll make short work of it." He positively grinned. "Won't we, Jones?"

Trenchard left then, taking Bates with him. Twas hardly nine in the morning, but those two were scandalous when it come to a sense of duty. As usual, poor Livingston had to stay behind to keep an eye on me.

The moment the door shut behind them, he got down on his knees and reached for the photograph.

"Don't touch it," I told him. And I snatched it up myself.

He stayed down there, doing the penance of picking up the glass. Without looking at me, he said, "Look out, will you? Charlie's really going to give it to you."

"I can handle the likes of him."

"You don't know Charlie Trenchard. He was always the champion. At Penn. Champion of just about everything. Rowing, boxing . . . and he's the best sportsman in the city when it comes to shooting."

"To hell with him." My speech had become a disgrace, I will admit.

He looked up. But as soon as he found my eyes, he cast his own down again. "Jones . . . yesterday . . . when you saw me . . . I had been accompanying a friend . . . you understand . . ."

"Go over to your chair, boy. And sit down."

He did as he had been told. Sitting with his hands dead in his lap and his eyes shy as a Musselman girl behind her veil.

"Are you going to tell?" he asked.

I let him sweat.

"I'm going to be cured," he went on. "It's guaranteed one-hundred-percent effective. And I don't have a bad case. I'll be cured by spring."

There was a crease in the photograph, diagonal down through the shoulder, where it had slipped from the frame. I looked at my beloved. And she was beautiful, I tell you. So beautiful she was to me.

There is a cruelty in men that would shame Satan.

"For God's sake, Jones. I'll be ruined."

I could not help myself. "And your Miss Cathcart? What about her? What about her ruination? Have you no decency, man?"

"I'll be cured before the wedding," he said. "Jones . . . please. I'll do anything. My father's a rich man. What do you want? Name your price . . ."

Again, I let him sit and sweat. I looked out of the window. Twas not yet the end of November, but the sky was gray with the winter's impatience.

"I want two things from you," I told him at last. "First, tell me you knew about Anthony Fowler's plans to marry."

The boy had a colorless face to begin with, but now the very life faded from it. He was a thin dead thing in the gray light. A thin, shocked-to-death thing.

"You do not need to speak," I said. "Just nod your head. But do it now."

He nodded, ever so slowly: Yes. With his eyes lost.

I looked beyond that room again, at all the sorrows I had come to know, at the follies of every one of us.

"And Bates and Trenchard knew, of course."

"Yes," he whispered. "Anthony told us. At first . . . we . . . just thought it was another one of his mad ideas. He was crazy, you know. Everything was some big cause . . ."

"That's enough for now," I said. "Let's get on to your second task."

He looked at me fearfully.

"I want you to sing for me," I said.

It would have been unreasonable to expect him to understand. But I had my purpose. I was going to go forward more methodically this time. To gather every shred of proof. Before I went strutting about trumpeting grand conclusions from here to the Rhondda.

"I want you to sing me . . . say, your favorite Philadelphia songs. You need not be loud."

"Philadelphia songs?"

"Something special. Something . . . only gentlemen from Philadelphia would know."

He still did not understand me. There is helpless, that look I remember on his face.

"Songs?"

"When the pack of you were together . . . all friendly like . . . didn't you ever sing? For the pure joy of it, man?"

He shook his head and his scanty eyebrows drew together. "We weren't the singing sort."

"At your university perhaps . . . or a club . . . wasn't there anything? An anthem, perhaps? Some convivial melody?"

He brightened from black despair to charcoal. "When we went boating. Sculling. We had a boat-club song. And there was a fraternity song, too."

"Sing them for me, boy."

He looked at me as though I were tormenting him for no reason.

"Sing," I said. "And we'll be quits."

Well, he would never have made a valley choir, I will tell you. Closer to contralto than tenor, he was, and like the droning of the bees in springtime, though with no honey at the end of it.

"Again," I said. This time I hummed along. I made him do it a third time, as well. To make sure I got it. Then I made him sing the other one.

When we were finished, he sat there with his mouth open for a fly trap. He looked a proper moron, which is what his sickness might have made him, had he lived out the week.

"Is that . . . all?" he asked.

"Yes," I told him. "That's all."

I left Livingston then. Twas all a shambles. They had taken my work away, and made me a dupe. And I knew the duel business was foolishness, but I cannot tell you of the anger in me. You may insult me, and I will only think you the fool. But you will not bother my wife with your wickedness. I would have died to spare the woman the inconvenience of a rain shower. All reason fled me where she was concerned.

Still, there were other matters that wanted attending. And more important those. A man cannot think on a duel any more than he should think on a battle beforehand.

Just as I walked from the War Department, Evans the Telegraph come running after.

"Captain Jones!" he called. "Wait you."

Twas as though he had been watching for his chance.

I stood by and let him come on. He was one of your slow Welshmen, and his bit of a sprint left him scarlet in the face.

He marked the stitches below the brim of my hat.

"Fighting is it?" he asked.

"A matter of no consequence," I said, for I had much to do and had no time for a proper conversation between valley men.

"And the Fowler business? Still not laid to rest, I think?"

"News, then?"

He scanned the street up and down. A few dismounted cavalrymen bantered on the corner, and a pair of rogues who looked the worse for the morning headed toward the President's House. Twas said Mr. Lincoln would see anybody that waited on him, and that the halls were filled with suppli-cants and office-seekers every day.

"Come round the corner, if you please, Captain Jones."

I followed the man. With another glance about for prying eyes, he handed me a scrap of paper. It was a telegraphic copied over in his own hand. And addressed to General McClellan.

G.B.M. Jones questioned Gowen. Danger. Stop him now. Matters pursued sufficiently. Cawber will no longer support abolitionists. L. Fowler agrees to rein in Greeley and press.

Wants no further investigation, we have her now. Goals achieved.
Suggest halt. Will Richmond negotiate if slave issue buried?
Bonds subscribed wife's name. Charlie must leave country.
Respond soonest. D. Trenchard.

"Disappointment, is it?" Evans asked.

My hand trembled to hold that paper. Nor could I speak.

"In code it was," Evans continued. "We received it yester-day. In military code, see. But there is no gentleman with the name of D. Trenchard receipted for a code book. I thought that was queer. So back I went. Through the listing of personal messages for General McClellan. And there was strange. A great flurry of messages between them, see. After the Fowler murder. But just before it as well. Strange, I call it."

"And . . . would there be copies of those messages?"

He shook his head. "No copies kept of the personals, only the log. And I did not have the night watch. So I do not know what they contained. And I cannot ask, see."

I put my hand on his shoulder. With my heart shriveling more every moment.

"You are a true buttie." I gave him back the note. "Burn this."

He had those gray eyes that always seem drawn to the chapel. A good man he was, Evans the Telegraph.

"Will you be finished with this business, then?" he asked me.

But I could not say more. For his sake.

"And how is Mr. Lincoln?" I asked him.

His smile was no smile at all. "Harried, I believe. For the general will not take the field, but only parades the army.

While the President is under great pressures to make an end
to the war. And Mrs. Lincoln is alarmed over the typhoid
reaching the city, for she fears for her young ones. Strife
there. He is a great sorrowful man, see."

Yes. And that made two of us.

I found Tyrone in front of his tent, bloody from pulling
a drummer boy's tooth.

"Little bugger bit me," he said, wiping his hands.
"You're early."

"The best-laid plans," I told him. "And the worst-laid,
as well . . ."

"And you're after talking to that sentry boy? Haney,
wasn't it?"

"Will you come with me? As a witness?"

He pulled off his gory apron and led me into his tent.
There were more French books about, and a thick one with
a thicker title, in German, by a fellow named Hegel.

"Every time I go near those damned New Yorkers," he
said, "the camp sanitation sends me into fits. But there's no
talking to them. Listen, Jones. You understand what happened now. You see it. Why not just get it all out in the
open?"

I sat down on his camp chair. The last leg of my journey
had been on foot, and the military roads were broken and
gullied, and hard on even the best of legs.

"I will be certain this time," I said. "Certain beyond certain. And there are still facts missing."

"I don't know what else that sentry boy could have to
say."

"We will see."

We went out then, past the infirmary tents set aside from

the rest of the camp. As we passed, a soldier screamed out at the horrors of hell.

I turned to Tyrone. "Typhoid, is it?"

He had a number of grim smiles in his repertoire. One of them tightened his lips.

"Delirium. A drunkard. The typhoid at its worst won't do to this army what drink, indulgence, and diarrhea are doing."

"Irish, is he?"

Tyrone gave me a hard look. "I think Davies is a Welsh name."

There was progress in the army, though. McClellan, for all that he would fail us later, and for all of his shenanigans, must have the credit for bringing a professional touch to the forces under his command. When we got to the New York camp, I found that the old colonel had been relieved and replaced by a regular. The man had no objection to our interview with young Haney, and even offered to accompany us.

Private Haney was emptying slops when we found him. A look of fear crossed his face at this sudden convergence of officers—with his new colonel, at that—but he remembered me then and put down his bucket with a dunce's smile.

"Salute, Private," the colonel said. He did not bark, but had that good, cold voice of command in him. As though every word he said had been tested and found of worth.

Haney got up a salute of sorts.

"Enough now," the colonel told him. "These gentlemen want to talk to you."

"Yes, sir. About that dead fella, I reckon."

"Will we go someplace where we can sit?" the colonel asked me. "Is there a requirement for privacy, gentlemen?"

"No, sir," I said. "For we won't be five minutes. Now . . . Private Haney . . . when last we spoke you made a curious remark to me, though I failed to appreciate it at the time. You told me you heard a party of drunks come singing up the road in the rain. In the night, before you found the body. You specified that they were officers. How could you know a thing like that? In the darkness of a storm? You couldn't see them, could you?"

"No, sir."

"Then?"

"Well, two things, Captain. First, only your officer fellas get to act that free-for-all, like. It was long after midnight. After the storm come over us. With tents blowing down and all. And all us soldiers were long since back to camp, and weren't hardly gone in the first place. When they come up the road singing like that, I knew they had to be officers. Cause of their liberties alone."

"And the second thing?"

God bless the boy, he made the story whole.

He worked his boot into the one cake of soil in Virginia that had not been turned to mud by the autumn. "Well, sir . . . it was that song they were singing. I know just about every song there is. I'm just singing all the time." He eyed his colonel shyly. "When it's time for singing, I mean. And I know 'em all. But I didn't know the song those fellas were singing. And they didn't sound like no foreigners. So they had to be officers to know some funny song like that."

"Do you think . . . you might recognize it again?"

He shrugged. "I don't know. I got a fair ear."

I braced back my shoulders and began to sing.

And didn't they all give me the queerest look.

When I had finished verse and chorus, I asked, "Was that the song?"

Haney's head twisted back and forth. "No, sir. I never heard nothing like that. That weren't it."

"All right. Listen again." I tried the second song, the fraternity ditty.

Not four bars had gone by when a change swept over the private's face. He began to nod along in time. Before I could reach the chorus, he broke in.

"That's it. That's the song, all right."

The colonel only looked baffled by the entire business. But Tyrone had my measure.

"You're sure that was the song? You're absolutely certain?"

Haney was excited. "Oh, yes, sir. I'm real good that way. And it's such a silly kind of tune, ain't it?" He tried a few bars himself, and made a fair job of it, though his tenor was reedy and he did not have the words.

As we walked back toward the brigade headquarters, Tyrone said, "Well . . . that locks it in. Is there any more proof you need?"

"Yes."

"Man, the business is clear as an August sky."

"No. There's more."

"And what more could there be?"

"I can't say. Not yet. You'd think me a fool. Or worse."

He grumbled to himself. Then he laughed and said, "And I thought all Welshmen could sing. For the love of God."

I ignored his remark, for he was in foul temper, and even an educated Irishman is no judge of musical ability.

As we approached the straight line of tents climbing his slope, I screwed up the nerve to speak of the other matter to him.

"Dr. Tyrone . . . there is a favor I would ask."

"What's that?" He seemed as gruff as he had that first day. My unwillingness to confide in him had put him in a temper. But I could not shape the words yet. For if I was wrong in my suspicions, I was horribly wrong. Fit for the blackest pit of Hell for even thinking such a thing. I needed one more piece for my puzzle. But I knew not from whence it might come. Twas a terrible feeling.

"I need a second," I said. "For a duel."

He stopped cold. His eyes contained all the ferocity of a northern sea during a winter blow.

"Are you insane?"

"I must fight a duel. This afternoon. At last light. Will you stand my second, Dr. Tyrone?"

"I will not. I should write you into the madhouse for even suggesting such a thing."

"It is with Major Trenchard."

He snorted. "Then you're twice the fool. Let justice take care of him. Anyway, duels are against the law. And all of it's nothing but nonsense for rich ninnies. For God's sake, Jones . . . let justice handle Trenchard."

"There is justice . . . and there is justice. I will have my go at him first."

Tyrone was exasperated. "And here I thought there was hope for at least one hard-nutted Welshman. But I see there's none. And what is it that the man did to you, then? That's so terrible you're after him like a whisky priest after the poor box?"

I could barely speak it. "He . . . insulted my wife."

I expected more mockery from him. But he surprised me. He settled and reached into his pocket for his pipe. "We'll none of us ever learn," he said. "Will we?" Then he looked at the lowering sky and said, "I will not be your second, for it's all a nonsense anyway. But you may be needing a doctor, and you can count on Mick Tyrone for that." He held the pipe halfway to his mouth. "You're a religious man, are you not?"

"I am. For there is strength in it."

"Do you pray? Every day, Jones?"

"I do."

"On your knees? Like a child?"

"On my knees. And, sometimes, when I am only walking about."

"And you have faith? You really have it? You really believe it all?"

These were difficult matters, but I answered as best I could. "I have faith when it is on me," I said, "and duty when it is not."

"But faith, then? At least some of the time?"

"Much of the time. I would it were more."

"Then tell me something, Jones. Just tell me one thing." I saw the clouds reflected in his eyes. "Why is your God such a bastard?"

Now I would not think on the duel. But there were matters that could not be avoided, and last things that wanted doing. Tyrone come back to the city with me, and we stopped by Mrs. Schutzengel's. She wanted to feed us both, but I told her we had no time. Though I mentioned no duel.

"Men must eat," she said. "For the strengths."

"Supper will do, Mrs. Schutzengel, when suppertime comes."

She regarded me dubiously, and looked to Tyrone for an ally. But he said nothing. He was a gaunt one, Mick Tyrone, with the look of one who fasts or at least finds no great pleasure in the world of tastes and aromas.

"Mrs. Schutzengel," I said, "I do have a favor to ask of you." Tyrone perked up at that, as if he thought I might ask her to be my second. And a fine second Hilda Schutzengel would have been, for she had more courage than ten of us, I think now. But I only said, "Lately . . . you've been complaining. About the amount of work you have to do. I thought perhaps—"

"Complaining? You are hearing me to complain? When am I complaining? *Soll ich alles einfach gehen lassen?*"

I took a step backward. "No need to get in a dudgeon, Mrs. Schutzengel. It's only that there does seem to be an awful lot of work for you since you let the last girl go, and I just—"

"You think I am weak, maybe?" She filled her lungs and filled the room. "Weak and sick like the *Englischen* roses?"

"No, Mrs. Schutzengel . . . you may be . . . the strongest woman I've ever met . . . it's—please just hear me out. There's a young woman I've come across. Of excellent character. She's looking for a domestic position, see. For she lost her last one through a tragedy, and no fault of her own. She's a good girl, I think."

Oh, the suspicion in her eyes. "And where do you meet this good girl?"

"She's at a boardinghouse for young ladies. Very tidy it is. The establishment of one Mrs. Flaherty, just over in Swampoodle. Her name's Annie Fitzgerald, and—"

"*Flaherty? Swampoodle? Fitzgerald? Irish?*"

"Well, yes."

"An Irish girl he wants to bring into my house. *Gott im Himmel.* What kind of house does he think Hilda Schutzengel is for keeping?"

"The Irish . . . can't all be bad," I said, with a careful glance at Mick Tyrone. But he only seemed amused by the conversation.

"Men she will come sneaking in! And then the stealing! And such mouths they have, these Irishes! And dirty!" She crossed her massive arms across her bulwark of a chest. "*Nein! No! Bis zur Ewigkeit!*"

It was not a day to intimidate Abel Jones. I fair squared off with the good woman. "Mrs. Schutzengel . . . if you just give the girl a chance . . . just meet her, talk to her . . . I will stand her bond. I will . . . assume liability," and how those words hurt coming out of my mouth, "*financial* liability for any . . . indiscretions on her part. Listen, she's a good girl, and she needs a chance. I just don't want to see her driven into the streets. And Irish she may be, but look at Dr. Tyrone here. Even the Irish can rise above themselves, given a chance."

"She is a drunkard, this Irish?"

"No."

"But dirty?"

"Spotlessly clean."

"With the badness in the mouth, though?"

"She is the soul of modesty and politeness. Listen . . . you have that attic room nobody will take. Annie Fitzgerald would be glad of it. Glad and grateful she'd be. Can't you just let the girl come over so you can judge for yourself? Just give her that much of a chance. Please, Mrs. Schutzengel. You said yourself justice would only come in America. But it will never come if we don't make it come, see."

Mrs. Schutzengel's face looked as though she had just pulled it from the oven.

"She will scrub," she said, "and clean the nightpots. Terrible things I will make her do. And then we will see about your Irish."

"Thank you, Mrs. Schutzengel. I just want you to have a talk with her. Just that. You'll like her."

The last bit was too much for her and she hurled herself back into the sanctuary of her kitchen. "Now he will make me like her, too," she grumbled as she went.

*   *   *

After that, I went upstairs and wrote a letter to my Mary Myfanwy. For accidents will happen. And the truth is that, for all of my experience of war, I had none of duels. They were not matters for sergeants, and rare they were in India even among officers, for death prowled all around us there, and few had the luxury of the silly quarrels that might have laid them low back in England.

I would not be maudlin, and time there was little. So I wrote of my love and of the small account in the bank. Then I went back downstairs and gave the note to Tyrone, with an explanation. He laid down the book in which he had been browsing.

"I pray we shall not need it," he said. "You know . . . this truly is madness, Jones. And you're a rare good man. I pray you'll see reason."

"And who do you pray to," I asked him, for my temper was not good.

"A figure of speech. You know what I mean. Listen . . . all these outmoded concepts of honor . . . I was certain you had more sense than that."

"There are fights in life," I told him, "from which we must not run. I look easily enough upon the cowardice of the body, Dr. Tyrone, but not on that of the soul."

Twas a poor choice of words, and I regretted I had spoken them to him of all men, but could not take them back.

We walked in silence to Swampoodle then, where we rounded up Jimmy Molloy. He was not too drunk and agreed to stand my second.

13

WE FOUGHT AMID THE CATTLE. THE COMMISSARY DEPARTMENT grazed hundreds of beeves on the Mall, and the herd had bunched by the obelisk at the day's end. The tower was to be a grand memorial to George Washington, they said, but its trunk stood unfinished. Discarded blocks of stone lay by the base, and the site drowsed in neglect. It might have been a broken pagan shrine. We shoved between the heifers, with their indolent unconcern and sudden trottings, until we reached the edge of the mud flats. At low water, all was stink and busted barrels, with broken wagon wheels and the bloated corpse of a goat. On top of all, the smell of ill-tended horses drifted down from the army's remount stables across the canal. Twas an ugly place for an ugly business.

Gulls swirled above us. Across the river, the mansion on the ridge held up a gray sky.

"This is idiocy," Tyrone said yet again.

"Watch where you step now," I told him.

Molloy was humming, happy as if he had a pocketful of gold. He wanted for companionship, I think, and this was a fine boy's excursion.

"You there," Tyrone said to him. "If you've known him

all these years, you tell him. He's out to get himself killed, and no sense to it."

"Oh, now," Molloy told him, "Sergeant Jones is become a fine officer, and they have taken all the sense from him. A very pukka sahib he is, sir. Sure, and there never was talking to the man, anyways."

"Madness," Tyrone said, shoving his medical bag against the flank of a bovine obstruction.

They were waiting for us. And pistols it was to be. I had expected Bates to be Trenchard's second, but Bates introduced us to a French fellow with a name that sounded like the Duke of Sharters. Twas the fellow with whom McClellan most liked to ride. And weren't they all just fine friends?

Trenchard stood there straight and still, in all his terrible handsomeness. He had stripped off his greatcoat and tunic, and the ends of his black cravat fluttered over the perfect whiteness of his shirt. I took off my frock coat as well, since it seemed to be the proper thing to do. I wished I had a lovely shirt such as the major's. Greatcoat had I none to bother with, for it was not yet cold enough to justify such a purchase for myself, though I had a good India rubber for the rains.

I felt small. The rich have a thousand ways of making us feel their lessers, even in America.

The Frenchy duke made a display of Trenchard's pistols, silver and sleek in their case. "They have been loaded," he said. "Captain Jones has now the choice."

Tyrone craned his neck to every side, and I knew he was wanting the provost marshal's men to come by, but such are rarely where they are needed. There were only the gulls and, across the brown river, a choring about of small figures in blue with no interest in us.

I hefted one of the pistols. Old-fashioned they were.

Single shot. But fine, with long barrels that would send the bullet straight.

Of course, my Mary Myfanwy crossed my mind. And the boy. And I knew there was only foolishness in this business, looked at sensibly. But there are times in life when good sense is not enough, if a man is to live with himself.

A cow come up curious. Molloy made a to-do of chasing him. Livingston, I noted, was not to be seen, although Trenchard had a doctor fellow of his own along.

Trenchard tossed a look toward Molloy, then toward Tyrone and myself, and said something to the duke. The two of them laughed while Bates strode out the measure of the killing ground.

"Now you will shake the hands," the Frenchman said.

I was loathe to do it, but I took the devil's cold paw in my own. Trenchard was steady, with no sweating or shaking about him. He just looked down at me with the scorch of those eyes and said, "This should make a neat end to it."

There was sorry to think that the last breath I might take was the bad air of those mud flats. I laid my cane where it was dry and clean, and Bates led us to our places. We set our bodies in profile, pistols back against our shoulders. The Frenchman stood between us for a moment, making things formal, then he retreated to the side.

"Jones, for the love of God, man," Tyrone called. "Tell him you're sorry. Just make an end to it."

"I am not sorry," I said. "And he may go to Hell."

I saw the flash of Trenchard's teeth.

"The count," the Frenchman told us, "is to the number of three. Then both parties have the freedom of the fire." He looked at me. "Captain Jones? You will have the satisfaction, no?"

"I will have satisfaction."

A gull squealed and banked away from us.

"Major Trenchard," he said, pronouncing the name long, without the last letter on the end of it, "you will give the satisfaction?"

Trenchard nodded. Just once.

"Gentlemen . . . please to cock your pistols."

We did so.

Oh, the thoughts that come to a man, and that must be kept down.

"One."

Behind Trenchard, a cow rose to its feet to see better.

"Two."

Trenchard looked ten feet tall to me, I will tell you. With those dark eyes burning like lamps and every muscle in him tightened.

"Three."

Trenchard was quick. Quicker than me, and steady of arm. But there are miracles on this earth, see. With all the fickleness of November, the last sun broke through behind my back. It struck Trenchard's eyes.

Something stung me on the side of the neck and I heard the crack of his shot. But I have stood at attention under the assault of mosquitoes the size of winged horses. I did not break my aim.

Trenchard's pistol smoked like a cigar as he lowered it. There was a startled expression on his face. A long time I looked at him. Killing he needed. And deserved. Had I known how much damage that man would yet do in his lifetime, I would have shot him down like a foaming dog. Yet I will credit him—he was a low swine and a human beast, but not a coward. He stood his ground like a man and waited for my shot.

When I could not bring myself to it, he even said:

"Do it, Jones."

And he said it without a ghost of emotion.

I pointed my pistol downward and fired into a cowflop. Then I wheeled on my good leg and hurled his fine pistol as far out into the mud as I could send it.

I took up my cane again, and turned my back on the lot of them.

"Captain Jones?" the Frenchy hollered. "Have you had the satisfaction?"

But all the Frenchies and the fine gentlemen in the world could go to black blazes.

Molloy come up on me first, waving my frock coat and calling, "Oh, Sergeant Jones, ye could have kilt the dirty heathen, and done it honest! Fair ye could've laid him out, and a fine wake there might've been in the town. What got into ye, man? And bleeding like a Punjab pig at a sticking, ye are . . ."

But Tyrone, when he stepped up by my side, just walked close for a bit, letting the cattle settle themselves again after the noise of the discharges. Finally, he said:

"If you had half as much sense as heart, man, we could change the world before breakfast. Now stop, damn you, and let me see to that neck."

"You, Molloy," I said, stopping in front of Mrs. Schutzengel's. For even after my thankful goodbye to Tyrone, that black son of Erin had kept on my heels like a mongrel pup. "You are to go to Mother Flaherty's and bring out Miss Annie Fitzgerald for the lady of this house to see. Bring her safe. And take her back, if need be. And we'll have none of your hooligan nonsense. You are not to set foot in this good door yourself, nor to bother any that goes in or out of it. Do you understand me?"

"Employment is it I'm having, sir?"

"There will be a gratuity for a job done properly."

"Carry the girl, I will, sir. Like I carried ye down to Attock Fort, all sweating and bleeding and groaning meself."

"Just mind your manners. The young lady is decent, and not of your ilk, Irish though she may be. And, Molloy?" He looked at me with the skulk and shrewdness of the eternal private. "There is other work, if you will do it honestly."

I thought of how we had finally caught him in the bazaar, dirty as the Devil's secret thoughts and kitted up like a wandering Hindoo holy man. Had he not been drunk as a sailor with an inheritance, we might have missed him. Nor had he lost his skills at masquerading, since he had made a most convincing cripple before I startled him back to health the night before.

"You were ever as quick to change your shape as your story," I said. "The good Lord bestows talent even upon the wicked. Now I would have you keep an eye, day and night, on the fellow who was party to the . . . little altercation this afternoon. I will give you his particulars. But you are not to be detected in your watching. And no free talk or drunkenness, see. Nor foolishness of any kind."

"A dollar a day it must be worth, for such a labor o' Hercules."

"You will have fifty cents."

The man was fit for the stage, such a disconsolate mug he put on. That was the blarney in him, of course. He made his face long, and then he set it all crooked besides. His eyes sorrowed as if his mother had just gone down in a shipwreck, and with the family fortune, too. The silence wailed around him. You might have thought he was suffering in the depths of pestilence and famine, and that all the seven plagues of Egypt were upon him.

"Oh, sir . . . an honest man cannot feed his missus and babes on fifty cent. Sure, seventy-five cent would be but the faint beginnings o' decency?"

"You have a family, Molloy?" Anything is possible in life, see.

He was not completely dishonest, I will say that for him. Only no-good, scheming, and given to blasphemy.

"Well, then, sir," he said, twisting his face into another portrait of agony, "Not exactly a family . . . tis more like dependencies, ye might call 'em . . . like poor India is dependent on the grace o' Victoria . . ."

"Molloy, it is repulsive and unsuitable for you to speak of yourself in the same breath as the Queen. Nor will I finance any disreputable web of gamblers, confidence men, and . . . women . . . in which you may find yourself entrapped. It is fifty cents a day, and not a penny more."

Never did a beaten hound take on a look of greater affliction.

"Ever a terrible man, ye were, Sergeant Jones, and never accursed with the quality o' mercy."

"I am *Cap*tain Jones, Molloy, and will not remind you again."

"And twenty-five cent, in advance, say, Captain, sir? For the ferrying o' your sweet colleen from the distant black depths o' Swampoodle?"

"She is not my 'sweet colleen.' And you just had two dollars of me last night, man. That should be a small fortune to you."

He twisted up his face again. "But investing that I've been, sir. A man must think on his future. And there is a lovely great cockfight to be held Thursday next, and a share o' the finest cruel rooster I've purchased meself . . ."

Now you have heard the great Lyceum speakers talk of

the incalculable worth of justice, of its sanctity and the like, and how no price may be put upon it. But Abel Jones can tell you exactly what justice cost in November of 1861, and that was fifty cents a day to the likes of Jimmy Molloy.

The summons arrived. I had known it would. I was seated at the table that was my bedroom desk, reading over my farewell letter. I had taken it back from Mick Tyrone, thankful that I was in condition to do so. Tyrone was frustrated by my unwillingness to hurry things along—for he was as set on justice as I was—but I saw the lay of the land now. Twas time for Welsh reserve, not Irish temper. So after I washed the scratch on my neck and took some soap to my collar, I just sat down with my foolish letter and waited for Mrs. Schutzengel's call to dinner, or for the other call that I knew would come soon.

Once the body's juices have stopped rushing about, the nearness of death casts things in a cold, clear light. I saw now how inadequate, how useless, my scribbling would have been to my wife and son. High-flown nonsense, and an insult to them. They deserved better. What man is not a fool?

Mrs. Schutzengel called up the stairs to tell me I had a visitor. Twas McClellan's murky cavalryman, as I knew it would be. I let him lead me to the carriage, then on through the wintering streets.

Again, we used the back door, the one for servants and the like, which was fitting. This time, Little Mac received me in a half-furnished parlor. He did not look well, and he was not alone.

Neither man stood up when I come in.

"Jones? Good to see you again. I don't believe you know Allan Pinkerton? Greatest detective in the country. Allan, this is Captain Abel Jones, the man I've told you about."

Twas the fellow I had seen that first evening in the general's office. And he looked as unsavory to me now as he had then. The Welsh rule, see, and it is a good one, is that a man should never own a suit he would not wear to chapel. Pinkerton wore a big brown check, with a fancy-man's rag about his neck, and glass rubies in his cuffs. He looked like a man who could not afford what he wanted and who did not want what he could afford. Only his shoes had a sensible look, and far away they were from his ape's face. I could not have fashioned a more fitting get-up for one whose profit lay in the miseries of others, and in lies, and who would hang good men for money. All that was to come later, of course, when the business with the Mollies exploded under Pinkerton and Gowen and all the rest of us. But let that bide.

"Jones," McClellan said, "I owe you an apology." There was a fine veil of wetness on his forehead, and his color was poor. His words seemed to come at an effort, though Little Mac was never short of them. "Now . . . you will appreciate . . . that I am not in the habit of . . . apologizing to captains. But you've fairly earned it. I'm afraid I allowed my enthusiasms and my prejudices—that's right, my prejudices—to carry me away. You're a very persuasive speaker, Jones. Had me convinced. No, it's a great embarrassment, those accusations against a respected citizen like Matt Cawber. Never should have let you go to Philadelphia that last time. But consider, Jones, how great a burden these shoulders must carry. The weight of the Union is upon me, and I must save it single-handedly." He sat back, and Pinkerton set a bootlicker's gaze of admiration upon him. "I can do it all, Jones. But mistakes will be made. Even by me. And I'm afraid it was a great mistake dragging you into all this. After all, as you said yourself, you had no qualifications . . ."

"Yes, sir."

"Now, Jones . . . see here . . . I can't very well turn you out into the street. What I mean is, I can't just send you back to your old job without an explanation. Wouldn't be fair. And I'm a fair man. Wouldn't you say so, Allan?"

Pinkerton nodded, crushing his beard down into his chest. "More than fair," he said, and I heard the grump of a Scottish burr.

"Well, Jones, I must confess . . . you will forgive me . . . I had doubts all along. So I had Mr. Pinkerton look into these matters, as well. In parallel, you might say." He sat up straighter for a moment, stuffing his hand into his coat just below his heart. But he slumped back almost immediately. "Is it cold in here? It seems freezing."

It was not cold.

"Anyway, Jones . . . Allan has uncovered everything. I just want you to know how it all came out. To put your mind at rest. And to thank you for your efforts, your good intentions." He forced a smile. "Although I will *not* have an old warhorse such as yourself potshotting at my young officers down by the riverside, as it were. We are civilized here, Jones. This isn't India, after all. And we old soldiers must be cautious not to prey on the follies of hotheaded youth." He shivered and called for an aide to bring his greatcoat. "Odd, how cold it seems," he said. "Time of year, I suppose. Allan, would you clarify matters for Captain Jones?"

Pinkerton ructioned about in his chair as if he felt a mouse in his trousers, then he leaned forward and set his elbows on his knees. He had those lifeless eyes you see in men who do not love.

"Well," he began, "it's simple, really. Case of good intentions gone awry." He emulated the speech of the native-born American, but his voice rang odd and forced, with Scotland clinging to its edges. He sounded as if he would never be at home anywhere. "Fact is, Anthony Fowler was shot down by an unknown assailant. Who he was, we'll likely never know. Some low criminal of the city. Certainly fled by now, given all the commotion." He sat back and placed his palms on his knees, just where his elbows had been. "Motive? Robbery. Clear-cut case. Trouble is, it happened while the lad was out on a rip with his pals. In a part of town," he smirked, "where the better sort pretend not to go. And drunk, all of them. When these friends of his run out to the sound of the shot, the poor boy's already dead. Now what to do? Well, they don't want to shame his poor, old mother by having him found dead at the steps of a bordello, do they? No, they don't. So young fools that they are, they lug his carcass right over the river in a commandeered wagon, pulling rank on the sentries, then drag him up toward the lines. And lay him down again. Where it just might appear he'd died a hero's death. Or at least not a shameful one. There it is."

His eyes were stones.

"Yes. There it is," McClellan repeated. He pulled his coat more tightly around him, with his color gone nearly green. "You see, Jones? There we were, you and I, playing amateur policemen . . . when there was really a simple explanation for all this. You see?"

"I see," I told him.

"Now here's what we must do," McClellan said. "As much as I despise—*despise*—these excesses of the press regarding Fowler . . . our best course of action at this point—given Mr. Pinkerton's discoveries—is to let them fade away on their own. Certainly, this abolitionist fervor is as dangerous as it is despicable . . . but we shall weather it. Determination is what's wanted here. Fortitude. Indeed, Jones, I was touched by your sympathy for Mrs. Fowler. It quickened an old soldier's heart. No, we must not bring shame to her door. We will let her son rest a hero. For if he was often misguided, his intentions were of the best. And there is no need to drag his name through the mud over a single youthful foray into this city's more questionable districts. No, let him die a hero, if the public will have it so. There are more important matters at hand . . ."

"Far more important," Pinkerton agreed.

"As for those friends of his," McClellan continued, "we'll pack them off for a time and see if they won't learn better judgement. Split them up and keep them out of trouble. They're good boys, only a little wild." He wiped a flush of sweat from his forehead. "Ah, the fine intentions of the young, and the follies that cometh thereof . . ."

We sat in silence for a moment. I suppose I was expected to say something. But well I remembered my Mary Myfanwy's caution. And it did give me an odd feeling of power to sit there knowing as much as I did by then. With the general blowing his tin whistle for all it was worth. That feeling of greater knowledge was just strong enough to keep my rage buttoned up in my shirt.

"Well, Jones?"

"I will not be needed more, then, sir?"

"No. No, of course not. But you did your best. I see that. No blame, no blame at all. Indeed, you have my thanks. Tell me . . . is there anything I can do for you? In reward of your service?"

"I'm to go back to the woolen accounts?"

The gas jets lit his mottled skin. "Exactly." He looked at me. Struggling. As if the focus would not come to his eyes. "We'll need your skills . . . your resolve . . . to clothe the troops for winter. Allan, it's cold. Isn't it damnably cold?"

I watched Pinkerton watching the two of us. Poor

McClellan sat shaking and trying to master himself. It was the typhoid on him, and it would lay him down until January, and save me his immediate wrath. But all I saw then was a frightened, shivering liar.

"Then, sir, if you'll allow me the boldness . . . I do have a request." I put on the sort of mask a sergeant will, if something is needed on a day when the colonel has had problems at home. "I have let go my personal affairs these weeks, and have interests that want tending. If I might have your parole through the week, and a writ to travel . . ."

"Of course," McClellan said, relieved. "Delighted . . . that I have not risen so high up I cannot help a worthy captain. Good for you to get out of town for a bit. Hearth and home, I know the joys myself." He looked around the room. "I'm awaiting my . . . own dear wife . . . you know . . ."

He called to that aide again and had the young major write me out a pass, then he scolded the boy for not putting enough coal in the stove. The room was steaming, but neither Pinkerton nor I said a word about it. Watching each other, we were. And for once I found joy in falling short in another man's estimation.

I declined the carriage and walked back to Mrs. Schutzengel's, although my dinner would be that much the colder for it. There was serious thinking to be done.

When I did come in, the dining room should have been dark. But who was sitting kingly at the table but that nogood Molloy, with a fine drumstick of chicken applied to his mouth.

At the sight of me, Mrs. Schutzengel heaved to her feet.

"You are ashaming yourself, Captain Jones!" she told me fiercely. "Oooch, now I know why you are liking them Irishes so." She managed a tender glance down at Molloy, whose smile was ghoulish with the death of an innocent chicken. "You have only half a brother, and missing all these years! *Und* now *der liebe Stiefbruder* is founded again, but there is nothing you say to your friend, the Schutzengel . . ." Oh, the glare of her eyes upon me. "How a man who I am thinking so good will starve to death his own brother . . ."

"Mrs. Schutzengel . . . I'm afraid—"

But that no-good Molloy was on his feet and prancing. "Pay him no mind, good lady, for tis only the shock that is on him. I seen him like this a thousand times in old India, in the wake o' a hundred murdering battles, and he'll be fiddlin' his usual jig in the morning." He thrust his arm through the crook of mine. "Oh, come now, brother dear, for I have news for ye from Phillydelphy."

As he led me out through the kitchen, there was Annie Fitzgerald, hard at the pots. When the girl saw me, she put a look on her face that gave me a richer reward than a hundred dollars in gold. Though no thanks was looked for, see.

We stopped in the yard. Between the smells of dinner and coal smoke and privies.

"What's this about Philadelphia?" I demanded. "And just what do you think—"

"Oh, a feller was here, he was. A great, awful messenger, like. With a great raging want o' your company. Only hanging about the kitchen, he was, and behaving all shameless with that Annie, and little enough to eat as it was, and wasn't the time pressing on him like sin on a young girl's heart? When I explaint I was your trusted agent, he give me the message for ye and off he went."

"What was it, man? What did he say?"

"Oh, a fellow name of Cobbler or the like wishes to

parley, and urgent as flames through the barn roof, thank ye, and he expects ye to just run off to Phillydelphy, like ye was at his beck and call, and ye a high captain now."

"I was going there anyway," I said, and it was true.

I had to make one more trip to Philadelphia. To know for certain. To look the full horror of it in the face. And if Cawber had something to tell me that might plug a few holes, all the better for it.

I settled Molloy's cock and bull with Mrs. Schutzengel, though not a few cross looks and snorts of disbelief I got from her for my trouble. Then I wrote a note to Tyrone, asking if he could meet my return train the day after next.

The note went into Mrs. Schutzengel's hand, just as she was about to ascend the stairs.

"I have to make a trip in the morning," I said, "though no one has use for the details of it. I need you to pass this message to someone you can trust—one of your German sutler friends perhaps—and have it delivered to that camp address tomorrow."

"A trip?" Mrs. Schutzengel said. "But the dinner of Thanksgiving is only until two days now! It gives everything *gutes* to eat! Such turkeys!"

"I will be back. That very afternoon. Save me a plate, please, Mrs. Schutzengel. And don't forget the note."

She pulled on her wounded face again. "Forget? Hilda Schutzengel should forget such a thing, when she is trusted? *Meint er, denn, dass ich so eine polnische Wirtschaft führe?*"

Germans, see. You will never speed them up, but they will not let you down.

"You are my faithful friend," I assured her. "And don't let that no-good Molloy in your house, see."

She grumped and groaned and lifted one leg onto the staircase. Then she looked at me, bless her, and said:

"But the girl. That Annie. She is not so dirty after all."

I would not put stock in dreams, for it is unChristian to make too much of such things. Our guard comes down in the dark, and it is a time of temptation and illusion. Still, I will tell you of the dream I had that night.

I might have sworn I woke, were I a man given to swearing. And there, all aglow at the foot of my bed, stood Anthony Fowler. His face had the chill of Little Mac's, though a thousand times fairer it was, and he looked at me with eyes that encompassed all the sorrows of the poor. It was the face of a saint, and beautiful, with its blond radiance of hair. Then I noticed the blood pouring from his chest. Oceans and seas of it, a deluge upon the floor. I sat right up to tell him he had to stop that, since Mrs. Schutzengel would go mad over the mess, but he only put a finger to his lips and hushed me.

"They'll hear you," he said. "You mustn't let them hear you."

Then he walked out through the door, just as his mother had described him going.

Oh, I woke up properly then. Sweating as if I had the typhoid fever myself. At first I thought my old malaria had come back, but a quick inventory assured me that the world and my insides were fine. Only my heart disturbed the quiet.

I will have nothing to do with apparitions, or omens, or spirits, or the like, for they are empty things, and heathen, and lead us where we should not go. But I wonder to this day if I did not see him there, in his murdered innocence, standing before me.

Perhaps the dead need settling before they sleep. Now

you will say, "There is silly," and I will agree with you. By daylight I will agree. But what if the poor departed must do up their accounts before the Good Lord takes them to his bosom? All sums will be credited, and all wages paid, see. It is a law of every counting house. And perhaps Anthony Fowler knew the value of a good clerk.

14

ALTHOUGH YOU WOULD NOT HAVE THOUGHT IT OF HIM, MR. Cawber was a great one for books. He received me in his library, and it was a splendid room. Perhaps those books were only a display, as the newly rich are apt to make, but it seemed a grand thing to have in one's own home, a luxury of merit, and I envied him. Keep your ballrooms and fancy salons, I would have a library. Even if only a small one. For I like a good book. Not your silly novels, mind. But the meat of men's thoughts. I do not pretend to be a scholar, but I will tell you it makes a man feel wiser having books about him, even when he has no pause to read. Just to hold a good book is to shake hands with the soul of him that wrote it. Which is why I will have no truck with these French writings, see.

All the while I hoped for just a peek at his wife, forgive me, though I did not envy him that greater treasure. I might as well have envied the stars in the sky, such was her indelible beauty. A man must have some sense, to say nothing of loyalty. I had beauty enough in my life. I only would have liked to set eyes on her once more, but the lady did not appear.

"Whisky?" Cawber asked. "Brandy?"

"I have taken the pledge, sir."

He made a dismissive sound and said, "More fool you." Then he poured himself a quarter glass from a decanter and shut the library door.

"Come and work for me," he said.

Now that was a surprise. "Sir, I . . . cannot pretend to understand . . ."

His paw landed along a row of gilt spines. "Wouldn't expect you to. You're a horse's ass, Jones. Now don't get riled. That's just one of the things you are. I've made inquiries, looked into the business. And I find you're an honest man, with a full ration of guts and a good head for figures, to boot. Courageous, stubborn—stalwart, you might say— and not entirely stupid. There's money to be made from such qualities."

"Sir . . . the war . . ."

"Oh, to hell with the war. Fools enough for it." His black hair bristled. "Strikes me you've done your part. And forget Washington. The place is nothing but a zoo where the animals eat each other. I can get you out of there anytime you say. Come up here, set your family up in a nice house, say over in Chester. Put you right to—"

"Sir, I thank you . . . but I cannot do such a thing."

" 'Cannot?' "

"I must stand to my post, sir."

He laughed as he prowled the room. "And just what post is that? Clerking? Under an avalanche of corruption?" He halted and gave me a look askance. "You like war, Jones?"

"No, sir. I have learned better."

"Then what is it?"

"I will do my part. That is all."

He shook his head. "Jones, there are fortunes to be made.

Right now. I'm not one of those sunny-siders who think the fighting will be over in the spring. I know how deep this business goes. Damned Southerners are crazy. We're going to have to plough them right into the ground. Oh, we'll win. Only a queston of capital, in the end. But it'll take us another year, maybe even two. Meantime, the smart are going to get very rich. And the smartest of 'em won't have to bend a law to do it. War means opportunity." He seemed an animal let loose in his refinement of books. His pelt glistened. "The men who come out of this war on top of business are going to run this country. It's going to change things mightily. I'm offering you a place in the coach, man. And all I ask is that you be the one honest man I can turn to. To know where my business and I stand. Banks will open their doors to you . . . railroad offices . . . brokering houses . . ."

"Is this General McClellan's doings, then?"

He made a face that set me straight on that. "Jones . . . this may be the first time in my life I have met a man who can be a pompous ass without knowing his own qualities. Nothing to do with that twit McClellan. On the contrary."

I shook my head, and not without a shred of regret, for there is greed and ambition in all of us. "I thank you, sir, but cannot do it. Is this the reason you wanted me to come, then?"

He sat down in a red leather chair with gold studs and settled his glass on the table beside it. "No. Matter of fact, hiring you on just seemed like a good idea. Had to turn out a number of people from my company. When I looked into it, they were serving two masters. Made for a good house-cleaning. Now I need good men, and soon. But that wasn't the reason for the message."

For the first time, he looked at me almost as if I were his equal. "Jones, the morning after you left . . . Monday . . . old man Trenchard showed up at my door. Before I'd finished my breakfast. Wanted an immediate meeting. About 'vital matters,' he said. The old bugger. Came in and sat right where you're sitting. Laid it out shamelessly. If I stopped giving money to the abolitionists and their newspapers, all of the 'misunderstandings' with the government would stop. And fat contracts to come. He said Secretary Cameron was anxious to help me out, as a fellow Pennsylvania man. Now what do you think of that?"

"It sounds . . ."

"Don't reach for words. It's damned corruption, at its worst. Terrible way to do business. Leaves you at their mercy. And Trenchard the most respected citizen of this town. To say nothing of that damned Cameron." He cleared the ghost of a cigar from his throat. "They make a man puking sick."

"What did you tell him? If I may ask, sir?"

Cawber smiled. "I told him, 'Fine.' Because he doesn't know what I know. Cameron's going to be gone by January. Hasn't had the sense to bury his droppings, and the War Department stinks to high Heaven. Stanton's coming in to replace him." He smiled. "Never settle for knocking out an enemy's teeth if you can rip out his heart. I'm going to set up old Dan Trenchard for the hard fall he deserves." He reached for his glass again, but only cradled it in his hand. "Know why old Trenchard's all wild to end this war and quick?"

"Bonds, sir?"

It was his turn to be surprised. He raised his brandy to his mouth, but lowered it without drinking. "Well, bonds it is. Old Trenchard's bank is sick to death with 'em. War caught him holding speculative bonds out of Charleston, New Orleans, Mobile . . . all backed up by the cotton trade. By slave labor, the glory of the South. Hell, man, if I was in those shoes of his, I'd want to end the war, too. And shut the mouth of every man, woman, and child who says, 'Boo,' about freeing the Negro. I figure . . . oh, by spring . . . the second-biggest bank in Philadelphia is going to go under. And there's a lot of old Philadelphia money thinks it's safe in those vaults." He took a drink then ran his tongue over his lips. "That bank's remaining assets are going to end up on the block. Cheap." Those wolf's eyes fixed me. "I've always had a yen to go into banking. And I'm going to shake the cobwebs out of a few Philadelphia attics along the way. Sure you don't want to come along?"

"We each have our duties, sir."

He gave me a smile. "Jones . . . you're priceless. How many men in this country do you think would pass up a chance like this? After all that blather about patriotism and the grand old Union is said and done?"

"More than me alone," I said. "And better men."

"It doesn't take good men to stand in the way of a cannonball. There's Irish and Germans and fools enough for hire." He grimaced. "Well, the hell if you're pigheaded, and stupid, to boot. A man makes his own fate. I take it you haven't quit on this Fowler business?"

"No, sir. Though I have been told it is no longer my affair."

He scratched his ear. You almost expected him to do it with a hind paw. There was something forever raging and clawing about the man. "Didn't think you'd let go of it. Well, I hope I haven't wasted your time . . . but I had some boys

I trust take a hard, quick look at things. Comings and goings, that sort of thing. And one matter came up quick. Did you know young Trenchard was in town here the day before Fowler was murdered?"

"No, sir."

"Well, he was. In and out quick. Just time for a shouting match with his father. And a three-hour assignation in private rooms with Miss Elizabeth Cathcart. Who, I believe, is elsewhere betrothed. Then a miraculous reconcilation with his father at the old man's office. Somebody saw the light, one way or the other. After that, there was one more very interesting visit. Young Trenchard—"

I held up my hand to stop him. "That night," I said, "he visited Mrs. Fowler. Am I correct?"

I had surprised him yet again.

"Really, Jones . . . how did you know that?"

I did not answer the man, though he deserved a response. All my "Welsh reserve" was blasted to the four winds now. I was out his front door before the servant could get his fingers on the handle.

I thought I had the puzzle done at last. In fact, I still had two pieces juxtaposed, but I would learn of that the day after. That night, though, I had enough of it put together to finish with Philadelphia.

I ran. Yes, I know. "What about his leg?" you say. Well, now you have seen a three-legged man run, scooting along on a cane still strong for all its chipping and nicking. It is amazing what we can do when the fire comes up in us. And I was ablaze. You know by now the silliness in me, the blindness to the ways of the world. But I will not have injustice. I will not bear it. Laugh if you will.

In the park square, the ladies and gentlemen were out, with their fur trimmings and pink cheeks and plumes of breath under the gaslamps. A few children ran down the paths, pursued by distraught nannies. Twas dark, but not yet the dinner hour for such high folk, and I suppose the holiday coming the next morning put them in a mind to parade their finery. There was strange to see them all so normal, and unsuspecting, when there was evil all around them. I remember one lovely hiding her lips with a velvet glove as she laughed at the sight of me. We must forgive the hard hearts of the young, for they do not know what awaits them.

I whacked on the door of the Fowler manse like a bill collector gone mad. And I kept on whacking. Finally, with a great undoing of latches and locks, the old Chinese fellow peeped out through the cracked-open door. His little beard caught the draft.

"Not at home," he said, "not at home."

Forgive me for a bully, but I fair knocked him over. I shoved my way into that house of darkness.

And dark it was. Especially after the doorkeeper shut back up behind me.

I blundered down the hallway, testing my path with my cane and banging my knees, nonetheless. I struggled to remember the distances and the lie of things. But the place was a madman's jumble. I veered wrong and tripped on the stairs. When I got back up, a bronze devil stared me in the face. He stood gleaming in the cast of a skylight, guarding secrets.

The Chinese grandpa did not pursue me, and a wise decision it was. He rustled off, croaking in his heathen tongue, and doors I could not see banged shut behind him.

Then there was stillness.

You have never known such eeriness. I could not hear

one sound of the great city, nor any hint of life beyond my own breathing and footfalls. Twas a tomb, not a house.

I felt my way onward as best I could, working my way down the corridor and groping along the wall for the door that had led me to Mrs. Fowler once before. I did sense a light in the place after a time, just a faintness, like the glow that ghosts through a mine gone bad.

Full darkness would have been kinder. Monstrous shapes tormented the house, and the air itself seemed twisted. The house was made of angles that would never be righted.

The floor changed pitch beneath my feet and I nearly toppled a great pot.

Behind it I found the door.

The red chamber was lit by its pair of sconces, just as it had been the day I waited there. The jets had been turned low, yet the suddenness of the light burned my eyes. I saw the dragon lurking at the back of the room. He jumped about in a frenzy as my eyes struggled to focus. The gas hissed in the walls.

I tore open the final door.

The lamp on the far wall of that cavern of a room drew me like the light at the top of a shaft. I stumbled through the clutter, and broke one thing of glass.

Nothing living responded.

I felt as if my eyes had been put through a series of magician's slides and tricked out of the world I knew. The shapes around me seemed to cheat gravity, floating in the corners of my eyes. Queer smoke filled the air like incense.

She was not in her chair. And I will tell you truly, I did not relish the need to search deeper into that house of horrors. But I steeled myself to it. I would have torn the place apart, brick by brick, to get at her.

Then I saw her.

A candle showed me the way. At first it was only a faint glow behind a lacquer screen, the least light in the world. I shoved great brambles of junk aside to get closer, cutting my hands. Then I saw the sputtering flame and, a moment later, the woman.

She lay on a low foreign bed, reclined on a mass of pillows. So tiny and white she was, with the glass eyes of a doll. A long pipe lay on the floor.

God forgive me for what I did then.

I hardly know if she saw me, or cared from the place where she had journeyed. But I grasped her by the shoulders—by her dry-wood bones—and shook her. A faint puff of sickness rose from her lungs.

"You killed him," I shouted. "You let your own son be killed. Out of your damnable pride . . ."

She smiled up at a lover.

"He lived out every word," I bellowed. There were tears on my face. "Didn't he? All the Christian love and the lot of it? And you wanted him dead . . . just so you wouldn't have to live with the shame of that marriage . . ."

She parted her lips. Her teeth were brown fangs. And her eyes were a demon's.

"Whoremasters . . ." she cackled, ". . . like father like son . . . only wanted their whores . . . I warned them . . . God would punish . . ."

I raised my hand to slap her face. Perhaps the wickedness of the house was infectious. But a shift of her eyes froze me.

"*My son!*" she shrieked. "*My son!*"

I whirled about, following her eyes.

A pale face stopped my heart.

Twas Mr. Lee. Staring down at the two of us. With a far continent of sadness upon him.

"My son . . ." she repeated, dropping down to a sob, ". . . oh, my son . . ."

Mr. Lee laid his hand, gently and carefully, on my shoulder.

"She's dying," he said. "Please leave her now."

AS AGREED, TYRONE MET ME AT THE DEPOT UPON MY RETURN.
It had rained in the night, and the city froze, then thawed.
We took Pennsylvania Avenue to avoid the mud of the side
streets. There was peace on the town, with the shops closed
for the holiday and the government quiet. Only the hotel
bars and saloons went at a roar. As we walked, I told Tyrone
all that I had held back. And I described my visit to Mrs.
Fowler.

When I was done, a silence fell between us. Winter
snapped in the air. Just past the National Hotel, a drunken
private begged liquor money, so far gone he was not above
approaching two officers with darkness on their faces. Twas
a sham, all of it. The rules against selling drink to the soldiers, and the great honor of the uniform, and my hero,
Little Mac. Oh, what is honor but the mask we put over
our wickedness? Chapel called me, and prayer. But there was
no time.

I have been lower, mind. But not often. The train journey
had left me too long alone with my devils.

At last, Tyrone gave a little whistle and said, "As a
doctor . . . you start thinking you've seen all there is. But

isn't humanity always ready with a surprise? And rarely a good one."

"There is goodness in us, too," I said. For I was anxious to believe it.

"My . . . attempts at religion," my friend went on, "always foundered on the idea of Hell. I've never wanted part of a God who would make such a place as that. But there are times . . . there are times, bucko . . . when I almost see the need of it."

Two provost riders loped past. One of the horses hiked up its tail, shameless.

"And Trenchard?" I asked. "Has he made any moves?"

Tyrone shook his head. "Your man's on him. That Molloy. He's not a bad one, you know."

"He had God-given abilities, but threw them away."

"Well, he's been on Trenchard like a terrier on a rat. The good major's packing out. Ready to run. Molloy says he'll leave on the Saturday morning train for New York. Then it's the steam packet to Liverpool."

"We have today and tomorrow, then."

Tyrone was every bit as glum as I was. "You'll need proof, man. And hard proof it must be. You were right, and I was wrong. I see it now. Especially if McClellan himself has decided to bury the matter." He sniffed at the cold and wiped his whiskers with the back of his hand. "Rumor has it the general's down with typhoid, by the way. Even so, it sounds like you've got the whole Union ranged against you, and more troubles than Ireland."

I gave the sidewalk a good rap with my cane.

"I will have justice," I told him. "And a witness."

Mrs. Schutzengel had held the dinner for us. It smelled rich, and heavy, and brown as sauce. She was a proud one, when it come to her kitchen. And if she never did mankind a great turn with her revolutions, she did many a fellow fine with her cooking. I could not tell her that there was no hunger in me. Only that I had no time.

"Save me a plate of your best," I said. "I'll be back as soon as I can."

She considered the sum of me. There was not much to strain her eyes.

"You are all only the bones now," she said. "When *der Herrgott* gives us good food on this day . . ."

"I'll be back as soon as I can. I promise you."

The other lodgers perched around the table, looking at me with hatred in their eyes. For a man would sooner wait on Heaven than on his dinner. And I had kept them waiting long.

I broke away, with last apologies, leaving Mrs. Schutzengel to her gravies and disappointment. Mick Tyrone followed me back into the hallway.

"You're sure you don't want me to go along with you?" he asked. He would have come with a good heart, for he was a man looking for sustenance that food could not provide.

"No. It is a thing I must do alone."

"We could both go. We could both look for him."

I shook my head. "It is between the two of us, see. But if you could look to the feeding of Molloy . . ."

Tyrone smiled his first smile of the day. "I think Annie Fitzgerald has that in hand. No nonsense to that girl. She's already got him to bathe once."

And I went. Pegging along through streets full of dinner smells and the musk of coal fires, with woodsmoke meandering from the shanties in the alleys. I went first to the rooms Livingston rented on K Street, but he was gone and the maid said only that he never left word of his destination.

Then I went back to the Avenue and checked the hotel bars. I suppose I see the convivial nature of such like, but there is sorrow in those places, too. Well, each man must deal with his own loneliness. There were fine buffets and handsome decorations, and there was endless laughter that day. The Union was forgetting its troubles. A fight broke out in the Clarendon, with blood and oaths, but there was laughter in that place, too. Laughter, but no Livingston.

The Willard was as crowded as a pit car at the start of a shift. Families got up grand ate in the big dining room, and there were parties in the smaller rooms. I checked each one, excusing myself before faces familiar and not. There were great politicos, and generals with their tunics opened over their bellies, and women in winter velvets. Officers I did not know invited me to share their celebrations. It only made me think of Mick Tyrone. For he and I seemed terribly alike. The two of us were great ones for sitting off to the side and thinking overmuch. I liked him, see. And if I could not be with my wife and son on such a day, then I would have been with him in the warmth of Mrs. Schutzengel's parlor, with a fine dinner inside me, talking over the ways of the world.

Oh, it would have been better so.

I checked the amber interiors of the costlier saloons and the restaurants with their harvests of smells. I went near all the way to Georgetown, but could not find Livingston. I began to worry that I had set Molloy to watch the wrong man, that the lieutenant had been the one to give us the slip. And I needed him.

The lamplighter was at his work by then, and the yellow beacons of carriages jolted through the streets, bringing the quality home from their visits and celebrations. There was hunger in me now, despite my sickness of soul, and I could do no more. I should have gone back to Mrs. Schutzengel's. That is what I should have done, and what I wanted to do. Yet, I did not. I walked the streets, feeling small and inadequate. Fearing that I was even more the fool than anyone had made me out to be. That all of this was a waste that would come to naught. That the world would have its way, whether I liked it or no.

I decided to stop by the War Department to clear my desk. For I did not want to do it under the eyes of those boys. If I could not hang them, I would not give them the satisfaction of seeing me go in shame and dismissal.

From the street, I saw a light up in our office.

Twas Livingston.

He sat behind my desk—Anthony Fowler's desk—in the radiance of an oil lamp. His skin was sallow and it looked as though he had not slept in days. That well-made uniform that never quite managed to make him soldierly hung open and his shirt showed stains where the tunic gapped. He smelled so powerfully of drink it was a wonder the flame of the lamp did not ignite the air between us.

"I knew you'd come back," he said.

I took Trenchard's chair. It left me in the shadows. All of the light belonged to Livingston, who sat round-shouldered, with his hands invisible in his lap.

"I've been to Philadelphia," I told him.

He nodded. "I know. We had a telegram."

"I lied to you," I said. "I want more. The price of keeping your secret has gone up."

"I know." His eyes had always seemed those of a boy, even when he was frightened. But now they seemed terribly old. He had seen far more than such a young man should.

"I want you to tell me that Trenchard shot Anthony Fowler. I want to hear it said out loud. And I want you to tell me exactly how he did it. And everything that happened afterward. Then you will tell it to the provost marshal."

"I can't," he said. If a whisper can capture all the agony of a man's soul, his did.

"You can," I said. "And you will."

"I *can't*." A single tear, big as a maharajee's pet pearl, broke from one of his eyes.

"You were friends," I said. "Like brothers. All of you. And you let Trenchard kill him." I gave him a smile in the darkness. Twas an expression of wonder at the doings of Man, not of kindness or indulgence. "I know his mother was for it. And Trenchard's father came around. I do not know Mr. Trenchard, though I know Mrs. Fowler is mad. But I can't see how you could let it happen. You . . . or Bates. His friends."

His head turned faintly back and forth, and he closed his eyes. "*Can't* you see, Jones? Don't you see it? We would've all been laughingstocks. Humiliated. We were . . . we'd always been so close. Always together, the four of us. Except when Anthony was off preaching about freeing the Negro and all that. His little enthusiasms." His eyelids lifted slowly. But he looked down at the desk top, not at me. "We grew up together, went to school together. We volunteered together. People thought of us as one. The association was . . . indelible."

Suddenly, his eyes searched me out in the shadows. As if he truly did expect me to understand, to condone, to forgive. "All Philadelphia society would have been made a laughingstock. And we would have been the laughingstock of Philadelphia. With one of us married to . . . to a blind nigger whore." He lifted his shoulders and hands in a plea. "For God's sake, Jones. You can't keep a thing like that quiet. And Anthony didn't want to. He wanted to tell the whole world. Can't you see it was impossible? All of it. Ridiculous. We couldn't let such a thing happen. Think of it."

"I have thought of it."

"My . . . my own marriage . . . would have become impossible." He leaned toward the desk. Twas a slight gesture, but one full of passion in its queer way. His eyes, his face, the long scrape of his body pleaded to be understood. I saw then that Trenchard had been right in his prejudice against me. For I did come from a different world than their kind.

"Anthony Fowler believed in what he was doing," I said. "Crazy or no. He *believed* in the words he spoke, man. There was goodness in him. And he was murdered for it."

Livingston laughed and let himself fall back into the chair. "Anthony was as mad as his mother. Worse. At least she understood . . . that society . . . that . . ."

"He wanted to do a good thing," I said. "Just that. To make his sacrifice. And who knows? Perhaps he even loved the girl?"

Livingston gave a snort. " A nigger whore?"

"Just say it," I told him. "Tell me that Trenchard killed him."

"I can't do that."

"Why?"

"I just can't."

"Oh, and is there loyalty to friends now? Now are we all going to stick together? With the best one of you shot down in the street."

"It wasn't in the street," he said.

I should have figured it out right there.

"I don't care where it was. Anthony Fowler was shot down for what he believed. For his generosity of spirit, for

the bigness of his heart. Madman or not. His murder was a
wicked act. And Trenchard will be damned for it."

"No."

But the anger was up in me. And anger clouds the mind.
"What do you mean, 'No'? He'll be damned to Hell for eternity for such a sin. Oh, you think he's your great friend,
Trenchard. For he's the one everybody looks up to. Yes, he's
a great friend, that one. And do you know what else he did
in Philadelphia, your friend?" God forgive me, for I will never
forgive myself for what I told him then. There was no need
of it. "He spent three hours in private apartments. With a
woman. Do you know the name of the woman, boy?"

"No," he said. "Don't, Jones."

Who knows what all he knew? And chose to overlook,
so long as it was not spoken. For that is the way of society.

"One Miss Elizabeth Cathcart," I said. With the cruelty
of a beast upon me. "And do you think they were planning
your wedding all that time? Or was he only telling her about
your little trips to the doctor?"

"Don't, Jones."

"Oh, you're loyal enough to him. You could let him
shoot Anthony Fowler down like a bit of game. For your
wicked, damnable pride."

"You don't understand."

"I *do* understand. And you're going to say it to me, and
to the provost marshal, and to the whole world, if that's
what it takes. You're going to say—you're going to *swear*—
that Charlie Trenchard killed Anthony Fowler."

"I *can't.*"

I jumped from my chair. Ready to beat him to the ground
with my cane. "Why can't you?" I shouted. "Why, man? Tell
me why, then."

"Because *I* shot him."

That put me back in my seat. Nor could I speak at first. And I saw myself clearly for what I was: a vengeful man. I had set my heart on punishing Trenchard. Justice was only my tool. I had stumbled from one blindness to another.

Livingston wept with his face in his hands. "I killed him . . . I shot him . . . when he got into the carriage . . . when he came for the carriage . . . I did it . . ."

"Why, man? For the love of God? Why?"

"Charlie . . . he said he'd tell. He was going to tell my secret. If I didn't do what needed to be done." He looked up, face shimmering wet. "I *had* to do it. Don't you see?"

We live to regret many things. I will always regret my harshness with the boy that day.

"Charlie's got you beat," he said. "Charlie's got us all beat. He always wins. He's leaving for England tonight, not Saturday. He's got everybody fooled. And he's just going to leave me here. Like this." He gave me an imploring look. "We were *friends*, Jones. Real friends. But I suppose you wouldn't understand a thing like that."

"No."

"Anthony was going to spoil it all. He didn't care about us. Or his family. How we'd all look to society. All he cared about anymore were his damned niggers. And they weren't real to him. Just some fantasy . . . some dream. He was crazy. He should've been locked up like his father . . ."

"Yes."

"You'll never get Charlie," he told me. "And you won't drag me down in shame."

His right hand rose from his lap again. This time it held a pistol. I thought he was going to aim it at me, of course.

Before I could move he put the barrel in his mouth and pulled the trigger.

*　　*　　*

I should have stayed there. But even as I bent over the body and felt that sudden heaviness of death upon the boy, I could think only of his claim that Trenchard had beaten us. And that he was leaving for England that very night.

There was gore on my hands from feeling the artery in his neck. I quickly wiped it off on the skirt of his tunic. For I feared the contagion of his bad blood. Then I plunged down the empty hallway and the stairs, hardly stopping to tell the bewildered sentry, "Lieutenant Livingston's shot himself. Call the provost marshal's guards."

I did not care what Livingston had said or thought or even done. Trenchard was the killer. Just as in war, where the real killers are not the boys with the bayonets, but the men in the rooms of state. Trenchard had killed Anthony Fowler with help from Livingston, and now he had killed Livingston with help from me. I was not about to let him dance off to England.

I found a cab just by the President's House and directed him to Mrs. Schutzengel's. We were long enough into the holiday that little groups of revelers dotted the streets, singing patriotic songs in their drunkenness. At our destination, I paid the driver quickly and did not even wait for my change.

Mrs. Schutzengel tried to greet me. Tyrone sat over a book in her parlor, pipe in his mouth. But I had not a word for them. Not yet. I hustled up the stairs to my room.

Tyrone came in as I was loading the pistol the boys from my company had given me.

"What's this?" he said. "Another duel?"

"Livingston's dead. Shot himself. *He* shot Fowler. But Trenchard was behind it. And he's not leaving Saturday. He's leaving tonight." I looked up at the sadness and trouble of the doctor's face. "I'm going to stop him."

"I'll help you."

I stood up and hoisted my frock coat, shoving the pistol into my waistband.

"It is a serious business, Dr. Tyrone. And not your business now."

"As much as it is yours."

There was no time to argue. And the truth is I was glad to have him by me.

"Let's go," I said. "We'll get Molloy on the way. He's good in a scrap."

Trenchard's rooms were on Franklin Square, which was not distant, though it was another matter socially. We found Molloy in the little park, which had been ruined by the bivouac of soldiers in the first months of the war. It had the look of an abandoned excavation.

Molloy had got himself up in rags again. His face was so dirty you could hardly tell him from a heathen. Had we not known he was there, we would have wandered past the colorless bummer he had made of himself. His talent for deceit was such a gift it made you doubt the truth of other men.

"*Cap*tain Jones," he said, proud of his alertness now.

"Where's Trenchard? Is he inside?"

"Oh, and they were pleasing the ladies today, him and the Bates fellow. Shining like lords, and saying their fond farewells, I'm thinking. While here's poor Jimmy Molloy, missing the cockfight o' the century for the terrible duty ye put upon him."

"Is he in there now?"

Molloy nodded toward the building. "His rooms are on the second floor. All full of meat and punch, he is. And full of himself, as well. He's a fine ripe portrait of a man, that

one. Tis sorry I am ye did not kill him when the chance
come to ye."

"I'm sorry, too," I said.

Perhaps our fates are set out for us, although it troubles
me to think so. I am not certain what might have been done
differently. My choices fled me when the coach drew up
before Trenchard's door.

His trunk must have been waiting, for the coachman no
sooner gave his rap than the butler opened and the two men
lugged the baggage down to the vehicle and strapped it to
the shelf at the rear.

"You, Molloy," I said. "You're to stop that coach from
leaving. Take what it will." I turned to Tyrone. "Go on with
you and get the provost guards. Tell them what you must.
Tell them murder. And tell them they'll need officers to
manage the business."

Tyrone stopped me with a hand on my upper arm.
"And you?"

"I'm going to hold Trenchard here. And Bates."

"But you have no witness now."

I looked at him. "God is my witness. I'll do what I must."

And I tore away from the two of them. I had no plan.
No idea of what I might say. Only my anger. And the Colt
shoved into my trousers.

Perhaps it was my uniform. The butler only gave me a
glance. I marched into that house as though I had a right
to be there. And I believed I did.

As I went in, I heard Molloy strike up a banter with
the coachman behind me. Then I caught the other voices.
Trenchard's joking, and the answering laughter from Bates
above my head.

Stairs were still difficult with my leg, but I took them as

quickly as I could. I made the second floor just as Trenchard and Bates stepped out of a doorway.

No need of firearms. I raised my cane before their startled faces and gave Trenchard a thump on the shoulder. I nearly crumpled him.

"Back in that room," I said. I stabbed the cane toward Bates, who retreated immediately. Oh, there was shock on their snouts. But Trenchard was no coward. When he did not move, I poked him in the chest. And I made it hurt.

"In there, you bastards," I said. "And we'll wait for the provost detail."

Trenchard was no coward. But it does not take a coward to feel fear. I saw it come to Trenchard's eyes then. It is like any fight, see. You want to catch your opponent off his guard. Attack in the morning, when their camp is asleep. That is how you do it. Only you must do your killing before they have a chance to recover. That I failed to do.

They did my bidding at first, though. I herded them into the room from which they had stepped, then shut the door behind us so no one could surprise me from behind. Twas a fine gentleman's parlor, thick of cushion and drape, with the marble fireplace going and glasses but half drained on the drum table.

"Are you mad, Jones?" Trenchard said. He rubbed his shoulder, but I could tell his mind was not on it. He would not have let me see his pain if he had not had greater concerns. "I'll have you jailed for this."

"You're the one who'll see the dungeon," I told him. Then I looked at Bates, who was watching for Trenchard's lead. "The two of you. Murderers."

Trenchard tried a look of bafflement. "Whatever are you going on about?"

"You know it," I told him. "And well. You killed Anthony

Fowler. By putting Livingston up to it. Out of no more reason than your pride."

"That's absurd."

"Is it, then?" It was time to bluff. "Then it will be Livingston's word against yours."

Their eyes changed. Trenchard's mouth tightened. You could feel the desire to strike come over him. Bates looked horrified. He smoothed his hand back over his ginger hair, again and again.

"I just left him," I said. "In the provost marshal's care." I worked up the smile of a sergeant who has the goods on a lazy private. "You should never put your faith in a drunkard. For they're given to blabbering."

"Whatever he says, it's a lie," Bates half-shouted. But a look from Trenchard silenced him.

"Livingston's a syphilitic fool," Trenchard said. "There was trouble . . . between him and Fowler. Fowler always had to be the do-gooder. He threatened Livingston, told him if he didn't do the honorable thing and break off his engagement, he'd let it out that Livingston was diseased."

"No," I said. "That was your threat. And Livingston knows about your appointment in private rooms with Miss Cathcart. Oh, that got the boy talking. He's already written out his statement."

"That drunk sonofabitch," Bates said.

But Trenchard did not take his eyes from me now. I felt as though I were facing down an animal that wanted to eat me alive.

"You've got it all wrong, Jones."

"No."

"Livingston shot him."

"I know. You may not hang. But you'll taste the society of a prison."

"What . . . do you want?"

"Justice."

He laughed. Bates tried to laugh with him, but could not manage it.

" 'Justice?' " Trenchard said. "Don't you mean revenge? Revenge on your betters? Look at you. You're a crumpled, soiled thing, Jones. A nobody. And you'll always be a nobody. You're wasting your efforts."

"There will be justice."

"You don't sound at all certain." He smiled. "You know this is only a charade. You know you're only making a spectacle of yourself. You have no one behind you, no one to back you."

I met his eyes and did not falter. "I will make a spectacle of you. And if I cannot have justice, I will have the public shaming of you. You'll never raise your head again. I'll make the world believe me. And if I cannot do that, I will still make them doubt you."

Trenchard shook his head. "Such an angry little man." He glanced sideward. "Isn't he, Bates?"

"Charlie . . . listen . . . this is no time to be fooling . . ."

Trenchard smiled again, easing his hands into the pockets of his trousers. "No. It's no time for fooling. So tell me, Jones. What do you really want? Money? Position? What's your price?"

"I will have justice," I repeated.

"Then have it," he said. He drew out a derringer. They are wee little guns, see, and cannot hit much beyond a few feet. But he was hardly a body length from me, and he pointed the two little barrels straight into my stomach.

I felt the Colt resting against my shirt. Useless. I should never have carried a pistol if I had not the intention to draw it and use it from the first.

"Anthony's death is a burden to me still," Trenchard said. "It was a regrettable necessity, and we all miss him." He smiled. "He was funny, did you know that? Made a man laugh. A lovely companion, when you got him going. Bit of a crank on the Negro, but those lectures attracted marvelous women. Positively swooning, every one of them. A man could take his pick. But Anthony had to get it into his skull that he could save the world by marrying a prostitute . . ." He smiled, and tilted his head to summon Bates. "Take that damned stick away from him, would you, Billy? And you, Jones. Make no mistake. Your death would not be a burden to me. Give him the stick, now. Nicely."

I let Bates have my cane. He tossed it into the fire.

"Now," Trenchard said, "I suggest we all go for a ride. You will see me off, won't you, Billy? Then you can see off Captain Jones."

"Charlie, I . . ."

"You know what you owe me, Billy. Your family would disinherit you."

"Charlie, they'll know. They'll know we did it."

Trenchard grinned. "They'll know *you* did it. But don't worry. Daddy's money will put it right." He looked at me, head to foot, then back again. "Do you really think anybody's going to care?"

"I'll see you in prison," I told him.

"Well, first you'll see me to the rail depot. Then you can discuss your future with Captain Bates. Out now. Down the stairs and into the coach. Or I'll put a bullet into your spine."

The stairs were harder going down than coming up. But I still had my pistol.

I heard Bates laugh behind me. "Don't he look like a little turtle, though, Charlie? Don't he just?"

We reached the street just as two provost men rode up.

I could not see Trenchard, who stayed behind me, but he must have slipped the derringer into his pocket again, for the cavalrymen did not alert to the danger. They dismounted behind the coach, weapons holstered, and paused in the cast of the gaslamp. Too many officers for them to feel confident.

Molloy stood in his rags, soothing the coach's lead horse, treating it to his blarney. Our eyes met and I said:

"Attock Fort."

Now there is only one man in the world other than me to whom such a battle cry would make sense, and though he was a lying, conniving, and blaspheming Irishman of the lowest orders, I was grateful for him that day.

"Get in the coach," Trenchard hissed. "No nonsense."

But Molloy come swaggering up the pavement, prancing like a minstrel in a blackface show. He called to the provost men and pointed, with a gesture big as the Hindoo Kush, at Trenchard and Bates.

"There's your murderers," he called. "Them two fine ones there. And they're bothering poor Captain Jones."

Mick Tyrone come legging it around the corner.

"Everybody stop," Trenchard shouted. "Stay where you are. Just *stop*."

Oh, there is beauty in surprise.

I turned and gave Bates the full of my fist in his jaw. I had not the force of my good-legged days, still it dropped him to his knees. And I caught sight of Trenchard, with the great fear in him now. His derringer was out again, and pointed at me. Not three feet off, he pulled one of the triggers.

It misfired. They are lovely, untrustworthy little weapons.

One of the provost men went for his pistol. Trenchard turned the derringer on him, jerking the second trigger. This time the little pistol worked.

The trooper staggered back a step, with a look of wonder on his face. The pistol dropped from his hand. "Cripes," he said, "I'm shot." And he sat down in the street.

Now the derringer was useless, with one misfire and the other barrel discharged. But the second provost man just put his hands in the air. "For the love of God," he said, "don't shoot me, sir."

Then it went wild. Trenchard dove for the fallen pistol, and got it. But I had my Colt up in my hand, the action primed.

I would have put him down then and there, if Bates had not slammed me behind my bad knee.

I went down flat. But Bates paid. The bullet meant for me caught him in the chest. And Trenchard was a deadly shot.

Trenchard was on his feet again. He pistol-whipped the second trooper across the face and leapt up on the man's horse. Mick Tyrone threw himself at the back of the animal, grabbing onto the saddle, and the horse spun round, lifting its hooves and dancing. Twas only the animal's confusion that saved Tyrone from worse than he got. Trenchard let off a shot with the trooper's pistol and Mick twisted back on the cobbles, with a bloody rip out of his arm.

Trenchard lashed the horse. He had no spurs, but he kicked it hard and brought it around. I strained for a clear shot, but the coach got in the way. And Trenchard went off at a gallop.

I ran into the street. Pistol raised. But I would as likely have hit an innocent as him at that range, with only the gaslamps to light my aim.

I will tell you of the size and shape of my anger. Twas so great it conquered the worst of my fears. Bad leg or no, I scrambled onto the other trooper's horse. I could only find one stirrup, and it sat me at a tilt. But I kicked the beast's flanks and lashed her neck with the reins and shouted as I had seen and heard men do.

They must have been stablemates and long companions, those two horses, for mine took off after Trenchard's mount as if reading my thoughts. I clung to the saddle with my left hand, the pistol and a great tuft of mane in the other.

Trenchard did not turn for the station. He galloped down K Street, heading west. I saw it all clearly then. He was riding for Georgetown and the Aqueduct to Virginia. Going South, where his father's bonds would save him.

Now I don't know if the horse caught my rage, or if it only wanted to rejoin its companion, but we seemed to gain on Trenchard as the blocks fell away. Perhaps I only had the better of the horses. It is certain I was not the better rider. I bounced and banged and clung.

Trenchard's white blur of face glanced back at me. Where strollers paused, I shouted, "Stop that man," and many another silliness. But those citizens who were out for the evening air only looked on in curiosity. The war had brought them stranger sights, and greater madnesses, and we were none of their affair.

I heard a frantic galloping come up behind me.

Twas that no-good Molloy, on a nag he stole. Waving a pistol the size of a ham haunch.

"Jaysus, Mary, and Joseph," he yelped. "I've jined the bleedin' cavalry."

Trenchard fired back over his saddle. The bullet sizzled by.

We came to the intersection with Pennsylvania Avenue, narrowing Trenchard's lead all the while. But that only made him more dangerous, a killer on a poor horse. He fired again. The sound passed closer. I had all I could do to stay on my mount and could not fire. But Molloy had all the fearlessness

of a drunk. He let go the reins and laid his pistol's barrel
across his left forearm. He must have seen a picture of a red
Indian doing it in a weekly illustrated. And he fired.

Trenchard's horse reared.

When Trenchard spurred the animal on again, blood shot
from its flank like the jet of a fountain.

Trenchard lashed the beast and hammered its neck with
his pistol. A carriage pulled into the avenue and he almost
collided with it. But he was horseman enough to pull up
in time.

He had not a block on us now. But the driver lost control
of the carriage's team and it come careening at us. My horse
bolted onto the sidewalk and a gaslamp nearly took off my
head. A fellow in a top hat backed against a building, with
a look of indignation on his mug. Molloy got in a tangle
betwixt the runaway carriage and an omnibus headed for
Georgetown.

I was more afraid to stop and think about what I was
doing than I was of the bullets. It is the way of the old
soldier. You go forward because it is the easiest thing of all.

Wounded, Trenchard's horse moped off its pace, no matter the whippings he gave it. He turned, saw me, and fired
again, shattering the window of a grocer's shop. Then he
kicked the animal to life a last time and turned its head off
to the left, leaving the avenue. Twas 21st Street, I think,
though that chase will ever be something of a blur.

I did not know where he was going, but I followed. With
Molloy coming on behind.

"Like old times, an't?" Molloy yelled. Then Trenchard
fired again and Molloy's horse crumpled, hit square in the
chest. I remember the shock in the horse's eyes, seen for a
sliver of a second, worse than the fear in a man's. Molloy

went flying over the mane and rolled along the street. The fall would have killed a man given to sobriety.

I could not stop. Getting Trenchard, bringing him down, was all that was left to me now. I did not think of wife or child, or of God or justice. I thought only of making that man pay.

Trenchard's horse began to buck him, trying to shake off his tyranny. Blood hosed the street. I saw the foam on the beast's mouth, and then the vomit of blood. But the animal kept its footing.

I smelled an ugly smell, ugly and big, as I followed him down that street. Then Trenchard was on foot, running. He fired backward toward me another time, then dodged to avoid the light of a gaslamp.

He dashed toward a row of low barns.

The Army remount stables. Had he led me into a snake pit, I would have liked it better.

Just before me, Trenchard's horse went down at last, saddle twisting onto its side. It lifted its head to look back, trying to examine its wound. Behind me, I heard Molloy shouting that I should wait for him. But there was no time. And I was out of my element. I did not even know if I could stop my horse to get off.

The horse helped. It broke its gallop and trotted over to its wounded companion. Then it stopped and lowered its head in sympathy.

I slid off its back, jamming my bad leg to the ground first, of course. But I had no time for pain, no more than I did for thinking. I took off after Trenchard, watching his back disappear into the door of one of the great barns.

The stables were vast. There were ten long barns, knocked up shoddy of pine, connected by covered ways and filled with horses by the thousand. I did not know how I would find him in that labyrinth. But I was determined to do it.

He would be after a horse. But he would be too clever to stop before he had left a confusion of distance and turns behind him. And he would want a saddle, if he could find one. For an officer with such commanding looks and an imperious tone may bully his way through many a guard post on a proper mount. But bareback would want explaining.

I could hear the turmoil of the place from a hundred feet away. The neighing and kicking. The sheer hatefulness of the brutes. But I did not hesitate. Not that night. I ran into the barn as if leading a bayonet charge, pistol up, fearless in my fury. Had Trenchard thought to hide in the first stall, he could have shot me dead and finished the business.

But he would be frightened now. I sensed that in him. For he was a man unaccustomed to reacting. He was the one who gave the commands, who pulled the strings, who captained the team. This was a new experience, see.

Lamps hung wherever the barns divided, but their wicks were turned low. Twas almost the darkness of Mrs. Fowler's house in there, and worsened by the thrust of great heads out of the stalls and all their nipping and meanness. I tried to hug the line of wooden gates, but the animals would not let me. So I ended by limping down the middle of the way, pistol ready, trying to hear past the noise of the disturbed animals.

Somewhere behind me, Molloy's voice called, "Sergeant Jones?"

I tried to recall the skills you learn as a young soldier on outpost, the hearing in between sounds and the reading of the darkness.

I worked my way from one barn to another, with the horse fear greater in me than any dread of Trenchard's pistol.

I knew that he might be hiding. Waiting for me anywhere. I tried to count back over the number of times he had fired.

He might have one round left.

One would be enough, if he fired first.

I hated the stink and grossness of the place. It clawed at my senses. The pulsing of blood in me seemed ready to burst my head.

Was that the sound of a man?

I paused.

It did not come again.

I was deep in the maze of stables. And had not seen a single groom or guard. The holiday it must have been. My misfortune. And that of the horses.

Well in the distance, Molloy called to me again.

I turned into another stable row. White heads and brown and black thrust over the ledges of their stall doors, curious, chewing, sensing only the presence of a man, but not his purpose. One of them gave the wall a kick as I went by.

Trenchard was probably gone, I realized. Escaped. And that would be that. Oh, I could publicize his doings, and shame him. But that was not enough for me. Perhaps it was revenge I wanted, perhaps Trenchard was right. But I still believe it was justice that I sought, behind my veil of anger.

I went softly, with the strewn hay muffling my footsteps. As it would muffle Trenchard's, were he still in the barns. Without my cane, my leg wanted to thwart my will. It was a miserable thing, that contrary pain, and it urged me to quit. But I refused. For weakness is the devil's door into our lives.

I was too close when I realized that the sounds ahead were different. I did not stop in time to do things properly.

Turning a corner, I saw him. Saddling a gray. With his

pistol flat on the ground by a stable lamp he had taken down.

"Trenchard," I shouted. Gun raised.

He dropped toward his pistol and I shot him. My Colt took a fine piece out of his shoulder and applied it to the door of a stall. Horses reared and screamed and thumped. The gray nearly trampled him, then came to a halt between us.

Beneath the horse's belly, I saw Trenchard strain his left hand toward the pistol.

The man was not a coward.

"Don't do it," I told him. I got the pistol up again, hammer cocked. Stepping to the side of the horse, I pointed the long barrel at the swell where his neck joined his chest. There was rage and aching on his face. "For I will kill you and like it."

He withdrew his hand.

I thought I had him then. But I made the mistake of watching the pistol, not the man. With an athlete's power, he rolled backward and grasped the lamp, hurling it down in the straw with his good arm.

The glass shattered, and flames spread quicker than the Mutiny.

The horse danced, with fire licking its hooves. I could not get a clear shot. Trenchard ran bleeding. Fire rose around me at a speed I would not have thought possible. I tried to plunge through the flames, but the horse nearly trampled me and I fell against a pillar. I put one last shot down the line of stalls as Trenchard faded into the darkness, his right arm hanging dead. But I did not aim well.

Then he was gone. And there was only the fire.

16

FLAMES EXPLODED AROUND ME. THE BALES OF STRAW AND PINE planking might as well have been gunpowder. The roof burned all along the stable, and patches of fire gnawed the walls.

The horses reared and kicked and let off nickering shrieks. Struggling to break from the prisons of their stalls. Such eyes they had.

I hate the beasts, as much as it is possible to hate any of God's creation. But I could not let them burn.

I jammed the Colt back into my trousers and began opening the stalls. The animals ran wildly down the barn, driving me out of their way, leaping through the flames. But many a horse I could not reach. They burned. Their tails took fire, and their manes, and they smashed themselves against their wooden cells in madness. Even after the smoke hid them, I heard their pleas. Baying they were, and pitiful.

"Sergeant Jones," Molloy called as he come up the way. There was a cough to his voice. And a tone of relief, too, at seeing me on my feet. For he was a good comrade, if a liar, cheat, and thicf.

"Open the stalls, man." My throat clutched up. The air was hot and thin, despite the stewings of smoke.

We ran down the rows like men possessed by battle. The fire chased us. Confused horses could not find their way out. A rearing, stamping herd of them shied at a surge of flames, blocking our path, and I had to shoot into the air to drive them on.

"Where's Trenchard?" Molloy called.

"Forget him. Free the horses."

By the time we reached the next barn, it, too, was an inferno. I have seen villages burn, and fortresses, but never a fire so swift as the one Trenchard left behind him.

A black horse charged us, burning. Its teeth opened to make a scream it could not sound. We leapt from its path, and Molloy rose back up with his sleeve on fire. I rolled him on the ground, and no harm done but a singe here and there. We were losing the battle to save the horses, though.

The fire roared like a cannonade. Braces collapsed and sections of the roof dropped in a blast of sparks. The heat seared the skin, the lungs. My sweat boiled under the wool of my uniform, and my eyes tightened and blurred.

"For the sweet love o' Jaysus," Molloy hollered. "We've got to get out."

But I could not let God's creatures burn alive. They bit me, and knocked me out of their way. They banged their unlatched stall doors back against me. Kicking. Wild. Yet I could not go from them.

Molloy dragged me from that barn just as the rest of the roof came down. But the fire had outraced us again. The stable that should have been our refuge was ablaze. The smell changed from the spunk of burning wood to the stink of cooking flesh not drained of blood.

I remember the noise. The groan of burning walls, and the big snap of the flames. Whinnies and hoofbeats and thumping at wood.

"Got to . . . get out," Molloy said. Choking. The floor burned in front of us, a quick hot scorch of hay. I unhooked another stall and blistered my hand on the metal latch. The horse would not come out, shy of the fire before her.

"We'll burn alive," Molloy gasped.

The smoke clouded between the walls of flame, making it hard to judge the best way to go. There were no water barrels, nor buckets of sand. Only hay and harness, cheap wood and horseflesh.

The horses made me think of souls in Hell.

"That way." I pointed.

We helped one another, taking turns pulling each other through walls of flames and spanking out the fire that teased over our clothing. Twas comradeship, that.

Drunk with smoke we burst into the night. And saw that we had company at last. The flames had called out drunken stable hands and lazing guards, then regulars from town. Citizens had come to do their part. They chased the horses, wild in their shouts, or freed them from the yet unravaged barns. They dragged out bales of hay and axed the walls to put a space between the fire and us, to save the stables still untouched by flames. A brick house stood amidst the great corral, asleep, as if it were not of our world.

Twas a dreadful scandal in the press. Congress had been unwilling to pay for a pair of steam fire-engines for the city, for they hated the mayor and his boys, and now ten times the cost went up in the blaze. Molloy and I pitched in. We put our shoulders to the job of tearing down pine boards beside a cursing crush of men. Freed horses charged in the background, neighing and clattering. Even with the howl and crackle of the flames going Heavenward, you could hear the stampede of hundreds of the animals loose in the streets. Like a cavalry charge without bugles it was. In the morning, they found them broken-legged on creek banks or fallen bloody down blind alleys. Many had to be shot. I heard that a lone horse, burned to the bone on its rump, stood whinnying to die inside the Treasury Department's yard.

Now I have seen worse. And I would never put an animal's fate above a man's. But I will always think that night a tragedy. You will say they would have been slaughtered on the battlefield, anyway. But it does not matter. No living thing deserves such suffering, and my hand was in the doing.

Twas the early morning hours before the fire come under control. Full half the barns burned up, while others were torn down to the ground or damaged. A great mess it was. Molloy and I plodded homeward without talking, the only sounds our footsteps, and the thunk of the axe handle I had borrowed for want of a cane, and the clatter of horses running on distant streets. We were black as miners at the end of the shift, the two of us.

"Tis better, I think," Molloy muttered, "to be the lowest of men than a damned cavalry horse." And then he said no more. But his voice that night was full of what we men are, of loneliness and the mix of bitterness and conviction that pushes us from one day to the next.

"Trenchard's gone," I told him. "I let him get away. I failed, see."

And then I thought of Mick Tyrone my friend, and the bullet he had taken to the arm. Where might he be? Surely, it could not have been a dangerous wound, I told myself, with a prayer in the thinking. And Livingston was dead. And Bates. The sickness of human vanity had been a plague upon us all, worse than the black cholera. Anthony Fowler's corpse hovered over the world.

A horse raced down the street.

They were waiting for me at Mrs. Schutzengel's. Enough

of them to storm a redoubt. They had no interest in Molloy, for which I was thankful.

"Captain Abel Jones?" the officer in charge of the detail asked.

"That I am."

"I have orders to take you into custody. And to remand you to prison."

He did not even ask for my pistol. But I gave it to him. For I am a great one for the orderly doing of things. Even when I am astonished.

"What charge against me, then?"

He read over his list in the lamplight.

"Murder," he said. "The murder of Lieutenant Howard Sneed Livingston. And arson. Destruction of government property. Housebreaking. Assault. Attempted kidnapping. Insubordination. Desertion." He looked up at me. "There's more, if you want to hear it."

They shut me in the Old Capitol Prison, up behind the house of government, and let me sit. I shared my cell with a liveliness of small creatures, but with no other men. No breakfast, see. Not for the likes of me. And not one word more. I did get a pail for my slops, though. And a basin of cold water for washing up.

There was foolish I had been. For when the great men will not have a thing, the little men cannot force it through, and even revolutions end with the same men behind the desks. But, God forgive me, I was not sorry. I had regrets, but only for the shame that would fall upon my wife and child. Even a man proven innocent, which I might or might not be, carries his charges through life in the eyes of other men.

And yet I was not sorry for my doings. Oh, there were

bits that might have been done better. I would not have seen young Livingston end so, despite the awful thing that he had done. Nor even Bates. And surely not the horses. But I felt as I had in my cell in India, after I refused to kill those old fakirs. I had done that which was right and proper, and I scorned the judgement of men. For a Christian must do more than kneel and pray in this world, or the devil will have it all.

How is it that we end in cells when all we want is justice?

Now you will say, "McClellan himself told Jones there was to be no more of his nonsense, and Jones was a soldier. He should have behaved himself." But what will come of this world if we do not take its weight upon our shoulders now and then? There is nothing easier than the turning of a back. But I would not be such a one as that for all the gold and glory in the world.

And even in those hard, black hours in prison, with secessionists and worse packed all around, I did not lose my faith in our great country.

Now there is foolish, you will say, and snicker. After all Jones saw, how could he think the Union that he served retained its worth? He saw corruption, and the hidden hands of power, hypocrisy, and wrenching of the law. Death for no good purpose, that he witnessed. And how the hand of man disfigures love. How could he still believe in our torn land? How could he keep his faith in men alive?

Well, I will tell you, see.

Perhaps I have a weakness of the mind—enthusiasms reach into my soul. Perhaps Tyrone had worked upon my thoughts, with all his longings for a better world. But faith is simpler than the learned say. I felt a part of something great and vast, of something mighty and yet undefined. Beyond the sorry scraps of daily life, a nation had got up on its hind legs—a nation we had never seen before. The men who volunteered to serve the cause, with all their thousand motives and their fears, became crusaders for a better world—although their thoughts were duller day to day. They did their fighting not for kings and crowns, and not for conquest or the spoils of war. They could not even put such into words, the reasons why they left their farms and shops, the mines or city slums or rough frontiers.

And yet they knew their purpose in their hearts. Twas greater than the fate of any man. You had to stop to see the picture whole, to feel that bigness of unspoken hopes. Oh, down with slavery, yes. For there is evil. The Fowler boy had seen that right enough. But up, I say, up with possibilities so long denied to little folk like us. Mine was the country of the little man, where each might raise himself, with help from God. And no man was born better than the rest, though he might think his pedigree a prize. A land of justice, decency, and merit—a new Jerusalem come down to earth. Such was the dream of eighteen-sixty-one, despite our squalid failures right and left. So let us all fight *for*, and not against. We hold the future in our trembling hands.

They would take my uniform away. And though I hated war, and would have loved to sit at home with my beloved, I could not bear the thought I might fall out of the great march. I wished to do my share. For my new country.

Twas a dream of a country, see. A sweet, good dream unrivaled in the world.

In the murk of morning, sitting under a dirty window, I considered my uniform. Singed and seared it was, with one sleeve burned through and the brass buttons dull with soot. My captain's rank was marred and shabby now. Embarrassed I am to tell you how proud I had become of those insignia.

They would take it all away. And then we would see

what else they would do to me. But a Welshman is a terrible thing when you spin him up, and they would never have my silence to console them. I would not give in. No, I was determined to fight on, as fiercely as Molloy and I did that day above Attock Fort.

I hoped no harm would come to him from my willfulness, for Molloy was fully able to harm himself without assistance. And Mick Tyrone. What might they do to him? It hurt my heart to think myself the cause of his damaging. Isn't friendship the Good Lord's second gift, just after love? I hoped I had not done him more harm than the bullet he had already gotten for his troubles.

At noon they fed me soup. A moment of weakness swept over me and I wept.

They let me sit the day out with my thoughts. In the cell next, a reedy voice sang, "The Bonnie Blue Flag," and cursed us all between verses. Footsteps passed my door unseen. I simply could not believe they would make such accusations against me. But money has its ways to power, and power is its own law.

I was as sober a man as ever you will find when they opened my cell door that evening.

"You. Jones," a voice called. "You're wanted."

Even the weak gaslights in the corridor bothered my eyes after the gloom of the cell. I must have looked a bummer in my rags, my hair awry and tunic mottled. The jailer did not even call me "Captain."

"In there," he said.

Twas a simple room, and empty of the flesh. With only a table and bench, one desk and a few rough chairs. No lap of luxury, the Old Capitol Prison. But there was a full window, if a barred one. I looked out on the coaches swaying past. The guards hunched against the drizzle, their rifles inverted. The outline of the Capitol rose beyond the bare trees.

The door opened again behind me. I turned to face a bearded man. He wore officers' trousers, a civilian overcoat, and no badge of rank. I did not know him. But in my vanity, it pleased me that I had not been shackled.

"You're Jones?" he said, eyeing me as if about to make a purchase.

"Captain Abel Jones, U.S. Volunteers."

"Right, right. Sit down." He pointed at a chair and I took it. Sitting down on the bench, he leaned his elbows on the table.

"Name's Baker," he told me. "Bad business, all this. One damned stinking mess."

"Yes," I said.

"Who the Hell do you think you are?"

There was a fine question.

"I did what I saw as my duty."

He banged the table. "You're a goddamned clerk. How the Hell . . . oh, forget it. Listen, Jones. I'm going to make you an offer. Straight up, man to man." He tested his beard with his fingers. A vulture's eyes the man had. "You swear to God almighty, and sign your name . . ." He drew a folded paper from his coat. ". . . that you will never divulge a single detail of all this . . . that you'll just put it out of your head . . . and you can walk out of here tonight a free man."

"No."

I do not know if it was the quickness or the force of the answer that so startled him.

" 'No'? You tell me, 'No'? Do you have any idea of the nature . . . the extent . . . of the charges against you?"

"They are lies. I will not be bullied with lies."

He shook his head, but kept those predator's eyes upon me. "Hell, you're pigheaded as a Carolina Democrat. And one damned fool." His head stopped moving and the room seemed impossibly still. "You're not afraid of hanging?"

I had not thought that far along.

"I am . . . afraid of many things. But I will not be a party to your lies. Anthony Fowler was—"

"Right. I know. Our boy hero. Murdered in all his innocence. And you're the avenging angel of the Lord."

"I would not put it so strongly."

"How would you put it, Jones?"

"I . . . only want justice. For the Fowler boy."

He slammed his hand down again. "To *Hell* with justice. There's a war to be won. Justice can wait. Do you have any idea of the effect this scandal would have on our nation? If it came to light? A scandal of this . . . this sordidness? Play right into the hands of the Rebels. Nothing but damned sordid. And the English interests who'd like nothing better than to take us on and rip away the South. They're all just waiting for an excuse. And there are traitors here among us . . ."

Someone knocked on the door. The fellow, Baker, answered it. I saw a lieutenant's shoulderboards. The two men exchanged whispers.

"You," Baker told me. "Stay right there."

It had not occurred to me that I had a choice.

I watched through the window and saw him go out in the wet. He stuck his head inside the door of a black carriage that had pulled to the side of the street. I saw the back of his head shake. Then he turned toward the prison again. I returned to my seat.

He strode back into the room.

"I'm going to ask you one more time," he said. "Are you willing to close the book on all this, once and for all?"

"No."

He grimaced. But there seemed to be a smile underneath it now.

"Come with me," he said. "We'll try another brand of persuasion."

The rain was so light it would have been no bother, but for the cold of it. And I did not feel my best. Baker led me to the carriage. I limped along like a fool. The coachman did not look down at me, nor did the two cavalrymen serving as outriders show the least interest. I might have been invisible to the world, nothing but a damaged, little man.

Its rain-streaked lamps shone golden, but the carriage was shut tight.

Tight as a coffin.

"Get in," Baker told me.

I would not let him see me falter and did as I was told. Mr. Lincoln sat inside.

I must have looked a silly one with the face I got on. I stopped halfway, with my backside out in the rain. Baker gave me a prod. "Just get in there," he told me. "It's wet out here."

Mr. Lincoln. His knees come up higher than the carriage bench and bulged under his lap rug like the humps of a camel. He seemed too big for the compartment and thin as a cracker all at once. Baker slammed the carriage door behind me. A whip cracked.

His eyes, though. That is what stayed with me. Lincoln was no beauty of a man, with his unkemptness and the lack of trim about him. His hair would go its own contrary way. The skin on his face was rough as a farmer's, spotted and moled. His hands were gigantic and knobbed at the knuckles. He could have got them halfway round a horse. But it was those dark, deep eyes—the sheer painful seeingness of them—that made me feel my place.

The carriage bounced along the bad streets, and he smiled. "So you're the feller won't let go of the bobcat?" he said. "And scratched half to death, it looks like."

"Mr. Lincoln . . . perhaps there's been an error . . ."

"Not if you're Abel Jones. Laf Baker tells me you possess a head harder than hickory wood." He smoothed the lap rug and drew his shawl closer around him. His hand half covered the gaunt chest. Twas a great spider of a hand when the fingers spread out. "He also tells me you may be the last honest man in Washington."

I knew not what to say. But saying was not my business.

"I'm faced with a dilemma," Mr. Lincoln told me. "I feel like the feller standing up on the top rail of the fence, with a bull all mad at him on one side and a nest of rattlesnakes stirred up on the other. I got a fine line to walk, and neither party's much interested in helping me keep my balance." He tapped me on my bad knee. "See here now. I'm just as sick as you are over this business. Lawyer sees a lot, and a politician sees worse. But this Fowler story takes the prize." He sighed.

"Mr. Lincoln, sir," I tried. "The man behind it all, Major Trenchard, he's taken off for the South and we—"

He stopped me with a squeeze of my knee. Then he withdrew his hand. "I made the decision to let him go. Though I hear he won't use that right arm again, if that helps any." He closed his eyes for just a moment, then looked straight at me. "The Union . . . this country . . . we cannot afford the scandal of a trial. Not now." And wasn't there sorrow in him then? "We've already had scandals enough. And there's going to be a passel more explaining to do about all this as it is. But a trial? The country . . . could not bear it. Not now, not now . . ."

A thousand other men might have said the same words and made no impression. But his eyes reached down into me, and his thin voice pierced my heart.

"Jones . . . there aren't but a few things I love truly. My family, that's one. Mary and the boys." He waved a hand toward the greater world. "This country, now that's another. And last there's the written law. But I . . . am prepared to sacrifice the first item and the third for the preservation of the second. That's what a president's got to do, when the choice comes up. It's his duty to save the nation first, and pick up the pieces later on. Know anything about *habeus corpus?*"

I was not one for Latin.

"Well, I've already suspended it. And done ten dozen other things that trouble my heart as much as they do the Constitution. And it does sound to me like young Trenchard wants hanging." He looked away. Far away. "But I let him go. I need his father's support, the support of his class. I need Philadelphia. And I need a country that believes in heroes, and that country needs heroes to believe in. I'd take up with the devil himself to preserve the Union." He brought his sad eyes back to me. "As a fellow lover of justice, I'm asking you to let this dog lie on down."

He tried to rearrange himself, and his rug and shawl both slipped. I helped him settle them again.

"Poor George McClellan," he said, "he's lying abed, raging in a fever. *He* thinks we ought to hang you just to keep things tidy. But I'll take that bear on." He chuckled. His voice was so high and thin it might have made a man laugh. He would never be known for his speaking or his rhetoric. "The general gets confused even when he's not feverish. He forgets which one of us is President." He looked at me, and the slight smile fell away. "But I *need* him, Jones. The country needs him. The soldiers look up to him, not to me. They want a hero, and he fits their expectations." He bulged his lower lip like a man who chews tobacco, though he chewed only words. "If Little Mac can win this war, I'll swallow all the pride I can fit down my throat and sing his praises." His eyes fell to the plaid of his blanket. "We must pray for him to get well. The country needs him. More, perhaps, than it needs me."

"Mr. Lincoln, sir . . ."

"Much is needed. So very much is needed now. And there is so little time." Unexpectedly, he grinned. Showing brown and yellow teeth, in two uneven lines. "You know, you owe a great deal to Allan Pinkerton. If he wasn't willing to sell himself to everybody in sight like a scarlet woman, I might never have learned the details of all this. But everything Little Mac heard, I heard. Pinkerton would sell his mother down the Mississippi—and his own soul, too, if anybody'd give him half a dollar for it." He drew a breath as if he badly wanted air. "Yet . . . we'll need men like that, too. We won't win this war with saints alone. Anyway, Laf Baker gathered up the rest of the story. You surprised the devil out of 'em all, you know. Not a one of 'em thought you'd get so far." He shared another smile with me. Twas a little, private one. "Of course, they never thought I would, either. I guess we're two of a kind, Major Jones. Both of us figured for fools by men who thought themselves our betters."

"Sir . . . it is but Captain Jones, begging your pardon."

He gave his lip another chew and playacted looking me over. "Major, I've been hatching generals out of rotten political eggs by the dozen. I reckon I can make one major out of a fine old soldier."

"Sir . . ."

He reached down into a carpet bag at his feet and brought up my Colt, the gift from my boys. It had been cleaned and polished.

"Devil of a piece of weaponry," he said, admiring it. "You like Sam Colt's poppers?"

"They do seem a fine gun, sir."

He nodded. "I'm trying to learn all that business. What equipment we should buy . . . how many men we really need . . . how we're to get them . . . and the money . . . strategy . . ." He turned the weapon over and traced the tooling by the flicker of the lamp. " 'Hero of Bull Run.' "

"It is a terrible exaggeration, sir."

He dismissed that. "Well, you're no picture-book hero. And I sometimes think the American people elected me to prove they have a sense of humor. But I'm also starting to think the real heroes never are the picture-book variety." He nudged his knees closer to mine. So high up they were I could have climbed them. He was a wonderful, awkward man.

"You have done your country a good service, Major Jones. But now we must go forward, and not look behind. I've come out in the rain to offer you a choice. You can get out of this carriage tonight and go back to your work, taking that major's rank with you—along with my thanks, for what that might be worth. Or you can help me."

"Sir?"

"The situation of our government . . . is terrible. Worse than all those wise men out there know. It's a close game, Jones." He smiled the saddest of smiles. "Chase says we have no money. Even Seward's losing faith. And Cameron's nothing but a thief. Congress wants everything done right now, just so's they don't have to belly up and do it themselves. And the generals . . . our generals can't seem to be got to fight. All they want to do is parade and buy up more supplies. And every day I feel this country slipping away . . ." He sat up straight, as if fighting his own thoughts. The top of his head scraped the roof of the carriage. "But I *will* not let that happen. I will do whatever it takes. What*ever* it takes to save the Union. And I need good men to help me."

"Sir . . . if there's any way . . ."

"Don't go buying before you've had a look in the sack. Now I need an honest man . . . for private matters. Matters of great secrecy. Of great delicacy, if you want to put it fancy. The kind of business where a moral acrobat like Pinkerton could never be trusted. Nor even Baker, who's a little prone to make his mind up in advance. I need a thoughtful man—and one who isn't afraid."

"There is fear, sir, in each of us."

"But they're different kinds of fear." He twisted up his mouth. "I wonder if my fears aren't much the same as yours." He laid his great hand upon my knee a last time. "I need a man who's not afraid to fail—which I'm beginning to believe is a problem of General McClellan's. I need someone who can keep the end of the race in sight and not shy at every little obstacle along the way. A man who's willing to take a bite out of the world's hide and put up with the kicking and bucking that follows. Will you help me, Jones?"

And what might I have said then?

He handed me the pistol, holding it out by the barrel. Then he tapped his cane up behind the driver's bench. The carriage jerked and the pace of the horses quickened.

It struck me how sad it was that Mr. Lincoln had to turn to the likes of me.

"Your friend," he said. "That doctor. He's just fine. Hardly a nick out of him. But that other Irish fellow gave us the slip. And Laf Baker was ready to hire him on. Born to be a secret agent, he said. Feller could fool his own mother."

I felt the good weight of my pistol as if he had laid an entire army in my hand.

"This chapter's closed," Mr. Lincoln told me. "But I have a new job for you, if you'll do it."

I looked at him and waited to hear more. But the carriage jerked to a stop. Mr. Lincoln leaned closer, just for a moment. With his cheekbones ready to burst through his skin and the woes of the world on his face. "When you get down, a feller's going to come up to you. His name's Nicolay. I trust him above all others. He'll tell you what wants doing." His lips tightened to the left side. "If you decide not to take the job, just walk away. With my thanks for what lies behind us."

"Mr. Lincoln . . . if I could just say . . ." But I did not know what I wanted to say. And he knew it. He understood his effect, and that of his position. I would come to know him well enough to see that he understood more than any of us. He was a great, good man, and I let him down in the end. As we all did. But let that bide.

"Better get down now," he told me. "Before the driver gets restless. I ain't got him but half trained."

"God bless, sir," I said, and got out of the carriage.

I descended into a startling brightness. It took me a moment to realize where I was, and by then the carriage had pulled off.

Twas the great gassy glow of Mr. Ford's theater before me, with a performance going on inside. Now I find theatricals corrupting to the morals of youth, and little less dangerous for grown men, though I have read Mr. Shakespeare to my benefit. For his part, Mr. Lincoln had a famous weakness for the blandishments of players. He said they made him laugh. Yet do not judge too harshly. No man is perfect, and may the Good Lord save the rest of us from the shameless temptations of the stage and the wickedness of actors.

A spry, quick fellow come up to me. With a neat little moustache and a shiny goat's beard on his chin. His hair shone under his hat. He smelled of lotions and there was a touch of old Europe about him.

"Do you think," he said to me, "you should now put away the gun?"

German. Though with little accent left. But when you have lived around them you can always tell. And I recognized that clerk's fastidiousness they all have.

I looked down at the pistol in my hand. I had forgotten I was holding it.

"Unless you are making a robbery," he continued.

I stuffed the pistol down beneath my faded coat of blue.

He held out his hand. "John Nicolay. Shall we work together, do you think?"

"Abel Jones." He had a good, firm grip. He had a good, firm grip on everything he touched, that man.

"I think the rain is stopped," he said. "Is your leg good for walking?"

I could have marched thirty miles with a good heart.

"Lead on, sir," I told him.

He gathered his coat around him and we strolled into the darkness.

"The first thing I am to tell you," he said, "is that it will be very dangerous. They killed the last man we sent up there."

THE ADVENTURES OF ABEL JONES WILL CONTINUE IN

The Vacant Chair

History and Thanks

In writing *Faded Coat of Blue,* I struggled for accuracy of detail. I walked the Welsh valleys—so different now than in their black heyday—and the streets of Washington were home to me for years. I grew up in the Pennsylvania coal fields, where the shadows of history and Philadelphia's old money fell heavily upon us. I even went to Attock Fort and old Lahore. Whether the high water along the first several blocks of Pennsylvania Avenue on the morning of Scott's departure, the books available in the shops, or the practice of the quack healer, Dr. La Bonta, the backdrop of this novel is drawn from contemporary and eyewitness sources, or from personal knowledge of the shape of the land and the many shapes of humanity.

There is so much richness in our Civil War era, so much beyond the oft-described battles and repertory heroes, that I yearn to draw the reader deeper into that age. The Civil War made the America we know, but we hardly know the America of the Civil War. It was a time of immeasurable courage and noble hopes, but also of stunning prejudice and the brutalization of immigrants—our New Jerusalem was built on Babel. The impact on the war of refugees from

Europe's failed revolutions goes largely unremarked, and yet it was enormous. Although not all immigrants relished military service, they brought with them expectations that reformed our country. We might say that the old Americans began the war, but the new Americans finished it, for the Union won with the blood of the foreign-born, who reinforced its manpower and material advantages. An ancestor of mine was killed before he mastered English.

It was also an age of sudden, splendid wealth, of whopping wartime corruption and deep moral reflection—and of levels of prostitution and its consequences that do not accord with our notions of the Victorian era on either side of the Atlantic. It was a time when ideas mattered, and men wrote well and wondered about God's design for humanity. It was a profane age of pervasive religion, of savagery, and of transcendence. We have contented ourselves with myth, when the reality makes the sacrifice on both sides all the more resonant.

I am fascinated by the details of daily life, of how men and women lived and thought, what they ate and used and desired. Without burying the reader under catalogs of description, I aim to tease him or her into thinking just a bit differently about the world behind the guns of our rebellion.

In the interests of accuracy, however, I must point out three instances where I have bent history to meet the demands of the plot. First, General McClellan's typhoid struck him in mid-December, 1861. I moved the onset of the disease up to Thanksgiving week. Next, the horrible fire at the government corral and remount stables occurred just after Christmas; that, too, I shifted forward to Thanksgiving. Otherwise, the details are presented as reported by the daily press of the period. The cause of the inferno has never been clarified.

Finally, I created a fictitious company for our hero to command at First Manassas. The sons of Pottsville, Pennsylvania, were among Washington's First Defenders in the spring of 1861, but they did not appear on the field of Bull Run where I needed to place our hero. Otherwise, the battle is described as accurately as such a confused event may be, down to that redheaded colonel's formation of a defensive square during the Union retreat.

Errors will emerge. I bear full blame. But any success in capturing the soul of the age owes much to the gracious assistance or merciful criticism provided by a number of experts on the sources, period, and locations. Two deserve special mention. My heartfelt thanks to: Mary Kay Ricks, director of "Tour D.C." and grand guide to the past, whose knowledge of the Civil War era in Georgetown and Washington is as daunting as it is revealing; and to Matthew B. Gilmore of the Washingtoniana Division of the District of Columbia Public Library, whose knowledge of sources and enthusiasm for his vocation are exceeded only by his courtesy. The library's Washingtoniana Division itself is a treasurehouse.

Our Civil War is an inexhaustible subject, and an interested reader must go through, literally, hundreds of books to get near the complexity of character and event. Yet, I would like to recommend a few key books for anyone who wishes to know more about the environment in which Abel Jones conducted his first investigation. Of all the books and monographs that deal with the period history of Washington itself, Margaret Leech's *Reveille In Washington* remains unsurpassed for precision, range, and readability. On Philadelphia, the remarkable historian Russell F. Weigley has edited a massive, yet readable text, *Philadelphia, A 300-Year History*. On Lincoln and his cabinet, there are innumerable works, and so much of quality that one can only name favorites. My two candidates are J.G. Randall's *Lincoln the President* and the highly readable *Lincoln*, by David Herbert Donald. That greatest of president's own words are a joy and inspiration to read.

On the dark side of the street, the interested reader will find *The Story the Soldiers Wouldn't Tell*, by Thomas P. Lowry, M.D., whose research makes it clear that not all of the dangers of the time waited on the battlefield. For intelligence operations, the best single volume by far is Edwin C. Fishel's *The Secret War for the Union*. On General McClellan, against whom I must admit the prejudice of a one-time soldier who encountered his descendants right and left, Stephen W. Sears has written the most attractive biography possible, *George B. McClellan, The Young Napoleon;* there is, however, no substitute for reading McClellan's own papers, with their misapprehensions and stunning vanity. And for the reader of deeper curiosity and sufficient time, the *War of the Rebellion, Official Records of the Union and Confederate Armies* teaches timeless lessons about war and timely lessons about the deterioration of our writing skills over the last century and a half.

Now, as Abel Jones would say, go on with you and do your duty. And may God bless.